Dead Goode
By Adrian Cousins

Copyright © 2023 Adrian Cousins

All rights reserved. This book or any portion thereof may not be reproduced or used in any manner whatsoever without the author's express written permission except for the use of brief quotations in a book review.

This book is a work of fiction. Names, characters, businesses, schools, places, locales, and incidents are either products of the author's imagination or used in a fictitious manner. Any resemblance to actual persons, living or dead, or actual events is purely coincidental.

www.adriancousins.co.uk

Prologue

February 2016

"Yes! I said I'll be there. So, I'll be there. Christ, woman, don't go on." Detective Chief Inspector Kevin Reeves stabbed the red button to kill the call. Before slotting his phone into his jacket pocket, he raised a finger at his sergeant, who sported a quizzical raised eyebrow as he stood leaning against the doorframe at the front of a large Edwardian house situated in a highly sought-after suburb of Fairfield.

"Guv? You alright?"

Kevin nodded. "Don't get married, and definitely don't have any kids."

"Problems?"

"I'm getting nagged about making sure I'm back in time for parents' evening. Christ, I only married the damn woman because she was young and fit. Now she's starting to sound like my over-bearing, sour ex-wife."

"Oh."

"Nag, that's all that bloody woman does," Kevin muttered as he stepped forward. "Right, what we got then?"

Detective Sergeant Richards nodded behind him as a gesture to the DCI to follow him into the hall. "Probably nothing for us. Uniform called it in, thinking it might be suspicious."

The DCI stopped short at the sight of a body awkwardly positioned at the foot of the stairs. Judging by the angle of the head, Kevin assumed the cause of death would be as a result of a broken neck.

"What's the liquid?" questioned the DCI, pointing to the splatter marks on the parquet flooring and splashes up the skirting board.

The DS indicated with an outstretched boot the cut-glass tumbler that lay half concealed by the leg of the hall console table. "Whisky, by the smell of it."

"Pissed, missed his footing and took a tumble, I guess," the DCI muttered, as he glanced up at the stairs, the landing now bathed in darkness caused by the fading winter light. "If your time's up, you might as well be shit-faced," he chuckled.

The DS nodded over his shoulder. "The cleaning lady discovered him. The old girl's a bit upset," he whispered. "She's in the sitting room with PC Horne."

"Horny?" quizzed the DCI, suggestively raising an eyebrow.

The DS side-eyed his boss. Although he was fully aware most of his colleagues called PC Horne by her station name Horny, Detective Sergeant Richards considered the name unnecessary, derogatory, and would never repeat it. Station nicknames were just a thing, but he detested the way some of his colleagues referred to female officers. The worst being his DCI, a throwback from the twentieth century, who dragged along his sexist, politically incorrect attitudes with him.

The DCI clocked his sergeant's disapproving glare. "Christ, man, don't be so uptight. It's just a bit of banter. I definitely wouldn't object to a fumble in the locker room with Horny. Police women didn't look like that in my day, I can tell you."

"Guv," huffed out the sergeant, reluctant to continue this conversation.

"Oh, don't give me that look, Richards."

"Guv."

"And don't shake your head. Jesus, man, your arse is so tightly buttoned up with the bloody rule book shoved up there, I'd be surprised if you can take a crap. Half the station wouldn't mind knobbing WPC Horne, me included."

DS Richards rolled his eyes and huffed.

"I think I'll have to get her transferred to my team. It will be good to have a decent bit of skirt to gawp at and would certainly be an improvement on having to look at your ugly mug."

DS Richards offered a snorted response but chose not to correct the DCI on the incorrect, outdated term, WPC. Akin to a character from the Sweeney, the DCI was a rough, hard-drinking, sexist bigot and wholly inappropriate for modern-day policing. However, Sergeant Richards's previous attempts at whistleblowing when calling the DCI out for his inappropriate comments had only resulted in denting his own career and damaging their relationship. Anyway, he believed tossers like DCI Kevin Reeves would get their comeuppance and, when that day arrived, the DS would be the first to dance on his grave.

"Right, this bloke got a name?" questioned the DCI.

"Doctor David Rawlings."

"You'd think they'd know better, wouldn't you? That said, doctors probably smoke and drink more than the rest of the population," he chuckled.

The DS nodded as he flipped open his notebook. "He's a surgeon up at Fairfield General and performs some private work at that medical place on the Haverhill Road. According to the cleaning lady, the doctor's a bit of a drinker. The stash of empty bottles of Glenfiddich shoved in the kitchen bin would confirm her story."

"She said that?"

"Not exactly. She said he was partial to the odd dram or two."

The DCI nodded. "What's Horny called us for, then? What's suspicious about it?"

DS Richards leaned forward and snatched up a clear plastic evidence bag from the console table. "This," he waved before handing the bag to his senior officer. "Unfortunately, the cleaning lady picked it up, so it's smothered in her dabs. However, she reckoned when she found him, the poor sod was holding it in his left hand."

The DCI glanced at the single sheet of lined paper, which appeared to have been torn from a reporter's notebook. "So, our pissed doctor had hold of this before he fell, which is unlikely because, during his tumble, he'd presumably let go of it when attempting to break his fall. Or, of course, someone placed it in his hand after death."

"Yes, Guv. I reckon after death."

The DCI frowned as he read the note aloud. *"How did I escape? With difficulty. How did I plan this moment? With pleasure."* He glanced up from the note, raising his eyebrows at his DS.

"No idea, Guv. Sounds like some proverb or gobbledegook."

The DCI nodded. "The bollocks, I know what that means."

"Dantès, sir," came a voice from the sitting room before PC Horne poked her head through the gap beside the sitting room door she held on to.

The DCI beckoned with his index finger for the young PC to step into the hall before he leaned around her and closed the sitting room door.

"Sir?"

"Mrs Mop. Who is she?"

"Susan Twyford, sir."

"As in the khazi makers?"

"Sir?"

"Shitters, bogs, toilets, you know, sanitary ware. Twyford's make urinals. Those white porcelain things that I wave my todger at, at least four times a day."

"Oh, yes. Yes, sir."

"Is she in any fit state to talk?"

PC Horne glanced at the sitting room door and then back at the DCI. "Yeah, I think so. She's a bit shaken up, but she's alright."

"Okay, good. Oh, what was it you said?" he questioned, waving the plastic-wrapped note.

"Dantès, sir."

The DCI bulged his eyes, presumably willing the young PC to explain.

"The words written on that note are a direct quote from Dantès ... the Count of Monte Cristo." PC Horne, clocking the DCI's continued bemused look, bashed on. "That quote is from Alexandre Dumas, the author. The main character in the book, Edmond Dantès, actually never said that line when Dumas wrote the book back in the 1840s, but it is a quote from the author which I believe was used in the film produced in 2002."

"And your point, Constable?"

"My point, sir. The quote is about revenge."

The DCI narrowed his eyes at her. "There's a brain inside that pretty little head of yours, too."

PC Horne huffed and shook her head.

"Oh, Jesus," he belligerently barked at her. "It was a compliment. Christ, you can't flash a flirtatious grin or offer a bird a compliment these days without the politically correct brigade throwing their arms in the air citing bigotry." The DCI offered a glare at his sergeant before returning his attention to the young constable.

"Sir."

"All I'm saying is you've got a brain to complement that fabulous chest of yours. You'll make some lucky bloke happy one day, that you will."

"I'm gay, sir, so I doubt it," PC Horne delivered with a deadpan expression.

"Oh … what a waste. You're not bloody offended, are you?"

"No, sir. Course not, sir," she huffed, dismissively shaking her head. "And just to correct you. Your comment was more sexist and misogynistic than bigoted. Of course, that's assuming you were stating that I'm pretty and surprisingly for a blonde, not a bimbo, sir," PC Horne calmly replied, emphasising the word 'sir' to enforce her point.

"Christ," the DCI muttered, shooting a disparaging glare at his smirking sergeant.

"Sir?" questioned the PC before sticking her tongue in her cheek and raising her eyebrows whilst desperately trying not to copy DS Richards's smirk.

"Right, before you impart the rest of your sociology degree upon me, what do you mean by revenge?"

"Okay. So, the short version?"

"It better be. I haven't got all day, and I have a bloody parents' evening to endure in about an hour with my ever-so annoying nagging wife, so make it snappy."

"The book, the Count of Monte Cristo, is about a man who is wronged and imprisoned. He escapes and then sets about exacting his revenge on those who crossed him."

The DCI waved the note. "And Mrs Mop reckoned the note was in the hand of our drunk doctor here?" He shot his arm towards the man lying by the foot of the stairs.

"Yes, sir."

DCI Kevin Reeves checked his watch and then glanced up at his DS. "Well, the good news is my nagging wife will have to attend parents' evening on her own. The bad news … we have a murder to investigate."

Part 1

1

1987

It's Raining Men

"Lizzy! For God's sake, stop fidgeting. You look fine."

"Fine ... fine? Christ, is that all you can come up with?" she hissed at her husband, somewhat annoyed after all the effort and expense that all he could say was she looked *fine*.

After three hours at the hairdressers followed by nearly half that time perched at her dressing table slapping on her war paint, Lizzy found his comment, although not surprising, infuriating. Despite their rapidly dwindling bank balance, Paul had been the one to insist that she invest in a new evening gown. Now, four hours later, after shimmying into the tight-fitting silk garment, and despite many friends and acquaintances complimenting her on her new dress, all he could conjure up was *fine*.

Although a stunning frock, purchased from a swanky boutique on the King's Road, Lizzy regretted the three-hundred-pound purchase. Notwithstanding their precarious financial situation and her husband's insistence regarding the purchase, Paul had also deemed it necessary to acquire a new dinner jacket and cummerbund despite last year's perfectly good suit still hanging in the wardrobe.

"You know what I mean. Christ, woman, I'm just saying, appear confident and stop fiddling with your ruddy hair. If we cock it up, that's it … we're bloody finished," retorted Paul from the side of his mouth whilst nodding and grinning at Brian, the Club Captain, who didn't reciprocate.

"Your cock up," she whispered, sipping her Martini and scanning the room, offering a forced tight smile towards a few golfing widows she vaguely remembered being bored shitless by during last year's New Year's Eve bash.

"If we're going to convince Mel to invest in the business, we have to appear successful," Paul hissed, whilst offering a polite nod to Celia, Brian's timid wife, who appeared to hover awkwardly at her husband's side whilst he entertained the group huddled around him, all of whom seemed to hang on to the bombastic tosser's every word.

"Well, I suggest you slow down a bit," she nodded to the glass that he upended, slugging the whisky back. "That's your fourth double, and you must have sunk a bottle of red on your own at dinner."

"What? You counting?"

"I'm just saying, that's all. If you plan to talk to Mel, getting plastered isn't a particularly good idea."

"Well, maybe I just fancy getting pissed," he hissed back, before nodding to the barman for a refill.

Seeing in the New Year at the Calthorpe Golf and Country Club's dinner and dance, which they'd attended for the past six years after Paul joined the golf club, was always a lavish affair that both Paul and Lizzy had, in years gone by, been an event they eagerly looked forward to.

In fact, until two years ago, Lizzy considered the event the highlight of the festive season, enjoying the seven-course meal and swilling it down with copious amounts of Cinzano. Notwithstanding the inordinate quantity of à la carte fare and wine on offer, and after she'd swallowed at least half a dozen of those aperitifs – made from those Italian wines suffused with herbs and spices, according to Leonard Rossiter before inadvertently throwing his drink over Joan Collins in those cheesy adverts – there was also the dancing to enjoy.

Paul would expertly glide her through a foxtrot in perfect timing to the live band's swing-style renditions or a quickstep to the jazzier numbers before the disco kicked off in the lead up to midnight. A point at which, when becoming slightly worse for wear, Lizzy would ping off her high heels and allow her inhibitions to be left in the passing year as she strutted her stuff to the Weather Girls and the Pointer Sisters, to name but a few.

Paul would sit out the disco dancing, preferring to swill brandy and puff on Cuban cigars with his golfing mates. That said, along with everyone else, he would join his wife when she dragged him onto the floor to perform the traditional dance to the Gap Band's *Oops Upside Your Head*.

After a night of partying into the wee hours, Paul would whisk her up to their suite and, despite the inevitable impending brewers' droop, still performed to an acceptable level that provided her with some level of sexual gratification.

Not anymore.

After that letter ominously landed on their doorstep on the 10th of July 1985, those hedonistic days had become a distant memory. The same day the French Secret Service bombed the Rainbow Warrior, a one-page letter from the NHS blew their marriage apart.

Despite the ravages of childbirth, and now creeping past her mid-thirties, weekly aerobics classes, and hours spent prancing around in front of the TV when watching her extensive collection of Jane Fonda VHS tapes, all attributed to Lizzy maintaining her youthful physique.

Tonight, with her hourglass figure shoehorned into a tight-fitting, plunge-back, split-leg dress, Lizzy became an eye magnet for the vast majority of the golf society's members, who allowed their lustful gazes to linger momentarily too long. Notwithstanding the fact she could still stop traffic, Lizzy only wanted one man to notice. However, despite all her efforts, Paul no longer looked at her that way since that day he received those damming test results.

Nine years on from the birth of their only daughter, Virginia, she and Paul had long since given up on the dream of a second child. In fact, Paul appeared to have completely lost interest, moving into the spare bedroom in July 1985. Paul's confidence and desires seemed to have frittered away when learning of his lack of virility and the knowledge that his daughter, whom he doted on, biologically couldn't be his.

Their marriage wasn't on the rocks, so to speak, but the lust had fizzled away, boiling their relationship down to that of one of convenience and staying together for Virginia's sake. The hurt had been too much for Paul, distancing himself from her by way of throwing himself into the business. However, unbeknown to Lizzy, until it all smacked the air conditioning a couple of months back, Paul had been systematically gambling away their livelihood over the last two years, leaving them facing financial ruin.

His claims of 'late nights at work' weren't illicit liaisons with some floozy as she'd feared and suspected, but evenings bent over the roulette wheel where he'd gambled and inevitably lost what they'd spent years building. So, now they faced two options – either allow the business to fold and lose their home or somehow persuade Mel Strachan, an acquaintance and thriving local businessman, to invest and buy a stake in their firm.

Although they hadn't openly discussed how to persuade Mel to come to their rescue, they both knew Mel had what was commonly known as a wandering eye. So, Lizzy parading leg, thigh and cleavage in Mel's eye line while Paul attempted to convince him to whip out his chequebook was probably their best tactic.

Despite her discomfort regarding her body being used to lure Mel into what could only be a lost cause, Lizzy accepted they were now in a somewhat tricky situation. So, if flaunting a bit of flesh to cloud Mel's vision would save their business and home, that's what she was prepared to do. Despite their difficulties, she would support her husband and do everything in her power to ensure Virginia wasn't going to become homeless.

Paul grabbed his wife's hand and affectionately squeezed it as he turned to face her. "Lizzy, I'm sorry."

"Sorry for saying I just look fine, snapping at me for checking my hair or for gambling our life away?"

"All three."

"One and two are forgiven. The third one, as you well know, I'm going to need some time."

Paul offered a resigned nod. The very same gesture he'd felt the need to provide all too frequently after his initial penitence last September when coming clean about the state of their finances. Whatever transgressions his wife was guilty of in the past, and although the chances that Virginia was his flesh and blood were slim to zero, his daughter deserved better. So, time to atone, grow a pair, and get himself out of this mess.

"You're stunning."

"Better," she smirked.

"It's a pity I can't show you how."

"Oh, Paul, don't spoil the moment. You're not impotent … well, I assume not. It's been that long—"

"Alright, alright. You know what I mean."

"Yes, but that doesn't mean we can't still be man and wife."

"No, I meant I can't put you in the family way like whoever did that gave you Virginia."

"Paul, I'm not doing this. Not here, and not now."

Paul dismissively shook his head and glanced away, dropping his wife's hand.

Two years had passed since that revelation landed on the doormat, stating that he couldn't procreate children and, by all accounts, never could. According to that letter, Paul was apparently the unfortunate one in the one-in-ten-thousand men diagnosed as infertile caused by a particularly nasty bout of mumps, which he'd suffered in his late teens. Of course, he had suspicions of the identity of Virginia's biological father, but Lizzy had remained tight-lipped on the subject.

"Mrs Goode, as gorgeous as ever." Mel appeared from behind them, laying his hand on Lizzy's bare skin of the small of her back as he leaned in to kiss her cheek.

"Oh, hello, Mel. Is Jean not with you?" Lizzy enquired, spinning around and arching her back to escape the waft of stale tobacco huffed from Mel's mouth as he hovered close.

Mel didn't take the hint, letting his hand drift lower to squeeze her bottom as he guided her close. "Evening, Paul," he nodded and waved his cigarette in Paul's direction, but kept his focus on Lizzy. "No, the poor woman's on call tonight. She's not having to go in, but can't drink in case there's some bloody emergency."

Lizzy shrugged his hand from her bottom. "Oh, that's a shame. She could have still come, though, surely?"

"Oh, no. I told her not to bother. The kids are staying at her mother's, and she's going to see the New Year in with Des O'Connor on the box with a mug of Ovaltine. Unless, of course, she's required to nip into theatre and whip out someone's appendix when Big Ben chimes," he chortled. "Now, enough about Jean and her scalpels. I think you owe me a dance."

"Mel, can we have that chat first?" Paul interjected, not oblivious to Mel's wandering hands, but fully aware he needed to keep the man sweet.

Mel, still with his cheek unacceptably close to Lizzy's, glanced at Paul and grinned. "Why not. Let's grab a table, and I'll talk you through my proposal."

Lizzy and Paul shot each other a look, praying Mel would come through for them. Paul had mooted the idea just before Christmas, suggesting to Mel that he could take a thirty per cent stake in his dwindling business for a cash injection of twenty thousand pounds. Although it wouldn't solve all their issues, an investment of that size would be enough to save their home.

After selecting a table at the far end of the room, Mel ushered Lizzy into the seat next to him before pointing to the chair opposite for Paul.

"Mel, I appreciate this. As I said a couple of weeks ago, my client base is strong. You'll see a good return on your investment."

Mel whipped out his packet of Dunhill cigarettes, extracting one before repeatedly tapping it on the lid and glancing up at Paul. "How have you got yourself in this situation?" he enquired, before lighting his cigarette and reclining in his chair.

Paul shifted awkwardly in his seat, glanced at his wife, and then back at Mel. "Just a run of bad luck. But, as I said, the business is solid."

"Bad luck?"

"Yeah, nothing that can't be sorted out."

"I hear that bad luck is regarding your obsession with the roulette wheel."

Paul's jaw dropped. "Err ... no. Well, sort of, but that's all in the past. I don't gamble now."

Lizzy huffed and shook her head. Paul had promised her that Mel was in the dark regarding his gambling problem. Unfortunately, she suspected the chances of Mel investing serious cash in the business had just taken a nosedive.

Mel stroked his knuckles up and down the side of Lizzie's dress. "I take it you're not best pleased with your husband's obsession with the casino. Does he still gamble?"

"Mel, hang on—"

Mel raised his finger at Paul, effectively stopping his pleading tone. "Sorry, Goode, but I was asking Lizzy what she thinks." He offered a salacious grin at her whilst allowing his fingers to drift to the side of her breasts.

Lizzy would normally slap his hand away, but this wasn't the time to rebuff his advances. Although touching had not been part of their plan, she suspected allowing Mel to flirt with her might help to seal the deal they so desperately needed. Despite managing to avoid flinching, Lizzy inwardly cringed at the feel of his touch. She felt exposed, almost naked, as he continually rubbed his knuckles against the delicate silk material. As she willed herself not to react, she contemplated how convenient it was that his wife, Jean, was on call and, therefore, unable to attend the annual bash. Although Mel had a reputation, openly flirting with another woman wouldn't be something Mel would dare perform in front of his wife.

Lizzy glared at Paul, who looked away. Although her husband couldn't watch as another man pawed at his wife, he'd clearly sunk so low to accept this was their only option. Christ, he was almost pimping her out to save their business.

"Lizzy?" Mel enquired, before taking a long drag on his cigarette.

"Yes. I mean, no. Paul doesn't gamble anymore," she huffed, trying to control the bile that rose in her throat caused by the repulsion of his delicate touch.

"Hmmm. Okay, well, that's not what I've heard."

"Mel—"

"No, listen to me, Goode," Mel interrupted, cutting Paul short with a disparaging glare. "I'm not interested in your pathetic lies. However, as your name suggests, you're a talented architect. So, I have a proposition for you."

Paul's breathing laboured, now detecting his moist shirt sticking to his sweating armpits as he waited for Mel to make the offer. Notwithstanding that Mel seemed more interested in touching his wife's breasts, Paul was past caring. They hadn't been 'a couple' for some considerable time. So, if allowing Mel to get off on pawing at his wife meant he could grab the offer to save his business, then so be it.

Whilst continuing to allow his fingers to glide libidinously across her silk dress, Mel turned to assess Paul's reaction. He snorted a chuckle and shook his head at the pathetic man opposite. "So, here's my offer. You allow the business to fold and declare bankruptcy. Then, you come and work for me. Fifteen grand a year and paid holidays … the usual benefits. You know the drill."

"Wha—"

"I haven't finished," Mel waved his cigarette in Paul's face, effectively cutting him short. "Also … I take your client base."

"What … I thought—"

"You thought wrong. It's a great offer, and I suggest you take it."

"No! I've worked years to build my business."

"You did. Now you're ruined."

"Christ, Mel, what about what we discussed? You said my proposal was interesting when we spoke last week."

"I've changed my mind."

"Oh, you git," spat Paul. "Come on, Lizzy. I'm not going to be strung along wasting my breath on this bastard."

Lizzy grabbed Paul's hand he'd offered and prepared to slide out of her seat.

"Your funeral, Goode."

"Piss off!"

"Elizabeth," Mel grabbed her arm before she could shimmy out of her seat.

Lizzy whipped her head around, shooting a ferocious glare at Mel.

Mel smirked as he allowed her to snatch her arm away. "Of course, there is another way to get out of this mess your husband's landed you in. I take it you do want to help your husband?"

2

2016

The Belfast Boy

Why am I not surprised? Christ, you'd think I'd be savvy enough to realise the futility of embarking on this pointless exercise at my age. However, apart from a few messages posted by weirdos, who I'm convinced stalked females on dating apps to seek out their next victim to murder, my relatively recent foray into the online dating world could only be described as tragic. No, scrub that, pathetic.

Although I presumed those who wished to 'hook up' with me weren't all serial killers and were fully aware appearances weren't everything, I needed to find at least one attractive feature on their profile picture. Hairy warts, pock-marked skin, and unibrows were not my thing. That said, maybe I was being overly shallow and any number of these potential suitors could be Mr Right.

Dream on, girl.

Anyway, my heart really wasn't in it. Karen had persuaded me to sign up to the app, even loading my scowling image and penning the profile.

I knew what GSOH stood for, but had to question and then delete FAF. Based on the fact my picture resembled some mug shot of a child killer, I guess it wasn't totally surprising the sort of men I seemed to be attracting. Kindred spirits, perhaps.

"Is that everything?" grinned the barista.

"Err—"

"Can I give you my number?"

"Sorry?" I blurted, shooting the boy a steely stare. Not too dissimilar to the disparaging, lip-curling expression I'd offered the profile picture of the latest suggested match that had just pinged up on my phone.

It appeared my barked response didn't quell the enthusiasm of the fresh-faced, barely-out-of-puberty barista, who nodded at my phone and the match-making app I'd been aimlessly perusing whilst he fizzed and banged various funnels and levers when preparing my drinks order.

He offered a winsome smile. "I finish at two. We could grab a Subway for lunch and hang out down by the river." He grinned, showing a full set of braces clamping his incisors in place. "Hey, you like the hearts?"

My mouth gaped as I swivelled my eyes downwards to spot the heart shapes in the frothy foam of both coffees, which he nudged a little closer to me across the counter.

"Hey, no drama. Just a thought," he shrugged.

"Christ, how old are you?"

"Me? Twenty-two," he grinned.

"So ..." I peered at his name badge sticker, displaying his handwritten name and a smiley face penned in pink ink.

"So, Callum, is this your usual chat-up line when trying to pick up your customers? Or have I just been unlucky and subjected to your worst one, based on the fact I'm nearly old enough to be your mother and clearly desperate?" I waved the picture of the latest serial rapist the match-making app suggested could be my soulmate for life.

"Hey, okay, okay. I was just suggesting we could hook up and have some fun. You're hot, that's all."

"Christ!" I chortled. "It must be my lucky day."

"Cool. I take it that's a yes, then?"

"Err … no. That is definitely a no. I'm flattered, I must say. But, sorry, a Subway by the river really doesn't do it for me."

"KFC?"

"No. And before you offer a dinner date in Maccy D's, or Five Guys, or rattle through a list of fast-food suggestions to woo me, it's still a no."

"Fair enough," he shrugged.

"How much do I owe you?"

"Nah, that's alright. On the house."

"Oh, no. Come on, how much? I wouldn't want you to get on the wrong side of your boss for ruining the profits."

"No worries. I'm the shift manager, and I like to offer up the odd freebie to hot girls."

"Oh, well, yes, I'm sure you do." I popped two pounds in the tip box whilst precariously holding my phone before grabbing the mugs and glancing up at him. "Although I've declined your kind offer of a footlong, you've made my day,

Callum. It's been a long time since anyone has referred to me as hot."

"Well, you are. You're well fit. How about I buy you a drink tonight?"

Still balancing the cups and phone, I hovered near the counter and offered the barista an exaggerated frown before stepping away to find a free table that wasn't splattered with crumbs and coffee rings from previous customers. However, going by the state of the place, not a straightforward task, I mused.

Whilst chuckling to myself about Callum's chat-up line, I settled into an uncomfortable chair and perused the picture of Stuart that the match-making app had churned out, presumably after applying some algorithm that suggested he and I were perfect for each other.

Frustrated and somewhat bemused as to why I'd even contemplated signing up to the app, I lobbed my phone into my handbag before plucking up my latte. Then, whilst attempting to ignore the boy behind the counter who continued to give me the eye, presuming he was into MILFs, I sipped my coffee, trying to block out the din from the table behind. Going by the sound of the argument, it suggested a visit to the divorce courts wasn't too far in the future for the couple, who, for some odd reason, thought the High Street coffee house was an appropriate venue to air their differences.

With curiosity getting the better of me, I furtively glanced around to match the raised voices with a face. The middle-aged woman facing me slumped back in her chair before slowly shaking her head at her husband – if looks could kill.

Not wishing to stare, or more to the point, be caught in the act, I became fixated on the dark wart positioned centrally on the woman's forehead. I imagine, to those less-kind types, she would be known as chocolate chip. Also, I presumed, if the two-inch dark roots of her easy-to-manage-shoulder-length lank hair were anything to go by, the days of caring about her appearance had long since departed. I figured back in the '70s, when perhaps in her early twenties, she probably wore her hair long. A time when her bot-bellied bald husband afforded the George Best look, or maybe that was just his accent.

Why I thought of Mr Best, I have no idea. Well, apart from my father being a lifelong Fulham fan and constantly banging on about how George was far more talented than David Beckham, who, incidentally, when I was at the tender age of sixteen, I kissed every night before going to bed – the poster on my bedroom wall, that is … a girl could dream.

Whilst I reminisced about my father, who passed six years back, I chuckled at how he used to trot out The Belfast Boy's quotes – *I spent a lot of money on booze, birds and fast cars. The rest I just squandered.*

The clipped Belfast accent of the chap behind me brought me out of my stupor, specifically to how he seemed to berate his wife. I risked another glance around. Chocolate Chip still held that rather pugnacious arms-folded pose.

I guess as the years rolled by, whilst his hair fizzled away and his beer gut grew, the woman lost interest in her appearance or couldn't be bothered to sit and blow dry her hair for hours on end. Maybe it was the other way around, and the poor bloke tried his best, but she just gave up. Whatever their back story, two slightly longer than furtive glances were all I needed to know they weren't candidates for *Love Island* or *Mr & Mrs*.

Anyway, who was I to criticise? Here I was, soon to be divorced, with my only friend, Karen, dragging me around the shops in an attempt to rejuvenate my wardrobe – and for what? It's not as if I had some hot date lined up with Mr Unibrow. So, akin to buying a lottery ticket, Karen constantly persuading me to squeeze into revealing dresses held a certain pointlessness to it. Both seem like a good idea at the time. However, both purchases, in reality, are a complete waste of money – disposable income I didn't have.

Also, since my soon-to-be ex-husband pissed off with Miss Blonde-health-freak with an on-trend thigh gap, taking our substantial monthly salary with him, funds were like those dresses – a smidge tight. On the subject of *Love Island*, the young floozy who Alistair had taken up with – no, hang on, *shagged*, is a more appropriate term – could easily pull any one of those sun-tanned, testosterone-fuelled studmuffins from that show. So apart from wrecking my life, I had no idea what she saw in my Alistair.

'Not your Alistair ... he buggered off with Love Island girl, remember!'

I raised my eyebrow at my mind talk whilst watching Karen shimmy her child-bearing hips through the packed coffee house on her way back from the toilets.

"Oh, that's better. I thought I was going to pee myself," she chuckled, sliding onto the chair opposite. "So, seen anyone you fancy?" she casually enquired over the top of her raised cup, the steam partially misting her glasses.

"On the app or in here?"

"Oh, either!" she chuckled. "Is there a bloke in here that takes your fancy?" She raised a seductive eyebrow before grabbing a quick glance at the gaggle of male patrons.

"Well, the couple behind aren't getting on too well. So, I reckon he'll become available soon. The boy with the ponytail behind the counter has offered to share his footlong, and there's that heavily tattooed thug near the toilets who looks a smidge lonely. So maybe."

"Ginny, come on!" she hissed. "Be serious. Let's have a peek at that dating app. I'm sure I can find you someone."

"Karen, leave it. I'm not in the mood for texting some saddo serial killer."

"You're not still thinking Ali will come back to you, are you?"

I chose not to answer. Karen knew as I did, there was a slight possibility, desperation induced, that I'd probably take him back if he suddenly decided Love-Island girl was a mistake and, despite her ever so well-proportioned sticky-out bits, realised he wanted his thirty-eight-year-old wife back. How pathetic does that make me? Although, as I said, I think that thought was born out of pure desperation. I was in a puddle of shite wearing open-toed sandals, metaphorically speaking, of course, but you get my drift.

"Ginny ... you know that's not going to happen. And anyway, why would you want him back after the way he's treated you? No way would I take Danny back under those circumstances, I can tell you."

"Yes, okay, okay. Don't go on."

"Hey, I'm just trying to help."

"I know … and I appreciate it. Honestly, I do." I offered a tight smile to cover the continued anguish that terrorised me each day for the past two months after discovering my husband and his personal trainer trying out some nude stretching exercises on our bed. Namely, Ali arching his back and *her* positioned beneath him whilst impersonating a panting starfish.

"Anyway, Danny would never cheat on you."

"Too right! He knows which side his bread is buttered."

"I'm sure the boy does," I chuckled. "So, listen. I've made a decision."

"Oh? A big one, or just which wallpaper you'll do your bedroom in?"

"Ah, well, now you mention it—"

"Not wood-chip or Anaglypta, per-lees!"

"No, neither. Anyway, remember, I don't have a bedroom."

"Oh, honey, I'm sorry, that was really crass of me." Karen placed her mug down and reached across to grab my hand. A nice gesture, but the pity etched on her face only added to enforcing home my dire situation. "You know Danny and I are more than happy for you to stay as long as you want, don't you?"

"I do. But, look, I need to move on. Because Ali is here, in this bloody town, I thought I'd make a fresh start and go back to London. I seem to recall enjoying my time there during my Uni years—"

"Twenty years ago!" Karen blurted.

"Yes, alright—"

"And Alistair should have moved out, not you. That's your home, and he's the one who's cheated."

"I know, but … it's complicated."

"How so? As I said, you can stay with us as long as you like, you know that. But Ali has done the dirty on you."

"He has. Look, Karen, I just think going back to London will be better for me, that's all. There will be plenty of job opportunities. If I stay here, I'm liable to constantly bump into him or his thigh-gap floozy. I know this is our town, and you've settled here, but I find Fairfield … well, let's just say a bit too provincial. To be honest with you, it's not really my cup of tea anymore."

"Oh, no, don't worry. I don't blame you. There's not much here, but it's good for the twins. Anyway, Danny and I couldn't afford a shoebox in London. Have you found somewhere that needs a few rolls of Anaglypta, then?"

"Oh, no. I've not even looked. Anyway, I think I need to get a job first."

"How's that going? You haven't said much about that lately."

Unintentionally, I huffed out an enormous sigh.

"Oh, that good?"

"Trouble is, the last ten years have just been about building the business with Ali, so I don't have what those employment agencies term as marketable skills. I've applied for this, that, and everything, but so far, I can't even get a damn interview."

"And what's the decision on that? I take it you'll allow that git of a husband to buy you out. I presume he'll have to secure a sizable business loan. Not that I'm prying, but I suspect your half of the business will be a hefty sum?"

I offered a wimpish smile. Although I knew I'd have to come clean with Karen at some point, actually admitting my utter stupidity wasn't something I relished.

"I presume the git can't afford to buy you out of the flat as well, so you need to push him to get it on the market."

I winced – Karen continued.

"There's no point letting him live there with that thigh-gap bitch, rubbing your nose in it. I imagine your swanky penthouse down by the river should sell easily. You need to push it through … be strong, Ginny."

I nodded and took a sip of my coffee as I built myself up to inform my best friend of just how dire my situation had become and precisely how deep that puddle of excrement was that I now wallowed in – way above my open-toed sandals and exponentially rising like a blocked Victorian sewer.

"I'd imagine with half the business and the proceeds from the sale of your flat, that will set you up nicely."

After huffing out a colossal sigh, I placed my mug down before cupping my cheeks with both hands. "It's not that straightforward."

"Oh, I know, honey, these things take time. But you need to push him. He'll be in no hurry to secure a loan or move out of the flat. So, come on, give Ali an ultimatum and set that solicitor upon him."

I shook my head while allowing my fingertips to massage my temples. I could detect the onset of a migraine.

"Yes! Don't shake your head. Tell that despicable waster of a husband of yours to get his finger out!"

"Of where?" I chuckled.

"Oh, don't! I really can't think about Alistair and where his fingers might be with that girl. And a girl is all she is! Christ, how old is she?"

"About twelve," I muttered. "No, twelve-year-olds don't have legs that long. She's twenty-three, I think."

"Ridiculous! She's a child. I thought men had to reach at least forty before they embarked on their midlife crisis."

I shrugged, not knowing what to say.

"You don't think losing his mother so suddenly has affected him in some way, do you? Maybe her tragic death has sent his mind skew-whiff."

"Oh, I don't know. I lost my mum a few months ago, and that didn't cause me to feel the need to bang the brains out of some young boy."

"Oh, God, sorry," she winced. "I keep putting my foot in it—"

I placed my cup down and grabbed her hand, detecting she was feeling somewhat awkward. "Hey, it's okay. Mum had been ill for a long time. So, I knew her death was coming."

"I know, but that was insensitive of me."

I shrugged and wiggled her hand. "Anyway, I think you're right. Ali is having a midlife crisis, but that's his problem. When Thigh-Gap girl gives him the boot, he can wallow in the mess he's made."

"Alistair seems to have gone early on this one. He's a bit young for a midlife crisis. What is he, thirty-nine?"

"Yes, slightly premature. Something Ali was always prone to."

"Oh, how disappointing," giggled Karen. "Well, make sure you test drive a few suitors before landing your next catch. Nothing worse than building yourself up only to find he's allowed the train to leave the station early."

"Yes, well, the offers so far have only come from a bunch of desperadoes on that bloody dating site or ponytail boy offering a footlong. So, I can't imagine trying out many suitors in the short term."

"Footlong?"

I nodded to the barista as he attended to some bloke who appeared to be talking to himself. Why idiots walked around with a damn great Bluetooth device stuffed in their ear was beyond me. "The lad behind the till asked me on a date. He wanted to buy me a Subway for lunch."

"Really?" Karen's eyes lit up as she swivelled around to grab a closer look.

"Don't look! The last thing I need is to encourage him."

"He's rather cute … in a pubescent way."

"Exactly!"

"Well, why don't you? You never know, it could be fun. I'm sure his train wouldn't leave the station early!" she sniggered.

"Oh, Karen, he's only twenty-two!"

"So?"

"Oh ... good God, it can't be," I muttered, as the Bluetooth man spun around before heading towards a free table, clutching his espresso and newspaper.

"Ginny?" Karen followed my gaze as my eyes followed the man. "Ginny, what's the matter? You look like you've seen a ghost."

"I think I might have."

3

Sunny Hunny

"Ginny, have you lost it? What d'you mean you've seen a ghost? Who's that man?" Karen whispered, effectively breaking the trance I seemed to have fallen into whilst studying the man with the Bluetooth contraption poking out of his ear.

After eventually prising my eyes away from him, I turned to Karen. "Sorry, I thought I knew him."

"Who is he?"

"I don't know."

"Well, he's a step up from Footlong Boy. Why don't you go and say hello?"

"Sorry?"

"Go and chat him up," she hissed, before tapping her wedding ring. "No ring. He's not married."

"Jesus, Karen. You suggesting I just waltz over there and say, hello, I'm Ginny? I'm a smidge desperate because my husband has run off with Thigh-Gap, so do you fancy whisking me back to your place for a quickie?"

"Alright! I thought he looked nice, that's all."

I slugged down the remains of my latte before folding my arms on the table and leaning forward. Karen raised an eyebrow whilst sporting a smirk, suspecting I was about to launch into some juicy gossip.

"You know that photo of my mum and dad and the bloke I call Uncle Terry? The one in that glass frame on the kitchen windowsill."

"Err … maybe. I think so. Is that the one you showed me after your mum passed?"

"Yes, that's it. Well, it can't be him, but that bloke is the spitting image of Terry. He wasn't my uncle as in a blood relative, but a really close friend of Mum and Dad's."

"Oh. Well, your uncle must have been something in his day because that bloke is seriously hot."

I studied the man over Karen's shoulder as he rambled on with his phone conversation, which gave the appearance he was chatting with the empty chair in front of him. Bloody weirdo.

"Well, it can't be your parents' friend, can it? I presume he would be a man in his sixties."

"He's dead."

"Oh, well, that seals it then! Go on. Why don't you go to the loo and accidentally nudge him? You never know, this could be fate."

"Karen, this is weird. But I'm convinced that man is my father."

"You've lost me." Karen bulged her eyes at me. "I thought you said he resembled your dead uncle … friend of your parents. What's your father, God rest his soul, got to do with this?"

"My dad wasn't my dad, if you see what I mean."

"Christ, girl, you really have lost me."

"Look, as I said, Uncle Terry wasn't my uncle. I never met the man, but he was my father."

"Ginny, have you succumbed to smoking weed? What the hell are you talking about?"

"Oh hell, he's looking at me!" I ducked down, effectively hiding behind Karen. "Don't turn around," I hissed, as Karen swivelled around to glance at Bluetooth.

"There you go then!" she grinned, spinning her head back after ignoring my instruction and having a good gawp at the man. "He clearly fancies you."

"Christ, Karen. You're acting like a dizzy schoolgirl! He's not some boy in class that you're suggesting I ask out on a date!"

Karen shrugged. "Well, I think he's hot. I guess he might be a little on the young side, but at least he's older than the boy who keeps giving you the eye from behind the counter."

"Karen!"

"Alright, alright," she raised her hands in surrender. "I'm only saying that he's good-looking, on his own, and not wearing a ring, that's all."

"I'm not going to ask a stranger in a coffee shop for a date, alright?"

"Okay! Anyway, what on earth are you on about, saying your dad not being your dad."

"He isn't. I've known the truth since Mum received her diagnosis. I think she knew she didn't have long left, so wanted to tell me the truth."

Karen raised her eyebrow over the top of her coffee mug.

"Mum had a holiday romance in 1977. Well, it wasn't quite like that. You see, before they were married, she and Dad and a couple they were friendly with enjoyed a week away in Sunny Hunny. You know, Hunstanton on the North Norfolk coast. Anyway, Mum informed me she and the other chap had a fling one night … right sordid affair, apparently."

"No … way!"

"Oh, yeah!" I exaggeratedly nodded. "The four of them rented a quaint little chalet near the sea. Anyway, one night, Mum nipped into the kitchen to grab a glass of water and Terry, that's her best friend's boyfriend, was doing the same. One thing led to another, and they ended up doing it on the sofa."

"Good God! Your mum?"

"I know! Who would have thought?"

"And while they bounced around like a couple of rabbits, your dad and her best friend were asleep?"

"Uh-huh," I nodded.

"Wow! Did your dad ever find out?"

"I guess he must have. When I was about seven or eight, Mum and Dad had some test to discover why they couldn't conceive again. Turns out Dad was a Jaffa and always had been. Apparently, they didn't discuss how I came into being, but Mum said Dad put two and two together."

"Well, not exactly difficult to work it out if his love train was devoid of passengers," she chuckled. "But … I can't believe it."

"I know. It's crazy, isn't it? So that picture of my parents with Terry, who I always thought was just a friend of theirs, was, in fact, my real father."

"And the hot bloke behind me looks just like him?"

I grabbed another glance before nodding. "He does. Since finding out about my mother's little antics, I've studied that picture. That bloke, who's still yakking away through that Bluetooth contraption, is the spitting image."

Karen offered a furrowed brow and leaned forward after gently placing her coffee cup down. I could tell her mind was whirring, and I knew exactly what was coming next.

"Julian?"

"My brother?"

"Yes!"

I shook my head and raised my palms. "He's not Dad's."

"Obviously! But does Jules know?"

"No! So, you must keep this to yourself."

"Christ, who was the father?"

"I don't know. Mum refused to say. All I know is she must have had some fling soon after those test results, and clearly, Dad must have known."

"This is unbelievable! I've known your parents for years. I always thought your mum was a butter-wouldn't-melt type of woman."

"So did I."

"How d'you feel about it?"

I shrugged. "I don't know. Of course, you always think your parents aren't capable of that sort of thing, but they're human, just like us."

"Your poor Dad."

"I know. He stayed with her for mine and Julian's sake, I guess."

"Well, you've blown me away."

"Remember, you can't ever mention this. I don't want my little brother to find out."

"No, of course. I take it his father isn't this Terry bloke."

"No, definitely not. Mum said he died in 1983. Heart attack, apparently."

"Oh, how sad."

"Yes, he was only in his early thirties. There must have been something about him because when Mum mentioned his name, her face would light up. I think she was in love with him. It's all so sad. My parents were a happy couple, but her true love was the man who wooed her over a glass of water."

"She said that?"

"No, what she actually said was he was the only man to give her multiple orgasms."

Karen spat her coffee out, snorting foam through her nose. "My God!"

"I know! Alistair could never achieve that, so I think I'm missing out."

"Really? Oh, how dull. Danny often—"

"Enough!" I held my palm aloft. "I don't want to hear how Danny makes you cum."

Karen smirked. "Very good with his hands, my Danny."

"I said I don't want to know."

"So, Julian's dad. Who's your money on for that position?"

"Hmm … no idea. Mum didn't mention his name and certainly didn't coo about him like she did over Terry. I guess Jules's biological father wasn't particularly good with his hands, and Mum decided to end the fling."

"Hmmm, I must admit I always thought it odd that Julian's a ginger, what with your parents and you being blonde."

"I know. It never occurred to me before."

"Well, I'm lost for words. I'm shocked."

"I know. It's one hell of a revelation."

"You're sure it's all true?"

"What d'you mean?" I quizzed, scrunching up my nose.

"Well, Lizzy, your mum, she lost her mind towards the end, didn't she?"

I sighed, recalling her final weeks and the utter devastation of watching my mother wither away. "She did. But Mum told me all this way before she lost her mind."

Karen nodded. "She was lovely, your mum."

"She was."

"Anyway, honey, before you shattered the illusion that your mother was a pillar of the community, God rest her soul, you were about to tell me about a decision that didn't involve wallpaper."

"Yes, I think it's time I moved on. I can't stay at yours forever."

"Honey, it's only been a few weeks. As I said, you can stay at ours as long as you want. Get yourself sorted, and when the money comes through, then you can search for a place in London."

"No. Look, Danny and the girls can't have me rolling around your house forever. You need family time, so it's time I moved on. Anyway, I've had enough of hearing you moan in the middle of the night when Danny is applying his perfected hand techniques."

"I can't help it … Danny has that effect on me," she sniggered.

"I'm delighted for you," I chuckled. "No, seriously, I need to move on."

"Honey—"

"No, please," I interrupted. "You've been so good to me, but I must give you two some space. Otherwise, you'll end up in the divorce courts, too."

"Where will you go?"

"Well, it's not ideal, but I've taken a short-term rent on a flat here in Fairfield, mainly because it's cheap. Hopefully, that's just a stopgap until I find a job and a flat in London."

"Oh, that's fab. At least you'll still be close."

"Yes … I can move into it tomorrow."

"Oh … so soon. Why ever didn't you say?"

"I've been building up to telling you." I chewed my lip, dreading what would come next. However, as I planned to move out of Karen's in the morning, I'd run out of time.

"What's going on?"

I shrugged, breaking eye contact.

"Ginny, where's this flat?"

"Not far … it's only about five or six miles from you."

"Where?"

"Look, it's not a particularly affluent area, but it will do for now."

"Virginia … where?"

"The Broxworth Estate."

4

The Tide Is High

"You enjoy your coffee whilst I just sit here, why don't you!" spat Deana, aggressively folding her arms across her chest.

"Excuse me?"

"Terry, I'm fully aware being cooped up in my house all day long is driving you stir-crazy, and you feel the need to get out and about, but it's not so easy for me, is it?"

"I don't follow."

"Err ... hello!" Deana waved her index finger at the minuscule espresso cup he'd just plucked up. "I can't very well enjoy a coffee when out and about due to it might appear somewhat odd to see a levitating cup."

Terry shrugged. "It's not my fault you're invisible."

"Darling, I'm well aware of that. This is how it works. We're both dead. I'm invisible, acting as your gorgeous guide to ensure redemption and retribution are applied where and when required. However, it would be nice if you occasionally thought of me when suggesting we nip out for a spot of lunch or a coffee because all I can do is sit and watch you."

Terry replaced his cup on its saucer and nodded. "I know. But I'm getting bored rolling around your house all day waiting for the Powers-That-Be to inform us about our next mission."

"Well, I can think of plenty of ways to entertain you."

"Oh, Deana, don't start that again."

"Uh-oh."

"What."

"Don't look now, but there's two women positioned near the window, and they're looking our way."

Terry spun around.

"What bit of don't look now did you not understand?"

Terry swivelled back and grinned. "They probably fancy me," he chuckled. "Not sure about the one with glasses. She's not my type, but I could definitely entertain the blonde."

"Could you now?" Deana sarcastically fired back. "I thought you were a pious celibate monk?" she raised her eyebrows and pursed her lips, still holding that aggressive arms-crossed pose.

"Well, you know. All I'm saying, Blondie's just the type I'd go for. She looks like you used to."

"Used to?"

"When you were younger."

"Oh, so that's it, is it? I'm too old … pensioned off, discarded, no longer desirable, and thus put out to pasture."

Terry rolled his eyes. "That Debbie Harry woman still singing? I liked Blondie. Had a fling with a girl in the late '70s who looked just like her."

"I'm in no doubt you did. And I have no idea. I suspect Ms Harry must be in her seventies now. Anyway, you're changing the subject."

"Yes, and on that subject, of changing the subject, this bucktooth thingy is making my ear canal sore. It can't be safe having these things shoved in your ears," Terry announced, fiddling with the gadget Deana had rammed in his ear before they left home. Although Terry found it somewhat uncomfortable, he was also keen to nudge the conversation away from Deana's favourite subject. "What you laughing at? You're wheezing like Muttley again."

"I'm sorry darling, but you make me laugh when you pull that Steptoe gurning face. Anyway, it's called Bluetooth, not bucktooth. A set of those shoved in your ear really would hurt," she chortled.

"Bloody daft name, and it's painful. It feels like it's stretching my ear out."

"My darling Dickie said they named it after a Viking king, who apparently was fabled for having a blue tooth."

"What has an earpiece got to do with Vikings?"

"Oh … I don't know. I didn't think to ask him that."

"Probably because they both cause severe pain." Terry winced as he fiddled with his ear.

"Stop fiddling with it. I think it's a rather inspired idea of mine. At least we can converse without everyone around us thinking you're some bloody fruit loop who's escaped from the funny farm."

"And these things are like radio receivers, picking up signals from those portable telephones?"

"Yes, darling. See that woman tucked into her seat near the toilets. She's tapping away on her laptop, and she has a Bluetooth in her ear so she can hold a conversation on her phone whilst she works."

"Oh, yeah, so she is. She looks just like me ... talking to an invisible friend. You don't reckon—"

"No, darling. If she were chatting to a ghost opposite her, we'd be able to see them, wouldn't we?"

"Oh, yes, I guess we would. It all looks a bit odd, though, don't you think?"

"Not really. It's what everyone does these days. Look, for the first time, no one is gawping at you as if you're wearing a space helmet while chatting to an empty chair."

"I feel like some spy ... Napoleon Solo, with this contraption stuck in my ear." Terry tapped his Bluetooth earpiece. "Open Channel D," he chuckled.

"What are you, five? Shall we nip over to the toy shop and see if we can pick you up a toy gun?"

"Oh, yes, I always wanted an U.N.C.L.E. Special with its long-range carbine attachment."

"Darling, I think you're mis-reminiscing. You were a teenager in the sixties when The Man from U.N.C.L.E. hit the TV screens. I, on the other hand, was about ten, and I do recall thinking what a lush David McCallum was."

"Blimey. Ten's too young to be having those sorts of thoughts."

"I was an early starter, darling. Womanly urges came early for me."

Terry offered a po-faced frown before re-twiddling his earpiece.

"Leave it alone!"

"It's like some form of ear torture. I'm surprised the bloody Gestapo didn't invent this when interrogating their suspects, because I'm quite convinced having my fingernails plucked out with a pair of pliers would be more comfortable."

Deana tutted. "Come on, drink that thimble of coffee, and let's go home."

"Or …" He raised his finger as if having a lightbulb moment. "It feels like I'm being experimented on as if I was that Alex DeLarge in *A Clockwork Orange.*"

"Well, I can't say I ever watched a film about a chocolate orange. However, I would have gladly accompanied Mr Kuryakin in his quest to defeat Thrush. God knows I've suffered the vaginal variety enough times," she chortled.

"Christ, Deana. Can you hold a conversation about anything that doesn't end up talking about your private parts?"

"Just making conversation."

"Well, hearing about the history of your bouts of sexually transmitted diseases is not a conversation I would like to participate in."

"Thrush is most definitely not a sexually transmitted disease. I have *never* had one of those, thank you very much."

"An amazing escape considering your history," mumbled Terry.

"And just so you're abundantly clear, thrush is a yeast infection ... a bit like Marmite."

"Marmite!" exclaimed Terry. "How the hell can Marmite be anything remotely like thrush?"

"Yeast ... they both have yeast."

"So does bread, but I can't see your average Mother's Pride white sliced loaf being associated with thrush."

"No, probably not. I was just making a point, that's all. Anyway, I'm not sure you can still buy Mother's Pride ... I think they would have to change the name to Parents' Pride, or Stay-at-home father's Pride, these days."

Terry screwed up his face. An expression Deana was fast learning meant her statement had totally lost him.

"Political correctness, darling. We can no longer say housewife, WPCs, woman doctors, manpower departments, salesman, mankind, and so on."

"Why?" Terry raised his hands, presumably bemused.

"Political correctness, darling. And quite right too, I might say. You bloody lot have had your way for thousands of years, so it's high time us girls fought back."

"You lot?"

"Men!"

"Oh ... well, what do you call that list you trotted out now, then?"

"Stay-at-home-parent, police officer, doctor, without stipulating it's a woman as if that's suggesting lesser capability, human resources departments, salesperson, and humankind."

Terry huffed out a puff and rolled his eyes.

"Anyway, back to bread … my mother—"

"Stay-at-home-parent, you mean."

"Don't get silly, Terry Walton."

Terry smirked. "Alright, tetchy Deana Beacham."

"My mother used to buy Mighty White bread. D'you remember that?"

"No, never heard of it."

"Yes, well, you've been dead for rather a long time. It was all unsliced Hovis in your day with a bit of beef dripping on top after a hard day down the coal mines for you, I suspect."

"We had sliced bread when I was at home."

"Yes, I know you did, darling. I'm just pulling your chain. And another thing, please do not refer to me by using my first married name. I'll have you know, Ian Beacham was a total bore. Why d'you think I copped off with you in that hotel room, eh? Well, it was to grab a bit of excitement, that's why."

"You said Sidney was boring. So, were all your husbands boring gits?"

Deana tapped her finger on her lips as she contemplated that question whilst Terry once again fiddled with his Bluetooth.

"Ian, Sidney, and Alan definitely slot into the lacklustre, pedestrian category. Mark, Adrian, and Alex were alrightish in a somewhat tiresome way, I suppose. However, my darling Dickie was a total lush."

"I can't understand how you came to marry them all if they were so awful."

"One of my faults, not that I have many, of course. However, I do have a propensity to fall in love at first sight. I'm sure if I'd invested the time to grab a second look, I might have avoided all the expense of those wasted marriages."

"Oh ... well, one out of seven's not bad, I suppose," he chuckled.

"Hmmm ... so, yes, if you feel the need to utter my surname, please use Burton ... my darling Dickie's name and not any of those other nitwits."

Terry offered his now perfected po-faced response when stumped with what to come up with as a verbal response. That said, knowing she disliked being called Beacham provided an ace up his sleeve when he fancied jibing her – anything to relieve the boredom. Unfortunately, despite what many movies and books suggested, Terry thought being a ghost wasn't that exciting.

"So, I take it you didn't regard me as boring or lacklustre?"

"No, darling. Stop fishing for compliments."

"What about all your other conquests? Were they boring?"

"If you're referring to my casual affairs, then no, most I recall were quite exciting. Unfortunately, I just stupidly chose to marry a plethora of turgid gits."

"How many casual affairs have you had?"

"Darling, I have no idea. That's not an appropriate question, is it? Some were quite long, like a few weeks, and others with slightly less commitment. I had a brief fling with some pop star before I met you."

"Really! Who?"

"Oh, I can't remember his name. I woke up underneath him in a hotel room. Back in the day, that was what was called going steady."

"Steady."

"Yes, darling. Staying with a man for longer than a few hours is definitely considered going steady in my book."

Terry's jaw dropped, contemplating that he could classify himself as relatively inexperienced compared to Deana. That said, she'd benefited from an extra twenty-five years to notch up her totaliser.

"You know, until I bagged my darling Dickie, I always preferred casual affairs. As they say, no need to lug around a whole pig, when all you want is a sausage."

"Who says?"

"Someone did. I don't know who, but it's a rather spiffing little saying, don't you think?"

"Do you?" Terry rolled his eyes.

"I do so. Oh, Dar—ling … we might have a problem."

Terry followed her gaze towards the counter, specifically the long line of punters as they shuffled forward to place their orders.

"Turn around!" she barked. "Don't look and cover your face. Open that paper and pretend to read."

"Sorry?"

"Read the paper," she hissed. "Being a scummy red-top, there probably aren't that many words printed in there that comprise of more than one syllable, so just cover your face and look at the pictures."

Terry complied with Bossy-Boots-Beacham, opening the paper and holding it aloft to cover his face. "What's going on? Who's spotted me? Christ, it's not that Marjory woman again, is it?" Whilst he furtively scanned the line of customers over the top of his paper, trying to identify who Deana had spotted, he chuckled to himself about the new nickname he'd conjured up for his invisible partner.

"No darling, it's not good-old twinset and pearls. However, be ready to go when I say so. There's a strong possibility that we may have to make a dash for it."

Due to Terry not being able to identify any potential issues from his scan of the faces waiting in line, he swivelled his eyes from the queue to the picture of a man called Boris Johnson. The article listed the politician's achievements during his tenure as the London Mayor. Specifically focusing on the Cycle Superhighway, which Terry thought was somewhat baffling, causing him to wonder why Londoners needed such a thing considering the plethora of black cabs and extensive Tube network on offer. Not for one moment could he grasp the idea that commuters would actually prefer to cycle. Momentarily distracted from Deana's concerns, it also surprised Terry that the position of London Mayor existed and wondered what had happened to the Greater London Council.

Terry swivelled towards Deana whilst lowering the paper. "What happened to the GLC?"

"Oh, no. I think he's about to head our way."

"Who?" Terry whisked his head around to assess the queue.

"Crackarch! The man whose testicles I realigned with Inch-High's laptop when he caught us in that pervert's office."

"Crackitch, not Crackarch."

"Whatever. That Czechoslovakian goalkeeper with the anal piles issue. Oh, dear God, it's definitely him, and it appears he's crawled out of that cesspool of a dump to buy a coffee. Hide your face; he's coming."

Terry whisked up his paper as instructed.

"Oh hell, I think he's making a beeline for my chair."

"Err, this seat free, mate?"

Terry recognised the man's gruff tones from a couple of weeks back when caught rifling through Hallam's laptop. Annoyingly, Bossy-Boots-Beacham was right.

"No, sorry, that seat is taken." Terry stealthily lowered his paper just enough to spot the man assessing the empty chair, noticing Deana pulling a face before vigorously wafting her hand in front of her nose. Terry speedily raised the paper again when Crackitch turned around.

"Oh, revolting. The vile, repugnant oaf, has just guffed!"

"Oi, you can't save seats, mate. It's a first come, first served type of place," he announced before adding further odious gases to the vicinity by way of an audible belch and a somewhat surprisingly lengthy, high-decibel flatulence that reverberated down his rather filthy joggers.

"Darling, he's about to sit on my lap!"

Keeping the paper high to cover his face, Terry jumped up. "Take my seat. My friend pissed herself a moment ago, so the seat pad is wet."

"Oh, right." With his free hand, he grabbed the top of the paper and scrunched the news sheet in his fist whilst peering at Terry. "Do I know you?"

"Pissed the seat! Terry Walton, I hope you're not suggesting that I have a weak bladder and suffer from incontinence! I have never needed to use, or ever have purchased, a pack of Tena Lady pads."

"Err … no, I don't think so." Terry nervously grinned. "Please take my seat. We're going now."

"We?"

"Me."

"You look familiar, mate."

"Deana, stop pulling that face, and let's go before Crackitch works it out."

"Who you talking to?"

Terry tapped his Bluetooth earpiece. "Do you mind? I'm talking on the telephone."

Deana shimmied away from Crackitch, pinching her nose as she bolted for the door. Terry offered Crackitch a winsome smile before whizzing after her.

"Door, Terry."

"Sorry?"

"Be a gentleman and open the door." Deana nodded to the handle.

"So much for that bleeding equality bollocks you keep trotting out," he muttered, before yanking back the door and dramatically waving his hand, indicating the clear path for Bossy-Boots-Beacham to pass. "After you, Deana Beacham. And just as a side point, when I mentioned that film A Clockwork Orange, I can assure you it has nothing to do with Terry's Chocolate Orange. It's a film about gratuitous nudity, sex and violence. Right up your street, I might suggest."

5

Danger-Prone Daphne

Karen's eyes bulged, her Coke-bottles glasses exaggerating the size of her eyeballs, whilst gripping her coffee mug positioned just below her lips. "Christ! You can't live there! Bloody hell, Ginny, the Broxworth Estate hit the country's top ten most dangerous areas according to a report I read in one of the tabloid papers."

"Oh, it's not that bad. I get it's a tad shitty, but the flat seemed relatively clean."

"You've been up there?"

"Course. I went and viewed the flat yesterday. Alright, as I said, it's a bit crap. The previous couple split up and moved out, so it's just become free, and the landlord was keen to have it occupied. I could tell he was desperate, so I managed to knock him down on the price."

Karen slammed her mug down. "No! You can't live up there. You'll get murdered, raped, or both!"

"Don't exaggerate."

"Oh, Ginny, please. It's awful up there," she whined. "I can't for the life of me understand why you think this is a good idea."

"I need my own space," I paused before adding a little less convincingly, "It will be alright, I think."

Karen shifted forward in her seat and wagged her middle finger. "Boot Ali out of your flat and send him and that floozy to live there. He should be the one moving out, not you."

"Don't have a go at me. I knew you'd react like this."

"For good reason!"

"Okay, I know there are gangs, and the place is full of criminals, but not everyone who lives there is a despot, murdering git. The landlord said the girl who lived there before was a porn star. Apparently, she's made a bucket load of cash and moved on."

"My God … you're not—"

"No!" I chuckled. "Christ, I know I'm in a bit of a pickle, but I'm not planning on making a career in the adult entertainment industry."

"I should hope not!"

"Anyway, that girl lived there without getting herself murdered, despite her boyfriend now languishing on remand in Brixton Prison."

Karen's jaw sagged.

I pulled a face and shrugged my shoulders, trying to deflect away what I said, now a smidge disappointed that I divulged that particular titbit of information.

"Prison?"

"Yeah. The landlord let it slip that the porn star's boyfriend got himself arrested for murdering some rival gang member ... drugs, I think."

"Jesus," she hissed. "You'll end up raped or murdered. You cannot go and live there."

"I'm more likely to suffer that fate by going out with some weirdo-nutter that dating app keeps suggesting."

"How long is the lease?"

"Six months. I've paid up in advance, but I'm hoping to be out of there in a lot less."

Karen slumped back in her seat, huffed and shook her head in the same manner Chocolate Chip still seemed to perform. "You can't stay there. You just can't."

"It'll be alright. Honestly, it's only until I get back on my feet."

"I'm not happy about this. Honey, I don't want to pry, but didn't your mum leave you enough so you could rent somewhere better in the short term? I know your parents weren't that well off, but you and Jules must have received some inheritance."

"It's all still in probate ... some dreadful backlog, apparently."

"Oh."

"Anyway, there isn't much to be divvied up."

Karen raised her eyebrow, indicating I should continue.

"When Dad died back in 2010—"

"Is it six years already?"

"Yeah, I know. It doesn't seem possible."

I momentarily became distracted by thoughts about my father. Paul Goode was a good man. Also, after my mother's revelations, that just went to show how good he was, staying with her to support Jules and me even though we biologically couldn't be his children.

"Ginny?"

"Sorry, I was thinking about Dad."

"Paul, I presume, not this Terry fella."

"Yeah. It was that bloody investigation and false accusations that broke poor Paul. I'm sure that's why he suffered that heart attack."

"Hmmm," Karen nodded. "I still can't understand how it all came about. I mean, they arrested him and then said there was no case to answer."

"I know," I shrugged. "Of course, the committee forced him out of the club, even though he'd done nothing wrong."

"I presume they never identified who actually misappropriated the funds?"

"No ... I don't think so. Alistair's dad said the police just filed it as an unsolved case. I guess they had more to worry about, and fifty grand missing and then reappearing from the club's accounts wasn't deemed a high enough priority."

"It's not fair, though, is it? That killed your father."

I straightened up and took a deep breath. Memories of my father's difficulties could quickly bring tears to my eyes, but I was determined today that wasn't going to happen. "Anyway, after Dad died, Mum was left with no choice but to tap up one of those equity release companies. As you know, Dad had always had a bit of a gambling problem, but it transpired that his finances were in more of a pickle than Mum realised."

"Oh, hell."

"Basically, the house will go to that equity release company. Jules and I will be left to fight over a few boxes of tat and a post office savings account worth diddly squat."

"Oh, I had no idea. Honey, I'm so sorry."

"It is what it is. We can't change it … it's just spilt milk."

"Well, get moving on selling your flat and force Alistair to pay up for your side of the business. At least with your share, you can then buy something decent."

This was it. We'd touched on the subject earlier before shooting off on a tangent about my mother's multiple orgasms with Bluetooth look-a-like. I had to come clean and tell her the truth.

"Ginny?"

"I have a bit of a problem on that front," I whispered, making an involuntary grab at my parents' wedding rings I wore on a chain around my neck. I guess they were my version of a set of worry beads, which I fiddled with at times of high stress.

Karen questioned that statement with a nudge of her head and open palms whilst sporting a gaping mouth.

"The business is solely in Alistair's name. Apparently, according to my solicitor, I have no right to any of it."

Karen's expression shifted slightly with the widening of her eyes. Maybe her jaw sagged a smidge further towards the table top.

I bashed on. "When we set the business up, we put it in Ali's name. He paid me a salary ... if you see. Because I now refuse to work with him, I've rendered myself unemployed. So, as I say, technically, I have no legal right to any of the assets."

"No ... no, that can't be right," Karen muttered. Whilst still holding her shocked pose, my closest friend continued. "You put all the legwork in. You built the client base. You're the one who secured all the contracts. Christ, if it weren't for you, there would have been no business. Jesus, Ginny, this can't be right!" Karen's voice crescendo ended her rant at a level that caused a hush around us, effectively hauling George Best and Chocolate Chip from their continued hissed argument.

I rubbed my eyes with the heels of my hands. Not to wipe away tears, but to prepare myself for the next crazy statement. "I know. But there's worse to tell you."

"Oh, Jesus, Ginny! What the hell can be worse?" she whined, appearing exasperated.

As I prepared to launch into my next revelation about my calamitous situation, I noticed Bluetooth step past me towards the door. Apart from becoming mesmerised by the uncanny resemblance to the man in that photo my mother had cherished, I couldn't help but stare because of his odd action when opening the door and the comment he muttered.

"Ginny ... hello, anyone there?"

"Sorry, sorry, I got distracted."

"Yes, I could see. You could run after him and ask him out."

"What?"

"Bluetooth ... you seem bewitched by the bloke. Look, he's still out there yakking away. That's got to be the longest phone conversation in history."

I swivelled in my chair to peer through the window at him as he waved his arms about, appearing to be holding an argument with thin air.

"I think he's a bloody nutter. Probably a good job you didn't ask him out. I reckon you dodged a bullet there."

I turned back and nodded. However, what I'd witnessed and heard played on my mind.

"Right, come on, let's have it. What else have you got to tell me that's worse than Ali swindling the business from you?"

"The flat."

"What about it?"

"It's owned by the business. Ali owns the flat, and I have no legal claim to it. We purchased it as a tax write-off ... basically using the business to fund the purchase. Although our solicitor said it wasn't completely ethical, it was legal and avoided a bucket load of tax."

There, I'd said it. At last, I'd unburdened myself by divulging my dire situation to Karen. Although a complete disaster, I almost felt relieved despite the tears pricking at my eyes. I rummaged through my bag and plucked up a tissue to dab the corner of my eye.

"Ginny, please don't tell me you have no right to any of the proceeds of the sale of your flat."

I shook my head. "My solicitor reckons I'm entitled to a settlement as we're married. The problem is Ali technically owns the flat. That's why I can't ask him and that thigh-gap floozy to leave."

"But you will get half?"

I offered a slight nod and a shrug of the shoulders. "Yes … eventually. My solicitor just said I would need to be patient. He said the situation wasn't ideal, but he thought he could secure proceeds from the sale of the flat."

"And the business?"

"No … I'm screwed on that front."

"Honey, you want another coffee," whispered Karen. I think she felt the need to say something. So, suggesting another coffee served up by Footlong was probably better than screaming at me or offering some platitude, like 'everything happens for a reason' or 'time heals'.

"No," I squeaked from behind the tissue as I prodded my dripping nose. "I just need a moment."

Karen nodded and took my free hand in hers. A gesture of comfort, presumably now recognising this wasn't the time to berate me. Although I continued to snivel, she couldn't maintain eye contact and presumably preferred to stare out of the window in the direction of Bluetooth.

"Is that weirdo still there?" I asked, keen to say something and change the subject.

"No," she confirmed by shaking her head, allowing her brown bob-styled hair to sway. "No, he's gone."

"I wish I could be more like you, Velma Dinkley." I peered up at her, trying to lighten the mood.

Karen snorted a laugh. My closest friend since secondary school had always been Velma due to not only her looks but her brilliant academic mind and being comfortable in her own skin. Danny was definitely Shaggy Rogers – not the most handsome man, but kind and loving with the propensity to start every sentence with the word 'like'.

Just like the auburn-haired cartoon beauty, despite my appearance looking nothing like Daphne Blake and irrespective of Karen's insistence I was FAF, I always seemed to attract problems and end up in some sticky situation. My husband, Alistair Strachan, had done the dirty on me. So, although nothing like Fred Jones, he wouldn't be there to save Danger-Prone Daphne this time.

"Did you hear what he said when he opened the door?"

"Who?"

"Bluetooth."

Karen swished her hair again.

I lobbed my tissue into my bag and sat forward, sniffing a few times. "When he opened the door, the nutter waved his hand as if offering the open doorway to what looked like an imaginary friend."

"So ... he's on a bit of a spectrum. I said you dodged a bullet."

"You didn't hear what he said?"

"No."

"He said ... 'after you, Deana Beacham'."

"Is that supposed to mean something?"

"Not to you ... but it does to me."

Karen shrugged.

"When Mum told me about Terry and her little fling—"

"Would that be multiple-orgasms-Terry?"

"Yes, the very same. So, although Dad never knew what happened on that sofa that night, they stayed friends with Terry despite Terry and his girlfriend splitting up. Anyway, Mum and Dad went to his funeral in the early '80s after he died of a heart attack when bonking some young floozy at a work's do."

"Blimey, your Uncle Terry put it about a bit, didn't he? I bet that shattered the illusion for your mother if she was still besotted with him."

"Oh, I don't know. Although, I have to say, hearing your sixty-four-year-old mother almost coo about the man was excruciatingly embarrassing. But, listen to this, she said she held nothing but contempt for that woman who he was with in that hotel room—"

"She blamed her for giving Terry a heart attack?"

"Yes ... unbelievably, I think my mother harboured ideas that she and Terry would end up together at some point, despite the fact the man was married."

"Christ, Ginny, I can't believe all this. What with all your issues and your mum's history."

"I know. Anyway, the woman he was with when he died in that hotel room also attended his funeral. According to Mum, they had words."

"Bloody hell ... what, like a cat fight?"

"No, I don't think so because Dad was oblivious about Mum and Terry's fling. However, the woman had an unusual name."

"Deana Beacham?"

"Precisely."

"And Bluetooth man, who you say is the spitting image of your biological father from the '70s, just uttered the same name of the woman who killed him."

"Yeah," I nodded and sniffed.

"Okay ... coincidence, I expect. Now, I know you probably don't want to talk about it, and the last thing I want to do is upset you, but we need to think of a plan of what to do about that bastard husband of yours."

6

Stand By Your Man

"Oh, yes, darling. Yes, yes, that hits the spot," panted Deana, as she writhed on the bed. "You're so good at this, my love. My darling Dickie could send tingles up my spine but, I have to say, your wonderful manly hands really know what they're doing when you touch me like that."

"Yes, well, Sharon used to always suffer from tense shoulders when she became stressed, so I suppose I've had plenty of practise." Terry knelt back from where he'd been massaging Deana's neck and shoulders as she lay face down on the bed.

Deana spun around, her black, sheer, silk dressing gown parting causing her naked form to become exposed. "Oh, that was wonderful. I feel like a new woman," she purred. "While we're here, we could, perhaps?" she expectantly enquired, sporting raised eyebrows whilst twirling her dressing-gown tie around like some cheerleader spinning their baton.

Terry scrambled away before hopping off the bed and backing up to the bedroom window.

"Oh, alright," she belligerently barked. "I take it that's a no, then?"

Terry disbelievingly shook his head.

"You don't have to scuttle away from me as if I'm some hideous insect. It was just an idea. I thought it would kill a bit of time, that's all," she huffed.

"Christ, Deana. I take it that your claim of needing a massage was just a ruse to get me to touch you?"

"No … no, not really. Whatever do you take me for? I was just suggesting how we could while away a few hours, that's all."

"Huh," he offered, with a shake of his head. "You weren't suffering from tight muscle spasms, were you?"

"I might have," she shrugged. "Well, yes, but perhaps not the sort of muscle spasms I hoped to enjoy."

"Oh, give it a rest, woman. And for God's sake, cover yourself up. You're posing as if some Baroque style painter is about to whip out his brushes and immortalise you in oil."

Deana lay her arm above her head. "Like this, darling? I look like the *Sleeping Venus*."

Terry tutted, turned away from her and snapped down the slats of the Venetian blind to survey the street – anything to curtail Deana's flirtatious advances.

"She was also known as the queen of pleasure. Something the Roman goddess and I have in common, you know."

Terry dramatically sighed and again shook his head. "Have that lot informed you of our next mission, yet?"

"That lot?"

"Yes, the Powers-That-Be, or whoever they are."

"Oh, I see. Yes, whilst you nipped out to the pub last night, something that is becoming a bit of a habit, I might add, I received an update on our next little jaunt."

Terry allowed the slat to ping back into position and glanced around at the queen of pleasure as she writhed semi-naked on the bed, raising her hips in his direction. "What are you doing?"

"Pelvic floor, darling. Muscle strengthening technique."

"Really? Anyway, come on, what did they say?" he questioned, whilst trying to ignore her less than subtle attempt to display her womanhood at him, not for one moment believing Deana was performing some floor exercise routine. That said, if he didn't know better, she appeared to be performing some weird gymnastic exercise as she repeatedly pumped her hips forward.

The nightly visits to the local pub were his way of securing some much-needed Deana-free time. He'd started this new evening routine when her dead ex-husband had turned up a couple of weeks back after killing Lee Parish by way of crushing the evil man's head in with a hefty silver candlestick snatched from the altar. Although Deana walked out on old Sidders thirty-odd years ago, and despite her rather diminutive opinion of his sexual prowess, Terry had hoped Sidney and Deana might have got it on – quenching her sexual desires – thus negating the need for her constant advances.

Disappointingly, although Deana had said that Sidders had been up for a tumble in the sheets, as he'd apparently put it, Deana rebuffed his advances due to remembering their previous somewhat lacklustre encounters and not wishing for a repeat performance.

When explaining her decision, Deana reminded Terry that Sidders was more akin to *'Jones the Steam'* from *'Ivor the Engine'* than any greased-up hunk of a man on the footplate of the Flying Scotsman. Also, renaming Sidders *'Ivor the Boneless'* followed by her trademark chortle. Then, Deana further added that she wanted a real man when her time was up roaming the earth as part of the community of the walking dead. Although Terry suspected it was all just bluster, the wanton woman suggested that she would happily seek out the real Viking chieftain, *Ivar the Boneless,* because she quite fancied partaking in a spot of rape and pillage.

Of course, that's assuming she was destined to traverse the circles of hell. However, Terry believed the punishment for lust and fornication, which Deana was undoubtedly guilty of, and if Dante's vision of Inferno was to be correct, was for the souls to suffer the ravages of a perpetual storm. Whereas the punishment for rape, pillage and murder, which he suspected would be the case for the Viking warlord, would be to be boiled in blood. So, although the vivacious Deana would most certainly be nipping down the fabled thirteen steps to hell, Terry doubted she would be afforded the opportunity for an introduction to many Vikings. Also, he presumed they all went to Valhalla.

Although he needed no reminding, Deana was like no other fifty-something woman he'd ever met or likely to wherever he ended up.

"We can only complete our next mission once you've made love to me," Deana panted, as she continued her Nellie Kim floor routine. Notwithstanding her exertions, Terry doubted the famous Soviet gymnast had ever performed her floor exercise in the nude.

"A woman of your age needs to be careful. You'll end up with a slipped disc if you carry on pumping your hips up and down," Terry nodded to Deana's midriff. "And I'm quite certain that the Powers-That-Be have made no such stipulation that you and I have to copulate like … well, like some sex-crazed bunnies."

"Bonobos primates, darling," palpitated Deana before collapsing on the mattress, exhausted and rather flustered from her pelvic thrusting.

"Sorry?"

"According to a programme on the National Geographic channel, I once watched, those lucky little monkeys are the most sex-crazed animals on the planet."

"I doubt they could lay a glove on you," muttered Terry.

"Sorry? You said something?"

"Nothing."

"Don't mutter, darling. I chose to ignore your vulgar ageist comment. However, please refrain from muttering. You're not a child. Only snotty-nosed, grubby little children mutter. Now, as I was saying, Bonobos copulate like humans might shake hands, and they shag each other's brains out to settle arguments. Rather wonderful, don't you think? Instead of those stupid politicians shouting at each other across the dispatch box, they could turn the House of Commons into a love nest and fornicate all day long. That would give a new meaning to cross-bench party support."

"Good God. Not only do you watch and read salacious material, but you're also into animal porn!"

Deana tutted. "Oh Terry, it was a documentary. I'll grant you that the subject matter wasn't what David Attenborough might commentate on, like the *Blue Planet*. However, I found it interesting that these little furry fellas enjoy sexual relations with all family members and apparently, with amazing regularity, perform all positions detailed in the *Kama Sutra*."

"Christ! Not exactly Animal Magic, is it? I really can't imagine what Johnny Morris would make of the merrymaking monkeys."

"Bonobos, darling. We could learn a lot from them. No more wars, just love making."

"Can we move off the subject of bonking Bonobos and get back to the details regarding our next mission?"

"Yes, alright. So, although we can't really claim to have solved our Damian's little crisis, the Powers-That-Be are satisfied with the end result."

"I take it that Sidders will be punished for his little rampage of murder. That's assuming he was responsible for Bridget's death in Paris, that is."

"Yes, it seems that way. I've stipulated that good-old Sidders requires the application of a leash upon him. I know he helped us out of a particularly tight spot with that horrible man Lee, along with throwing that awful woman to her death, but I'm a little worried that I might be on his hit list, so to speak."

"Sorry? What are you on about?"

"He might try to kill me, too. I cheated on him all those years ago and rebuffed his advances when he stayed with us a fortnight ago."

"Deana, you're already dead. I can't see how he can kill you again."

"Oh, darling, you're right. Oh, thank God for that," she chortled. "You've put my mind at ease. Thank you, darling."

"So, come on, spit it out. What's our bloody mission this time? Now we've saved my two children from the evil gits who wanted to destroy them, who else needs the help of a couple of ghosts?"

"Darling—"

"And can you please cover yourself up? It's not easy conducting a conversation with you whilst you lay spread-eagled in the nuddy."

"Oh, alright," she tutted, whilst whisking the dressing gown around her body and dramatically tightening the tie. "And please step away from the window. Dreary Drake was prowling around in her sensible brown loafers yesterday. If she spots you standing by the bedroom window, we could find ourselves in a spot of bother."

Terry flung open the wardrobe to select some clothes from Deana's dead husband's extensive collection of designer apparel. After grabbing a pair of jeans, a polo shirt and underwear, he turned to Deana. "Well?"

"Well, what?"

"Our mission?"

"Oh, yes. They were a little tight-lipped on the details this time. All I managed to glean from them was we needed to save a woman called Virginia Strachan."

"Never heard of the woman. The only Virginia I can think of is Wade, the tennis player."

"What about Tammy Wynette and Patsy Cline?"

Terry lobbed the jeans and polo shirt on the ottoman positioned at the foot of the bed, holding on to the clean boxers as he contemplated changing. "What the hell have they got to do with anything?"

"Darling, both ladies' real name is Virginia."

"Oh. Anyway, as I said, I don't know a Virginia Strachan."

"Well, they suggested you would know her."

"Me?" spat Terry, as he prepared to change.

"Yes, darling."

"Can you turn around or close your eyes?"

"Why?"

"So I can change my pants."

"If you think I'm going to miss you whipping off your boxers, you're very much mistaken. I have a front-row seat, and I'm not missing this event for anything."

Terry tutted and swivelled around before shimmying out of his underwear. "Why would I know this Virginia woman?"

"Lovely bottom, darling. I don't know. They just said you would."

"Well, I've never heard of her. Who is she?"

"You've put them on inside out," she giggled. "Apparently, you were friendly with her mother."

Terry glanced down, noting he had, as she suggested, applied his underwear inside out. He turned around and whisked them down. "Who's the mother?"

"Your bottom is all hairy, darling. Did you know that? It's covered in fine, downy hair like one of my mohair jumpers."

Terry huffed and dismissively shook his head as he quickly flipped his pants around and reapplied them.

"The mother is a woman called Elizabeth Goode."

Terry's hand hovered near the ottoman when making a grab for his shirt before glancing up at her. "Goode?"

"Yes. I take it you can remember her. As they intimated you were friendly, that suggests she must have been one of your many conquests."

"Oh … I can't recall. The name sort of rings a bell."

"I suppose there were that many, it must be difficult to remember all your little love affairs. How many, exactly?"

"Oh, I don't know. Anyway, who tells you the missions? And why don't they talk to me?"

"It's complicated, darling. And, as you well know, I'm your beautiful guide whose sole purpose is to support you to set things straight, so to speak. Whilst looking gorgeous, of course."

Terry huffed and grabbed the clothes from the ottoman. Although frustrated she wouldn't divulge the information, he knew it was fairly pointless to push her for answers, knowing the woman would turn every conversation around to her sexual desires – something he was rather keen to avoid.

"So, that's it, is it? We have to help this woman called Virginia, and her mother's name was Goode, who, apparently, I once knew."

"Yes, darling. They suggested there was some issue with her husband. They also said to mention Sunny Hunny. I have no idea what that meant, so I googled it. Apparently, it's a term used as a nickname for a girl with a vibrant nature or the golden nectar Pooh Bear enjoyed. Although, quite frankly, I really can't see how that helps much."

Terry halted his leg mid-air as he prepared to slot it into the leg of his jeans. "Christ almighty … it can't be …"

"Darling?"

"1977 …"

"Oh, yes, the Silver Jubilee. I recall my mother wanting me to help serve jelly and ice-cream at the street party to all the little shits from the neighbourhood. But I was having none of that, so I snuck off to the cinema with my boyfriend. I think we watched *Confessions from a Holiday Camp*; you know, those saucy films with all those funny innuendos. Not that I can remember much about the story line because I recall my boyfriend and I were otherwise engaged when romping around in the back row. Anyway, darling, what about 1977? What did you get up to?"

"I went to Sunny Hunny."

7

Guess Who's Coming to Dinner

"Ginny, I'm not happy about this. The whole place is full of despots, rapists, murderers and drug dealers. Did you see the look those hoodie thugs gave us when we turned up? When Danny makes it back down the stairwell, I'd be surprised if our car has any alloys left on it."

"Karen, it will be alright. I'll keep the door locked and bolted and only go out in the daytime. As I said, it's just a stopgap until I can get back on my feet."

"Christ, this place has even got a steel meshed gate to cover the front door. Didn't that indicate this might not be the best place to rent a flat?"

"Well, that will keep me safe, won't it?" I quipped.

"Hilarious. You know what I mean. D'you want me to stay tonight? Or I could ask Danny to kip on the sofa and keep guard."

"Karen, stop fussing. If Danny stayed here tonight, what about the next night and so forth?"

"Alright, alright."

"Look, it will be fine. Now, come on, it's gone half-three, and you have to pick the girls up."

Karen hovered, chewing her lip.

"Go! I'll be fine. You can't leave my goddaughters stranded at the school gates. This place might be full of undesirables, but perverts lurk around schools, so go and get the girls. I'll call you tomorrow."

After persuading my closest friend that all was good, I closed the front door of my new humble abode, crouched down by the letter box, and proceeded to howl. Although I now realised the mistake I'd made when moving in here, I really couldn't admit that to Karen. On the way over with my collection of suitcases filling the back of their people carrier, I nearly bottled it and asked Danny to turn back. However, I'd stayed strong, knowing sleeping in Karen's spare room was not a sustainable solution to my current predicament.

I covered my mouth to muffle the sound of my sobbing whilst the tears streamed down my cheeks. I knew I'd be alright in a moment, but I just needed to sob, and sob I did.

2016 was panning out to be a particularly tough year. It was only May, but I still mourned for my mother, lost earlier in the year when taken by cancer; my husband had cheated with Love-Island girl; and now I was pretty much penniless after Ali had employed a crack team of lawyers to ensure I would soon depart our failed marriage with nothing – zip, bugger all – apart from a collection of clothes rammed into an assemblage of suitcases, a slim hope of a settlement of the sale of our flat, and a bucket full of regrets.

2016 – my annus horribilis.

The Queen might have had her issues in 1992, namely the split of three of her children's marriages, topless shots of Fergie with her toes being sucked, and a book by Andrew Morton revealing Charles's affair with Camilla. Not to mention Squidgygate – that article in the tabloids about Diana and some Gin heir, culminating in all sorts of revelations about the Wales's failed relationship. And to top it all off, her precious castle burnt.

Well, I could steal a march on all that. Although I didn't own a castle and disappointingly hadn't managed to bring any children into this world, so no issues about my offspring's potential future divorce proceedings, I now resided on a hideous estate inhabited by characters that could have taken the leading roles in *Scum*. Also, I was stone-broke, jobless, and loveless whilst heading towards my forties and shooting down the helter-skelter of life at breakneck speed towards oblivion.

I huffed out a sigh and a slightly hysterical giggle at the steel box that covered the back of the letter box. I'd assumed it was there because the previous tenant owned a dog, thus preventing chewed mail. However, I learned from the landlord that wasn't its purpose, but rather to prevent fires when fireworks or Molotov cocktails were shoved through the letter box – apparently, a regular occurrence. Perhaps that snippet of information, along with the steel mesh covering the front door, should have been enough of a suggestion to explain the low rent.

I'd willingly stepped into a war zone.

Like my marriage, I'd moved into this damn place without heeding the warning signs. When I'd started dating Alistair, my parents were not best pleased.

Of course, at the time, it somewhat bemused me why they would take umbrage about my choice of boyfriend. Ali was clean cut, degree educated, attentive and generous. Also, Ali's parents were successful, middle-class, upstanding citizens and members of the same golf club – so what was the problem? It's fair to say, despite their frosty attitude to Alistair, my parents' dismay at the announcement of our engagement took me by surprise. My mother had said it would end badly, even pleading with me not to go through with it when Karen and my other maids of honour fussed with my wedding dress when arriving at the church.

"You should have listened to your mother," I muttered, straightening up and smearing the tears across my cheeks with the heels of my hands. "Come on, Ginny, get a grip. Christ, you're even talking to yourself now." I scrunched my neck and rolled my shoulders, contemplating that I better nip over to the convenience store and stock up on a few essentials – like wine.

After grabbing my purse, I hopped out onto the landing, shooting a furtive glance left and right to assess my surroundings. Then, whilst on high alert, I closed the front door, not bothering to secure the steel mesh gate because that all seemed a bit of a faff.

"Oi, bitch."

Assuming that rather offensive shout wasn't aimed at me, I scooted along, head down, praying I could reach the stairwell before some altercation kicked off with whoever had called out and the recipient of that vulgar address.

"Oi, bitch. You from flat one-twenty."

I glanced around to spot who presumably was my new neighbour with her head poked out of the doorframe of the flat next door as she raised her chin at me and flared her nostrils.

"Come 'ere."

Somewhat nervously, I complied. Although not overly chuffed about being referred to as bitch, a new term of endearment that my soon-to-be ex-husband had chosen to call me during our brief calls over the past few weeks. However, I thought it might be prudent to introduce myself.

"You ain't locked your gate."

"Oh, ha, thanks. I was only nipping down to the shops, so I didn't think it would matter," I squeaked, mouse-like.

"Bit of a dippy cow, are ya?" Those nostrils flared again.

"Sorry?"

"You will be when some wanker bust your bleedin' door down and nicks your gear."

"Oh … really?"

"My little'un, Gabriel, can't resist an easy target."

"Sorry?"

"Jesus, is that all ya gotta say?"

"Sorry, are you suggesting you would allow your son to break into my flat?"

The woman shrugged, folded her arms across her chest and flared those nostrils at me.

"Well, I'm shocked! First of all, I'm surprised you're old enough to have grown-up children. And secondly, I'm aghast you would allow such a thing." Lord knows why, but I seemed to have employed a hoity-toity accent.

"Gabe ... he's ten. And what has my age got to do wiv ya?"

Realising I was overstepping the mark – although somewhat shocked that this woman allowed her ten-year-old to dabble in breaking and entering between completing his homework and watching children's TV – and as I now had to live next to this family, I moved to a more conciliatory tone. "You're right. It's none of my business. That was kind of you to say about the gate ... mesh thingy over my door."

The woman nodded and smirked.

"I'm Virginia ... Ginny. Apart from my soon-to-be ex-husband, I'm not usually known by the name bitch."

"Deli ... most people call me Deli."

"Is that short for Delilah?"

"Nah ... Delfina. Reckon my mum were pissed when she chose my name. It's some Greek goddess or something or other. I mean, how many Greek goddesses do ya see with cornrow braids? I don't look nuttin like no goddess."

"Oh, right. Lovely name. Nice hair too." I offered a thin smile, nodding to her long, braided hair that hung almost to her waist.

"I could braid yours for ya, if ya like?"

"Oh," I reached up and twizzled my ponytail, lost for words. "Err ... no, but thanks. Your hair is adorable, though."

Deli jutted her chin and snorted at my compliment. "You know, you're like that posh boy, Damian, who used to live a couple of doors down." She nodded along the landing. "He and Courts from your old flat took off into the sunset. Bleedin' lucky bitch, I can tell ya."

"Oh, was that the porn—"

"Courts?" she interrupted. "Yeah, she dabbled in all sorts. Bit of prossy work, films, that sort of stuff. Bit of a stunner is our Courteney."

"Mum, where's my fucking Coke?" boomed out a child's voice from somewhere deep in the flat behind Deli.

"Get it yourself, ya little wanker," Deli threw over her shoulder. "Kids, who'd have 'em, eh?" she raised her eyebrows and chuckled. "Course, I've got the figure to do what Courteney done, but wiv my back along wiv needing to convince the Social about my disabilities, writhing around with some punter ain't possible."

"Oh, I see," I mumbled, still shocked at the verbal exchange between mother and son.

"Yeah, those bastards from the Social always try and catch me out. But, hey, if they're dippy enough to pay me disability benefit so I don't have to work, that's their problem."

"Yes, I can imagine."

"What's your game then? You a hooker? I suspect a fancy bit of blonde skirt like you can earn a few quid. Punters pay well for blondes with nice tits," she nodded at my chest.

"Oh, hell no!" I blurted, feeling myself blush due to being gobsmacked by her suggestion and not knowing whether to be flattered by her compliment; if that's what it was.

"Alright, keep your bleedin' split-ends on. I was only asking."

"No, I'm … I'm between jobs at the moment."

"On benefits, then?"

I shrugged, thinking that may well be something I needed to sort out.

"Ex-husband, and unemployed. I reckon you've hit rock bottom and ended up in this shithole."

"Something like that."

"Oh, shit." Deli straightened up and turned on her heels to shout into the flat. "Gabe! Nelson's coming. Hide the gear."

I glanced down the landing, where I spotted a black guy wearing what appeared to be a t-shirt at least two sizes too small, causing his arm and chest muscles to stretch the garment to the seams as he purposefully strode towards us. Although with only an hour under my belt, I surmised through my experience of living on the estate that this bloke was not here to exchange pleasantries. Also, going by my new neighbour's reaction, it suggested he was someone best avoided.

Now concerned for my safety, I pondered whether to dart back to my flat or make a bolt for the other stairwell and thus avoid becoming embroiled in whatever was about to go down; either a drug exchange or a violent encounter. As he quickly closed the gap between us, and based on the fact the thuggish man appeared capable of snapping Conor McGregor in half – that cage fighter chap who my husband hero-worshipped – I decided on option two. However, I halted my getaway when Deli bellowed at him.

"Nelson the nark. What you 'ere for, then? You come to nick your little sister or bang up your nephew?" Whilst straining her head around the door frame, she turned to me and whispered. "My brother's the bleedin' filth."

Presuming Deli meant her brother was a police officer, and as all officers of the law were upstanding citizens, I scrapped my plan to flee. Perhaps this was fortuitous, and I could report the youths who'd intimidated Danny when hauling my suitcases up the stairs.

Although ripped, I think that's the term, his demeanour suggested anything but a cage-fighter type. As the thirty-something, debonair and affable appearing man approached, he flashed me a heart-melting, Sidney-Poitier-styled smile before turning to face Deli.

"It's Mum. She's suffered another relapse," delivered in a warm but gravelly tone that befitted his appearance.

8

Brief Encounter

Sidney Poitier's lookalike's statement appeared to shrink the brash woman, causing her to lose that rough persona, regressing to almost becoming childlike. Akin to watching her transform back through her twenties and teens, the rotating time clock halted at about the age of ten – an age of innocence – similar to the age of her thieving son, Gabriel, who probably lost his innocence whilst still in nappies.

The aggressive body language she'd presumably perfected over the years of living on the estate evaporated as quickly as her chin began to tremble. Her youth and vulnerability became apparent as her persona altered to display a young woman who'd probably led a somewhat harsh existence.

Nelson reached out and grabbed her arm. "Look, I just spoke to the Pastor and he don't fink she'll last the week. I've checked online, and I reckon I can get a couple of seats on a flight tomorrow. I fink we should go."

"What about Gabe?" she mumbled.

Nelson huffed. "I can't afford three flights. Anyway, he's never met his grandmother, and I fink he needs to stay at school."

"I can't just leave him here on his own. The bleedin' Social will do me for that. In fact, I wouldn't mind bettin' you'd shop me to the Social before we left."

As I stepped away, Nelson again huffed and groaned, presumably frustrated at the constant jibes about his career choice. Something I imagine his younger sister trotted out with some regularity.

Whilst attempting to secure the steel mesh over my door, I wondered if her son was still scrambling around the flat, shoving the 'gear' into well-used hiding places before Deli allowed her brother to step inside.

"Deli, please. Just for one moment, can you stop the constant aspersions about my job?"

"Aspersions! Listen to yourself. Fuck sake, you've forgotten where ya come from. Fucking aspersions," she tutted, before returning her attention to me. "Oi, Ginny, whatever your bleedin' name is," she bellowed at me, that aggressive tone now fully reformed.

For the second time, whilst attempting to nip down the landing on my way to the shops to grab some much-needed wine, I spun around after this woman called out to me. At least this time, she didn't refer to me as *bitch*.

"Ya reckon ya could take Gabe in for a few days, so I can visit my dying mum?"

"Me?" I questioned, whilst involuntarily poking my chest. The palpable quiver in my voice confirming this was an uncomfortable situation.

"Yeah. What else ya gotta do? Ya reckon you're unemployed. So, keeping an eye out on Gabe shouldn't be that hard."

Whilst exaggeratingly shaking my head and nervously stepping back towards her, it appeared her brother's expression suggested he could detect the sheer panic which must have oozed from my every pore.

"Oh, no. No, sorry. I couldn't possibly do that."

"Some bleedin' neighbour you're turning out to be. Courteney would have stepped up to the plate in a heartbeat."

"What about another friend?" quizzed Nelson.

"Yeah, well, it ain't gonna be that easy at this short notice. Not now this posh cow reckons she can't help." She turned and waved her middle digit at me. "We look after each other up here. Ya gonna live here, ya need to start playing by the rules. Ya fink with your fancy clothes and plummy voice that you're better than us. Well, bitch, ya ain't. You're gonna find it tough, that I can tell ya."

"Deli, come on. Leave the woman alone." Nelson offered me a tight smile and a slight nod that suggested I should go.

Despite his non-verbal suggestion, I stepped forward, offering my thrust-out index finger in return for hers. "Excuse me? I've only just met you, and you expect me to put my life on hold to babysit your son?" I belligerently batted back.

Although this odious place seemed to have sucked away my confidence, her thinly disguised threats appeared to provide a resurgence of my fortitude that I'd previously left at the threshold to my bedroom when witnessing my husband perform on top of that panting starfish.

"Bitch!" Deli leapt forward, only to be held back by her brother as he grabbed her around the waist whilst grappling with her flailing arms in an attempt to stop his sister from landing one upon me.

"Deli! Jesus, hold up."

I hopped back, shocked at her barbarous attitude and somewhat concerned about the type of woman I now dubiously called my neighbour.

"Hey, I ain't here to tell you what to do, but I suggest you do one," Nelson threw in my direction as he maintained a firm grip on his Rottweiler younger sister whilst trying to avoid a slap from her flaying arms. He nodded down the landing, reinforcing his suggestion.

"Alright! Christ, get off me. I ain't going to slap the bitch."

I scooted towards the stairwell, not waiting to discover whether Deli had decided against meting out violence. Whilst traversing back down the concrete steps, that only half an hour ago I'd hauled up my suitcases, I pinched my nose and held my breath to avoid sucking in gulps of the stale, piss-ridden air which hung like a heavy fog in the enclosed space. As I reached the bottom, I gulped in a breath and hovered to compose myself before stepping into the central square.

Although not used to confrontations, I'd always benefited from a strong character. Alistair used to call me his rock as in reference to possessing the strength of character to stay focused and calm him when the going got tough in the early days of growing our business. However, the events that transpired over the past few months resulted in that hard-shell persona cracking and becoming fragile, leaving me constantly vulnerable with tears never far away.

Whilst willing myself not to cry, I stepped forward around the corner of the stairwell to come face to face with a pack of hoodie-clad youths who circled around as they employed a tactic which suggested they'd regularly used when intimidating their cornered prey.

"You lost, sket?" questioned the youth who entered my personal space, offering me a minacious smirk. His yellowing eyes suggested his diet was deficient in the correct vitamins to promote a healthy lifestyle or perhaps a touch of jaundice. He offered a slight upward jut of his chin, which I took as an indication that it was now my turn to speak.

Although I wasn't lost, I surmised he wasn't there to offer directions or likely to whip out a copy of an A-Z street map, but more his opening line to suggest I'd unwittingly stepped onto his turf. As for calling me sket – I could only assume it wasn't a particularly endearing term.

As I nervously glanced around, Yellow-Eye snatched my purse and stepped back a pace as I reeled around. "Hey," I whimpered. Although he was still within easy reach, I knew the futility of making a grab for my purse, a decision reinforced by one of his disciples as he held out an arm blocking my path.

Yellow-Eye grinned back at me as he prized apart the press stud. "You got any Ps?"

"Ps?"

"Cash, you sket."

"Sket?"

Yellow-Eye sucked his teeth before jabbing his chin forward. "Bitch ... you got cash, bitch?"

"There's nothing in there ... just a few notes and receipts." I stammered. Notwithstanding the imminent separation from my last remaining two ten-pound notes, which was annoying, but I felt violated.

Yellow-Eye thumbed out my bank cards, indiscriminately pinging them into the corners of the stairwell whilst holding that perfected nefarious grin and allowing those discoloured eyes to penetrate through to my soul. As I watched my cards scatter across the concrete floor, I wished their credit balances were just as easy to distance myself from.

The ever-so-welcome sound of footsteps thumping on the concrete stairs above offered some hope that this gang of reprobates would take flight. Now, feeling concerned for my safety, I really couldn't care less if they skedaddled with my purse. That said, that would negate any way of being able to purchase my much-needed bottle of wine.

A woman came into view as she turned the corner on the stairs. Although I guessed she would be of about my age, going by her unkempt look, enhanced by the washed-out-cracked lettering *'This Cute Babe Takes No Shit!'* blazoned across her t-shirt, that's where any similarity ended. She halted as she turned the corner and took in the scene below.

I shot her a pleading look.

Although I guess desire is in the eye of the beholder, I doubted many would describe the woman as a 'cute babe'. However, I desperately hoped she would be the sort that 'takes no shit' and her presence would be enough for this posse of reprobates to take flight.

"Piss off." spat one of Yellow-Eye's disciples, which was all that was required for her to retreat up the concrete stairs and disappear, suggesting she didn't live up to those printed words across her chest.

As I listened to the woman thud her way back up those concrete steps, I realised that hoping another resident of this hideous place might intervene and do the right thing had been nothing but wishful thinking.

Yellow-Eye held the last card aloft, my Amex maxed-out gold card, which I believe now sported a ten grand balance and a somewhat scary twenty-nine per cent APR. "Virginia Strachan. This card got a pin number?"

"No … no, it doesn't have one … I don't have it," I stammered, unsuccessfully trying to lie my way out of this mess.

Yellow-Eye scrunched his nose at me as he pocketed the notes and flung my pink Radley purse in the general direction of my discarded cards. "You better pick up the one you can remember, then." He stepped forward. "Phone."

"Sorry?"

"You will be, bitch. Give us your phone."

Despite his lack of a healthy diet, his grin revealed a perfect set of teeth and, surprisingly, his breath offered a clean, fresh waft as he huffed in my face. Despite her apparent lack of culinary skills, I surmised his mother had managed to impress upon her son the need to maintain a half-decent oral hygiene routine.

The hoodie-clad youth who'd previously blocked my path pulled my phone from my back pocket, rubbing his hand across my bottom as he did so. I shuddered at his touch but fought to maintain eye contact with Yellow-Eye as I desperately tried to strengthen my resolve.

"Nice arse for an old bitch," he snorted, before passing my mobile to the leader of the pack.

My hand involuntarily shot to my necklace, that nervous reaction I always performed in situations of high stress, and, let's face it, getting mugged when on my way to buy wine was pretty high up there on the stress scale. I'd read somewhere to manage stress, one should apply the five-by-five rule. If your situation won't matter in five years, don't spend more than five minutes stressing over it. Bloody easy suggestion for the author to make, but I'm presuming that they weren't faced with Yellow-Eye and his disciples when penning his not-so-helpful ideas. Unfortunately, as Yellow-Eye accepted my phone, my actions drew his eye, thus alerting him to the fact that I sported two gold rings attached to a gold chain around my neck.

Yellow-Eye slapped away my hand and snagged the chain, resulting in my head jerking forward before he relieved me of my parents' rings. Although the value of the gold was, I suspect, minimal, the sentimental value was priceless.

"No, please. Not those," I whimpered.

While contemplating grabbing my rings, the git to my left blew a cloud of cigarette smoke in my face, causing me to wince. He definitely needed to take some advice from Yellow-Eye in the oral health department. "You need to pay up for protection. Us heads just seen you move into that flat up there." He raised his eyes, indicating the second level up one flight of stairs where the *'This-Cute-Babe-Takes-No-Shit!'* woman had sensibly and rather hastily retreated to. "So, bitch, pick up your cards and get us two hundred from the cash point. That will do for this month."

I reeled around upon him. "No!"

Yellow-Eyes slammed his hand on Stinky-breath's chest, forcing him back against the wet iron-ore-stained concrete wall that sported a floor-to-ceiling splash of faded graffiti. As Stinky-breath's back thumped against the wall, he offered up no protest, suggesting Yellow-Eye called the shots. "It's two hundred a month," he calmly asserted, stepping close and laying his hand on the crotch of my jeans. "I could make it one-fifty and take the rest in kind … Friday afternoons are good for me," he delivered, whilst offering a wide nefarious grin. "So, if you're a decent shag, I can offer a discount—"

"Oi! Piss off. Go on, piss off," bellowed a voice from behind me.

Unlike earlier, when hearing the approach of the unkempt woman who'd attempted to traverse the stairwell, I hadn't detected the footsteps of this new arrival. Now, as we all swivelled around, Deli's brother stood at the corner of the stairwell above us, pointing at Yellow-Eye.

The gang momentarily held their ground before Yellow-Eye held his hands up and backed up a pace. His disciples sped past him, disappearing into the labyrinth of alleyways that served as access through this grotesque estate.

"We ain't done, Virg–in–ia," he delivered with his trademark grin before turning and hot-footing after his mates.

For the second time today, I covered my mouth to dull the sound of the sobs that involuntarily took hold whilst I shook, simultaneously detecting my knees starting to buckle. Before I hit the ground, Nelson took hold of my arm.

"Hey, hey. Come on." He gently lowered my hand away from my trembling lips. "Come on. It's okay. They've gone." He nodded to my purse and cards, which lay in the damp corner of the stairwell, nestled in the puddle with various items of litter and discarded needles.

"My stuff," I stammered, pointing down.

Nelson extracted a plastic bag and a pair of blue nitrate gloves from his jeans pocket. "Always prepared," he muttered, as he snapped them on and knelt down before gingerly plucking up my purse and cards, plopping them into the bag.

Although not cold, I wrapped my arms around myself, hugging my shoulders, desperately trying to control the shakes. "Is that all evidence now? You need to fingerprint it?" I whimpered.

Nelson swivelled around in his crouched position and glanced up as he slotted the last card in the bag. The sun streaming into the stairwell caught the face of his watch, causing the glare to blind me. I jolted my head sideways, noticing the highly polished sheen emanating from his black Chelsea boots. Nelson appeared to be a well-heeled man who took pride in his appearance.

"No … I'm just popping them in a bag for you. There's dirty needles and piss down here, not to mention what the rats have deposited. I suggest you wash your purse and cards."

"Oh."

"Is that your phone?" he pointed to my now smashed-screen mobile that lay tucked around the corner of the stairwell. I presumed Yellow-Eye must have inadvertently dropped it when taking flight.

I nodded. Although relieved to have it back, the cracked face would suggest it might not be in full working order.

Nelson reached out and grabbed the phone, brushing some dirt off with his Nitrite-gloved fingers. "It looks like it still works," he grimaced before straightening up and handing it to me with the police evidence bag. "Sorry, but muggings in this place are a daily occurrence. I'll let Uniform know what's happened. They might get time to pick up that bunch of wallads, but don't hold your breath."

"Wallads?"

"Lowlife. Scum, if you like—"

"I don't like."

"No, I guess you don't. It's a street term. But listen, this estate is teeming with gits like them. Not much chance of nicking them, I'm afraid."

I glared at him. "What? So, they can steal my cash and threaten me, and that's it? You lot not going to do anything about it?" I barked, his suggestion that muggings were just an acceptable part of everyday life on the estate bolstering my resolve.

Nelson shrugged. "I know it ain't right, but it's just how it is. We'd need to double the size of the force to investigate every crime. It's about prioritisation, I'm afraid."

I dropped my arms, the frustration bubbling up inside me, effectively halting my tears and controlling the shakes. "Oh, well, that's just bloody charming! So, you witness a crime, but you're not prepared to do anything about it?"

Nelson huffed, something he seemed to perform quite often in our two brief encounters.

"Christ! I've always defended the police, but this just goes to prove that the media are correct. The entire force is full of corrupt, useless wasters."

"Hey." Nelson reached out and laid his hand on my arm.

"Oh, sod off." I shrugged away his hand and stomped past him, heading for the convenience store. If my piss-covered cards were declined due to lack of funds or they'd reached their credit limit, I planned to steal a bottle of wine. There was certainly no fear of being arrested because, according to that useless git, shoplifting wouldn't be classed as a priority.

9

Perfect 10

"I must say, for an intransigent philistine dragged from the 'me decade', you've taken to this new technology rather well. I'm impressed, darling. Very impressed." Deana gripped Terry's left biceps as she cuddled up close whilst he surfed on her dead husband's Apple Mac. "I love squeezing your muscly arms. They're so … so manly."

Terry tutted and shook his head. "What does 'me decade' mean?"

"The 1970s, darling. An eminent journalist coined the phrase to describe the decade that post-dated the '60s … the era of free love and concerns about social and political injustice. The 'me decade' means we all became selfish in the '70s when concerning ourselves with self-improvement. A less caring society, I guess you could say."

"Bloody hell, what namby-pamby load of socialist crap have you been reading?"

"Excuse me!" Deana pulled her head away from where she'd been rubbing her cheek on his polo shirt. "Just because I hold different political views from you, that does not make me namby-pamby. You might well have been one of Mrs

Thatcher's loadsamoney black-shirt disciples, but I, like many, believe in a more socially caring and loving society."

Terry continued to tap away at the keyboard, purposefully keeping his eyes forward due to Deana hovering by his side in her skimpy silk dressing gown. "Well, I'm a little surprised. You're not the typical type to wave a banner for that lefty idiot, Worzel Gummidge. Never had you down as a Bennite."

"Darling, what are you drivelling on about?"

"You ... a socialist lefty. Waving your union banners with Tony Benn and that donkey jacket bloke, Michael Foot ... they call him Worzel Gummidge, you know. I tell you, that was an utter outrage when he turned up at the Cenotaph a couple of years ago dressed like that."

Deana patronisingly patted his arm. "I see, darling. Now, I know that all seems like recent history for you but, for me, that time was over thirty years ago."

"Still an outrage," he muttered.

"Well, whatever. Now, as it happens, I recall Michael Foot didn't stay long as leader of the Labour Party. There was Neil Kinnock after him, although I didn't like him much ... pasty, ginger Welshman. However, before you rattle your capitalist sabre at me, the Labour Party won the election in '97 and stayed in power for thirteen years. That, dear boy, is a lot longer than that Thatcher woman, I'll have you know."

"Oh, I remember Kinnock. He was elected leader of the Labour Party just before ... before—"

"You died in my arms, darling."

"Yes, I did, didn't I." Terry pursed his lips and slowly nodded, contemplating his death. "Anyway, I can't believe that socialist lot were in power that long."

"Well, they were. Google it, now you're proficient on that thing," Deana nodded to the Apple Mac, which Terry continued to peruse. "My darling Dickie was a fully paid-up member of the Labour Party and campaigned at all the elections. Dickie was such a clever, caring man. So, so brilliant, you know. Did I ever tell you that?"

"Champagne socialist," muttered Terry.

"I'll ignore that, Terence. At least my Dickie knew how to woo a woman."

"Ah! That's what it's really all about, isn't it?"

"Sorry?"

"You're not actually a socialist."

"I am!"

"Piffle! To quote what you said to me a couple of weeks ago …" Terry swivelled his head away from the screen to face her. "My darling Dickie was sooo clever," he squeaked out in a high-pitched voice.

"Oh, grow up, Terence," barked Deanna.

"Huh." Terry swung back to face the screen. "Anyway, you accused me of mis-reminiscing. I think you're conveniently forgetting the political disasters of the late '70s. The damn country was in freefall before Mrs Thatcher got a firm grip on it. I see she stayed in power right through to the '90s, so she must have been popular."

Without Terry noticing, Deana stuck her tongue out at him and shook her head. "About as popular as a bout of herpes. If I were you, I'd temper your enthusiasm for the woman if you happen upon nipping into a working men's club up north."

"Well, that's not going to happen, is it? Christ, you're a soft southerner who believes anyone living north of the Watford Gap is a whippet-wielding heathen."

"Dickie came from Daventry, I'll have you know. That's way up there somewhere. So, please don't lecture me with your right-wing prejudicial views. Dickie's father was a shop steward and a local government official back in the '70s ... he was very well respected, apparently."

"Daventry?"

"Yes ... that's a northern town."

"Hardly. You might do well to study geography instead of pornography. Then you might get your facts straight."

Deana scrunched her nose up and shook her head at him.

"I saw that!"

"Sorry, I don't know what you mean?"

"You, pulling a face behind my back. I can see your reflection on the screen. Anyway, it's lunchtime, woman. Aren't you going to get dressed at some point today?"

"It's lovely and warm. So, there's really no need for unnecessary clothing. I've just enjoyed a stroll around the garden. I must say, now summer is nearly upon us, and the little gardening chap we used to employ doesn't come around anymore, the flower beds are looking rather shabby and unkempt."

Terry shot her a disparaging look and tutted again when faced with the sight of her breasts that her loosely tied gown struggled to cover before refocusing his attention back on the screen.

"Although gardening has never really floated my boat. Now that I'm dead, I thought I might take it up as a little hobby. I had a rummage through the potting shed and found a pair of secateurs and quite enjoyed myself indulging in a spot of pruning."

"Not dressed like that, I hope?" Terry exclaimed, willing himself not to turn and look at her.

"No, of course not, darling. I took my dressing gown off. I didn't want to snag the delicate fabric on any brambles. It's pure silk, you know."

Terry swivelled around. "You're not serious?"

"Yes, of course. It's so liberating to skip around without clothes. You should try it. Although, if I can prise you out of my husband's finery, you need to stay away from the bottom of the garden because that nosey cow, Dreary Drake, can see the end fence if she strains her head against her bedroom window. Apart from the house supposedly being unoccupied, I think copping an eyeful of you wandering around naked would be a bit too much for the old prune to cope with."

"I have no intention of cavorting around naked."

"No, I don't suppose you have. Which is a pity."

"Well, it's okay for you. You're invisible. Despite your insatiable desire to flash, at least no one can see you."

"Yes, that's a shame."

"Sorry?"

"I enjoy exposing myself ... it's fun," she giggled. "Dickie and I made love against that fence last summer, and Dreary Drake made a complaint to the police, citing indecent exposure. She was only jealous. The silly old moo."

"Is that what you've been up to all morning? Prancing around naked in the garden like some nymph whilst snipping away at the rose bushes."

"No, I've also been performing my beauty treatments. Although I benefit from a gene pool of a long line of exotically gorgeous women, you don't think I can look this good without my regular beauty routine, do you?"

"No comment."

"Anyway, grumpy guts, what are you researching?"

"I, dear woman, whilst you skylark around like a fairy, have been getting on with the task in hand. Namely, investigating Virginia Strachan."

"Oh, very good. What have you come up with?"

Terry swivelled around in his chair. "Quite a lot, actually. Look, please, can you put something on?"

"Darling, I have my dressing gown." Deana let the cord slack as she performed a twirl.

"I meant clothing. It's quite disconcerting chatting whilst you stand there with it all hanging out."

"Oh, darling, you should be pleased. You're a lucky boy to have my gorgeous womanly frame to feast your eyes upon." Deana reclined on the leather Chesterfield sofa behind him, posing with her arm above her head. "Ooo, this leather's a bit chilly on my bottom."

"Get dressed then."

"No, it'll be alright in a moment. Anyway, as a little treat for you, for our next jaunt out into town, I plan to go naked. I'll pop on a pair of my Prada brushed-leather slingback pumps, but that's it."

Terry's mouth gaped as he bug-eyed gawped at her.

"It'll be titillating, darling. I can't wait. In fact, let's go out somewhere this afternoon."

"You're—"

"Unbelievable! I know, darling. Such fun, isn't it?" she chortled. "Now, come on. What have you discovered whilst you've been silver-surfing?"

"Silver-surfing?"

"Yes, darling. I noticed a few grey hairs poking out of your crown ... very distinguished looking, I must say."

Terry shook his head, opening his palms.

"Silver-surfing is a term for old crusties as they navigate around the internet."

"Oh."

"Now, come on, what have you gleaned from your hours of tip-tapping away?"

"Well, as I said, quite a lot. Why have the Powers-That-Be not supplied more information this time? Just saying Virginia has a problem with her husband doesn't leave us much to go on, does it?"

"Hmmm. Yes, well, to be honest with you, darling, although we've successfully fulfilled our previous two missions, they're slightly miffed at our somewhat lacklustre performance thus far. Citing that we would have failed without the help of a couple of other ghosts."

"Lacklustre?"

"Yes, I know. I said to them, how rude! However, they do have a point, I suppose. Anyway, to cut a long story short, they were somewhat tight-lipped with intel on this one, saying they need to see a marked improvement in our performance this time."

"Or what?"

Deana swivelled her head towards Terry. "Oh, I don't know. I didn't think to ask."

"So, we have the threat of something ... something unpleasant if we don't pick up our performance, and you see fit to prance around in the nude amongst the daisies."

Deana shrugged. "I'm not in the mood today. Anyway, darling. You've been busy, so what we got?"

"Right. So, I've researched the names, Strachan and Goode. Now Strachan is Scottish—"

"Really!" Deana mocked. "Is that it? Four hours of internet browsing, and all you can come up with is that," she smirked.

"Deana!"

"Sorry, darling. Do carry on. I'm all ears and boobs." She cupped her breasts and squeezed them together, glancing down at her puckered chest. "You know, since dying, I'm no longer ageing. My skin is as supple as it's always been."

"Jesus," he muttered. "Look, Strachan, apart from being a Scottish name, isn't that popular around here—"

"In the beautiful south."

"If you say so. I've discovered that Virginia is married to Alistair Strachan ... presumably the man she has an issue with. They run a small accountancy outfit in Fairfield. Now, Alistair's father, Melvyn Strachan, owned a firm of architects back in the day, but it seems he hit hard times after his wife left him five years back."

"Oh, poor man. Perhaps he was a turgid git, like some of my unfortunate husbands. If he's no fun, you can't blame the woman for binning him off, can you?"

"If you say so."

"I do so."

"I've been racking my brains all morning because that name rings a bell. I'm sure I know a Melvyn Strachan, but I just can't place him."

"Oh ... one of your old chums? Old drinking partner, perhaps?"

"No. It will come to me. Anyway, an old newspaper report details a case where Melvyn Strachan was accused and tried for raping one of the young secretaries who he employed. He claimed the girl came on to him, and nothing actually happened. Although, as he was sixty and the girl only twenty, that's somewhat hard to believe. Anyway, unbelievably, he was acquitted, but the mud stuck, so to speak. Unsurprisingly, his business folded."

"No one wanted plans drawn up by a pervert."

"I imagine so."

"Oh, good God. What a revolting man. Why do we have to deal with perverts all the time? First, there was Sam Meyer, then that little pervert, Hallam, and now this hideous excuse of a man."

"Quite."

"Oh, darling. You don't think the problem with her husband is that he's some pervert too?"

"Like father, like son?"

"Could be. That might be our mission to sort him out."

"Who knows? I haven't found any reports suggesting Alistair Strachan has been up to no good. Anyway, far more interesting is the death of Melvyn Strachan's ex-wife, Jean, a couple of months ago."

"Oh?" Deana shifted up the sofa to a sitting position. Terry was relieved she crossed her legs. Despite having to chat with a semi-nude fifty-seven-year-old ghost, at least some of her modesty was no longer on display.

"She was discovered by her daughter, Alistair's younger sister. Now, the reports state that Jean Strachan—"

"The wife of the pervert?"

"Yes. She recently retired from her position as head of Clinical Services up at Fairfield General Hospital, and the police were treating her death as suspicious."

"Suspicious?"

"Yes, drowned in the bath."

"Oh, that sounds like suicide."

"Well, who knows? But, as I said, it states the police are treating it as a suspicious death."

"The husband?"

"Again, who knows? That's where the trail goes cold."

"What do you think? Are we here to help Virginia shimmy out of the problem with her husband or to solve the murder of her mother-in-law?"

"No idea. Perhaps they're the same thing?"

"Oh, hell, I'm not sure how comfortable I feel about this. I know we dabbled in a bit of murder with our Damian's situation, but I honestly thought our game was solving wrongdoings of a less violent nature."

"Technically, your ex, Sidders, committed the murdering."

"True, darling."

"For the moment, all we know is her death is suspicious."

"What about the Goodes? Presumably, the couple you knew and enjoyed a jolly with up in Hunstanton *are* Virginia's parents, as the Powers-That-Be suggest?"

"Yeah … I think so." Terry glanced away.

"Darling?"

"As I said this morning. I knew Elizabeth and Paul Goode. We were friends in the late '70s, but we drifted apart after I split up with my girlfriend of the time. The last time I saw them was when I married Sharon."

"Your perfect little Sharon."

"Yes."

"Your wife, who you regularly cheated on."

"Yeah," he muttered, hanging his head.

"Hmmm. So, this girlfriend you went to Hunstanton with, why did you split up?"

Terry shrugged.

"Oh, don't tell me. You were caught dabbling in a spot of carnal pleasure with another woman, and your girlfriend was a bit put out about it all."

Terry nodded.

"You randy little thing, you. Pity you changed."

Terry rolled his eyes.

"So, come on. You're holding back on me."

"Lizzy … Elizabeth Goode and I had a bit of a thing."

"A thing?"

"Yes, you know—"

"You bonked her brains out?"

"Sort of."

"There's no sort of when it comes to sex. You shagged her, or you didn't."

"I did. One night in Sunny Hunny. We kind of got it on, so to speak."

"Oh, no wonder her husband and you were no longer friends after that. Now, I've enjoyed the company of many a married man, but mostly in the full knowledge of their wives. Usually, the very woman Dickie would be pleasuring himself with either in the next room or beside me as we partook in a little foursome. I've always enjoyed group sex. It's… well, it adds variety, don't you think?"

Terry huffed.

"Anyway, so, you bashed good-old Lizzy's brains out, but I still can't see why Virginia is our new mission or what the actual problem is, which we've been assigned to fix. It sounds like she might have a spot of husband trouble. Lord knows I've experienced enough of that in my time. Also, the poor girl, unfortunately, has a pervert for a father-in-law.

However, unlike little Kimmy and our Damian, there doesn't appear to be an obvious issue."

"The night of Lizzy and me ... you know—"

"Played hide the sausage?"

"Yes."

"What about it?"

"7th June 1977."

"Blimey, darling. She must have been special if you can remember the date of a casual fling you enjoyed half a century ago."

"Date of the Jubilee street parties. The day you had a fumble in the back row of the cinema whilst rummaging around in your boyfriend's Y-fronts."

"Oh, I see. And your point is?"

"Virginia was born 13th March 1978."

"Very good. You have been busy surfing—"

"Deana ... there are exactly forty weeks between those two dates!"

"So, what? You're good at maths. Is that what you're telling me? What d'you want, a little gold star and a ten out of ten on your school report?"

"Deana ... that's nine months to the day!"

10

In the Heat of the Night

I thumped open the door to the convenience store, the front of which, with its steel shutters covering the window and plethora of security cameras, afforded the place the appearance of a high-security prison. The unshaven, stinking fat oaf perched on a stool behind the Perspex screen, who appeared to be thumbing through the pages of a dirty mag, glanced up at me as I made my entrance before refocussing his attentions on the pictures whilst taking a hearty drag on his cigarette.

I shimmied up the aisles, searching for the alcohol section with a plan to purchase or steal as much as I could carry. Then, I would retreat to that concrete box positioned on the second level of that noxious tower block, bolt the door and get royally shit-faced in the shortest time possible.

After two complete tours of each aisle, twice bashing into an elderly chap who squinted at the cooking instructions on the back of a packet of Super-Noodles with his glasses perched on his forehead in an attempt to read the minuscule writing, I couldn't spot the wine and became concerned the store didn't hold an alcohol licence.

Like an alcoholic, which I wasn't, but probably soon would be, now in a state of panic, I bolted to the counter and tapped on the Perspex security screen. Two hefty knuckle raps were enough to gain the attention of the fat oaf as he huffed and apathetically glanced up and away from a magazine depicting glossy pictures of some nude dolly bird.

"Where's the wine section?" I blurted.

Fat-Oaf rather disinterestedly thumbed over his shoulder towards the shelves behind the counter, mainly displaying cans of dubious branded beers and spirits.

"Oh," I muttered, as I scanned the shelving for wine.

Although I'd never partaken in shoplifting and very much doubted that I had the stomach for it – also, although Nelson seemed nonplussed about apprehending criminals – the position of all alcohol behind the counter removed shoplifting as an option.

My eyes settled on an inviting bottle of Prosecco – or perhaps two.

"You buying or just sightseeing?"

I lifted my police evidence bag and inspected the cards through the plastic. I considered my bank debit card would probably secure the purchase. However, it appeared to be the one at the bottom of the bag, and the dubious-looking sludge that now coated my cards gave rise for concern about what may be splattered across them.

"I don't suppose you offer credit?"

Fat-Oaf dragged on his cigarette as he eyed me up and down from his position on the higher ground before pointing to the tatty sign taped to the Perspex screen.

'Credit can only be offered to patrons over the age of 95 who are accompanied by both their parents.'

"Right. Great. Bleeding hilarious," I somewhat sarcastically announced. "Do you have a cloth or a tissue I could use?"

"Top of aisle two," he nonchalantly replied before plucking a cigarette from a packet on the counter and lighting it with the stub of the one already lit.

"No, I don't want to buy tissues. I just wondered if I could borrow one to wipe my cards." I pointed to my police evidence bag, which now contained a slick of yellow liquid which pooled in the bottom.

He glanced up, closing his left eye to avoid the smoke that drifted up his face from the cigarette welded between his lips. "Does this look like a bleeding charity shop to you?"

"No. You misunderstand what I'm saying. I just want one tissue. As in singular. Tissue as opposed to tissues."

Fat-Oaf shook his head, then turned before rummaging through a bin. Finally, after what seemed like a lifetime, he extracted a scrunched-up tissue, straightened it out whilst peering at whatever had previously been deposited, and passed it through the serving panel.

"That's a used one!"

"New ones are top of aisle two."

"Oh, for Christ's sake! If I ask for a couple of sheets of toilet paper, you'll presumably pluck some shit-splattered specimen out of the bloody u-bend, would you?"

Fat-Oaf shrugged. "Toilet roll is top of aisle two. Next to tissues."

I glanced back at the piss-covered cards, then longingly at the Prosecco. I momentarily wondered if I could tap the card on the machine through the plastic, but decided I'd have to nip back to the flat, wash the cards and come back. Of course, that would require another jaunt across the square and up the stairwell, probably resulting in another meeting with Yellow-Eye and his band of merry men – or wallads, as that useless idiot Nelson had called them.

"You want it?" he nodded to the disease-ridden tissue that lay on the counter.

I tentatively reached for it, then snatched my hand away, realising it might very well contain worse than what now coated my cards.

"Oh, piss off!" I blurted, before spinning around, nearly flattening the elderly gent holding his packet of Super-Noodles, and stomping towards the door only to realise the door opened inwards when my nose met the glass, resulting in tears forming once again.

Slightly stunned, I stepped back and checked I hadn't ruptured any blood vessels in my nasal cavity. Fat-Oaf peered over the Perspex screen as I gingerly felt around my throbbing nose.

"There's a sign on the door. It says pull, as in pull, as opposed to push."

"Oh, fuck off!" I barked, before yanking back the door and barrelling into the central square.

I took a moment to compose myself, as I had at the bottom of that stairwell. In the space of ten seconds, I'd twice instructed the shopkeeper where to get off. That wasn't like me. Apart from the recent blazing rows with Alistair, such terms were not part of my everyday vocabulary – certainly not to a stranger. Well, there was that girl who came onto Ali in that nightclub when we started dating, but that's another story for another time. Anyway, I could only deduce my circumstances had altered my character – rat in a corner scenario – or perhaps an hour or so of living on this estate had somehow transformed me into some gutter-slut like the rest of its inhabitants.

"Hey, you okay?"

I spun around, half expecting to fend off another gang of youths who were about to demand protection money or suggest payment in kind. Perhaps on Thursday afternoons because, apparently, I had a date lined up with Yellow-Eye on Fridays.

"Oh, it's PC Plod who doesn't enjoy catching criminals. What, you hanging around street corners trying to catch shoplifters? Is that higher up the priority list for the useless police than street muggings and threats of sexual violence?" I barked.

Nelson backed up a pace and spread his hands wide. "Hey, Virginia … it's Virginia, ain't it?"

"So? You going to arrest me for telling that fat oaf in there to fuck off, are you? What's the charge? A breach of the peace?" I thrust out my arms, placing my wrists together. "Well, PC Plod, be my guest. Slap me in irons and drag me back to the station because, after this shit day, a night in the cells sounds quite appealing!"

"Hey, I guess you're having a tough day."

"Oh, I can see why you made it into CID. What with those amazing powers of deduction you have, you must be their lead detective! Christ, I bet the vast majority of the criminal underworld are quaking in their boots with your razor-sharp brain masterminding operations."

"Virginia—"

"Oh, but hang on. I'm forgetting; you don't arrest people, do you? Now, fuck off!" I stomped past him, head down, barrelling towards the stairwell, slightly concerned that instructing a police officer where to go could be construed as slightly more severe than verbally abusing that grotesque, porn-obsessed shopkeeper.

Nelson trotted after me and grabbed my arm. "Hey, Virginia, you okay? You need some help?"

"Get off!" I blurted, shrugging his hand away.

"Frig sake, woman, I was just offering some help, that's all. I reckon you don't come from around here, and I should know 'cos this is where I come from."

I spun around. "What d'you mean, this is where you come from?"

"Well, this is my ends—"

"Ends?"

"My manor if you like … I come from this estate. I know most people assume I come from Africa or the West Indies. But I was born here, right up in that tower block." Nelson pointed to the graffiti-covered block I now called home.

"No, sorry, I don't mean—"

"Hey, it's no issue. I'm used to it. I get asked all the time where I come from. When I say from here, they always say, no, where from originally."

"Oh, that's shocking."

"I'm a copper ... it's part of the territory. In fact, my senior officer keeps telling me to perform some black magic, as he calls it, when we're investigating a case. *'Come on, Kananga, use some of that witchcraft all you coloured lot possess'*. That's what he always spouts."

"Good God, you should report him. That's racist!"

"It is. The bigoted, racist, misogynistic, sexist git retires later this year, so I'm just biding my time."

"Oh ... well, I think that's awful. Anyway, I was questioning your comment about *I* don't come from here, not about your heritage."

"Oh, shit ... I assumed—"

"Wrongly," I barked.

"Look, I'm sorry ... I thought ... sorry, what I mean is Deli said you've just moved in, got divorced and lost your job. This is one hell of a crap place to live, and I just wondered if you were okay ... y'know, needed some help?"

The man offered that Sidney-Poitier-styled heart-melting smile. I thought of my mother and how she loved those old movies, especially anything with Mr Poitier as the leading man. That affable expression which oozed from him halted my barrage of abuse that I was about to launch into, namely that – it had bugger all to do with him, his gobby sister should mind her own business, and as he wasn't prepared to arrest Yellow-Eye – he could piss off.

Although a stranger, he appeared to harbour genuine sympathetic tendencies. I thought he should offer up his services as a part-time call handler for the Samaritans because I considered him just as capable of lending an empathetic ear as the chap I'd chatted to some weeks ago when my life imploded.

"Nelson, that's really kind. I'm sorry I told you to fuck off. You're right; I'm having a bad day. However, unless you can offer me a job, persuade my husband to do the decent thing and offer up half the business, which morally I'm entitled to, get the hell out of my penthouse flat and take his thigh-gap floozy with him, then no, I don't think you can."

Nelson nodded. "Alright. You want me to walk you back to your flat?"

"Will you be there whenever I want to venture onto the estate? Shall I ring the station and ask if you can turn up when I plan to nip out to the shops just in case some group of youths, who appear to have free rein to terrorise the neighbourhood, fancy indulging in a spot of mugging?" I sarcastically batted back.

"Hey, lady … I was just trying to do the right thing."

"Don't bother." I spun on my heels and marched towards the stairwell.

"Virginia."

I halted and turned. "What now?" I barked.

"Look, I guess the answer's no, and I know it's early, but can I buy you a drink?"

I raised my eyebrow, somewhat taken aback. "A drink? So, you can't arrest muggers, but you can take me for a drink. Christ, no wonder crime is on the up."

Nelson shrugged his shoulders. "Hey, just thought you could use one after what's just happened."

I stepped back and aggressively jabbed a finger at him. "What I want is for you to catch criminals. So, I suggest you sod off and do your job."

"Alright." Nelson backed up and stepped away. "Just be careful, Virginia. This ain't a safe place to be, let alone live."

I spun around and hot-footed towards the stairwell. "Fat load of good he was," I muttered. "Useless prat." As I approached the stairwell, I stopped short when spotting two youths appear. Although dressed in a similar style, neither were Yellow-Eye nor his disciples. However, their demeanour suggested that both harboured similar intentions.

"Shit!" I spun around, searching for my useless police officer. "Err … Nelson," I squeaked out, almost in a whimper.

However, it appeared he'd taken my advice and sodded off. I weighed up my options while tightly gripping my plastic evidence bag of piss-covered possessions. Do I front them up, then march past and get back to my crummy flat? Or do I run? Whilst chewing my lip, the decision appeared to be made for me.

"Oi … get your cute booty over 'ere," called out one youth who stepped towards me.

That puddle of excrement I'd been wallowing about in for some weeks just got deeper. I feared I was now up to my neck in shit, and I'd just firmly instructed the one person who could offer assistance to sod off.

11

Basic Instinct

"Ah-ha! Now it all becomes slightly clearer! Well done, darling. So, little Virginia Strachan is probably your daughter."

"It seems that way."

Deana started to chuckle. "Oh, darling, this is hilarious."

"Sorry?"

With both hands stretching her hair back, Deana tipped her head upwards whilst continuing to chortle. "Oh, darling, considering the high volume of illicit affairs you've dabbled in throughout your younger years, there's a strong possibility that you've produced enough offspring to field a rugby team!"

"League or Union?"

"Oh, is there a difference?"

"Two … but when we're talking those sorts of numbers, I guess it makes no difference. Anyway, we don't know for definite that Virginia is mine."

"Just think, darling. If all your little progenies have landed in a spot of bother, we could be completing missions together for some years to come."

"Oh, please, no. And do you have to do that?"

"What, darling?" she quizzed, still wheezily chuckling, causing her shoulders to bounce.

"Braying like a donkey."

"I don't bray! Anyway, what a lovely thought. You must be delighted with the idea of having me forever by your side," she hee-hawed whilst tipping her head forward.

"Not something I can bear thinking about. And you are braying, which is causing your chest to wobble like a couple of blancmanges."

"Oh, come on. My boobs are firmer than a blancmange!"

"Stick a couple of cherries on them, and it'll look like the jelly moulds my mother used to proudly present for Sunday tea."

"Oh, how lovely. I used to do something quite similar. As a little treat for Dickie and some of his friends, I'd lay out on the dining table with various fruits and blobs of cream strategically spread across my body for them to lick off."

"My ... good God."

"It's called human body plate dining. It was all the rage in our little circle of friends. We often tried sushi, but Dickie preferred desserts and especially lickable ones. Although, we never tried it with blancmange ... hmmm, pity that."

"You're—"

"Unbelievable. Yes, I know, my darling. I'm slightly bemused to hear that you've never tried it. We could do that for supper if you like. That said, it loses its erotic tilt when it's only dinner for one. Unfortunately, because we're now ghosts, we don't have a large circle of like-minded friends to come and join us ... such a shame."

"What a relief," muttered Terry, as he swivelled around to continue his research.

"I heard that, Walton. That was quite rude."

"Rude," he muttered. "Pot, kettle, black. You constantly flaunting your naked wares is rude."

"Oh, such a prude. You weren't prudish when you licked my body in that hotel room."

Terry tapped away, searching for more information on the Goodes whilst rhythmically shaking his head. Although fully aware he'd enjoyed more than the average amount of sexual encounters, those had always been with only one woman at a time. Deana's experiences made him wonder if he'd missed out – missed an opportunity that would now never present itself. As he walloped the return key, a familiar box appeared. Although this seemed to appear on every search, he always hit accept, but still regarded it somewhat odd.

"Deana?"

"Uh-huh."

"Why does this thing keep pinging up on the screen?"

"What thing, darling?"

"Well, I don't know ... it's like a flag or banner asking me if I accept biscuits."

"Biscuits?"

"Yeah, I assume so. It actually says cookies, which is an American term for biscuits, isn't it?"

Deana started her blancmange-mould shaking routine again. "Oh, Terry, darling, you're so funny."

Terry swivelled around. "I tell you one thing I've noticed since coming back from the dead. There's been a disturbing erosion of the English language."

"How so?"

"Americanisation ... if that's a word?"

"Yes, I think it is," she replied with a smirk.

"So, cookies, instead of biscuits, for starters. That woman in that fast-food place wanted to know if I wanted regular fries—"

"They were called that in your day."

"Maybe, but they're chips! And what's regular got to do with anything? I hardly want irregular, do I? I understand she was asking about portion size, but what happened to the word medium?"

Deana uncrossed her legs and recrossed, Sharon Stone style, whilst continuing to smirk and enjoy Terry's little rant.

"And another thing ... sneakers! They were pumps or trainers in my day. And ... and, math ... what happened to the s?"

"Darling, you're getting het up."

"And trash, there's that folder thingy on email that says trash ... surely, it's rubbish as in rubbish bin? I could go on. Jesus, one of these web thingamajigs asked for a Zip code! I wondered if that was something to do with my fly, and I'd inadvertently landed on some dodgy web thingy which your Dickie was probably more familiar with."

"Oh, darling, you should do stand-up. You're such a comedian."

"And please cover up those wobbling jellies!"

"Okay ... now listen." Deana complied with his request by pulling together her gown and loosely knotting the tie. "You are going to have to get used to these Americanisms. Like it or lump it, that's just how it is. The global village we now live in means that new terminology is spreading fast by way of advanced media technologies."

Terry frowned, which Deana spotted and realised she was already losing him.

"Darling, don't worry about that. Now, two points. Firstly, I and my darling Dickie enjoyed the odd session watching porn ... nothing wrong with that. Secondly, cookies, as in what is flashing up on the screen, is not referring to biscuits."

"Oh."

"Cookies are a name given to website files ... like an embedded message in code. I believe I asked Dickie this very question, and he said that the name came from fortune cookies because the code holds a secret message, if you see what I mean."

"Oh ... I see. Sharon used to like those when we went up the Chinky on a Friday evening."

"Oh, my darling. That really isn't acceptable."

"What isn't?" Terry barked, now becoming slightly miffed that she constantly corrected him as if he were a child.

"Chinky. That's quite offensive … racist, even."

Terry pulled a face.

"As you have pointed out, language has changed, dear boy."

"It seems everything is offensive now. So, what is it called now, then?"

"Chinese restaurant."

"And an Indian? What's the new term for that?"

"I think that's still an Indian."

"Oh, well, at least you can still nip out for a ruby without causing offence."

"Quite. Now, what's the website that you're researching?"

"Well, I looked at it earlier and thought I'd ask your opinion."

"Intriguing! I like it when we start investigating." Deana hopped up and deposited her right bottom cheek on the armrest of Terry's swivel chair, supporting herself by flinging her arm around his neck and laying her cheek against his. "You haven't shaved, darling. I like that rough, rugged feel."

"Really?" Terry sarcastically responded, whilst tapping the keyboard.

"Manly … very manly."

"Hmmm."

"This is like *Treasure Hunt*. We get clues and then have to zip off and investigate where to go next. Pity we don't have a helicopter. You know, she won the Rear of the Year award, probably because she paraded around in that tight-fitting jumpsuit. However, I must stress that I'm quite certain my bum is perter than Anneka Rice's."

"What are you on about?"

"Treasure Hunt ... helicopters ... Anneka Rice."

Terry moved his head to the right before glancing around to negate the chance of receiving a silk-covered nipple in the eye as Deana snuggled up. "Sorry, I have no idea what you're on about. And what's Rear of the Year?"

"That's an award for the celeb with the cutest arse."

"Oh ... very cultured."

"Yes ... it's been around for years, long before you died, I'm sure. Barbara Windsor was the first winner, and I'm quite certain Lynsey de Paul and Melinda Messenger won it at some point."

"Ah, Lynsey de Paul, what a woman. Boy, would I have liked to, well, you know?"

"Yes, the lustful glint in your eye suggests I do. I always thought she and I looked quite similar. We could be sisters ... me being the younger one, of course."

"Do you?"

"I do so. And lose the sarcastic twang, please."

"Well, I remember when Lynsey de Paul—"

"Oh, Insta!" interrupted Deana. "I love a bit of Instagram. You can glean all sorts of beauty tips on here. Not that I need them, of course. However, always prudent to keep up with current trends, I say."

"I'll take your word for it. Now look, Helen Strachan, that's Virginia's sister-in-law, regularly posts pictures on her account about her mother." Terry clicked on an image, which displayed a bunch of funeral white lilies with a quotation printed over the top. Terry read the quote—

"Every Man is guilty of all the good he did not do."

"Oh, very cryptic, darling."

"Next to it she's written that funny square symbol—"

"Hash … it's a hashtag."

"Really?"

"Uh-huh. #JusticeforJean."

"Why aren't there spaces between the words?"

"Good question. I don't know; there just aren't. That's not how it works."

"So, she's put, *'The police do nothing – they're as guilty of my mother's murder as is the perpetrator. Justice for my mother Jean Strachan.'* Bit odd, don't you think?"

"Oh, so this Helen woman is blaming the police for failure to satisfactorily solve the case."

"Probably. Is that what this Insta-thingy is for? Like Facebook, people post things about their life? Not very British, is it?"

"What d'you mean, darling?"

"Well, you know, stiff upper lip and all that. From what I've gleaned so far, it seems everyone wants to share their innermost thoughts with the world."

"Hmmm. Well, I suppose in your day, you'd just phone a friend."

"Yes, but I wouldn't phone a friend to tell them I had chips for tea or that I'm sad because some character died in a soap opera like this lot seem to do."

"No, I see your point. I think some psychologists regard it as the *Diana Effect*, as in people feeling more comfortable to share their feelings."

Terry shook his head. "*Diana Effect*? Who's Diana?"

"The Princess of Wales, or was."

"Oh, her. Yes, I proposed to Sharon on that very day she married Charlie. What did you mean, was?"

"That's for another day, my darling. Google it when you get a spare moment when you're not obsessing with social media."

"Talking of which, when I flicked through Facebook, it seems Elizabeth Goode died last year. Her Facebook account has the word *'Remembering'* next to it, which states the account is for someone who's died."

"Yes, I believe that's correct. Oh, well, she can't have been very old."

"My age, I think."

"Not in suspicious circumstances like this Jean woman?"

"No. From what I can glean, it appears to have been cancer."

"Oh, thank God for that!" she chortled.

Terry frowned.

"No, I mean, at least it's not another potential murder."

"Oh, I see. Christ, you're right. I don't relish the idea of chasing down a serial killer."

"No, quite," Deana shuddered. "Anyway, let's recap. Virginia is probably another one of your many offspring. It appears her mother-in-law, presumably, Jean Strachan, dies in suspicious circumstances which, some months on, the police have failed to satisfactorily investigate. So, that would suggest the ex-husband, pervert Melvyn Strachan, is not under suspicion. Also, it appears that Virginia's sister-in-law is somewhat miffed at a lack of progress with apprehending the culprit."

"Yep, that about covers it."

"Oh, and Virginia, the poor girl, recently lost her mother, too."

"Yes, that as well."

"However, we only know we're being tasked with helping Virginia because of some issue with her husband, who may or may not be a pervert like his father. Whatever the mission is, we can't bring her mother or mother-in-law back from the dead."

"No, I imagine that is out of our remit. However, whatever this issue is, we better find out. I reckon it has something to do with her in-laws. Also, I discovered my old pal, Paul Goode, is dead. Died some years ago."

"Oh, how sad. The poor girl's lost both parents, and there's something up with her husband. I must say, I'm mightily impressed with your surfing skills. Quite the little internet ferret, aren't we?"

"Yes, while you prance around like some siren, I've been busy."

"Good for you," she patronisingly patted his lap. "Now, what's the plan then, darling?"

"So, tomorrow morning, I think we need to start with a trip out to visit Strachan Accountants."

"Good idea. I'll go and have a shufty through my dressing room and decide which shoes to wear."

"Just shoes?"

"Of course, my darling. Now summer is nearly upon us, and as I'm invisible, it's nudity all the way from now on."

12

The Windies

As the youth swaggered towards me, offering me a nefarious grin that suggested this encounter would pan out no better than the one with Yellow-Eye, I considered my procrastination over the decision of what action to take unhelpful.

"Shit, shit, shit," I muttered, glancing between the advancing youth and the empty square where, only moments ago, that useless police officer had stood. Unfortunately, due to the stairwell being barred by a couple of reprobates and not wishing to re-enter Fat-Oaf's emporium after telling him where to go, my options appeared to be dwindling.

As I swivelled around and marched across the central square with no idea of my destination, I caught the sound of the youths laughing. I assumed they were amused that I'd scarpered and intimidating lone females made them feel all big and important.

Nelson, although not keen on catching criminals – which in this place would be as simple as shooting fish in a barrel, based on the fact I suspected I was probably the only law-abiding resident in the whole odious shithole which I now dubiously called home – was quite correct in his assessment that I didn't belong here. What seemed like a good idea yesterday, as in renting a flat on the Broxworth, now joined in with the rest of my imbecilic and witless decisions, which I seemed to have developed a frightenedly good skill at making.

Whilst nipping around the burnt-out community centre, which I was led to believe now housed the vast majority of Hertfordshire's crack-heads, I spotted Deli's brother just inside the alleyway next to the Chinese restaurant. Feeling relieved, I was about to call out his name but halted when spotting him thumbing out some notes and offering them to a hoodie-clad figure skulking in the shadows.

Although confused and concerned as to why a police officer would be passing out wads of cash to some low-life, I knew I had no option but to ask for his help.

"Nelson," I called out, surprised at how shaky my voice had become.

Nelson glanced back down the alley where the hoodie-clad low-life had scurried away before turning to me. "Virginia. Everyfink alright?"

"Err ... no."

After taking another furtive glance around whilst sporting a furrowed brow, he closed the gap between us.

"What's up?"

"You mentioned a drink." I nervously grinned whilst shooting a look back at the two youths who appeared to still be on sentry duty at the foot of the stairwell.

"Thought you wanted me to catch criminals," he smirked.

"Who was that man?"

"What man?" he stabbed back.

I inadvertently stepped back a pace, concerned that perhaps Nelson was no better than the men guarding the way back to my flat. His sharp retort to my question suggested that whoever he'd just made a financial transaction with wasn't the sort an upstanding officer of the law should be associated with.

When presumably sensing what I was thinking, Nelson offered a surrendered hands gesture, keeping them at chest height. "Virginia, he's a snout … an informant of mine. I just asked him to give me the name of that wallad who accosted you in the stairwell." Before I could respond, Nelson tugged my arm, encouraging me to walk with him. "Look, that's how it works around here. If my snout gets rumbled, he's as good as dead. So, you didn't see anyfink, alright?"

Although he appeared honest and sported that heart-melting smile, I wondered if he was duping me. Let's face it, my recent decisions had mostly been on the poor side, so trusting Nelson could be equally idiotic.

"Virginia, you look terrified. Come on; I'll take you for a drink … get you out of this dump for an hour or so."

I opened my mouth to speak, but nothing came out.

"Hey, I'm a police officer. According to you, a friggin' crap one, but I won't cause you any harm."

"Oh, Christ. Sorry," I winced. "I didn't mean to be so rude."

"In my line of work, what you said was tame. Scum, pig, black filth, are the polite ones."

"Oh, hell, this place is horrible. What am I going to do?" Frustratingly, my chin wobbled, and the more I focused on controlling it, the worse it became.

"For starters, let me buy you a drink. You look like you need one."

I nodded, maybe slightly too enthusiastically, but the thought of escaping the estate for a few hours seemed like a heavenly option, irrespective if Nelson wasn't the upstanding officer of the law that he seemed keen to portray.

"Good, come on. Let's get you off the estate for a couple of hours. I'm a police officer, so I'm not some dick or a serial rapist."

"How does being a police officer guarantee that?"

"Fair point. It doesn't, I guess. But I'm not, alright?"

Based on the fact that I didn't fancy re-entering Fat-Oaf's convenience store to purchase a bottle of Prosecco, and Nelson probably wasn't a serial rapist, like I suspected most men whose profiles were pinged to me on that matchmaking site, I guessed it would be okay. And, boy, did I need a drink.

"I thought you lot weren't supposed to drink on duty."

Nelson checked his watch. "As of an hour ago, I'm on compassionate leave."

"Oh, God," I winced. "Shit, sorry, I forgot. You're going to see your mother?"

"Yeah, probably. So, can I buy you a drink, then? Or perhaps we could stand outside the crappy Chinese all evening."

"Yeah ... get me out of here."

"Are you a celebrity? A film star, model, perhaps?" he smirked.

"Jesus, please don't tell me that was a chat-up line. Because, if it was, I've heard better," I laughed, feeling relief starting to ebb in, forcing the fear away.

Nelson offered that affable smile. "Let's just say I'm not famous for my chat-up lines. My car's parked off the estate. I know a nice little pub out on the Haverhill Road. Will that be okay?"

"Is that the Hornblower out near Treddington?"

"Yeah, is that alright?"

"Sure, why not? Why are you parked off the estate?"

Nelson halted, swivelled around, and shook his head at me. "Virginia, you have a lot to learn about the Broxworth."

I nodded. "I guess if you parked here, it wouldn't be in one piece when you returned."

"You got it in one. Also, I ain't that popular around here."

"Because you're a police officer?"

"Sort off. It's a long story. Now, come on, let's get away from here. I can buy dinner as well if you fancy it … save you cooking later. Oh, and never go in that Chinese. The place only offers up road kill disguised as prawn balls."

"Nelson, *are* you asking me on a date?"

Nelson smirked. Whether that was confirmation or surprise, I couldn't tell.

"Oh, hell, sorry. Foot in mouth time," I nervously giggled. Christ, that was embarrassing. Although he seemed a nice fella, he was clearly younger than me, and I imagine he already had a girlfriend who probably could rival that bloody Love-Island girl who Ali enjoyed panting with.

"Yeah, sort of," he shrugged. "I'd like that."

"A date?"

"Ah ... I get it. I guess you don't date black guys."

"No ... yes, I do. Well, no, actually, I haven't. But I would ... if ... if I was going to date ... if I got asked ... if you see what I mean," I grimaced, realising I'd just spouted a load of gibberish.

"I fink I do," he chuckled. "Look, I get it. You're going through shit, and timing is off. I understand."

I nodded. "Yeah, probably."

"Drink and dinner still alright?"

"Yes, Mr Nelson, police officer, or whatever your name is."

Nelson offered his enormous arm for me to latch onto, which I duly accepted as we hot-footed towards the alleyway beside Fat-Oaf's store.

"You don't look or sound like you come from here. I take it you've escaped and live somewhere less hideous now?"

Nelson halted again and turned to face me. "Yo blud, I ain't no greezy wallad. And I deffo ain't no gallis. Now I'm a fed, all ma fams turned," Nelson delivered in an accent similar to Yellow-Eye.

"Oh. I think you might have to translate."

"It's street talk. Basically, what I grew up on. I guess ten years in the force has bashed it out of me. I said ... hi, I'm not an idiot talking nonsense. I'm not a womaniser, and since becoming an officer of the law, I've lost all my previous acquaintances and friends."

"Nelson, I'll take your word for it," I chuckled as we picked up the pace again.

"Err ... call me Viv. I don't like my name much."

"Oh, okay. Is that your middle name?"

"No, it's my station name. All coppers have nicknames. Mine is Viv, which I'm alright wiv."

"Right. Why, Viv."

"After Viv Richards ... the greatest cricketer of all time. My surname is Richards."

"And your boss, the misogynistic, sexist, racist tosser. What's his station name?"

"DCI Reeves is known as Fox ... or sometimes Foxy."

"Oh," I chuckled, as we trotted along, bounding towards Coldhams Lane, the relief oozing through me as we increased the distance between me and my flat. Although, initially, he appeared not to be of a mind to hunt down Yellow-Eye, I felt slightly safer with an officer of the law at my side. "I imagined your boss would have a slightly more, shall we say, derogatory name based on your description of him. Foxy conjures up images of an alluring, pouting, sexy woman waving around a long cigarette holder."

"It's Foxy if he's not acting the twat, which he is most of the time. Fox is more commonly used."

"Like, in the henhouse. Fox in the henhouse causing havoc?"

"No, not really. He thinks his name is because he's cunning. But, what the wasteman don't know, Foxy is shortened from fox hunt, which rhymes wiv … well, I guess you can work it out."

"Yes, I think I can. What do you mean by wasteman?"

"Sorry, that's street slang. If you're gonna live here, you'll have to learn a whole new language. Wasteman means twat or muppet if you like."

"Oh, like Constantine?"

"Who?"

"Oh, you don't know your Muppets," I chuckled. "Constantine is the evil doppelgänger of Kermit. Constantine is the most evil frog in the world."

I noticed Viv side-eye me.

"I think I'll be quiet for a little while. It's been a stressful day," I nervously giggled, fearing Viv would change his mind about drinks and dinner. Apart from looking forward to some company, I needed that drink.

13

Pachelbel's Canon

"Virginia, can I get you another? Or shall we order food now?"

"Oh, call me Ginny. Like you, I'm not a huge fan of my name. But the shortened version is okay. My parents struggled to come up with Virginia, so they gave up trying to think of a middle name."

Viv nodded and pointed to my now empty wine glass.

Although a little early for food, I thought I'd better be careful how much alcohol I tipped down my throat. Despite my earlier plans to get wasted by downing a couple of bottles of Prosecco, that would have been in my flat, not whilst chatting to a man I hardly knew in a public place. During the twenty minutes of enjoying his company whilst nestled into a comfy armchair in the quaint little establishment, I'd already sunk a large glass of Pinot Grigio. So, there was a real possibility I could be bladdered before I even plucked up a menu. However, today had been one hell of a day.

"Yes, thank you."

"Same again?"

I nodded as Viv hopped out of his seat, heading for the bar, leaving me to contemplate what I was doing visiting a pub in the late afternoon with my slapper-of-a-neighbour's brother. To be fair to the man, who appeared to have dragged himself from the gutter and forged himself a half-decent career, despite sporting an acerbic twang to his voice, which I imagined could grind granite, that's where his similarity to his sister ended. Although he displayed a caring, calm manner, which seemed at odds with his physique, I suspected Viv Richards had fought hard to gain the position of Detective Sergeant before the age of thirty. Also, I hypothesised that being a previous resident of the Broxworth Estate must have compounded the issue. Something suggested to me that his career choice wouldn't have gone down too well with the natives.

"There you go. I've got some menus as well. John, the landlord, said to give him the nod when we're ready to order."

"Cheers, thank you. So, you're on first name terms in here, then?"

"Yeah, sometimes I can't face cooking. So, I nip in on my way home."

"So, come on, then. How did you manage to escape the Broxworth?" I asked, making a grab for the wine.

"The long or the short version?"

"I'm in no hurry, and I have no desire to return to my flat anytime soon. So, the long one if you like."

"Ha, yeah, that might be a bit boring, so I'll condense it down."

"I can't imagine it is. After only a few hours in that place, I'm going to need to formulate a plan to get out of there myself."

"Yeah, it ain't recommended, that's for sure. And I should know. Back in the day ... well, let's just say I got myself into a situation."

I expectantly raised my eyebrow, sipping my wine whilst maintaining eye contact.

"I was part of a gang—"

"Like those who accosted me in that stairwell?" I interrupted, somewhat surprised by his statement and more than a smidge concerned about who I'd agreed to share dinner with.

"Yeah. Not proud of that part of my life. Anyway, I got myself in a few scrapes and ended up in an interview room up at Fairfield Police Station."

I raised that eyebrow again whilst sipping my wine.

"Although I wasn't involved, I witnessed a stabbing. Two blokes from rival gangs got into a fight outside the bookies, and one shanked the other ... killing him. That's where I met the woman who changed my life."

I narrowed my eyes. Was he married but chose not to wear a ring? Did he trawl the estate during his down time to pick up women who he thought could be a bit on the side and thus add some variety to his life before nipping home to bathe the kids?

Viv, ever the detective, read my mind. "Oh, no, not like that. I promise you I ain't married, and I don't have a girlfriend."

"And why not?"

"What?" my question seemed to stump him.

"Girlfriend?"

"Oh, right. I was in a long-term relationship, but we broke up nearly a year ago. Basically, she couldn't put up with my long hours and decided to naff off with some bloke who would be more attentive."

"Oh, sorry. I do have a tendency to pry."

"No, no, it's fine. That didn't paint a very good picture of me, did it?"

"She couldn't have loved you enough."

"I guess you're right. Sometimes, in my job, you just have to put the hours in. She wasn't prepared to put up with my long hours and constant calls to my mobile in the middle of the night when in the middle of investigating some big case."

"At least she was honest with you. My husband just decided he wanted a newer model. As far as he was concerned, I'd passed my use-by date."

"The bloke's a twat."

"Deffo," I chuckled.

"Oh, look, sorry. I don't know him. I shouldn't have said anyfink," he shrugged, appearing a wee bit embarrassed.

"No, you're spot on. I knew Alistair liked to window shop. I guess I put up with that knowing he wouldn't take it any further … well, so I thought."

"I take it that's all still a bit raw?"

"The aftermath is. As I said, he's stiffed me. As for Alistair … no, I'm over him. I should have realised years ago we would never make it, but when you're in a relationship, you don't always see that, do you? His mother died a few months back. He was always a mummy's boy, and it hit him hard. Something must have clicked in his brain, sending him off the rails, resulting in me walking in on him and his personal trainer while performing exercises requiring penetrative contact."

"Wow."

"Yeah, it wasn't great." I offered a tight smile before gulping my Pinot. "Anyway, you were saying … the woman who changed your life, who wasn't your ex-girlfriend."

"Yes, no, Heather."

"That's your ex, Heather?"

"No, Heather is the woman who changed my life."

"Oh. Sorry, I'll sip my wine and stop interrupting you," I giggled.

"No, that's okay …" Viv paused and leant forward. "You're stunning. You know that?"

I blushed and dropped my eyes.

"Shit. That was well bad, sorry. Christ," he muttered. "I said I was crap at this."

I glanced up and smirked. "You're the second man within the space of two days to offer me a compliment. I'm flattered."

"I hate him. Who is he? I'll have him arrested—"

"Clamped in irons and left to rot in a cell?"

"Deffo!"

"Well, Officer, if you are going to apprehend him, he's a barista in that coffee shop in the High Street. I didn't take his compliment too seriously because I'm old enough to be his mother. I think you could get him on a charge of owning an offensive ponytail with intent to swish it."

"Serious crime, then. You can get life for that or even a seat in the electric chair."

"At least," I chuckled.

"Although being a minor, he may get his sentence commuted down to thirty years."

"Minor?"

"I assume, as you said you're old enough to be his mother, he must be barely out of puberty."

"Oh … he said he was twenty-two."

Viv frowned, although somehow, his eyes still maintained a smile.

"I imagine I'm a smidge older than you."

Viv shrugged, maintaining that warm smile.

"Quite a lot, probably," I winced, awaiting his reaction.

"Ginny, are you trying to let me down gently?"

"I'm just being straight with you. So, I'm thirty-eight. I assume, as my ex probably believes, I'm too old. Am I?"

"No. I'm thirty-one. Am I too young?"

"No."

"That's alright then," he smirked.

"Come on, before I blush again, you were saying about Heather, the angel of Fairfield Police Station."

"Yeah, I was interviewed by this right old dragon of a DCI, who royally ripped me apart. The woman was ferocious. However, I owe everyfink to her. Basically, I had a choice. I could either say nuffin, which was advisable for anyone living on the estate, because speaking to the filth is like signing your own death warrant, or I could squeal. Course, the problem I faced, everyone knew I was being interviewed. So, whether I squealed or kept my gob shut, I was as good as shafted."

"Shit … what happened?"

"Well, to start wiv, I trotted out the 'no comment' reply to all her questions. Then, after she'd booted me into a holding cell, threatening to charge me wiv perverting the course of justice, DCI French gave me a parent-child-type speech. The sort of bollocking I'd never received before. Mum had tried her best, but she was a single parent … money was tight, she worked three jobs, so was never around much."

"Your father?"

"No idea." He clamped his hands together and shook his head. I could tell this was a difficult subject. "He naffed off after Deli came on the scene. To be honest, I can't remember him. That grizzly old DCI, although brutal when educating me about my life path if I continued in that gang, hammered home the need to change."

"So, you squealed, as you put it."

Viv nodded. "I did. My evidence got the scrote twenty-five years."

"What happened when they released you? Y'know, you said something about grassing was a death sentence."

"Heather said the best protection I could get was to become a copper. Join the force, and I would be safe. Even the scum on that estate won't kill a copper ... they know that carries a life sentence wivout any chance of parole. As I said, I owe her everyfink. She was the one who sponsored me to join the force and basically sort myself out."

"That's why you said you're not popular on the estate."

Viv smirked. "I fink that's an understatement. People move on or forget as time passes, but some of the long-standing families, like the Gowers, still reckon they have a price on my head."

"Oh, Christ. Aren't you worried?"

"Nah ... that's just wasted energy. As I said, even the Gowers are sensible enough to know cop killing ain't a sensible path to tread."

"Wow, you don't hear stories like that when the media constantly trot out their police-bashing hype."

"You're right. I still keep in touch with retired DCI French. Of course, I keep that to myself because my DCI would be pissed if he knew. Anyway, it's good to have someone in the know to talk through difficult cases. Although she came from the same era as Foxy—"

"Your bigoted boss."

"That's him." He waved his glass at me, confirming I was on track. "But she was forward-thinking and determined to always do the right fing. That woman made fundamental changes to the institution and dragged Fairfield Police into the twenty-first century."

"Apart from Foxy."

"Yeah, apart from him. He was one of her DCs back in the day. She reckoned he was a nightmare back then and had to constantly deal wiv his, well, let's just say outdated attitudes."

"He sounds like that TV detective ... what was his name?"

"I know who you mean," he chuckled. "The character has the same rhyming name. Gene Hunt, from *Life on Mars*."

"Yes, that's it!"

"Yeah, if you picture that character, you have DI Kevin Reeves clear in your mind ... without the humour, that is. There ain't nothing funny about my DCI."

"What about your mum? Sorry to hear that she's unwell."

Viv sipped his pint, offering a slight nod over the top of his glass. "Mum's never been that lucky with her health. Although I'll be in Bridgetown by the weekend, I'm worried I won't make it in time."

"Sorry, I never listened much at school. Where is that? My geography is a bit crap. Christ, I can't even find my way through the shopping centre without a compass and an Ordnance Survey map. I think even Bear Grylls would find guiding me to the right path one challenge too far," I giggled, before halting my schoolgirl act, now concerned the alcohol was going to my head.

"Barbados. Mum and Dad came over here in the early '80s. She returned when her mother got sick nearly ten years ago. After my grandmother died some years back, Mum met this guy she used to go to school wiv and decided not to return to the UK."

"And presumably, you persuaded your sister to go with you to see her?"

"Nah ... no, she's staying put." He shook his head before gulping down a mouthful of lager.

"Oh. I feel guilty now about not helping out. You know, with your nephew."

"Nah, don't. That ain't your responsibility. Deli could find help from somewhere if she really wanted to. No, the reason she's not coming is that, according to her, she ain't got no passport."

"Oh ... yes, well, that could be tricky."

"Deli's got a kind heart, you know. I've tried to get her off that estate, but she's deep-rooted in the culture now. I know she and Gabe deal in stolen goods, but I can't be the one to investigate and nick her."

"Oh, no. I agree."

"It's all petty stuff, so that's for Uniform to deal wiv. I've told her, though, she gets herself nicked, she can't expect me to sort it out."

We both plucked up our drinks as an awkward silence descended like a thick, ominous fog rolling in off the sea. I'd endured several first dates in my time, and although this wasn't a date, all previous experiences had these moments where neither one knew what to say next or was concerned about blabbing out the wrong thing.

As Viv lost eye contact and glanced out the window, I wondered if this was a date. We hadn't said as such, just that awkward conversation whilst standing next to that burnt-out community centre on the Broxworth after I'd told him to fuck off. Previous dates, if I can remember back that far, had been as a result of being chatted up in a bar or club. This felt different, more grown up. That said, he was probably just at a loose end and thought he'd be kind and offer to buy me dinner, so he didn't have to eat alone. So, did he really fancy me, a thirty-eight-year-old with no prospects? Was that stunning compliment just a throwaway line? Did I fancy him, and was I looking for a toy boy?

'Well, he's a step up from Footlong with the braces and the swishing ponytail.'

I considered my mind talk made a valid point.

Viv swivelled around in his chair to face me. I presumed he'd become bored with the view of the car park. "Sorry, I'm a bit crap at this."

I furrowed my brow, wondering where the conversation was going.

"Hey, I'm … well, I'm enjoying this. You and me having a drink."

"Me too." I flashed my best smile. Probably too much teeth, but hey, I was blessed with a good set. Like Footlong, who I met yesterday, braces in my early teens had resulted in owning an impressive set of gnashers. "I like your company. Despite not arresting that git with the vitamin deficiency, I'm having a really nice time."

Despite Viv and my husband visually being on either end of the spectrum regarding their appearances and assuming two glasses of wine hadn't metaphorically applied 'Pinot Glasses' to how I viewed this gruff-voiced, ripped black man with that gorgeous smile, I decided I fancied him.

Viv nodded, offering that smile. Despite his awkwardness and almost self-protecting attitude, which was probably born out of his tough upbringing, I found it surprising some gorgeous woman hadn't already nabbed him. I momentarily wondered what was wrong with him and if there was some dark secret that would come to light.

'Jesus! So, a good-looking bloke takes you for a drink, and you're already convinced he's some sleazebag. Ginny, please, for the love of God, drop your guard and live a bit. The man's buying you dinner, not asking to marry you. Enjoy the moment because you're royally getting on my tits!'

"What were you going to say?" I quizzed him, ignoring my mind talk, which I knew would only lead to trouble.

"You fancy … d'you wanna …" he exhaled a hefty huff and shook his head. "Nah, leave it. Forget it. Shall we order?"

I glanced at the menus as he plucked them up and offered me one. "Forget what?"

Viv opened the folded cardboard and peered at me before scrunching up his nose. "Don't suppose you would … well, maybe go out with me when I get back early next week."

"A date … proper date?"

Viv nodded. "You probably can't tell, but I'm blushing."

I flipped open my menu and smirked as I glanced at the extensive offer. "I'm thirty-eight. That's seven years older than you."

"Good at maths, despite a lack of attention during geography lessons."

"Yes," I smirked. "Talking of school … the menu looks comprehensive."

"The grub here is always good."

"I live on the Broxworth. I'm currently between jobs with somewhat limited prospects."

"Hey, don't worry, I'm buying. Are you practising your spiel on me for when you apply for benefits?"

"D'you think that will work? Quite fancy the salmon with dauphinoise potatoes and French beans."

"You got me. I'm welling up. The benefits officer is bound to crumble with that little speech. What sauce you want wiv it? There's a choice between honey and mustard or lemon and garlic."

"Hmmm, not sure. I might be forced to declare bankruptcy if my solicitor fails to secure any kind of divorce settlement. Those credit cards you kindly placed in that plastic bag after snapping on those blue gloves have some pretty scary balances. I'll probably have the honey and mustard. I'll avoid the garlic just on the off chance you try to kiss me later."

"Good choice. I might have the same."

I raised an eyebrow in surprise, expecting him to order two large porterhouse steaks with a double helping of chips – he didn't look like a salmon type of man. However, as I was fast learning, despite his gravel voice and ripped appearance, Viv Richards was a gentle man, not the thug I had him pegged for when first spotting him on that landing.

"On the subject of self-denigration, I'm a public servant, forced to beg for overtime to make ends meet, living in a shitty maisonette in town, spending most of my free time trying to make sure my delinquent sister doesn't end up in a prison cell."

I gulped my wine after lobbing the menu down on the table. "You going to order, then?"

"Two salmons, no garlic, I'm on it." Viv waved to the landlord, who held his hand aloft, acknowledging him, before grabbing his order pad. "Oh, you want another wine?"

"You trying to get me pissed?" I raised my eyebrows, offering a smirk. "Yeah, go on then."

Viv nodded. Then turned to the landlord as he approached and hovered by our table.

I held my hand up to the chap, indicating I wasn't quite ready, before grabbing Viv's hand. "Remind me, what was your original question?"

"Shall I come back?" quizzed the landlord, presumably sensing this could be an awkward moment.

"No, we're ready. Just hang on one sec, please."

Viv closed his eyes before slowly opening them and flashing that Sidney Poitier's heart-melting smile. "Can I take you out?"

"Yes … yes, I would like that." I turned to the poor chap, who now fidgeted with his shirt buttons. "Two of your salmon, with honey and mustard sauce, and another glass of Pinot, please."

"Great choice."

"Him or the salmon?"

"Both!" he chuckled, before nodding at Viv. "It's about time you found a woman." He glanced at me, offering a grin. "I'm fed up with serving Billy-No-Mates here, three times a week, you know. Viv might look like a club bouncer, but he's a top bloke. Top, top, bloke. You've made a good choice, almost as good as the salmon, which is sublime."

"Good, because my life choices so far have been anything but good."

"Two salmons with honey and mustard," he muttered, noting them down on his pad. "Shall I take the menus?"

I nodded, still rubbing the back of Viv's hand.

The landlord grabbed them off the table and repositioned the condiments next to the vase containing a small posy of fresh flowers. "We offer wedding services in our barn if you're interested. If you make it past your first date, pop in, and we can talk prices. I can also bang out a half-decent rendition of Pachelbel's Canon on the old ivories ... oh, ebonies, in your case," he nodded at Viv, smirked and disappeared.

"You made me work hard for that."

"I did. Listen, Viv Richards, I really like you. However, I'm damaged goods, and I really can't be hurt. I'm up to my eyeballs in shit, and it won't take much to break me."

"Trust me. I'm a police officer."

14

A Woman Scorned

"Thanks." I offered an unintentional cheesy grin, although four glasses of wine probably had some say in my inability to effectively control my face muscles. Fortunately, I'd narrowly avoided getting wasted, and the salmon, which was sublime, helped soak up a fair swathe of the alcohol before I made a complete tit of myself. Despite my overactive jaw muscle working overtime as the fourth glass flowed past my lips, Viv didn't seem to mind.

We hovered as I rammed my newly acquired door key into the lock of my front door.

"You're welcome," he grinned, hovering behind me with his hands rammed in his jean pockets whilst shuffling the soles of those highly polished Chelsea boots on the piss-stained concrete landing.

"It was nice, and thanks for walking me to my door."

"Well, I could hardly let you walk up here alone. Remember, I used to be part of a gang that terrorised these stairwells and alleyways. Those twats, who you had an unfortunate meeting with today, are just some scrotes who finks they're tougher than they really are. Just a bunch of low-life tossers who all need a good slap."

"Is that DS Viv Richards talking, or are you impersonating your DCI?"

Viv held his hand up. "You're right." Dipping his head, he continued. "Sometimes the DCI's language rubs off."

"No, I'm deffo with Foxy on this one. String them up by their balls would be a good start, never mind a slap. Bigoted tosser, he might be, but I bet he can deal with a few wrong'uns."

Viv snorted a laugh. "Although he is a tosser, he has a certain way of persuading the criminal fraternity to talk. Most of the time, through illegal methods."

"Grab 'em by the balls, and their hearts and minds will follow," I chuckled.

Viv raised his eyebrows whilst whisking his hands out of his pockets and folding his arms. "Sounds like you've met him. That's just the sort of line he would trot out when instructing the team to question a suspect."

"It's a direct quote from Gene Hunt. It's all coming back to me now. My dad loved that series. Dad was one for quoting funny lines."

"I'd like to meet him one day."

I shook my head. "Dead … six years ago."

"Sorry."

"It happens," I shrugged.

Viv slotted his hands back into his jeans pockets, leaned back, and puffed out a huge sigh. "Well, better get going, I suppose."

'Well, Ginny? I know it's only the first date, but are you going to drag him in and enjoy a rampant night of sex ... christen the mattress, so to speak?'

"I don't know."

Viv frowned. "What, sorry? What don't you know?"

I waved my hand slightly more exaggeratingly than I intended to due to the effects of the alcohol. "I was talking to myself. Ignore me. I'm a nutcase."

Viv raised his eyebrows.

"Well, not as in certifiable, but I hold these little chats in my head and sometimes answer myself out loud," I nervously laughed, concerned I was giving reasons for Viv to make haste back to his car. I didn't want him to do that – I don't think.

"Right," he nodded. "Well, as I said, I'd better get going," he extracted his right hand and dramatically waved it down the landing, as if offering himself to step forward. "I'll call you when I get back."

I nodded and flashed a full grin. "Yes."

"Oh, what's your name ... surname?"

"Strachan ... well, no, come to think of it, I'll probably change it back to my maiden name, Goode. Anyway, for the moment, I'm Strachan. It's Scottish. Everyone assumes my husband," I paused and shrugged. "Ex-husband is Scottish, but he couldn't be further from it. The name Alistair Strachan conjures up some strapping Scotsman with a ginger beard wearing a kilt whilst roaming the Highlands with a fair maiden in his arms. The truth is, he's only my height, with pipe-cleaner legs and looks ruddy awful in a skirt," I giggled. "Sorry, I'm babbling."

"Skirt?" Viv leaned his torso forward. "Did you say skirt?"

"Oh, he's not a cross-dresser … well, I assume he's not. He's stick thin, so he may have tried on a few of my dresses because they would probably fit. I'm an odd size, you see. I'm an eight on the hips and ten up top … top heavy, that's me. It's any wonder I can stand up," I giggled again, rocking from side to side like one of those Weebles toys. "Alistair's only got a thirty-eight-inch chest, so he may fit in a size ten, although I'm not sure."

I clocked Viv's smirk.

"You're laughing at me."

"No … absolutely not. But you make me laugh. Anyway, I'm now wondering about the skirt incident."

"Oh, yes, Ali once wore one of my leather mini-skirts to a tarts-and-vicars New-Year's-Eve party. Men were tarts, and women were vicars. As I said, he looked ridiculous in it. I had to pin the back with a safety pin because it was too small for him."

"Leather mini-skirt," Viv raised his eyebrows, that salacious male look which all men seem to be born with, and the ability to make it appear suggestive.

"Oh, that was years ago. I'm not sure I'd feel comfortable wearing it now, not at my age."

"Shame. I was looking forward to that."

"Were you?" I giggled.

'Christ, just take him in and shag him. If Karen were here, she would be demanding you do so.'

Whilst considering my mind talk's instruction, I detected the change in Viv's demeanour. Subtle facial muscles altered, which suggested our flirting session, if that's what it was, had now come to a rather abrupt end.

"Ginny, are you related to Mel Strachan?"

I leaned against my unopened front door and huffed. Although positioned on the second level of the most grotesque shitty estate imaginable, and the pungent, stale odour that hung like a permanent fog in the alleyways and landings did little to add to the moment, I knew this romantic encounter had reached its termination point. Unfortunately, my father-in-law harboured the ability to destroy anything good.

I nodded before sucking in lungfuls of air to calm my breathing – Mel Strachan had that effect on me. My parents had always despised the man, but I never knew why until a few years ago. I guess I've come to realise that they were a good judge of character based on what transpired when Mel was arrested. Although he'd always been the touchy-feely type, his true colours emerged when charged with rape, which, unbelievably, he got away with.

"Unfortunately, Mel Strachan is my father-in-law. Although the good thing is, very soon, he'll be my ex-father-in-law."

"By unfortunately, I take it you were referring to his arrest a few years ago?"

I nodded and bowed my head. "You know, when I was dating Ali, his father touched my breasts. When it happened, he claimed it was accidental. Although I was shocked, I naïvely chose to believe him. I think I blocked it out because

I didn't want to upset the applecart with Ali, who I'd become besotted with. I take it you were part of that investigation?"

"Nah. I was a DC back then, but not on that case. Vice were dealing wiv that one. But, yeah, course, I remember it. The DCI, not Foxy, threw his toys out the pram when Mel got acquitted."

"Why did you assume I was related to him? Strachan's not the most common name, but it's not that unusual."

"It just came to be. Your husband being Alistair, and I remembered you said he'd recently lost his mother."

"You're investigating her death?"

"We were, or still are, I should say. Look, I need to be careful what I say, because this is an ongoing investigation."

"Oh ... right, well, this is awkward." Despite my alcohol consumption, I was now stone-cold sober.

"I interviewed your husband some weeks ago. We understand you were away on holiday together at the time of Jean Strachan's death. So, when your husband's story checked out, we didn't see the need to talk to you. Your husband mentioned that you'd since separated."

"Did he?" I barked.

Viv nodded. "Gotta say, I thought what he said was a bit rude. In fact, I can remember his exact words because I thought it was a well weird fing to blurt out in a police interview."

"Oh, go on."

"Nah, leave it. I can't say."

"Viv! You can't say that, then hold back."

"Alright, but friggin' hell, this didn't come from me, alright?"

I nodded before raising my eyebrows to enforce my suggestion that he should spill the beans.

"Well, he said … he said you were … frigid."

"Frigid! Alistair said that? Fucking hell, he's got a ruddy nerve!"

Viv winced. "No, not that exact word, but I thought it was politer than what he actually said."

"Viv!" I thumped my hands on my hips and flared my nostrils.

"Jesus, Ginny, this is awkward. Taped interviews are confidential. I could land myself in all sorts of shit."

"Shit! I'll bloody well give you shit if you don't start talking. Hell hath no fury like a woman scorned, I might remind you," I barked, my infuriation bubbling to volcanic proportions.

"Bleedin' hell, I wouldn't want to get on the wrong side of you."

"Then don't! Spit it out."

"He said you were a cold bitch, and humping you was like shagging a corpse. Said somefink like you were as dry as a bucket of sand. He reckoned he decided to end the marriage after your holiday and mentioned somefink about a new woman he'd started seeing who could fulfil him … properly."

My jaw sagged.

"Look, I told you I shouldn't have said anyfink. As I said, I thought it was odd but just put it down to the stress he was under. Y'know, what with losing his mother so tragically and being interviewed to explain his whereabouts."

"Wanker! I'll fucking kill him!"

"Please don't … I'll have to arrest you," he smirked. "Hey, it was just a throwaway comment. He said it in anger, and I'm sure he didn't mean it."

"Jesus. He's the one with the bedroom problems. Not exactly a studmuffin in that department."

Viv raised his eyebrows.

"Oh, please don't think I put it about and regularly fill out an extensive spreadsheet that compares my conquest's performances. Let's just say Ali wasn't the most exciting man in the bedroom, that's all."

"Yeah, well, I thought the bloke was a bit of a dick, if I'm honest." He waved a finger at me, still with that smirk plastered across his face. "Don't quote me on that."

I tutted and folded my arms. "Yeah. well, just goes to prove I'm well shot of the git. Anyway, I take it you still believe her death to be suspicious and not suicide?"

"Ginny, we're keeping an open mind. There are factors I can't disclose because it's an ongoing investigation. The other consideration to take into account, it's not that easy to drown yourself in the bath."

"How so?"

"Well, it is if you swallow drugs or swill enough alcohol to dull your senses. Jean Strachan had no such toxins in her bloodstream. When you're fully compos mentis, intentional drowning in shallow water is difficult."

"Are you saying she was murdered, then?"

"Look, I've said too much already."

"I guess you're aware of Helen's campaign against your lot?"

"Your sister-in-law? Yeah, fully aware. Ginny, although I'm pissed off about this situation, I fink we may need to put us on ice for a bit."

"Oh."

"Just for the moment, you understand?"

"Concerned I'll perform like a frigid corpse."

"Err—"

"Sorry. That was awful. I wasn't suggesting that we should have sex."

'Why not?'

Ignoring my mind talk, I bashed on. "You know, first date and all that, so I wasn't saying that I wanted ... I ... I was just. Oh shit, I don't know what I was saying. Just forget it."

"Ginny, it's the case ... I'm involved. It's an ongoing investigation."

"Yeah, I get it."

'Should have dragged him into your bed when you had the chance.'

Viv stepped forward and tentatively held out his hand to touch my arm, but held back an inch or two. "I really like you, but I'll be compromised if we get involved."

"Viv, it's alright. I said, I get it. Look, we probably wouldn't have lasted more than a week, despite that landlord offering his barn up for the wedding ceremony."

"Perhaps we could—"

"No, Viv. Let's leave it at that. Thanks for dinner; it was nice."

Viv bowed his head and groaned out an exasperated huff. "This is why I'm single. My bleedin' job always gets in the way."

"I guess it can't be helped. Hey, if you still fancy that date in the future with some old bird, then you know where I am. That's assuming you or your colleagues don't have to arrest me for bankruptcy in the meantime, that is. If I'm super lucky, I'll still be living in this crap hole, collecting my benefits cheques whilst contemplating acquiring a cat to keep me company. So, unless you get a better offer, which I doubt would be too difficult, I'll be here growing old and sad."

Viv touched my arm and offered that smile – a smile I now regretted not dragging through my front door. He leaned down towards me. As I slowly lowered my eyelids, anticipating the touch of his lips, he leaned back. "Sorry," he whispered.

'You could have had the lemon and garlic sauce.'

I offered a resigned nod, accepting his apology. "I hope your mum's okay," I whispered.

"Cheers." He stroked my arm before stepping away and pointing those polished Chelsea boots in the opposite direction of my flat door before disappearing towards the stairwell.

As I watched him retreat, I wondered if he had hoped to come inside when walking me back. Then, remembering my tossy husband's comment, he thought better of it because he didn't fancy experiencing sex with a corpse.

I chewed the inside of my cheek, willing myself not to cry. Although I'm aware blubbing can have the effect of easing emotional pain, some bollocks I read in an article of some women's magazine I thumbed through when slowly dying of boredom in a doctor's waiting room last winter, I thought three times in one day could be classed as overly obsessive.

15

The Man From the Pru

"Look, that's it, darling. The building across the street, next to the chemist. Now, pop your Bluetooth thingy in your ear so we can talk if we need to. Remember, if you're going to answer me in there, then tap the button on your earpiece as if you're accepting the call like I showed you."

Terry fumbled with the Bluetooth contraption as he rammed it into his ear. "I think your Dickie must have had bigger ears than me. The damn thing is so tight, it hurts."

"Oh, don't whinge and whine so much. If you're not berating me about my dress sense, you're whinging about something else. Now, come on, there's a break in the traffic. Let's nip over the road and see if we can't have a little chat with your daughter."

"Well, at least I don't have to moan about your attire or lack of. I'm pleased you've seen fit to come out fully clothed this morning."

"Yes, disappointing that. There seems to be a chill in the air this morning. So, rather than suffer goosebumps and have my nipples poking out on stalks, I thought it prudent to pop on some appropriate designer apparel. Sunny days will soon be with us, and then you can savour the delights of strolling along with a ravishing, nubile, nude woman hanging off your arm, you lucky boy."

Terry side-eyed her as they dashed across the carriageway, heading to a frosted-glass-panel door, the blue-glass plaque by its side indicating this was the offices of Strachan Accountants.

"Okay, darling. So, you remember the back story we've come up with? You're going to have to be vague because none of it will stand up to any scrutiny. However, with a bit of luck, we can assess the lie of the land and hopefully fit some of the pieces together to grasp the situation."

Terry nodded.

"Good. So, remember, to get some time with Virginia, you need to state that you would like an audience with her to glance over your accounts. Then, when we have her in private, you casually drop in that you're an old friend of the family and see if you can get her talking. With a bit of good fortune, she might let slip what the problem is with that husband of hers."

"Yes, you don't have to repeat yourself. I've got it."

"Alright. Please don't get tetchy. Now you have your file, so we're all set."

Terry rolled his eyes and waved the cardboard file that only contained a few sheets of blank paper.

"Good boy. Here's my mobile. Just hold it and don't fiddle with it. Last thing we need is you inadvertently calling some sex-chat line whilst we're trying to con our way in."

"What's that?"

Deana peered up at him. "Good grief. I don't suppose those types of services were around in your day."

"Not that I can recall, no."

"No, I'm sure you don't. I suspect it was all nipping into the local phone box to pluck up a card displaying pictures of scantily clad tarts offering their wares."

"I did not! I had no need to pick up those types of women. And, I'll have you know, I received more offers from the fairer sex than I could shake a stick at."

"Yes, I imagine you did. However, now that you're a fully paid-up member of the walking dead, you only have one offer. So, I suggest you think on, Terence, and realise what you're missing out on."

Terry tutted and rolled his shoulders. "I'm going to regret asking this, but what exactly is a sex-chat line?"

"It's a service where you phone a premium rate number, and some woman talks dirty to you. Ear-porn, I think, is the term."

"Oh. Something I expect you're fairly au fait with, I imagine."

"No, darling. Neither I nor my darling husband felt the need for such services. We enjoyed erotic group-sex orgies with like-minded acquaintances. So, listening to some obese housewife pretending to be some smooth sex goddess whilst ironing her working-class husband's Y-fronts was not necessary, I can assure you."

"You've lost me, as usual."

"I'm quite sure I have. Now, I suspect your daughter and husband are some boring Yuppie types. That's what accountants are, so don't be too surprised if they're both a couple of turgid boring gits with calculators stuck up their derrieres."

"Well, my other two children weren't exactly captains of industry before we stepped in to help. Kim cleaned toilets, and Damian was an insurance collector. At least Virginia and her husband are probably degree educated."

"Damian was a call handler, not a door-to-door policy payment collector."

"Oh. I thought you said he was like the man from the Pru? My father used to pay his ten-shillings a week when the Pru-man turned up on a Thursday evening."

"Oh, darling. Men don't pound the streets collecting payment or offering their wares from suitcases anymore. Digital age, darling. It's all online."

"Right, course not. Anyway, what the hell is a Yuppie?"

"Young, urban professional people. I would imagine they are also Dinkies."

"I guess that's not a toy car, is it?"

"No, darling. It stands for dual income no kids."

"Right, got it. Well, if they do have offspring, that could very well mean I'm a grandfather."

"Oh, yes. How funny. We'll have to get you a pipe and a pair of those nice tartan slippers. Perhaps a suitable leather-buttoned Aran-wool cardigan, as well."

"Hilarious. I'm only in my early-thirties. I'm still young."

"You are, darling. Young, fit, and manly, with a beautiful hairy bottom and bulging biceps. And dead, of course. Can't forget that we're dead."

"Hmmm. You know, I wish I'd attended university. I might have landed a fancy job instead of running a supermarket."

"Then you wouldn't have met me at that conference."

"No. What a shame," he muttered.

"Excuse me? And I told you about muttering. Now, I don't recall you being overly disappointed when you ravaged my body that evening. Quite the opposite, I might suggest. You're forgetting that enjoying carnal pleasure with me is a voluptuous hedonist treat to be savoured."

"No, I don't regret that. Just the dying bit afterwards."

"Regrets are like farts, darling. You can't get them back. Once they're out, they're stinky and gone. Anyway, I suspect in your youth, if you weren't pleasuring some floozy in your locker-room-stinking bedroom, you were vegging out on the sofa watching the TV. So, study time was limited and thus failed to secure the necessary qualifications to secure an Oxbridge degree. My Dickie got a first from Oxford. Did I ever tell you that?"

"Only the few times," he sarcastically replied. "Anyway, what's vegging?"

"Vegetate ... slothish behaviour."

"Loafing around being idle, as my mother used to say."

"Precisely."

"Hmmm, well, after our session, I died. So, even if I'd fancied a new career, I couldn't because I was dead. Now

I'm a ghost meting out retribution. Not exactly a career choice I would have picked out during careers lessons at school."

"I know, darling. Although, I must say I'm a little disappointed because it feels like you're blaming me for what happened. Semelparity cannot be laid at my door."

Terry pulled a face.

"Semelparity ... suicidal reproduction. It's what gave the name to Black Widow spiders, who have a good munch on the males after he's had his wicked way. I'm led to believe that some species of Praying Mantis actually eat the male alive whilst he's giving her a good old rogering ... can you imagine that?" she chortled. "And then, of course, there's that little furry fella, the Antechinus, sort of an Australian rodent, who is so randy that after copulating for hours on end, he keels over and dies, poor little furry fella. A bit like you did, my darling, when we made Damian."

"I take it you gleaned this pointless information from another one of your animal sex programmes that wasn't presented by Johnny Morris?"

"National Geographic, darling. Not animal sex; that's perversion. It's nature, the beautiful natural process of a female and male bonding to make love. All very educational and quite fascinating. Something you now seem to have forgotten how to do."

"Well, rather than go down that route, let's get on with it. I just don't know how you manage to turn every conversation around to sex."

"It's a skill, darling. Perfected over many years of wooing luscious men."

"Come on," Terry nodded towards the door. "We'd better get on with it, I suppose."

"That's the ticket. Best foot forward, darling." Deana waved her hand, gesturing for Terry to push open the door.

Terry complied, holding it for Deana to step through before approaching the reception desk where a heavily trowelled-on-make-upped twenty-something woman sat slumped in her chair filing her nails. Terry cleared his throat.

"Yeah?" she apathetically questioned without looking up, choosing to inspect the three-quarter-of-an-inch protruding nail she'd successfully filed to a point, which Terry presumed, apart from appearing to be some offensive weapon, could also double up as a tool to punch holes in inch-thick steel sheets. He feared for her boyfriend's back later that evening.

"Clearly, there's no HR department in this firm! She needs to cut those nails to an acceptable length, scrape off some of that tarty make-up with a paint stripper, and learn some damn manners!"

"Good morning. I wonder if I could have an appointment with Mrs Strachan, please. I'm aware of the short notice, but I have to submit my accounts later today, and I'm just looking for a half-hour appointment to check them over." Terry waved the file, indicating said accounts.

"Mr Strachan?" she mumbled, before sucking her pointed nail and only glancing up at Terry when he didn't respond.

"I'd prefer Mrs Strachan if that's possible?"

"Pity Alistair didn't ... I might not be out of a job."

"Err ... sorry?" Terry questioned whilst sporting a knitted brow before glancing at an office door from where he could clearly hear a woman shouting.

"Whatever is that damn racket? It sounds like all-out war in that office. Not exactly professional, is it?"

"You'd have to be deaf not to hear them." Pointy-Nail thumbed towards the office door. "They've been shouting at each other for at least half an hour ... long enough for me to do five nails."

"Sorry, who has?"

"Him and her. Mrs Strachan no longer works here. And now, because there's only Mr Strachan, he reckons he needs to cut costs and has let me go. Tosser."

"Oh, I see."

The apathetic woman carried on whilst refocusing on her nails. "Stay until the end of next week, he said. So I had time to find another job, he said," she stated in an exaggeratedly deep voice whilst shaking her head from side to side. "Wanker!"

Terry glanced at Deana, who offered a roll of her eyes.

The receptionist glanced up, taking a break from wielding her nail file. "I nearly told the git where to shove it, but I need the money, so decided to keep my trap shut and see it through. Although, after that bitch slapped me, I'm half tempted to do one. I only told her the truth to get back at him. How was I to know she'd go off on one? Could have the bitch arrested for assault for doing that. What d'you reckon?"

"Sorry, I'm a little lost."

"You can't have an appointment because the bitch don't work here no more. Got it?" she barked at Terry.

"Oh, right," Terry muttered, shooting his head backwards, keen to distance himself from her aggressive demeanour.

"She's in there screaming at her husband because he's dumped her for some tart who works up at that fitness centre place. Also, me telling Ginny about what me and him used to get up to when she was out of the office ain't helped much."

"Oh."

"Yeah, I know, oh! The bastard was quite happy to slip me one whilst she was out. Now he's taken up with that vegan yoga tart, the bastard reckons he no longer needs me in reception or bent over his bleeding desk. So, the git's dispensed with my services. Got it?"

"Got it."

"If I were you, I'd make an appointment somewhere else. The bastard can bin me off, but I will make sure I tell everyone what a wanker he is before I leave at the end of next week." She shrugged and set to work on the next nail that required shaping into a steel punch.

"So, the husband has been playing away. That explains the problem, and the bellowing coming from that office suggests all is not happy in the Strachan household. Sounds like your little Virginia's husband likes to play hide the sausage on a regular basis. And, by the looks of this little tart, he's not overly fussy where he hides it, either."

"Reckon my dad's gonna punch his lights out when I tell him what's happened. Although Dad's no angel, always got his hands on some bit of skirt." She glanced up at Terry. "You know what he's like, though. He ain't gonna be happy when I tell him what's happened," she announced, offering a knowing nod.

"Sorry. Do I know your father?"

She pulled a face at him. "I don't know, do I? What's that got to do with anything?"

"You said, 'you know what he's like' ... but I don't, do I?"

"Yeah, whatever." Pointy-Nail repeatedly glanced between the attentive Terry and the particular nail she continued to sharpen. "He's a leg man, y'know, my dad. Can't resist long legs in heels. Whereas Alistair's definitely a tit man. Tit! Good description for him." She temporarily halted her nail scraping and waved the file at Terry. "I said to him this morning, both me and his bitch of a wife have got bigger tits than that yoga-spouting tart at the fitness centre, so I can't see what the attraction is."

"No, I'm sure," Terry replied with a nervous grin.

"You know, darling. I did that Courteney, who our Damian has hooked up with, a disservice. Compared to this little piece of trash, Courteney could be described as a perfect lady."

Terry's eyes followed Deana's walk as she nipped over to the closed door to listen in on the slanging match. Although clear to hear, not all words were decipherable. Notwithstanding what Terry presumed was a volley of verbal assaults emanating from a male voice, Terry could clearly make out the string of expletives fired back by the female, who he presumed was his daughter Virginia, or

Ginny as Pointy-Nail had described her when taking a break from referring to her as bitch.

Deana hovered by the closed door, standing on tiptoe as she scrunched up her nose and squinted her eyes closed whilst listening to the exchange. "Darling, I think your little Virginia is deranged. She needs to nip down the doctors and secure a prescription for a year's supply of Prozac. You know, I might go in. They'll probably just think a draught or something caught the door."

Terry tapped his earpiece, cleared his throat, and straightened his spine. "Err ... Terry, here."

"Ian! We agreed you'd use my first husband's name just on the off chance that Virginia knows your damn name. Come on, Terence, buck up!"

"Err ... yes, Ian here. Can I help you? Over," he boomed, before nodding to Pointy-Nail and gesturing to his earpiece. "I've got a call. I've got a call on my telephone. I can hear it through my bucktooth," he nodded, then winked.

"And?" she shrugged, opening up her palms, taking a nanosecond break from filing her nails into a dangerous-looking point. "Frigging weirdo."

Ignoring her put down, Terry bashed on. "Hello, yes, this is Ian. No, no, I really don't think that is a good idea. I don't think you should open the door. Over."

Deana turned around and rested the heels of her hands on her hips. "Darling, you're acting as if you're auditioning for a part in a play. You're pretending to be on the phone, not addressing the audience at the Globe whilst informing them that act two of The Merchant of Venice is about to start. You need to act more natural. If you carry on like that, this little tart here will probably call the police, informing them she's holed up with an escaped lunatic."

Terry rolled his shoulders and wiggled his hands before clearing his throat as if preparing to re-perform his lines after receiving some less-than-favourable criticism from the producer about his performance thus far.

"You alright, mate? You having some kind of hissy fit?"

Terry glanced to his left to spot Pointy-Nail glowering with her nailfile poised in mid-air.

"You one of those epilectric types?"

"Sorry?"

"You know those epilectric weirdos who lay on the floor, flinging their arms around and foaming at the mouth, or whatever you call them. Epi-something or other."

"No. I'm on an important call." He tapped his earpiece to reinforce his point.

"Well, there's no point hanging about here. Them two will probably end up killing each other. Even if they don't, you ain't going to get an appointment with that git anytime soon."

"Well, I'll wait if that's alright with you?"

"Suit yourself," she shrugged, refocusing back on her nails, before waving her nail file at Terry again. "Just don't have an epi fit while you're in here, that's all I'm saying. I ain't got no first aid training, and I deffo ain't doing mouth to mouth with you."

"I'll bear that in mind."

"It'll be alright, darling. I'll just take a quick peek." Deana reached for the door handle, grimacing as she tried

to perform her act with poise and stealth to avoid being noticed. Although Pointy-Nail seemed focused on her manicure routine, so Deana presumed the girl wouldn't spot the handle magically depress.

"No, as I said, I think that would be a mistake. I suggest you refrain from that action. Over."

"Oi. If you're gonna wait for Mr Strachan, can you stop shouting?"

"First sensible thing that little slut's said," muttered Deana, as she nosed around the door into Alistair Strachan's office.

As Deana released the handle, the door flung open. To avoid being flattened, she hopped back as a ruddy-faced woman barrelled into the reception area. Then, with her long ponytail swishing from side to side, she dramatically swivelled around and jabbed her finger back at the suited gent who filled the space in the open doorway.

"Fuck you. You waster!"

"Your daughter seems nice, darling," quipped Deana, smirking back at a shocked-looking Terry.

16

Convoy

My tossy husband grabbed hold of his office door, ready to fling it shut. "No thanks! I'd rather stick needles in my eyes."

"I'll do it for you; you utter prick. In fact, I'm in a good mind to—" I halted my rant due to sensing that we weren't alone. Although I knew our tarty receptionist would be slouched behind her desk, my words caught in my throat when I detected the presence of someone standing behind me. As Alistair held his hand up, I spun around to spot a thirty-something chap sporting a bug-eyed expression as he gawped at me whilst hovering near the reception desk.

Although Viv had stated he would land in a difficult situation if I divulged the confidential interview he'd enjoyed with my knob of a husband, sixteen hours on from that conversation outside my flat, I still hadn't managed to calm down.

My loose plan when bashing through Alistair's door this morning involved ranting, of course, whilst putting him straight on a few points – namely humping corpses and references to buckets of dry sand. However, when Miss Manicure enlightened me about her and Alistair's regular weekly sessions across his antique leather-topped desk, a piece of furniture I purchased for him for our wedding anniversary last year, I might add, my utter fury notched up a level.

Now that I no longer held the position of business manager at Strachan Accountants, I thought I might partake in a spot of business ruining. Well, he'd successfully cut me free, so if I could inflict a modicum of damage on his accounting firm, then why not?

I aggressively pointed at the gawping chap. "Well, if you're looking for accountancy services, I'd go someplace else!"

"Ginny, stop!"

Ignoring his plea not to abuse a potential client, I bashed on, now enjoying myself. "He might have a string of letters after his name, suggesting he's perfectly qualified to assist you, but the git might struggle to perform to the required standard due to constantly becoming distracted with his regular sessions when entertaining our receptionist across the top of his fancy leather-topped desk. And that's, of course, when he can fit it in, no pun intended, between bashing the brains out of some tart from the local gym." I stepped forward, jabbing my finger at the chap who appeared to take a pace backwards towards the door. "So, if you're looking for accountancy services, I suggest you try Clarkson's on Timber Hill!"

"Oh, isn't she good? I'm going to enjoy helping this woman. Now, I have to say, the cheating git looks like a right loser. I do hope our mission is to ruin him. What fun, darling."

As I ran out of steam, I dropped my wagging finger, somewhat surprised that the poor chap, who'd unfairly been on the receiving end of my wrath, remained in the reception area and hadn't taken flight. As the red mist receded and my behaviour returned to a slightly more conciliatory demeanour, it dawned on me that I recognised him.

"Oh ... it's you. Bluetooth man."

"Sorry, have we met?"

"Darling, I've always been rather top-notch with faces. I have a feeling this woman is that blonde woman you referred to as Blondie in the coffee shop a couple of days ago." Deana circled around Ginny, inspecting her face whilst tipping her head to one side and tapping her index finger on her bottom lip. "Hmmm, it's definitely her."

Alistair stepped forward. "I'm so sorry, sir. Please excuse my wife. She's having a difficult time of things at the moment." He adopted a slightly stooped, open-palmed stance whilst sporting an embarrassed wince.

"Because of you, dickhead," I barked.

"Oh, hell, she made me jump." Deana hopped back, startled by Ginny's outburst.

"Sorry, I don't know your name. But I recognise you. I think you were in that coffee shop on the High Street the other day, and you remind—"

"Ginny, please stay out—"

"Oh, shut up!" I spun around on my husband, interrupting him whilst aggressively thumping my hands on my hips. "Take her ..." I waved my hand at Serena, who appeared fully focused on her nails rather than performing her office duties, the full extent of what they were, now becoming apparent, "… into your office and do with her what you want! The girl is only twenty. Christ, that thigh-gap bitch is young enough; now her! As I just pointed out to you … like father like son, eh! I expect you'll be preying on schoolgirls next, you depraved pervert."

Alistair stepped forward, entering my personal space. Although he'd never displayed an aggressive tendency during our relationship, the exchanges following our earlier spat seemed to have brought his animal instincts to the surface. "You've got a bloody nerve, woman. That's slander. My father was acquitted."

"A jury of twelve idiots might have concluded that. I can only assume they must have been asleep or in a coma whilst the poor girl gave evidence—"

"You supported him throughout the trial—"

"Only to stand by your side. Misplaced loyalty on my part! Everyone in their right mind knows what your father is like. Christ, you're more stupid than I—"

"Loyalty? Loyalty—"

"Yes! Even your mother knew the truth and dumped him—"

"Don't you bring my mother into this."

"As entertaining as it is, like watching one of those trashy soaps, this could go on forever. Do you think you might want to intervene, darling?"

"Your poor mother killed herself because she could no longer live with the shame."

"I'd do it myself, but being invisible has its disadvantages, if you see what I mean?"

"No, she didn't!"

"So, you're hanging on to this wild notion the police are still banding about that she died under suspicious circumstances?"

"She did. You know she did."

"Darling, refrain from catching flies. One of us is going to have to step in and break this up. These two going at it hammer and tongs isn't going to move us forward. As I said, I'm invisible, and that dippy tart appears content sawing her nailfile back and forth so that only leaves you, my darling."

"Oh, whatever! I've had enough, and I can't listen to your bloody annoying imbecilic theories anymore." I dismissively waved my hand at him.

"Excuse me. Excuse me … err … excuse me."

Before Alistair had the chance to respond, we both halted our rant because of that Bluetooth man interrupting. His third request to be excused became audible as we took a breath.

"Sorry, sir. Sorry about that. How can I help? Do you have an appointment?" Alistair stepped past me, extending his hand to the Bluetooth man.

I huffed before sucking in lungfuls of air to calm my nerves. Although I'd always possessed a tendency to fly off the handle, many years had elapsed since I'd bashed out a performance to this level.

"He said he popped in on the off chance," Serena, our hussy receptionist, offered as she held her hand out to inspect her nails.

Bluetooth man nodded at the girl, presumably confirming her statement while she remained focused on appraising the results of her manicure.

"I understand this may be a difficult time, but I was wondering if Mrs Strachan could take a gander at my accounts," he stated, as he accepted the offered hand from my tossy husband.

"I'm the accountant, sir. My wife is the business manager."

"Was!" I snapped back.

Alistair swivelled his head and scowled. "You still here?"

"I wonder if I might have a private moment with Mrs Strachan?"

I smirked as I watched Bluetooth man release his hand from Alistair's limp handshake and proceeded to wipe the sweat down his polo shirt. My soon-to-be ex had always offered a sticky, wimpish handshake, and it appeared this chap wasn't too enamoured with the exchange of fluids.

"She's not qualified. As I said, I'm the accountant, sir. My wife used to complete bookwork, but it's me who you'll need an appointment with, sir."

"Darling, I thought you said their website suggested they were both qualified accountants? I don't think, at this point in our mission, we need to talk to her husband. However, this is starting to blow rather hefty holes in our plan."

"Why d'you want to talk to me?" I stepped forward, narrowing my eyes, now becoming concerned about who this man was and what he wanted. I considered the possibility that he might be stalking me, although that notion seemed somewhat bizarre. Now my brain whirred as I recalled that comment he made when leaving the coffee shop, uttering the name Deana Beacham, a name that my mother would only utter when followed by a string of expletives.

"Err, it's a delicate subject, shall we say," he offered, with what appeared a nervous, shifty-type grin.

As I'd assessed him when in that coffee shop, I now concluded he held an uncanny resemblance to Terry, my mother's lover, my biological father. Clearly, he wasn't that man my mother cooed over because he was dead. And if she had, for some odd reason, lied about that fact, the man would now presumably be somewhere north of sixty and not the thirty-something man who I'd just rather unnecessarily berated. "Sorry, do we know each other?"

"Darling, remember what we discussed. Although this conversation is unfortunately diverting off-piste, trotting out that ridiculous line about being her dead father risen from the grave would not be advisable."

Bluetooth man tapped his earpiece whilst holding the palm of his hand aloft. "Sorry, I'm on the telephone," he grinned. "I can hear it through this transceiver that I have in my ear," he nodded before turning around, presumably wanting a little privacy to take his call. "Yes, I'm fully aware that is not the way forward," he hissed. "We discussed the plan this morning, and although there appears to have been some unexpected developments, I intend to stick to what we discussed. I know what I'm doing, woman. Over."

"Alright. Please don't get tetchy. I was only saying because, with both little Kimmy and Damian, you blurted out ridiculous statements that landed us in a right old pickle." Deana wandered around the office to face Terry as she

responded. "And darling, please refrain from using outdated phrases regarding your Bluetooth. It's not a bucktooth, transmitter, or transceiver. You're not a trucker in Convoy, and your call sign isn't rubber duck. Also, you do not need to say 'over' after you speak, or 'roger and out' or any other ridiculous radio speak."

"Oh, okay. Wilco."

I couldn't help but wonder about his odd conversation. He clearly wasn't happy with what the woman on the other end of the call was saying, and I thought it rather bizarre that he said the word 'over' to conclude his sentences.

Alistair swivelled on his heels and marched back to his office. Before slamming the door, he turned and pointed at me. "I suggest you chat to this bloke someplace else because you sure as hell ain't using your old office."

Leaving my dead father's lookalike to finish his call, I scowled at Alistair as he threw his office door closed, an act that caused the framed certificates mounted on the wall to the left to vibrate. I stomped towards them and yanked one from the wall before unceremoniously lobbing it towards the carpet tiles and ramming my foot into the cracked frame before grinding my heel on the splintered glass.

When satisfied that I'd sufficiently destroyed Alistair's professional qualifications certificate and reduced each sliver of glass to a size that, if so inclined, I could ram into my tossy husband's eyeballs, I glanced up to see my biological father's lookalike gawping at me. I presumed he'd completed his call now that he'd stopped talking. His expression suggested he probably regarded me as some deranged, crazed nutter. Serena continued her manicure, appearing nonplussed with my antics.

"I think your girl is a bit miffed with her husband. We'd better be wary of this one. I'd venture that this woman could be somewhat unstable. Is that from your side of the family, or did her mother suffer from bats in the belfry?"

"Right. Sorry about that," I smirked, now feeling better, as I lifted the heel of my trainer from the mashed frame. "So, as you can see, I'm unable to conduct any business from here. My husband and I are no longer in partnership, in all meanings of the word, if you see what I mean."

"Yes, I can see," he chuckled, glancing at the debris under my foot. "Look, it's a private matter, really. Presumably, we can't use your office," he stated, checking his watch. "As it's gone midday, can I buy you a drink?" he enquired, surreptitiously nodding to Serena, who occasionally glanced up whilst continuing her manicure routine, taking in the conversation.

"Darling, what are you up to? I know the other day you said you fancied Blondie, but she's your damn daughter. And, if you ask me, seriously unstable, going by that performance. I suggest, if you're planning on asking her on a date, that is wholly inappropriate!"

Although a smidge concerned regarding who this man was or what on earth a 'private' matter could be about, I certainly didn't want to conduct this conversation in Serena's earshot.

"Mrs Strachan ... a drink?"

I chewed my lip, weighing up the offer. Although I'd agreed to accompany Viv yesterday, at that point, I'd needed a drink after the trauma of being mugged. My hand shot to my necklace, the panic now setting in when unable to feel the rings before remembering that Yellow-Eye had relieved me of that possession. Sensibly, I considered that accompanying strange men to the pub at lunchtime didn't seem a good idea. However, based on the fact I had bugger all else planned for my day with no burning desire to return to my flat, a busy pub would be a safe environment. Also, he'd intrigued me regarding that comment made the other day when uttering the name Deana Beacham – fair to say, Bluetooth man had piqued my interest.

I nodded. "Yes, okay."

"Great," he grinned. Then, for some odd reason nodded to his right, muttering something into thin air before waving his hand to the door, presumably suggesting I should lead the way.

"Alright. But, for Christ's sake, don't screw this up! Go to the Murderers Pub across the road. I'll meet you over there. I think I'm going to have a quick nose around and see what I can unearth about this despicable git."

17

The Electra Complex

Whilst settling onto a bench seat near the window, I considered that my mystery man might be hitting on me. Not that I usually courted male attention, but that pubescent barista had made that offer. Also, Viv had shown an interest before pulling out the rule book, stating police officers aren't allowed to be involved with anyone connected to an ongoing investigation. So, two members of the opposite sex had made their intentions clear within as many days. Perhaps I was on a roll, and this guy was the third. If I continued at this rate, I could cancel my subscription to that woeful dating site.

My new date, if that's what he was, ordered the drinks, leaving me pondering what he'd have to say for himself. For sure, if he had spotted me with Karen and intended to ask me on a date, I thought it somewhat creepy that he'd discovered my name and shown up at my old office. That said, perhaps I was reading this all wrong, and that 'personal' matter he referred to was nothing to do with wanting to date a soon-to-be-divorced, potentially desperate, thirty-eight-year-old.

Despite my disappointment that Viv had decided not to continue our somewhat fleeting relationship – alright, only one dinner date – and my stupid decision to sign up to that match-making site, I honestly didn't believe I was in any fit state to jump into the merry-go-round of dating – irrelevant to what Karen believed. *"Get back on the horse as soon as you fall off,"* she'd said.

Thirty years had elapsed since I sat on a pony. A Saturday morning treat that my father thought I would enjoy, despite my scowling face and preference for watching *Saturday Superstore*. *"All little girls like ponies,"* he'd said, whilst I trotted around on the back of some smelly animal in an equally stinking courtyard with ten other annoying juvenile, pompous miss prissies whilst displaying my perfected curmudgeonly expression. Paul was wrong, not all little girls liked ponies, and Karen was also wrong, because I probably shouldn't get back on the 'horse' too soon.

Despite Karen's attempts at matchmaking, I was out of practice in the dating game after twelve years of marriage. Also, in my current predicament, I thought I needed to take a breath and sort my life out before diving headlong into a relationship so soon. Anyway, agreeing to date a man who appeared to resemble my mother's lost love in that grainy 35mm snap from over forty years ago would be a smidge odd. I remember the term I'd learnt when studying for my A-level sociology exams was the *Electra Complex* – as in a daughter when attracted to men who resemble or act like their father.

Paul Goode was nothing like Alistair Strachan in physicality or personality. Although Terry Walton, according to my mother, was my biological father, I believed the *Electra Complex* was a product of nurture, not nature. So, as my new date placed my glass of Pinot on the table, I considered, as I had when studying for my A-Levels exams, that theory was a load of bollocks.

"Thanks," I offered, making a grab for the glass.

"My pleasure."

My new date settled in the chair opposite, extracted and pocketed his earpiece before offering me a grin. At that moment, I considered that I'd made a potentially grave mistake due to his exaggerated facial expression resembling some sicko serial killer sporting a slasher grin with malevolent eyes.

"What are you grinning at?" I rather aggressively spat, whilst shooting a look at the barman, hoping he might spot the fear in my eyes. Unfortunately, when reciprocating with a Peter Kay styled pervy wink, it suggested he clearly got the wrong idea about my raised eyebrow. Christ, the barman, who appeared similar age to the barista-boy, also seemed to be hitting on me. Lord knows why, but since splitting from Alistair, I'd developed a propensity for attracting younger men.

Shaking toy-boys from my mind, I turned back to face the grinning man. "Well?" I snapped.

My rather pugnacious bark about his continued stupid facial expression appeared to haul him from his stupor. "Oh, sorry, sorry. I was just …" he hesitated.

I raised my eyebrows at him. "Just what?"

"Nothing."

"Nothing? Well, you said we have a private matter to discuss. So, instead of grinning at me, I suggest you start talking. Who are you, and what do you want?" I barked again, slightly surprised at my aggressive tone. However, I guess since barrelling into Alistair's office earlier, that seemed to be the conversational tone adopted for the day.

"I'm Ian. Ian Beacham."

"Beacham?" I narrowed my eyes. That name Beacham again.

"Yes, look, I knew your parents. I needed someone to cast their eye over my accounts," he tapped the folder lying by his side. "And while I was at it, I thought, why not pop in and introduce myself."

"Oh ... well, sorry about that. I was only the business manager, not a qualified accountant. You will need Alistair for that, or as I suggested, try Clarkson's. But you said you knew my parents; how come?"

"Yes ... sort of ... old friends," he nervously laughed.

"Presumably, you're aware both have now passed."

"Oh, yes," he nodded, reaching for his pint glass. "Very sad news. I'm sorry for your loss."

"Ian, when exactly did you know my parents?" I plucked up my glass, keeping my narrowed eyes on him as I took a sip whilst awaiting his answer, which I fully suspected would be bullshit. Whether I was being overly cautious, who knows? However, I detected there was something not quite right about the man.

Ian appeared to wriggle nervously in his chair, his body language confirming my suspicions. After a few seconds with his head down, he looked up and dismissively waved his hand. "Oh, it was years ago. Long time ago."

"Ian, if you don't mind me asking, how old are you?"

"Good question! I've been trying to get my head around that myself," he chuckled, before his expression changed, presumably realising what an odd statement that must have been. "I'm thirty-two ... at the last count."

"Oh," I muttered, whilst performing some quick calculations. "So, you're suggesting you knew my parents when Dad was still alive? So, that means you were younger than twenty-six when you knew them."

"Err ... yeah, that's about right."

I detected he wasn't overly confident with his answer. Either he hadn't concentrated during maths lessons at school, or he was bullshitting – I suspected the latter.

"Okay, so I left home when I married that cheating git, Alistair. That was in June 2004 when I was twenty-six, and you would have presumably been about twenty." I raised my eyebrows, not as if suggesting I'd posed a question, but letting the maths sink in. I bashed on as Ian appeared to be attempting to compute the numbers. "So, tell me, Ian Beacham, how come, as I lived at home right up until 2004, I've never met you before, or my parents never mentioned a young lad called Ian, for that matter?"

Ian widened his palms and shrugged whilst losing eye contact. "Well, we weren't close friends, as such."

"No, I imagine you weren't," I scoffed. "At that time, my parents were in their fifties. So, unless you'd joined the local indoor bowls association or regularly attended my mother's weekly slimming club, which I doubt, that would suggest you hardly knew them."

"Look, Virginia—"

"And another thing," I interrupted. "If you knew my parents, as you reckon you did, you would know full well that I haven't been called Virginia since I attended primary school. My name is Ginny."

Ian nodded and pursed his lips.

"You didn't know I was called Ginny, did you?"

Ian offered a slight shake of his head. "Not before today, no."

"Okay. So, listen, whoever you are, I don't need all this aggro. I'm having a piss-shit time of it at the moment, and whatever your game is, I don't need any more hassle to add to my ever-rising festering heap of crap which I'm trying to deal with."

"Ginny ... I'm ... err, this is difficult ..." He made a grab for his pint, presumably trying to conjure up his next line of codswallop.

Whilst Ian slugged his pint, the penny dropped. Although unsure how he'd acquired the name Beacham, his uncanny likeness to that picture of Terry Walton would suggest he could be my half-brother. I figured his stumbling was due to trying to build up the fortitude to introduce himself as such. However, that would mean he knew about Terry and my mother on the sofa in Sunny Hunny. Not to mention there appeared to be a problem with the maths – Terry Walton died before this man was born.

"Ian, are you related to Terry Walton, or even Deana Beacham, for that matter?"

Terry slowly lowered his pint glass. "Oh ... err," he frowned, shaking his head. "Why would you ask that?"

"Well, it's just that you appear similar to a man in an old photo who my mother knew back in the '70s. So, I'm guessing you could be his son, perhaps?"

As I waited for him to answer, the thought of the possibility of him being my half-brother marinated in my mind. If that turned out to be the case, that would throw up some tricky conversations with my brother, Jules.

Ian, still seemingly stumped by my question, fiddled with his glass, turning the base around clockwise, like shifting a dial. I could only presume his fiddling was a distraction whilst he took a moment to think before answering.

"Well, come on, then. Is that what this is all about?" For some unknown reason, I ran the tip of my finger around the rim of my wine glass. Either this was my new nervous tic to replace fiddling with my rings, or I felt the need to rotate my hand and thus copy the bullshitter opposite.

Ian shook his head as he gently rotated the glass counter clockwise. "Look, I do know the name Terry Walton."

"But you're not his son?"

"No," he chuckled, almost breaking into a laugh.

"Sorry, Ian, I fail to see what's so damn funny. Have I missed the joke?" I raised my open palms and shrugged at him.

"No, nothing. I take it you believe Terry to be your father. Is that correct?"

I leaned back in my chair and folded my arms, choosing not to answer. As far as I was aware, only my mother and I knew Terry was my father. So, I had to be careful about what I divulged. Despite my concern that he may be an unstable lunatic, it's fair to say he'd more than piqued my interest.

Ian raised a palm and leaned forward. "I take it you do, based on the fact you haven't denied it. But that aside, can I ask how on earth you would know a certain Deana Beacham?"

I shifted forward again. "Are you Deana's son? Is that it? You knew my mother's utter disdain for the woman and thought you'd hunt me down to put her side of the story, perhaps?"

"Ginny, no, it's not like that. Anyway, for the record, Deana is dead."

"Dead?"

He nodded. "Yes, she's dead ... sort of."

With knitted brows, I peered at him. "Err ... how can someone be sort of dead? You're either dead, or you're not." I wondered what game of vagaries we were playing. For sure, Ian seemed to perform some mental acrobatics as he spun out his bizarre comments.

"That's what I thought," he chuckled. "Anyway, why did your mother hate Deana? I'm not aware they ever met."

"Oh, that's a long story for another day. Now, come on, what's this all about? If you're not related to Terry or Deana, who are you and what d'you want?"

Terry pursed his lips and glanced away, appearing distracted as he aimlessly gazed through the window at the street busker who strummed their guitar and belted out their rendition of *Yesterday*. Apt, really, considering my predicament and how I longed to return to better times. That said, I was coming to realise that my past wasn't as rosy as I thought. I sipped my wine, musing that the busker was a step up from anyone I'd seen on *Britain's Got Talent*, whilst also contemplating whether it was time to leave. Slugging back glasses of wine at lunchtime with an overly loath man who resembled my biological father probably wasn't a good idea.

After an elongated pause, he returned his attention to me. "Look, Ginny, you said you were having a difficult time of it. So, as an old friend of the family, so to speak, I wondered if I could help in any way ..." his voice trailed off, I guess due to realising the ridiculousness of the offer.

"Ian, we've never met before. Well, I recognise you from a couple of days ago in the coffee shop but, other than that, we don't know each other, correct?"

"Correct," he winced.

"So, as we've established that we don't know one another, tell me how you thought you would pop into my old office and offer to help me resolve a situation that you are blissfully unaware of?" I raised my eyebrows whilst plucking up my wine, ready to slug back a mouthful before making a swift exit. With the glass hovering at my lips, I assessed the feasibility of my ability to shimmy out of my seat and make a run for it before this nutter could make a grab for me. That said, if he harboured ideas of kidnap or violence, there would be a fair-few witnesses based on the fact the pub had now started to swell with lunchtime drinkers.

Ian nodded. "Ginny, I'm aware there's a problem between you and your husband—"

"No shit! Well, what you just witnessed back in that office might suggest Alistair and I aren't getting on too well. Bloody hell, not exactly rocket science to work that one out, is it?"

"No, I mean, I knew before going there today."

"How? How would you know that?" I blurted, slamming my glass down. "Christ, man, if you're not my half-brother, who the hell are you?"

Ian leaned forward, folding his arms to rest them on the table. "Judging by what I witnessed in your office this morning, I take it you're getting divorced. I also presume—"

"No," I interrupted, "You tell me how you're related to Terry or Deana and how the hell you know he is my father before you conduct any more presuming."

"Terry told me he's your father," he winced, I guess, in that instant, calculating the impossibility of that statement. Ian presumably wasn't born when Terry died. Also, I very much doubted Terry penned a letter to his unborn son whilst copping off with Deana Beacham, just on the off chance a steamy session with a colleague turned out to be too much for his weak heart.

I snorted a laugh. "Christ, you've boxed yourself in there, haven't you?"

Ian nodded, then slowly shook his head before sinking his forehead onto his folded arms.

Of course, I should leave this peculiar man to his musings regarding his cock up and lies, which had effectively tied himself up in knots. However, I needed some answers. Sensible answers to how he knew Terry, and specifically that the dead man who he resembled was my biological father.

"So, you say you want to help me? Now, is that to skewer my despicable husband on a spike, persuade him to do the decent thing and pony up half the business that we built together, or save me from getting murdered in my bed now that I've made the ill-thought-through, moronic decision to rent a flat on the hellish Broxworth Estate?"

Ian slowly raised his forehead, peering up at me. "You're living on the Broxworth Estate?"

"Uh-huh," I nodded. "I made a bit of a blunder and rented some hellhole up there. Of course, I've always known it was a bit of a dump, but I never realised how awful it is." Now a little concerned I'd divulged far too much information to a stranger, I thought it was high time I left. Notwithstanding my dire predicament, blurting out my life story to this bloke could be a seriously stupid mistake.

"Ginny, I take it from what you said earlier, you don't believe your mother-in-law was murdered? Unlike your sister-in-law, who's claiming the police are failing in their duty."

Half out of my seat, I turned and narrowed my eyes at him. However, before I could interrogate him further, the chair between us appeared to slide backwards of its own volition. I glanced down, noting Ian's feet were a million miles from the legs of that chair. When the chair shifted forward a couple of inches, I assessed my wine glass, noting I'd only swallowed a mouthful. So, based on the fact I'd only consumed less than one unit of alcohol, I could safely assume I wasn't pissed but must be hallucinating. A frightening thought entered my head that this man had slipped one of those date-rape pills into my wine and, now a few minutes on, my mind was playing tricks.

Ian, who maintained his slumped position, glanced sideways, addressing the empty chair. "Please don't shout at me, but I think I've ballsed it up," he mumbled.

I shot him a look, then back at the empty chair, before focusing my attention on him again. "Who are you talking to?"

"Oh, terrific! I can't leave you alone for five minutes, can I?" Deana shifted forward in her seat, ignoring Virginia's quizzical expression as her head played tennis between her and Terry.

"You seem pretty pleased with yourself. What's happened?" he quizzed, keeping his head resting on his arms.

"Oh, darling, you won't believe what I've just discovered!"

Part 2

18

1987

The Fall and Rise of Reginald Perrin

With only an hour before midnight and the dawn of a new year, the band elevated the party atmosphere by bashing out a sequence of up-tempo rock and roll numbers. As a result, the dance floor swelled with a plethora of half-cut revellers who lacked the grace and poise of those who preferred to perform the more dignified ballroom dancing. No one paid any attention to the back table where Lizzy and Paul Goode continued their heated discussion with Mel Strachan regarding his less-than-favourable job offer and the impending failure of their business.

Seething with frustration about their dire situation, Lizzy glared at Mel. "What d'you mean there's another way? What are you suggesting?"

"I suggest we all take our seats and calm down," Mel nodded at them both, indicating they needed to sit before he enlightened them any further.

Notwithstanding her desire to slap him, Lizzy waited whilst he seductively grinned at her. Despite her husband's foolish acts, leaving them on the brink of financial ruin, Lizzy knew Mel was probably their only salvation. Paul had rebuffed the offer of allowing his business to fold and work for Mel, and she understood why. Although, as Mel now appeared to be suggesting there may be another option, she held back from whacking her hand across that smug face of his.

Mel winked at her before shooting a look at Paul. "As I said, there is another way to solve this conundrum. I have another proposal for you." Mel sipped his whisky, taking his time to leave the Goodes sweating. Whilst the pathetic Paul bug-eyed him, Mel took a moment to savour Lizzy's slender thigh, which lay exposed by his side. He ran his index finger along her pale skin before making eye contact with her.

"This second proposal will require a certain input from you, my dear." He raised his eyebrow expectantly.

"Mel, what's going on? What proposal?" Paul chimed in, oblivious to Mel's wandering hands. "What's Lizzy got to do with this?"

Lizzy closed her eyes and looked away. Unless she'd read this wrong, she feared Mel was about to suggest something she couldn't go through with – not at any price.

Keeping his hand on her thigh, Mel glanced up at Paul. "This is non-negotiable. I'll make that investment we discussed last week, but I want fifty-one per cent of the business."

"You're fucking joking," Paul hissed. "We agreed thirty per cent."

"We didn't agree anything. You suggested thirty per cent, and I said give me a few days to think about it."

"Jesus, Mel. You're taking the piss. How can that be fair?"

"So?" Mel shrugged. "I'm giving you another option. I could walk away and leave you in the shit." Whilst keeping his hand on Lizzy's warm, soft skin, Mel leaned across the table to force home his point. "You're forgetting that I'm doing you a favour. You've lost your business through your obsession with gambling, and now your gorgeous wife can only look at you with disdain. You're a pathetic excuse of a man."

Unable to argue with Mel's accurate assessment of his situation, Paul huffed and laid his palms out whilst glancing at Lizzy. Although his demands would provide Mel with a controlling stake in their business, this offer was significantly better than allowing his business to fail, thus succumbing to accepting the nine-to-five job offer.

"We don't have any choice, do we?" Lizzy shrugged. Despite Mel's wandering hands, she felt a relief he hadn't suggested what she'd feared. However, despite Mel's suggestion to take a controlling stake in their failing business, that didn't explain what he mentioned regarding an input from her.

"Before you accept my terms, I'm afraid that's not all I want."

Lizzy glared at him as he offered a concupiscent smirk at her.

"Christ Mel, what else, apart from a controlling stake?"

Mel turned to Lizzy. "I have a suite booked for tonight. Last thing Jean wants is me rolling in three sheets to the wind in the early hours," he chuckled, allowing his hand to drift up her leg.

Lizzy squirmed in her seat, desperately trying to arrest the git's hand from advancing any further towards her knickers while also attempting to appear calm and thus avoid alerting her husband to Mel's groping. Although repulsed by his touch, she could ill afford to make a scene which might result in Paul resorting to using his fists. When Lizzy discreetly tried to force the lecherous bastard's hand from her thigh, Mel tightened his grip, almost pinching her skin.

While maintaining his grip on her upper thigh and holding that lascivious smirk, Mel ran his tongue across his top lip before addressing Paul. "So, my old mucker, to add to the fifty-one per cent stake in your business, I want your wife in my bed tonight. Call it a deal sweetener if you like."

"Piss off!" Lizzy exclaimed, slapping his hand away. Whatever the consequences, she wasn't going to sell her body to fix the issues her husband had caused.

"You're fucking joking!" blurted Paul.

"No ... I'm not fucking joking." Mel turned and replaced his hand on her thigh. The force of his grip effectively preventing Lizzy from moving. "Lizzy, don't look so shocked. One night in my bed, and you'll save your husband's business."

Paul lashed out his hand, grabbing the lapel of Mel's dinner jacket. "Who the fuck d'you think you are?" he hissed. "You utter bastard, suggesting my wife would sleep with you."

Mel swivelled his eyes from the crumpled cloth in Paul's hand to glare at the pathetic man. "Goode, I suggest you let go. You're causing a scene."

Paul shoved Mel away as he retook his seat. "You've got a nerve, Strachan."

"Twenty grand to have sex with your wife … that's a great offer."

Lizzy squirmed sideways before grabbing her glass and shooting the content at Mel's smug face. Despite scoring a direct hit, his glasses formed a barrier, thus preventing the liquid from stinging his eyes. "How dare you!" she hissed.

Seemingly unperturbed, Mel plucked up a napkin and dried his face and spectacles before smirking at the two of them. "I don't see the problem. I'm offering a more than fair deal to solve your little issue," he chuckled.

"Fuck you, Strachan," spat Paul, jumping to his feet before grappling with the table's edge in order to regain his balance. The mixture of the grape and the grain now causing his head to spin.

"What about Jean?" hissed Lizzy, as she attempted to extract herself from the tight space Mel had purposefully corralled her into.

"What about her? I'm not going to tell tales. Our little arrangement can be kept purely between us. I have no intention of announcing one night of sex with you from the rooftops."

Lizzy leaned towards him as he popped his glasses back in place, forcing them over the bridge of his nose with the tip of his index finger. "I'll tell her! She needs to know what you've suggested, you pig!"

"Be my guest. She isn't going to believe you. Also, go down that path, and you can forget any investment and that job offer."

"You bastard," mumbled Paul, holding on to the back of the chair for support.

"Oh, without a doubt, and I've been called a lot worse. Look, Goode, I didn't get where I am today through being nice, to quote CJ," he chuckled. "That's where you've gone wrong. You're a weak man, and you know it."

"Who's CJ?" stammered Paul, as he white-knuckle gripped the back of his chair for fear of collapsing.

"The Fall and Rise of Reginald Perrin, dear boy … CJ is his boss. Now, you can come and work for me, or Lizzy succumbs to my offer." Mel raised an eyebrow at Lizzy before returning his attention to Paul. "Of course, you could actually do a Reginald Perrin or a Stonehouse. Fake your own death and claim the life insurance. However, I wouldn't recommend it."

Paul slithered down onto the chair to retake his seat. Although not for the purpose of continuing the conversation, but more as in a need to due to feeling the effects of a few hours of solid drinking.

Lizzy leaned towards Mel. "Get your bloody hand off my leg, you disgusting pervert," she hissed.

Mel slid his hand away as instructed.

"I'm going through to reception, where I fully intend to call Jean and tell her exactly what you've just suggested."

"Oh, Lizzy, I don't think you're going to do that."

"Don't you, now?" she raised her eyebrows, calling his bluff.

"No ... you want to blow my marriage apart? What about my two children, Alistair and Helen? You want to be responsible for them growing up with divorced parents?"

"Me! It's you who made that suggestion."

"And you're intending to tell Jean, are you?"

"Yes!" she spat through gritted teeth.

"And even if Jean believed you ... you think you'll still be friends after you've told her, do you?"

"I'll risk it just to destroy you."

Mel nodded and smirked. "Be my guest. Go and ring my wife if you must."

"Paul, come on." Lizzy shimmied sideways, preparing to drag her husband away and make that call.

"Just one thing to consider before you trot off."

Lizzy grabbed her husband's arm, who appeared to have fallen into a catatonic state, before glaring back at Mel. "What?" she spat.

"You're forgetting one minor point."

Lizzy glared at him, concerned that he held another ace up his sleeve.

"Tell Jean, and the job offer for Paul comes off the table. Also, as chair of the Guild, I can ensure no one else employs him."

Lizzy, who, after a couple of tugs on Paul's arm, hadn't managed to encourage her pissed husband to stand, continued to glower at the smug bastard. As feared, Mel had that ace up his sleeve, and he'd just played it.

"Tell Jean, and you're doomed. You'll lose your home, and that pretty little daughter of yours will probably have to grow up in some squalid shithole of a flat on the Broxworth Estate." Mel leant forward, dropping the smirk and wagging a finger at her. "With my connections on the Council, I can engineer it that the only place they offer you is one of those flats on that hellhole of an estate. Your pretty little daughter will grow up with no prospects and probably end up as a prostitute because no good comes to any kid from that bloody place. So, if you want that for little Virginia, go ahead and make that call."

Still with her hand hooked around her husband's arm, Lizzy took a deep, shaky breath. Paul glanced up at her, his eyes glassy with tears.

"Well?" questioned Mel, as he dropped his pointing finger and leaned back before grabbing his cigarettes.

"Paul will take the job," she whispered.

"And I take it you'll reconsider your suggestion about ruining Jean's evening in front of the telly whilst enjoying Des O'Connor singing in the New Year."

Lizzy nodded.

"Good. Jean's always had a thing about Des O'Connor. It would be a shame to ruin her evening," he chuckled. "Now, let go of your pathetic husband's arm and take a seat." He patted the chair seat where Lizzy had just alighted. "Come on, it's still warm," he smirked.

Lizzy slid back onto her chair whilst holding her husband's stare. She knew they were beaten. Also, the doleful expression on her husband's face suggested Mel's description held a certain accuracy to it. Paul was pathetic – a sad, pathetic fool who, since those test results landed two years ago, had become a shadow of the man she once loved. Although Lizzy had always lusted after another, namely Virginia's biological father, there was a time when she'd loved Paul. However, the cause of his low self-esteem and the spiralling fall into self-pity directly resulted from her actions ten years ago when in the embrace of Terry Walton – Virginia's biological father.

Because of that night in Hunstanton when Virginia was conceived, she had as good as condemned Paul. Now, ten years later, she faced the consequences of allowing Terry to woo her on that sofa while her husband slept in the next room. There was a heavy price to pay for a stolen moment of illicit passion.

Mel lit his cigarette before lobbing the box of matches onto the table. "So, that's your decision, is it? The business folds, I take your clients, and Goode here comes and works for me."

Lizzy shot Paul a disparaging look. Paul dropped his eyes to focus on the tablecloth.

"Well?"

"Yes," whispered Lizzy.

Mel frowned before taking a long, satisfying drag on his cigarette. "So, Goode, you agree with your wife, then?"

Still focusing on the tablecloth, Paul fiddled with the red plastic 'Happy New Year' table confetti and nodded. "Yeah ... I'll take the job."

"Pity."

Paul peered up at Mel, questioning that statement with narrowed eyes.

"It's a pity because, with the salary on offer, you'll have to sell up and buy a semi ... fifteen grand a year isn't going to cover your mortgage."

Paul threw his hand in the air and flung himself back in his seat. "Well, I don't have any choice, do I?"

"There's always a choice, Goode. Now, I'm off to the bar. I'll let you two discuss your options. All I'm asking is for your lovely wife to join me in my bed, and your business will be saved. A small price to pay, I might suggest."

19

2016

The Count of Monte Cristo

After Terry and Virginia vacated the office, heading for the Murderers Pub, Deana rummaged around the reception, searching for useful information. Pointy-Nail, seemingly satisfied with her manicure, now slouched in her chair scrolling through Instagram, her long nail rhythmically tapping the screen as she glided her finger up and down.

Just at the point when Deana sidled up to her and tentatively peered at the heap of post lobbed on the desk, Alistair ripped open his office door.

"Coffee!" he boomed.

Pointy-Nail tutted before apathetically glancing at him. "How about, please?"

"How about now?" he threw back before flinging the door shut.

"Tosser," she muttered, before lobbing her phone down, groaning, and hauling herself from her chair.

Deana grabbed the opportunity to rifle through the heap of unopened mail, spotting one from a firm of solicitors. Whilst Pointy-Nail rhythmically drummed her nails on the top of the coffee machine, waiting for the coffee to pour, Deana carefully teased open the envelope and extracted the letter.

"You despicable git," she muttered, when scouring the text, which stated that Alistair's solicitor confirmed his belief that his wife, Virginia, couldn't claim any entitlement to any proceeds from the business. Also, because Mrs Strachan had chosen to no longer be employed by her husband, that negated her claim for a financial settlement regarding lost earnings. As for the marital home, Mrs Strachan could not seek legal compensation due to the property being owned by Strachan Accountants and, therefore, a business asset. The letter concluded they had advised the petitioner's legal representative of this fact. "So, my darling, it appears your girl is jobless and homeless," she muttered, when noticing Pointy-Nail entering Alistair's office.

Deana rammed the letter into her handbag and nipped across the outer office to follow the receptionist into Alistair's lair. Pleased to be afforded easy access, Deana stealthily squeezed around the girl and hovered by Alistair's side as he hunched over his desk, poring over some documents.

Serena unceremoniously thumped his mug on top of his desk, causing almost half of the hot, black liquid to slop over the side onto his splayed-out paperwork.

"Oh, Jesus, this is an important contract, you stupid girl." Alistair, still sporting a ruddy face caused by his bluster when in the throes of the slanging match with Virginia, flung his arms in the air whilst shunting his swivel chair backwards to avoid the running liquid, which speedily headed to the edge of his desk, directly aiming at his lap.

Serena shrugged. "Well, next week, you'll have to get your own sodding coffee. I expect that enema, yoga-loving cow will have you drinking green tea or some vegetable smoothie, so I suggest you enjoy your coffee while you can."

Alistair shot her a contemptuous glare. "After your little escapade this morning, when informing my wife about our little arrangement, I suggest you get your coat and piss off."

"Whatever," she nonchalantly replied, swivelling around and stomping towards the door before turning to face Alistair, who now stood, mug in hand, preparing to take a sip. "Oh, just so you know …" Alistair peered at her, mug poised at his lips. "Ginny smashed one of your poncy certificate frames. There's glass all over the floor." Alistair gave a slightly dismissive shake of his head. "Also, unless you fancy spending the afternoon in the accident and emergency department at Fairfield General, I wouldn't drink that coffee if I were you."

Alistair moved the mug away from his lips and peered at the liquid before glancing back at Serena as she held the door frame and handle.

"I laced it with slivers of glass." With that, she slammed the door and then, by the sounds of the ensuing commotion, performed a similar frame-smashing routine that Virginia had started earlier.

Alistair dipped his finger in the coffee, swishing it around, seemingly trying to assess if she told the truth. Then, after a couple of finger swishes, he offered a resigned huff and placed the mug on the desk before slumping onto his chair, allowing his arms to sag limply over the sides.

"Christ, what a mess," he muttered.

"Your desk, the paperwork, or your life?" Deana chortled, as she folded her arms and leaned against the stack of filing cabinets. *"I know you can't hear or see me. However, I thought I'd let you know Terry and I are going to make your life a living hell. Now, there is nothing wrong with multiple sexual partners, as long as that's in full agreement with your wife. Of course, my darling Dickie and I had such an arrangement, but I understand it's not for everyone, including your soon-to-be ex-wife, Virginia. You've been thoroughly rotten to her, you know."*

Alistair shook his head and huffed again before he set about mopping up the carnage on his desk, only to glance up at the door when hearing Serena thrashing about in the reception area.

"Also, be warned, I'm aware of your plans to make the poor girl destitute, so Terry and I will be interfering in your little game. When we've finished with you, you'll wish you were dead. Like me!" she guffawed. *"You know, I'm not only gorgeous, but I'm also full of wit."*

After rummaging around in the wastepaper bin, Alistair attempted to mop up the spilt coffee with a used tissue. Before lobbing the soggy item into the bin, he teased it apart to scrutinise it. "Little bitch," he muttered, as he extracted and laid in the palm of his hand a vicious-looking sliver of glass.

"Oh, don't even think about confronting the girl. From what I've assessed of the little tart so far, she's liable to gouge your eyes out. Idiots like you never learn, do you? Hell hath no fury like a woman scorned, eh? What was it ... oh, don't tell me, you promised to leave Virginia for her? I expect she thought you were her meal ticket to riches. Right, well, of course, you're not going to answer, so whilst you busy yourself with a spot of spring cleaning, I'm going to have a rummage around."

Alistair dropped the sodden tissue and sliver of glass into the bin, placed his undrunk coffee mug on the windowsill, and shuffled the damp pages together before lobbing the heap onto the floor. Then, with a previously discarded envelope plucked from the wastepaper basket, he attempted to mop up the remaining streaks of spilt liquid, only managing to swish it about and thus smother the desk in coffee. "Sake," he hissed, leaning forward, nudging his mouse to awaken his PC before performing a few clicks.

Deana hopped forward and stealthily reached under his torso to tease free his pale-pink tie from inside his buttoned suit jacket. Then, while holding her breath and gritting her teeth, she allowed the tie to flop onto the coffee-smothered surface of his desk before dabbing it to ensure decent contact was achieved.

The printer, positioned near the door that Serena had moments ago slammed, sprung into life, performing its warm-up routine. When Alistair leaned back, he noticed his stained tie. "Oh, bollocks!"

"Oh, that's a shame. By the feel of it, I assume it's pure silk. Never mind, eh." she smirked.

After a couple of attempts to remove the stain by way of vigorously rubbing it with his fingers, he ripped it off and slung it across the room before tearing open the top button of his shirt.

"Temper, temper, dear boy."

Whilst balling his fists on the desk and holding a position akin to the stance preferred by an aggressive Silverback gorilla, he snorted air back and forth through his nose.

"Oh, come on, it was only a tie. Silk one, I attest, but really, you need to calm down." Deana spouted as she scanned the desk, searching for anything remotely interesting. "I don't suppose you could shimmy out of the way, could you?"

"Bloody woman," he muttered before stepping away from his desk and over to the printer, now holding his hand out as he waited for the machine to spit out the pages.

"Ah, good." Deana took up position at his desk, minimising the document and proceeding to scour the inbox of his email account. "I hope it's a long document and a slow printer," she muttered, whilst scrolling through his inbox.

Although she didn't know what she was searching for, any information gleaned could give her and Terry the upper hand. Due to the Powers-That-Be's displeasure regarding their rather lacklustre performance thus far, they'd been somewhat tight-lipped on relevant information for this mission. However, Deana's somewhat aphoristic conversation with them suggested they fully expected a significant uptick in performance, thus being able to discover the required information without the need to be spoon-fed and, in turn, lead to a satisfactory outcome.

Although it appeared Virginia was facing divorce proceedings, a broken relationship wasn't something Terry and she could fix. So, Deana presumed their mission comprised securing a more favourable settlement than the few paragraphs in that letter had suggested. However, not benefiting from legal training meant they'd have to find an angle to blackmail Alistair.

"Where are you, Odette, when I need you," she announced to herself, realising that her old dead friend would come in handy for this mission, just as she had when they were saving little Kimmy.

Alistair's mobile, which lay abandoned on the far side of the desk, started to vibrate. With a wedge of paperwork in his fist, Alistair nipped across the office, leaving the printer to continue regurgitating the remainder of the printing.

Deana glanced at the phone, which flashed up 'Dad' as the caller ID. "This should be interesting. I see it's your perverted father on the phone."

Alistair stabbed the green and speaker buttons whilst standing opposite Deana, glancing at the first printed page in his hand. "Hi, Dad."

Whilst listening in, Deana continued to scroll, hoping he wouldn't notice the mouse wheel slowly rotating as she scrolled through his inbox and a rather interesting file called 'Divorce'.

"Hi, there, Ali. Look, I'm in town. I've got a couple of things to do, bank and building society stuff, but d'you fancy a quick pint up at the Murderers at lunchtime?"

Alistair glanced away from his reading material, peering down at his phone. "Yeah, why not? I'm not having the greatest of days, so a pint sounds good."

"Oh?"

Alistair refocused on his paperwork. "I'll tell you about it over a pint. I've only one appointment this afternoon, which I can move. So, I think I'll call it a day."

"Okay …"

When sensing his father's hesitation, Alistair glanced back at his phone. "Dad?"

"Look, son, I'll fill you in on the details later, but are you sitting down?"

Alistair lobbed the paperwork onto his desk before leaning over his phone whilst resting his palms on the edge of the desk. "No, should I be?"

"Don't you dare … I'm busy reading your correspondence from your solicitor. I have no desire to have your boney backside perched on my lap. Like that letter, I see from these emails that you've royally stiffed poor Terry's girl."

"I didn't tell you because I didn't want to worry you. However, your sister and I met with Kevin this morning."

"Kevin?"

"DCI Reeves. You remember, Kevin is a member at my club?"

Alistair's eyes widened. "Oh … what about?"

"Look, Kevin wanted a word about Helen's campaign. You know, her posting on social media about the police letting us down—"

"Bloody right! They weren't putting the squeeze on her, were they?"

"Oh, no, no. But basically, Kevin's asked her to put a halt to it."

"Bloody cheek—"

"Son, Kevin has divulged some information to help us understand why they need her to halt her campaign. Now listen, son. Kevin shouldn't have but, as we're mates, he's trusted us with some confidential information."

Alistair narrowed his eyes whilst he continued to glare at the phone.

"Ali?"

"I'm here, Dad."

"Look, I'll tell you all about it at lunch."

"Dad!"

Mel sighed. "Alright. Listen, you remember that doctor who used to work for your mother?"

"The bloke who died just after Christmas? Fell down the stairs, or something or other, and broke his neck. I remember Mum went to his funeral."

"That's the one. So, here's the thing. Apparently, his death is suspicious and under investigation."

"Oh, I thought he just had an accident. Mum said he was a drinker. She assumed he was drunk, tripped and fell."

"Apparently not."

"What's his death got to do with Mum?"

"Son … when the police discovered his body, he was clutching hold of a note."

"Oh, no … no way."

"Yes, son. The note in that doctor's hand had precisely the same quote as the one in your mother's—"

"You're joking?"

"No, I'm afraid not. It was word for word."

"How did I escape? With difficulty. How did I plan this moment? With pleasure," Alistair muttered.

Deana glanced away from the screen to peer up at Alistair, who now appeared to have fallen into some sort of trance. "Ah, Dumas, if I'm not mistaken. So, it appears someone is running around murdering doctors on a campaign of retribution. Now, this is interesting."

"Yes, son. That's it. Not something we're ever going to forget, is it?"

"No … we're not. But … shit, this is nuts."

"I know." Mel sighed again. "Son, I think it's safe to say your mother was murdered."

"And it suggests that the police know that because her colleague was presumably murdered earlier in the year."

"I would assume so. Your sister was right all along. As I said, I think that confirms your mother didn't commit suicide. I know we had our problems over the last few years, but I knew Jean would never take her own life."

"But … Dad, why would anyone want to kill Mum and that surgeon who worked for her?"

"That's the question. The police said they have ongoing enquiries and would keep us in the loop. However, DCI Reeves asked Helen to stop her social media posts because she might compromise their investigation."

"How?"

"Well, I don't know. I presume they don't want the killer alerted to any information, I suppose."

"What the hell does that mean?"

"To be honest with you, son, I got the distinct impression that they aren't making much progress with it. What is clear, someone murdered your mother and that David bloke. By all accounts, both murders were revenge motivated."

"Jesus," Alistair muttered.

"I know."

"Well, it's damn bleeding obvious that the murderer must be someone connected to the hospital. Someone, Mum, and this David bloke must have pissed off. That quote pretty much states it's a revenge killing. What have they said about that quote or the writing on the back? What was it on the back again? I can't remember."

"Tetralogy, not trilogy … or something like that."

"And have they commented on that?"

"No. They just said they need us to keep this information to ourselves and trust them to do their job."

Alistair tutted. "We knew this all along. How could Mum have drowned herself whilst holding that note? It's ruddy obvious that someone placed it in her hand after they murdered her. Christ, Dad, I can't believe they haven't caught the culprit. What the hell are they doing?"

"Ali, I don't know. Look, your sister is in a bit of a sorry state. I told her to take the day off … just throw a sickie. I think it would be good if you popped around and caught up with her later. I know she'd appreciate it."

"Yeah, alright." Alistair glanced up. "What the ..." he exclaimed.

"Son?"

"Oh, nothing. I'd better get on, I'll see you up at the Murderers at, say, one-ish." Alistair killed the call. Before straightening up and with furrowed brows sported a quizzical expression as he gawped at his swivel chair.

"Oh, dear. This is tricky," Deana chuckled, before realising she needed to remain perfectly still. Unfortunately, whilst listening in to the conversation, she'd forgot herself and started swishing back and forth on the chair. Alistair's expression confirmed he'd spotted the odd phenomenon of his self-swivelling chair.

The printer, although completed its task, started up again, presumably running through a cleaning sequence. Fortunately, the noise created a distraction and presumably reminded Alistair about the remainder of the document he'd earlier printed.

"It's the stress," he muttered, glancing away from the now still chair. "I'm seeing things because of the stress," he mumbled, whilst padding towards the printer.

"Phew!" Covered by the noise of the printer, Deana opened up a blank Word document and, whilst grimacing at the noise of the depressed keys, carefully typed a sentence in large font—

Lust and Greed – two of the seven deadly sins you have committed. Alistair Strachan, be warned – you, and your pervert father, are going to hell. I will make damn sure of that! Beware the wicked diva of the dead.

XXXXXXX

After affording herself a little snigger, Deana clicked print, leaving the document on the screen before hopping out of the chair and plucking Alistair's coffee mug from the windowsill. Then, keeping half an eye on Alistair, ensuring he continued to focus on the printer, she gently poured the glass-sliver-infused liquid across the keyboard before placing the mug back in position. "There, sort that out, you git," she chortled.

After plucking up her Chanel bag, Deana skipped across the office heading for the door. Fortunately, with his position at the printer, Alistair wouldn't notice the door open. If she maintained her stealth-like flit, Deana thought she could escape without further incident – presuming the hinges were well-oiled.

The printer whirred and spat out the single sheet of paper displaying Deana's message. Alistair read the note, then spun around before barrelling over to his desk, only stopping short when his mobile vibrated. Tutting at the display, Alistair snatched up his phone.

"What? I'm not in the mood, Jules."

Deana hovered, although unable to hear the other end of the conversation, she thought it prudent to hang on a moment longer before nipping to the pub, whilst in the back of her mind praying Terry hadn't already ballsed it up with Virginia by blurting out something stupid like he was her long-lost dead father.

"No. You listen to me, you little shit. Your game of blackmail is over. You can't threaten me because if you squeal, I'll engineer the evidence to ensure Ginny takes the fall. So, Jules, I suggest you back off unless you want to put your sister in a difficult position. You ain't getting a penny out of me. Now, piss off!"

Alistair killed the call and lobbed his phone on the desk, aggressively scrunching Deana's note in his balled fist before thumping both palms on the desk. Whilst holding his gorilla pose, he snorted through his nose before expelling a guttural growl.

"Oh, dear, a bad day, I suggest. Also, that animal grunting routine leads me to assume you have anger management issues. Perhaps if your crummy little accountancy outfit benefited from an HR department, they could advise you on some courses or management training skills workshops that could improve your behaviour. Pity you can't hear me, really. That said, even if you could, I imagine they would be wasted words. I've unfortunately met many of your sort throughout my working career, and experience tells me no amount of behavioural training can help idiots like you."

Alistair pawed at his screen, yanking it around. Then, as he spotted the text of the Word document, he straightened up before chaotically spinning around on his heels, scouring his office. "What the ... who ... who's there," he stammered, before glancing back at Deana's typed words.

Deana turned the door handle, allowing the door to glide open, the very act distracting Alistair from the screen displaying her typed note.

"Toodle-pip, dear boy. Terry and I will be in touch. I'm sorry you've lost your mother, but I'm afraid there will be a heavy price to pay for your philandering and your rather shoddy treatment of your wife."

Deana paused for a moment before pointing at Alistair. "Revenge is sweet but not flattering, to quote a certain Mr Hitchcock, I believe. Well, Virginia really doesn't need to worry about that, because Terry and I will do the dirty work for her."

20

Deliverance

Deana shifted forward in her seat, ignoring Virginia's quizzical expression as her head continued to play tennis between her and Terry. "Darling, did you hear me? I said I've discovered some rather interesting facts when rummaging around in Alistair's office." Deana nudged Terry's arm, a little bemused by his sullen demeanour.

"Ian, who are you talking to?" I quizzed, sliding my bum sideways preparing to hop off my seat whilst nervously glancing at the empty chair, which now appeared to have halted its poltergeist activities.

"Oh, bugger ... I keep forgetting I'm invisible. No wonder that woman looked a little shocked in the ladies when I came out of the toilet cubical. When I flipped on the tap to wash my hands, I asked the poor woman if she was alright because the distress slapped across her face suggested she'd spotted a ghost. No wonder she didn't reply and just gawped at the running water when stumbling back against the tiles." Deana chortled. "I must say, Virginia appears to be sporting a similar expression to that poor woman."

Whether Ian, as I had, also noticed the self-moving chair, I couldn't tell. However, his demeanour changed, now furtively glancing back and forth between the empty chair and me.

"Oh, darling, this is a little awkward. I don't think you can slot your earpiece back in and feign a call. We're just going to have to revert to our old ways of communicating."

Ian nodded at the chair before raising his palm at me. "Sorry, I was mumbling."

"Did you see that chair move?"

"Oh, I nudged it with my foot, I think," he grinned, that odd creepy, somewhat nefarious, serial-killer-styled facial expression he liked to pull.

"Darling, I'll try not to fidget and keep perfectly still. However, as I said, I've discovered some rather interesting revelations. Oh ... I've just thought, you know, the last time I was in here was when I murdered poor portly Peter before we set about helping your little Kimmy. That was fun," she chortled.

Although a blatant lie, which his nervous grin confirmed, I shrugged off the thought about poltergeist and self-moving chairs whilst considering that this conversation with Ian Beacham was still worth persisting with based on the fact he knew about Terry Walton and my mother.

Notwithstanding my concern about being drugged, but because nothing else concerning appeared to be happening to my brain or vision, I concluded perhaps Ian hadn't laced my wine with Rohypnol. I hadn't suddenly acquired a feeling of losing my inhibitions, I didn't feel partially

233

unconscious, and although that chair definitely moved of its own volition, I felt fully in control of my faculties.

So, with the only other prospect for the rest of my day involving unpacking my meagre possessions in that squalid flat whilst avoiding Yellow-Eye and Viv's sister, I decided to stay and push this odd man for some answers – preferably sensible ones. However, just to be on the safe side, I moved my half-drunk glass of wine to the windowsill.

"So, Ian, tell me, why were you asking me about Jean Strachan, specifically the circumstances around her death?"

"Darling, you need to listen. Now, I know men struggle to perform two tasks at once, but you're just going to have to try. So, without me distracting you, you need to hold a conversation with your daughter whilst listening to what I have to say."

Ian seemed to hesitate again, that odd act of thinking carefully about his answers. The man was definitely reticent about what he divulged, but what he'd said so far didn't add up. I noticed he nodded to the empty chair.

"Terence! Stop nodding. You're like a nodding dog or giving the appearance that you're suffering from Parkinson's disease."

"Look, when you were arguing with your husband earlier, you both touched on the subject of your mother-in-law's death. Alistair stated that he thought his mother didn't commit suicide, but you disagreed with him."

"Darling, she didn't. Jean Strachan was most definitely murdered."

Ian side-eyed the empty chair. Either that, or he was grabbing a sneaky glance at the woman wearing a pair of

234

skin-tight jeans who sashayed past, presumably heading for the ladies.

Choosing to assume the latter, I pushed on with my questions. "So, let me get this straight. You're an old friend of my parents, who reckons you've had a conversation with Terry Walton, although he just happened to die before you were born. You want to help me out with my situation," I performed the old bunny ears. "And you're now enquiring whether I agree with my husband and his family about how his mother died. Have I got that all correct?" I sarcastically quizzed before adding a couple of cynical 'Hmmms' to finish off.

Terry grimaced, offering me a slight nod.

"Oh, and, of course, how could I forget? You also happen to know Deana Beacham, who my mother, God rest her soul, would like to tear limb from limb."

"Oh, bloody charming! What the hell have I ever done to this woman's mother? Christ, you're the one who bunked up with her on that settee all those years ago. I've never met the damn woman."

Terry glanced left again, just at the point the tight-jeans girl whizzed past. For most of my married life, I'd endured and become immune to Alistair constantly checking out the opposite sex. Although a repugnant sexist act, I guess he openly gawped rather than pretending not to ogle. To be honest, I didn't know which was worse; my ex-husband's salivating stares or Ian's furtive glances. I wondered if all men were like this, or had I just unwittingly married one and now met another?

"She's a stroppy one, don't you think? Did she inherit that trait from you or this bloody Lizzy Goode woman who wishes to dismember me? Now, apart from discovering that Jean Strachan was murdered, it also appears that we have a serial killer on the loose who's specifically targeting the medical profession. Good job I plumped for a career in HR and not nursing, which is a career I thought about when leaving school."

"Ginny ..."

"Oh, it's Ginny, is it? Well, that didn't take you long to become friendly, did it? Remember, Terence, Blondie is your daughter, not some woman you can casually pick up and whisk back to your love nest."

"Yes?" I blurted. "Christ, conducting a conversation with you is like talking through a faulty satellite link. What's all the pregnant pauses for?"

Ian leaned forward again. "Okay, so here's the thing. I can't divulge how I know ... knew Terry or Deana Beacham. However, I do know Terry was your biological father. I made that bit up about Terry telling me because, unfortunately, Terry never knew. Your lovely mother ..."

"Lovely! Piffle! She wants to cause me harm. I'm not sure that constitutes lovely."

Ian momentarily hesitated, then carried on after performing his dodgy satellite connection impression. "Your lovely mother chose not to tell Terry, leaving your father, Paul, to assume you were his."

"My mother told *you* this. But why ... why tell you?" I yanked my phone from my pocket, tapped through to the 'Photos' app and scrolled through to the picture I'd taken of that grainy snap before spinning it around and ramming it in his face. "Also, Ian, tell me how you just happen to be the spitting image of the bloke with his arm around my dad's shoulder in 1977."

"Can I?" he asked, reaching to take my phone.

I placed my phone on the table in front of him. Although, thanks to Yellow-Eye, the screen now sported a spider-web of cracks, plus the definition of the photo wasn't that brilliant. However, there was no denying the likeness was still clear to see.

Deana carefully extracted herself from her chair and peered over Terry's shoulder. "Spread your fingers like you do on the iPad, darling."

Ian squinted at the screen before enlarging the image with his fingers.

"She has a point. That man in the photo is instantly recognisable as you. I take it that woman is Lizzy Goode. I must say, she looks the spit of Debbie Harry back in the day. OMG," she sniggered, pointing at the picture. "That moustache of yours, and those damn great flares you were wearing. Not very on-trend, were you, darling? Flares had all but faded out by then. And that awful tan leather jacket," she chortled. "Though, I can't deny you were very handsome. A Burt Reynolds look about you, you could say."

Ian nodded and smirked. "Your mother was stunning."

"Alright, don't overdo it. The woman couldn't lay a glove on me, despite looking like she could give Ms Harry a run for her money."

Whilst plucking up my phone, my mind drifted. "She was … she really was," I muttered as I gently stroked my finger over her image whilst wishing she could be here for me now. It didn't matter how old you were; everyone needed their mother. However, that hideous disease had cruelly taken mine away from me. Shaking away thoughts of my mum, I focused on the here and now. "So … you agree? The man in that picture, Terry Walton, and you look very similar."

"A certain likeness, I suppose," he shrugged.

"And you say you're not related to him … nephew, cousin, or something like that?"

"No, I'm not a relative."

"Oh …" Surprisingly, I felt somewhat disappointed he wasn't my half-brother. "So, I presume you must be a relative or connected in some way to Deana Beacham." I raised my eyebrows but bashed on whilst he appeared to be searching for answers. "You said she's dead. Was she your mother?"

"Christ, this is getting difficult. Just say nephew. At least that will stop her probing."

"Yes, you're right. I am related to Deana. She was my aunt."

"Oh … but," my mind whirred. "Hang on. Did Deana know Terry was my father?"

Ian side-eyed left again towards the empty chair just as a twenty-something builder-type man wearing a skin-tight t-shirt and hi-vis vest passed by. I momentarily considered the possibility that Ian swung both ways.

"Yes, Deana told me."

"Your aunt Deana."

Ian nodded.

"Is that how you met my parents? Although, I have to say, I had no idea that my mother was in contact with this Deana woman. Christ, when she told me about Terry being my real father, she had nothing but bad words to say about her."

"Oh, I know who she is. Christ, she was at your funeral. The bloody woman had a right old go at me. I remember now. She cornered me, and accused me of taking her precious Terry from her."

"Well, they must have been. I guess, Deana and your mother must have chatted. She told me all about her fling with Terry Walton, and I suppose both women had something in common ... both were besotted with Terry." He offered a mischievous grin, like a cat that had got the cream.

"Don't get above your station, darling. We both know my feelings for you back then. However, just because this Lizzy woman and I both had the hots for you, that doesn't mean every woman succumbs to your charms."

"Okay, although I must say that is a bit of a surprise. Anyway, why would you want to help me? And more to the point, what the hell has my situation got to do with you?"

"Because Deana was special to me."

"Ah, how sweet. I hope I still am, darling." She leaned forward and affectionately rubbed his thigh.

"She was special to me," he repeated. "And I'm aware that Terry was special to her. I know Deana wouldn't have wanted to hear that his daughter had landed in a spot of bother."

"Really?" I whined, struggling to believe his story. "This all sounds a touch flimsy, if you ask me," I huffed, leaning back in my chair. "You're a good Samaritan type, are you? You're at a loose end and thought, I know, I'll go and help some woman I've never met before," I scoffed.

"Okay, I see how you might think that. But it's complicated—"

"Complicated?" I sarcastically batted back at him.

"I knew you'd have to trot out that line sooner or later."

"Yeah ... as I say, complicated." Ian parted his hands and leaned back in his chair before making a grab for his pint.

I snorted a laugh and tipped my head back. "Oh, why does it always happen to me?" I chuckled, before glancing sideways at the wineglass on the windowsill. Although I seemed to be in the company of a man who afforded tenuous links with my parents, I figured he wasn't out to cause me any harm. So, I decided I'd risk the rest of my wine.

"Ginny, can I get you another?"

I checked my watch, not that I had anywhere to be, a train to catch, or a meeting to attend, but just that involuntary action of needing to know the time for some reason.

"Go on then, why not." I shrugged before slugging back the last mouthful and handing him the glass.

Terry extracted his earpiece from his pocket and exaggeratedly grimaced as he slotted it in his ear. "I'll grab the drinks and make a quick call."

"Okay, I'm just going to nip to the ladies. When I get back, I'm expecting some sensible answers," I threw at him as I slid out of my seat.

As I placed the palm of my hand on the table to haul myself out of my chair, I glanced out of the window, where I spotted Viv strolling down the hill, linking arms with a young woman. I leaned forward, narrowing my eyes. Either he was a fast worker and had secured a date with another woman in the sixteen hours or so since he took me out for dinner, or all that spiel about being single was a load of old tosh, meaning he was already attached. "Huh," I muttered as I padded towards the ladies.

So much for his mother being ill. By my reckoning, he should be at Heathrow, preparing to board a flight to Barbados, not swanning around Fairfield with some woman. "Men," I muttered as I thumped open the toilet door. I was right; Karen was wrong. Pretty much all the men in my life had let me down. Paul had frittered away my inheritance with his gambling; Alistair had binned me off for a newer model; his father, Mel, was a pervert, and now the first decent man I'd met since splitting with Alistair was a bare-faced liar.

I slammed the cubical door shut and leaned against it. "No … don't you dare, Ginny Strachan. I'm not crying today." Whilst willing myself to hold my shit together, I gulped in a few deep lungfuls of sweet-scented air emanating from the air freshener perched on top of the toilet cistern. Although we'd only enjoyed dinner together, the vision of Viv with that woman seemed to be whizzing me towards breaking point.

21

Thriller

As soon as Ginny disappeared from sight when heading for the ladies, Terry hopped back from the bar with the drinks in hand.

"You enjoy your drink, won't you? I'll just sit here and watch," Deana huffed.

"Deana, you can have a drink when we get home."

"Oh, well, thank you. So kind of you," she somewhat sarcastically batted back. "I told you the other day. It's not fair that I just have to sit here whilst you sup your pint and enjoy yourself."

"It's not my bloody fault you're invisible, is it? Now, come on, we've only got a few minutes, so you'd better quickly fill me in about what you discovered. And another thing, I'm hardly enjoying myself. All I've achieved so far is to successfully tie myself up in knots. Ginny's probably thinking I'm some crazed lunatic who's managed to shimmy out of their straitjacket."

Deana smirked. "Very perceptive of the girl."

"Hilarious. Now, come on, spit it out."

"Yes, okay. But first, whilst you stood at the bar, I spotted a woman in the corner gawping straight at me." Deana shot a furtive glance to her left and back again. "She's still doing it. The woman is staring at me."

Terry shifted in his seat, about to turn around.

"Don't look," she hissed.

"She can't be looking at you, can she?"

Deana side-eyed to her left again. "She is!"

Terry shook his head. "Well, she just can't be. Now, come on, before Ginny comes back, enlighten me regarding what you discovered and how the hell you know Jean Strachan was murdered." He bulged his eyes and pointed at her.

"Darling, please remember, I'm invisible. The couple at the next table are now frowning at you, probably a little concerned that you are some nut job."

Terry dropped his hand and huffed.

"Darling, please don't huff, and try to act natural. Now, tap your ear and say hello, as if you're accepting a call. There's a good boy."

"Hello," Terry petulantly announced, dramatically folding his arms and offering a gurned expression.

"Oh well, if that's your best natural pose, I suppose that will have to do." Deana poked a finger at him. "Don't blame me if you attract attention just because you want to be all childish about it."

"Come on, spit it out. What did you discover in that bloke's office? I take it you didn't witness him and that receptionist getting it on over his desk again."

"No ... I think the girl quite fancied murdering the git."

Terry raised an eyebrow.

"Right, so I had a rummage around and read some correspondence from Alistair's solicitor. It seems that Alistair has left the poor girl destitute, taking the business and their home. So, not only does the girl have a pervert for a father-in-law, but her damn husband has manipulated the situation to leave her with nothing. I have a letter here in my bag from his solicitor that attests to just that."

"Oh ... that explains why she's moved into a flat on the Broxworth Estate."

"Oh, dear. Not that damn place again."

"Quite."

"Now, whilst I was having a rummage, Alistair took a call from his father."

"Melvyn, the pervert?"

"The very same. It appears that Melvyn and his daughter—"

"Helen?"

"Yes. They attended a meeting with the police to discuss Jean's death—"

"Why wasn't Alistair at this meeting?"

"Terence ... for pity sake. If you keep insisting on interrupting me, we'll run out of time. Virginia will have performed her ablutions and return at any moment, thus leaving us with no option but to converse by way of sign language."

Terry shrugged. "Like you never interrupt me," he muttered.

Deana tutted. "You're very vexatious at times. You know that?"

"And you're persnickety, did you know that?"

"What is this, Terence? A competition about who can conjure up different words. If you're suggesting I'm formidable, then yes, I accept I am."

Terry raised an eyebrow.

"I'm a force of nature, darling, and don't you forget it. Now, shove a sock in it, and pin your ears back."

Terry offered a po-faced frown.

"So, it appears that Jean was discovered drowned in the bath. However, in her hand, she apparently was clasping a note that stated, and I quote, 'How did I escape? With difficulty. How did I plan this moment? With pleasure'."

"Dumas."

"Darling, I'm impressed." Deana pouted and rubbed his knee.

"English Literature classes."

"It's a French novel."

Terry shrugged. "Whatever. We read it at school, that much I can remember."

"Very good. Now, listen up. Apparently, one of the surgeons who worked for Jean Strachan was also discovered some months back clutching a note with the very same quotation."

"Dead?"

"As the proverbial doornail."

"Christ … you're right. We have a serial killer on the loose."

"Precisely. Either that or those two doctors upset a particular patient who decided to dabble in a spot of revenge."

"Do you think this is relevant to our mission? I mean, as you said, it could just be a pissed-off patient of theirs. I believe we are here to sort out Alistair, not get involved with what the police are investigating."

"Maybe … I don't know. The odd thing is, Alistair mentioned the note also had words written on the reverse … tetralogy, not trilogy."

Terry shrugged. "Never was that good at Scrabble. Enlighten me."

"Well, it appears that the police or anyone connected are similarly incompetent at that word game, as you profess to be. It means four, not three … usually four pieces of art, like a trilogy in books or films."

"Like *Star Wars?* Well, the original ones I watched at the cinema before I died, that is?"

"Yes, if you like. So, I think it's fairly safe to suggest the murderer is planning to take revenge on four … tetralogy. Unlike Edmond Dantès, who targeted three."

"I can see that your time as a personnel officer was well spent. What d'you do all day? Read the dictionary?"

"I'll ignore that epithet."

"My point exactly. Anyway, I still think these murders, or future murders, have bugger all to do with us."

"That as may be. Now, as I was leaving, Alistair took another call. Unfortunately, I could only hear his side of the conversation. But, darling, listen. Whoever he was talking to, appeared to be threatening him."

"Oh?"

"Yes. He said, and I quote, 'You can't threaten me because I've ensured your Ginny goes down as well. So, Jules, I suggest you back off. Otherwise, I will engineer it to ensure your sister is also culpable'."

"He said that?"

"Yes … sort of. I'm paraphrasing, of course."

"Christ … what does that mean?"

"Darling, I have no idea. I mulled it over on my way over here. I can only assume that Ginny has a brother called Jules, who is trying to blackmail Alistair with something."

"And whatever it is, some dodgy dealings, presumably, Alistair intends to frame Ginny."

"Precisely."

"Bloody hell. This has got to be our toughest mission so far. What the hell are we going to do? I don't know where to start with this one."

"No, it is a smidge more complicated than our Damian's and little Kimmy's situation."

"And if you're correct regarding the Powers-That-Be being somewhat miffed with our performances so far, we're going to have to pull this one out of the bag. And sharpish, I might suggest."

"Quite. We need to up our game, darling."

"What's the plan, then?"

Deana shot Terry a disparaging glare. "Darling, how many times do I have to explain myself? I'm your guide. My sole purpose is to chaperone you through the mission, employ my exclusive invisible skills where required whilst looking gorgeous, of course. All three of which I demonstrate the performance of a high achiever. So, be clear, I am not here to formulate plans."

"Yes, okay, okay," he huffed.

"Now, I'm prepared to summarise for you if that helps?"

Terry raised an eyebrow and frowned. "Go on, if you must."

"Hmm. Terence, I have to say, I'm not too fond of your mardiness. We'll have to put a stop to this, I'm afraid," Deana pursed her lips whilst raising her chin.

"Oh, get on with it, woman."

"Okay, you peevish little thing, you. As I see it, our mission is clear. We have to help your girl obtain a decent settlement from her divorce. It appears she inherited your stupidity and somehow boxed herself into a position where Alistair holds all the cards. Now, that will probably have to involve a spot of blackmail, assuming we can find an angle, that is. Perhaps something to do with that phone call with that man called Jules. If that fails, we revert to scaring Alistair half to death with ghostly acts."

"A great synopsis."

"Thank you, darling. As I say, I'm here to help," she smirked, whilst patronisingly patting his knee. "Of course, we may also be required to put a halt to a serial killer who appears to be systematically working their way through the clinical staff of the surgical department up at Fairfield General. Presumably, two more doctors are about to join our rather exclusive club."

"Right, when Ginny eventually returns from the ladies, I'll probe her about this chap, Jules."

"Yes, I think that would be a prudent starting point. Now take hold of this solicitor's letter I pilfered from his office. It confirms what I said about her rotten husband, so you might consider allowing your girl to have a wee gander at it."

Deana scanned around the bar, ensuring no prying eyes, because a letter appearing out of thin air might cause those spotting the odd enigma to wonder how much alcohol they'd consumed. When suitably relieved that the odd woman who'd previously stared at her no longer appeared to be in position, Deana slipped the letter out of her handbag and onto Terry's lap.

"Good job you women shilly-shally around powdering your nose forever and a day."

"We don't shilly-shally."

"Faff, then."

"Darling, it's important for a girl to take time on her appearance. At least this daughter of yours has a certain pulchritudinous quality, a marked difference from your plain little Kimmy. I suspect she has her mother's genes."

"What are you on about? Pulch-what?"

"She's what you could describe as easy on the eye."

"Why didn't you say that?"

"Nothing wrong with possessing good diction, darling. Now—" Deana halted mid-sentence when an elderly woman, the one who'd earlier stared in their direction, slotted into the seat vacated by Virginia.

"Hello, Terry," she croaked as she gingerly eased herself down onto the chair.

"Oh, hell, it's that bloody woman! I told you she was looking at us. Christ, how does she know you? Good God ..." Deana pitched forward in her seat to grab a close-up inspection of her face. *"Oh, what an ugly old moo. The poor woman's not exactly a picture of health, certainly not a face that could promote anti-wrinkle cream."*

"I can honestly say you haven't changed one bit ... maybe a little grey poking through the temples," the woman smirked, as she tipped her head sideways, looking at Terry, before embarking on a particularly hoarse, rasping coughing fit.

"Christ, she can talk. Death warmed up would be an apt description. She looks like she could be an extra in Thriller. Although, that wheezing chest and unsteady gait would suggest she might struggle to perform a backsliding moonwalk shuffle without causing herself a serious injury." Deana chortled.

Terry side-eyed Deana, knitting his eyebrows.

Deana, clocking his expression, was fast learning when she'd shot off on a tangent after citing something that had happened whilst he lay in his grave. Although not quite sure when Michael Jackson's award-winning, groundbreaking music video was released, she presumed it must have been after Terry died. Never mind, she'd explain later.

"Err ... sorry, do we know each other?" Terry quizzed when the woman finally stopped croaking.

"We do," she wheezed in a husky voice. "Terry, I need to warn you. Pursuing that road of investigating Jean's killer is a path you do not want to tread." With that, she hauled herself up by way of gripping the back of the chair.

"Sorry, but who are you?"

"Take heed, Terry Walton. I'm the winged messenger. Goodbye."

Terry leapt out of his seat, preparing to grab the woman as she stepped away, but halted as she swivelled around and pointed at Deana.

"Oh, yes, I can see you, Deana. Just because the years weren't so kind to me, there is no need for rudeness. You always were a conceited, vainglory bitch. And I see nothing has changed."

22

Ay, Caramba!

As I shimmied through the tables and back to my seat, I noticed Ian stand, which I thought was a somewhat outdated gesture for a man to perform. Although Ian demonstrated some peculiar mannerisms and clearly wasn't being totally honest with me, I considered it a polite and welcome gesture. Anyway, outdated or not, it certainly wouldn't be something Alistair or his father would have performed.

Pleased that I'd managed to hold my shit together, complete my ablutions and not allow my chin to tremble, I decided to stop tip-toeing around this Ian bloke, go straight for the jugular and discover what the purpose was of this meeting. Then, I'd plan to set about getting my life on track. Time spent collecting my thoughts when holed up in that toilet cubicle had reminded me to slip on my suffer-no-fools protective armour and put a halt to those around me who seemed to be sucking my mental strength.

After properly unpacking my stuff, I planned to put in a good few hours job hunting, tear a strip off my solicitor for allowing Alistair to ride roughshod over me, and then perhaps wallow in a vat of Prosecco. That would conclude day one of my new life, post living in limbo at Karen's, post Alistair, and post any man who thought they could mess with my emotions.

"Blimey, that's a bit old-fashioned. Can't say I've met many men who stand for a lady when she returns to the table."

Ian, open-mouthed, seemed mesmerised by something happening near the pub entrance.

I glanced around, following his gaze before returning my attention to Ian, who appeared stuck in some strange trance. "Err ... hello, anyone there?" I waved the palm of my hand in front of his eyes.

"Darling, how could she see me? And how rude! Bitch, I accept, but vainglory ... really?"

"Ian?" I peered at him, my hand gesture failing to raise him out of his catatonic state.

"Oh, sorry," he grinned, turning his attention from the pub entrance to me as I settled back onto my chair before slowly lowering himself to his, whilst clutching what appeared to be a folded letter.

I glanced at my wine and shrugged to myself. If Ian were intent on drugging me, he would have presumably poisoned my first glass. So, I plucked it up, confident I would be okay. "Thank you." I raised the glass at him before taking a sip.

"Oh, you're welcome."

"Yes, you enjoy it. I'll just watch and slowly dehydrate," Deana spouted whilst aggressively folding her arms.

"Ian, besides being Deana's nephew, I know nothing about you. I think I've already said far too much and, based on the fact that we don't know each other, I'm concerned about the direction of where the conversation is heading."

Ian offered a knowing nod, presumably accepting my concerns. "Just to offer some assistance, that's all. I've been asked to see if I can step in and help you out."

"By who?"

"Oh, not well thought through, was it, darling? What are you going to say now? I suggest you don't tell her it's the Powers-That-Be who have set the mission. Christ, Terence. Come on, sharpen up a bit."

"Shush, woman!" he shot out of the side of his mouth.

"Are you shushing me?" I barked back at him, somewhat shocked by his rudeness considering his polite gesture from earlier. If I didn't know better, he appeared to be poorly attempting some ventriloquist act without the dummy.

"Don't shush me! You're as rude as that bloody woman. In fact, she couldn't have got far. I'm going to find out who she is." Deana leapt to her feet, causing her chair to nudge back as she barrelled through the pub towards the exit. *"Get out of the damn way,"* she boomed at a group of suited gents, who, of course, didn't hear or notice her. *Frustrated, Deana slapped the bottom of the chap's pint glass which he held to his chest, causing the majority of the liquid to tip down his shirt and tie.*

Once again, Ian appeared distracted by whatever was happening near the pub entrance. Whilst choosing to ignore my question about shushing, he continued to gawp open-mouthed over my shoulder.

After offering a confused shake of my head at that self-moving chair, I swivelled around to witness a commotion, the centre of which was a suited gent, his shirt covered in spilt beer, who appeared to be accusing the bloke wearing the high-vis of knocking into him.

"Jesus," Ian muttered, shaking his head.

Although there appeared to be a volley of verbal exchanges between the two men, an all-out pub brawl seemed unlikely when another suited chap hauled his mate away from the builder type, who appeared ready to larrup him one.

I glanced at the now motionless chair, giving it a nudge with my foot. "That chair moved again," I mumbled.

"Oh, did it?" Ian offered a nonchalant shrug.

"Yes, it did. And you keep glancing at it."

"Do I?"

I huffed. "Look, before you rather rudely shushed me, I asked you who has asked you to help me?"

"Sorry, I wasn't shushing you."

"Who then? Who were you shushing, and who is instructing you to get involved in my life?" I exclaimed, becoming frustrated with his vague answers.

"Ginny, I can't say."

I grabbed my wine, ready to take a mouthful before intending to end this conversation. "Well, unless you do say, I think we're done here."

"Ginny—"

"Uh-uh," I interrupted him, swallowing my wine and raising a finger to indicate I wanted to speak. "Ian, it was nice to meet you … I think. But I'm going to get going if you don't mind. However, I will admit that some of what you've said today has got me thinking. So, just hypothetically, if I were to take your offer of help, what exactly were you thinking of doing?"

"Okay, so I'm led to believe your husband has manipulated the situation that cuts you out of the business and also your home. He plans to ruin you financially and leave you destitute."

I slowly blinked as I gawped at him. "Err ... how on earth could you know that?" I considered that only my solicitor, the useless git, and now Karen, could know. Of course, Alistair, and presumably his new bit of fluff, were also fully aware. However, Ian Beacham wouldn't be holding this conversation with me if he was somehow connected to them.

"Ginny, can I show you this letter?" Ian slid the folded sheet across the table.

Confused as to why he'd be offering me a letter to read, I placed my wine down and plucked it up, my eyes shooting back and forth between the page and Ian as I unfolded it and held it out to read.

I scanned the letter, only choosing to start again and read in detail when realising it was correspondence from Alistair's solicitor. I glanced at Ian, who supped his pint, then continued to read.

Although my solicitor had suggested that gaining a settlement regarding the business could prove tricky, he had assured me I would be entitled to half the proceeds from the sale of our flat. Unfortunately, the information printed in just two paragraphs suggested that not to be the case.

Notwithstanding my divorce and renting that cesspool, it now appeared I was truly destitute.

Despite the promise I'd made to myself that I wouldn't succumb to tears, I felt it necessary to dab the corner of my eye with the back of my hand. "How ... how have you got hold of this?"

"Ginny, you seem a bit put out. Is this new news?"

I nodded without looking up from those devastating paragraphs. "But how," I mumbled.

"Let's just say I have an acquaintance who can access certain things."

"How? Do you know someone who works at Alistair's solicitors?" I lifted my head to offer a quizzical frown. Apart from the devastating information printed on that page, I was now totally bemused about how Ian could have accessed this confidential letter.

"No, but she can obtain certain documents and acquire information that others might find ... well, let's just say difficult to access. She's quite an asset, really ... wherever she is," he muttered.

Ian offered the empty chair another side-eye glance. As no attractive woman, or man, for that matter, had shimmied past, I presumed he wasn't eyeing up any potential talent. So, I assumed he just suffered from an odd tic.

"I'm sorry, I don't understand," I mumbled, as I waved the letter at him. "How could someone you know get hold of this?"

"Okay. So, I have a friend who possesses certain skills, shall we say. She acquired this letter that confirms what I've said—"

"Skills?" I interrupted.

"Yes, hear me out. Now, tell me about someone called Jules, and why would this person be in cahoots with Alistair?"

"Jules? Sorry, did you say Jules?" A wave of fear swept over me. Despite our sibling relationship being on the level of Bart and Lisa Simpson, as in our joint propensity to bicker, fight and disagree on almost everything, I became concerned about what pickle Jules had landed himself in, especially as Ian had mentioned Alistair in the same sentence.

"Yes, my acquaintance overheard Alistair on the phone to Jules. Apparently, the conversation appeared heated and, from what she could gather, it seems this Jules chap was trying to blackmail Alistair."

"When?" I snapped. "When did this so-called acquaintance overhear this conversation?"

"A little earlier. After we'd left your office."

"Today?"

"Yes."

"But ... but who ... there was only Serena there when we left?" Terry opened his mouth, but nothing came out. "Oh, I see." I folded my arms and leaned back in my chair. "Serena ... you and Serena ... you two an item, are you?"

"No—"

"You do know that Ali has been banging her, don't you?"

"Ginny—"

"Is this her way of getting him back for letting her go? Is that it? The silly girl was more than happy for Ali to entertain her across his desk each week. But now he's given the girl her marching orders, she's finding any old angle to get back at him."

"Ginny, I've never met Serena until this morning."

"Oh."

"Jules? He's your brother, yes?"

"Yeah, but whoever your friend might be, she must be mistaken. Jules always thought Ali was a bit of a dick. There's no way they would be cooking up anything together."

Or was he? Jules Bart-Simpson Goode had always acted the clown, often getting into stupid scrapes and making the wrong decisions which added a tragic layer to Jules's arc as he stumbled chaotically through life. Perhaps my idiotic brother and Alistair were entwined in something stupid or illegal. To quote Bart – *Ay Caramba!*

"No … as I said. Jules appeared to be threatening Alistair … blackmail or something."

"With what? That call you made when I nipped off to the ladies, is that when you found out?"

Ian nodded. "It is. But listen, whatever they were discussing, Alistair warned this Jules chap not to blackmail him because he would ensure that he engineers it so *you* took the fall and not him."

"I don't get it. Fall for what? And as I said, Jules wouldn't be talking to Ali."

"Ginny, I don't know. However, what my friend—"

"Hang on, how come your friend could overhear Alistair's conversation? He said this morning that I needed to leave his office because his next appointment was at two, and he needed a couple of hours to prepare. Apart from that silly girl filing her nails, there couldn't have been anyone else there."

"Don't move the chair," he hissed out of the side of his mouth, performing that odd ventriloquist act.

"Sorry?" I quizzed, glancing from Ian to the empty chair and back.

Deana grabbed the back of the chair but halted from dragging it backwards upon hearing Terry's hissed warning. "Darling, I may have inadvertently forgotten to mention one small piece of information," she winced, whilst catching her breath from running.

"Oh, great. What?"

"Ian, who are you talking to?"

"I may have forgotten to mention that Alistair was planning to meet his father here at one. Those two despicable good-for-nothing gits are about to step into the pub."

Ian glanced back at me before appearing to glare over my shoulder again. "Ginny, sorry, but your husband and his father are on their way here."

I swivelled around, jiggling my head around, trying to grab a clear view of the entrance. As a loved-up couple, whilst cooing at each other, shifted their stance, I spotted Mel Strachan push open the door. My pervert father-in-law halted as he clocked my stare.

Although it held no consequence that Alistair and I were in the same pub at the same time, being as our split was still raw, the last thing I needed was to continue our spat in a public place. Alistair joined Mel, hovering inside the doorway as the three of us locked eyes.

Despite the scowl offered by both men, uppermost in my mind was how Ian could have known they were about to walk in. The view from our window seat only provided a view of the hill. The front door, positioned at a ninety-degree angle to the hill, meant there was no way he could have spotted them ten to fifteen seconds before they entered.

"Oh, hell's bells. Now I remember why I could recall that name. The snivelling git is a lot older, but I remember Mel Strachan … that party back in '75," Terry vacantly muttered.

I broke eye contact with Alistair to turn to Ian. "Did you say 1975?"

23

Rockin' All Over The World

Ian failed to answer, and for a moment, whilst the hum of chatter in the busy pub faded into the background, the four of us held our positions, eyes flitting back and forth akin to the Mexican standoff situation in *Shaun of the Dead*. Although none of us were threatening each other with a gun, broken bottle, or corkscrew and, as far as I knew, there wasn't a zombie in the room, we appeared to have reached an impasse.

Mel broke the deadlock by way of wagging a finger at Ian. "I know you … but … but it can't be," he stammered.

"Oh, this is a bit of a quandary, darling. We do seem to have the ability to land ourselves in a spot of bother," she chortled. *"Would it help if I performed a few ghostly acts and cause a scene? Perhaps I should knee him in the privates; that might help. What d'you think?"* suggested Deana, whilst stepping towards Mel and raising a knee.

Ian appeared to be catching flies and Mel held his accusing finger, while Alistair and I played head tennis between the two men.

"Terry—bloody—Walton … but you can't be," muttered Mel.

"Oh, bugger. That's put the cat amongst the pigeons. You should see the look on your daughter's face. She looks just like Chief Brody when faced with that rather nasty little shark," Deana guffawed, still finely balanced on one leg with her attack knee poised and ready. *"Shall I?"*

Although I'd considered that Ian resembled my biological father depicted in that holiday snap, I'd come to realise that was probably due to my mind playing tricks. I'd suffered a difficult time of late, and obsessing about that photo had probably implanted delusional thoughts in my mind. However, I was now somewhat shocked that Mel spotted the resemblance to a man I didn't know he knew and, more to the point, how Ian could remember my father-in-law from a party nearly ten years before he was born.

"Mel–sodding–Strachan," muttered Ian.

"What?" I blurted, Ian's statement dragging me from my trance. "How do you know Mel?" I shot a finger in my father-in-law's direction. "Him?"

"Terence," barked Deana, lowering her knee. *"Please remember you are impersonating my first husband. Well, using his name because the last thing I would want to witness is you displaying any similar traits to that turgid git. Come on, buck up before this situation gets completely out of hand."*

Ian eased himself out of his chair, seemingly still mesmerised by Mel.

"Dad, that's the bloke who came to see Ginny earlier," Alistair whined, like a kid telling tales, as he waved an accusing finger in my direction.

I scowled back.

With his hands rammed into his jeans pockets, Ian stepped towards Mel and nudged his head forward. "So, you married Jean Allsopp, did you? I can't believe she actually ended up with you after that night. Christ, what would a woman like that see in a wanker like you?"

"Darling, what's going on? Apart from blowing your cover, I'm a little concerned to what's got your goat. I can honestly say I've never seen you so angry." Deana tugged on Terry's arm, attempting to haul him back from where he'd advanced upon Mel, now almost nose to nose with him.

When Mel hopped back a pace, I spotted Ian with his hands in his pockets enacting some odd twisting movement back and forth as if performing some weird cowboy line dance. Or perhaps the 'Quo Dance', which I recall my father, Paul, and a few of his cronies embarrassingly attempting at some hideous social event. A memory that's best forgotten.

'The bloke's a frigging nutter,' my inner thoughts suggested.

I nodded to my mind talk, thinking it may be time to get the hell away from all three before this Ian chap and Mel came to fisticuffs.

"How could you know my wife? Who the hell are you?" spat my rather flustered father in law as he took another pace away from Ian.

"Who is this bloke?" Alistair turned on me before stepping forward to take up the position Mel had vacated.

"I have no idea," I slowly whispered, my head desperately trying to compute the ridiculous.

"Terence! We'd better go. Come on." Deana tugged hard on his arm.

Still performing that odd twisting, Quo-dance movement, Ian stepped back from Alistair, nodded to his left, and then turned to face me. "Ginny, remember the letter and what I said about that phone call. You need some help, and I'm your only option."

Mel and Alistair shot me a look as Ian stepped around them and disappeared through the pub entrance.

"Well? Who the hell was that?" demanded my soon-to-be ex-husband.

As I assessed his flustered face, I began to wonder what I'd ever seen in him. They say that as you grow older your feelings for your partner change. Perhaps morphing from desire and lust to love and companionship. A point where your relationship evolves into a partnership, and you learn to accept and tolerate each other's annoying traits. As he pinched his face at me, I struggled to grasp where desire and lust had come from. I could only conclude, back in my twenties, I must have set my sights low. Any number of those demented, unibrow-sporting, serial-killer types looking for love or a victim to murder on that dating app offered far more alluring appeal than the weasel of a man who stood before me. Miss flexible, vegan, panting starfish was welcome to him.

"Terry–bloody–Walton," I quipped, raising an eyebrow at Mel, now pleased with myself for redeveloping some modicum of my previously withering backbone.

"Is this some joke?"

"I have no idea, Mel. You tell me."

"Well, it can't be him, can it? Although he looks the spitting image, Terry Walton left this earth thirty-odd years ago. And bloody good riddance."

The fact that Mel seemed to detest my biological father just notched my admiration for Terry up a few pegs. Although he was dead, and Ian wasn't Terry.

'Could he be?' my mind questioned.

'No! As I said, Terry is dead.'

'So how come that Ian bloke knows so much about you, and your tossy father-in-law seems to recognise him?'

'I don't know.'

'No, well, Ian seems to know Mel from 1975, so explain that.'

'I can't.'

'No, I'm sure you can't. Also, can you explain how Ian could possibly know your mother-in-law as well?'

"I can't," I muttered to myself, verbalising the end of my mind-talk exchange.

"You can't what?" Alistair barked.

Ignoring his question, I fronted him up. "Why are you talking to Jules?"

"What?"

"Jules rang you earlier. What was it about?"

"How …" Alistair paused mid-sentence, narrowing his eyes whilst jutting his chin forward. "How would you know Jules phoned me? Has he rung you?"

I nonchalantly shook my head.

"Huh, well, I guess that twat of a brother of yours must have." Alistair stepped closer and jabbed his index finger in my face. "Don't go down that route. I told Jules he's mistaken if you both think you can get back at me by reporting insider trading. If anyone comes looking into my affairs, I have laid a trail that leads back to you. You were the business manager, and that breadcrumb trail I've laid leads all the way to your door … not mine. So, if anyone is getting charged, it's *you*, not me," he hissed.

"What d'you mean, insider trading?"

"Keep your voice down," he hissed in my face. "Well, your twat of a brother knows, so I assumed you would, too. The Hutton's account … the shares Dad purchased before the takeover announcement."

"That's illegal," I spat, leaning my head back to avoid his jutting head.

Hutton's, a small tech company to whom we'd provided services to, were involved in a takeover from one of the giants in the industry. All of us employed at Strachan Accountants were bound by the laws governing such sensitive information.

"It is. And as I just told your brother, if you choose to whistle blow, all the evidence will point to you, and only you, acting outside the law. Yes, okay, Dad will be in the shit, but *you, dear wife,* will face the fine and a potential prison sentence."

My eyes shot towards Mel as he stepped forward, both men now bearing down upon me. I glanced around, searching for an escape route, my eyes dropping on Ian's half-consumed pint of beer. I contemplated shooting the content at them both before making a run for it, only to be hauled out of my musings when Mel took over from where Alistair had momentarily left off.

"Open that mouth of yours, Ginny, and my God, girl, you won't know what damn well hit you. I suggest you get out of Alistair's life and be thankful that if you keep that pretty little mouth shut, you'll not be facing the full weight of the law against you. You've lost, girl."

Both men continued to bear down upon me, thus pinning me into the small space afforded near the window. As if some higher being had hit mute on a remote control, silence descended, rendering the chatter and clinking of glasses in the busy pub almost imperceptible, with only the thudding of my heartbeat audible. Now, faced with two ignominious men hissing and spitting their words with fury as they attempted to berate me, that backbone I'd just rediscovered crumpled.

Alistair had clearly carefully planned and plotted against me, taking my livelihood, my home, and now holding the insider-trading-threat-styled Sword of Damocles over me. I knew Alistair possessed the skills and know-how regarding ensuring that any wrongdoings would be laid at my door if I chose to use this knowledge against him.

My ex-husband had me cornered – literally and metaphorically.

The scene unmuted as Mel barked at me after Alistair turned and stepped away.

"You're just like your weak father. Paul Goode was nothing but a pathetic waster, and it appears you've inherited his traits."

Out of the corner of my eye, I noticed Ian's half-drunk pint glass levitate, then tip forward before shooting through mid-air only to then abruptly halt, thus allowing the liquid to fire out and splatter across the side of Mel's face.

Stunned, Mel jolted backwards before shooting his hand to his wet cheek whilst spinning around to identify the culprit. "What the …" he blurted.

Alistair spun around just after I witnessed the glass gently settle back on the table. When spotting his father whip off his glasses, bend double, and paw the beer from his eyes, Alistair leapt towards me as I gaped open-mouthed at the glass. In that moment, I considered Ian *had* spiked my drink, and not only had I witnessed a self-moving chair but also a levitating beer glass. However, as I turned back to Mel, his face dripping with beer, the vision in front of me suggested I wasn't hallucinating.

Before Alistair could grab me, he appeared to stumble and grab the back of that previous self-moving chair before wheezing out a pained grunt whilst clutching his left shin.

"Hey, love, you alright?"

I glanced up from my wincing husband and bent double father-in-law to spot that builder chap dressed in his tight-fitting t-shirt and hi-vis, gesturing with an outstretched arm for me to step towards him and away from my pinned-in position.

Stupefied by what I'd witnessed, his gesture acted like a cattle prod, jolting me from my wool-gathering daze. I nodded and gingerly stepped around Alistair, allowing the builder chap to usher me away from them.

When safely on the other side of him, and in the protective circle of his mates, he turned to Alistair and Mel, who appeared to be recovering. "Oi … dickheads. I've had my fill of twats today. What with that bell-end earlier reckoning that I spilt his beer over him, and now you two knobs losing your manners. So, fuck off, or I'll nut the two of you."

"A little coarse, but well said, young man." Deana eyed up his bulging biceps that flexed and stretched the sleeves of his t-shirt to almost splitting point. "What truly wonderful manly, muscly arms you have. You and I could have hit it off before I was dead, you know." Deana raised an alluring eyebrow at him before shimmying around his cement-stained, hi-vis-clad, ripped body and stepping up to Mel, who appeared to be processing the builder-type's threat. "I suggest you take heed, you git. Florescent-Tarzan boy, here," she thumbed over her shoulder to the chap who appeared ready to thump his head into Alistair's nose. "Might want to pulverise your ugly mug, which I attest would hold a certain entertainment value. However, Terence and I are going to make both yours and that contemptible son's lives a living hell!"

24

Sophie's Choice

Whilst gently easing down my eyelid, pinched between my forefinger and thumb, I inspected the sclera areas, trying to detect any reddening or discolouration that may indicate that I'd unwittingly consumed a mind-altering substance. Fortunately, as I peered into the bathroom mirror, which afforded an antique effect – although I suspected this was due to dilapidation rather than any hip, shabby-chic attempt at interior design – I couldn't detect any concerning issues.

Notwithstanding my apparent healthy reflection from my newly acquired bathroom mirror, and taking into account that my vision appeared to be as close to twenty-twenty as it had always been, what I'd witnessed in that pub at lunchtime had left me in a state of bewilderment.

"Chairs don't move on their own. Glasses of beer don't magically fly," I muttered to my reflection.

I glanced at the Victoria's Secret's soap pump, one of the many items left by the vacating porn star when running off into the sunset with that posh boy who, according to Deli, used to live next door. Going by the plethora of half-used lotions and body mists liberally scattered across the windowsill, Courteney, I believe her name was, must have regularly frequented that store. I pointed at my reflection. "If she could get her life on track, so can you. Alright?" I nodded in reply, although my eyes suggested they knew my gesture of agreement to be a lie.

I straightened my back and removed my hair-scrunchy, allowing my hair to flop down from my practical and preferred ponytail style. After repeatedly tipping my head from side to side and combing my mid-back-length hair with my splayed-out fingers, I pulled my strawberry-blonde locks around my face to hide my eyes, as if that act could shield me from the ravages of the past few months. I snorted a laugh, remembering how I used this tactic when lying to my parents. I recalled when my mother would scold me, saying I looked like some scary onryō. Also, hiding my pretty face wasn't going to cover my untruths.

They say the eyes always radiate the truth, whatever the mouth is saying. Alistair had been lying for months, probably years, but I'd subconsciously chosen not to see what was right in front of me. Perhaps I was just plain stupid. Further confirmed when, in desperation at the thought of being alone, I'd allowed Viv to suck me in and spin out a load of bull. Why hadn't I seen through him, and why did he trot out all that crap about liking me?

I chewed my lip, thinking about that conversation last night on the doorstep. I'd been with Ali for over fourteen years, and like all previous boyfriends, I'd made him wait before taking him to my bed. Last night, although on a first date, I would have invited Viv in. Was that reckless? Perhaps that was just a foolhardy thought born out of desperation and fear of ending up alone with only a clowder of cats for company. Also, surely Viv could spot, after four glasses of Pinot and my obvious imprudence, sex was on the menu for afters.

Apart from that lie about going to Barbados to see his mother, his jaunt through town with that woman on his arm suggested Viv wasn't single. So, I presumed he'd taken me out for dinner but decided not to indulge in extracurricular activities because he suddenly put two and two together and remembered my husband's comment. So, that bollocks about not getting involved with a person connected with an ongoing investigation was just a cover because he wasn't into necrophilia.

After shaking cheating police officers from my mind, flying glasses filled the void. Although fully aware of the futility, stupidity and childishness of the idea, I prepared to twitch my nose, now convinced if I could move that soap pump through only employing the power of my thoughts and a nose wiggle, then perhaps I *had* subconsciously willed that pint glass to shoot its content over Mel's face.

Notwithstanding my valiant attempts, unfortunately, whichever way I wiggled my nose or scrunched my face, my efforts were in vain. As I suspected, this technique didn't work. Neither did the act of pointing my finger because no flurry of witch dust emanated from my nail as I wagged it at the soap pump, which continued its inanimate existence on the side of the sink. Although I used to sloth out on the sofa in my student digs watching daytime showings of *Sabrina the Teenage Witch* and old episodes of Samantha's antics in *Bewitched*, it appeared that I hadn't suddenly been blessed with spooky powers.

"Oh, Ginny, get a grip." I pointed at my reflection. "But that glass did fly, didn't it?" I nodded back before shaking my head to allow my hair to flop over my eyes again.

Holding that position, I huffed out a puff of air, shooting a few strands from my eyes, thus allowing my reflection to once again become clear. "I'm losing my mind. That's what's happening, isn't it?" I nodded a reply before padding back to the kitchen to flip the kettle on, intent on brewing a cuppa before setting about completing my earlier plan. That said, since traversing back from town, I'd lost the enthusiasm for flat sorting or job hunting. Certainly, any fervency for ripping my useless solicitor a good'un had evaporated, and even the vat of Prosecco idea seemed to have withered and died.

I unfolded that letter that Ian had somehow secured, re-reading the part about my sodding husband's intention to wriggle out of selling the flat and thus leaving me destitute in this shithole. The anger that bubbled up was enough to jolt me from my oh-woe-is-me stupor and get hold of my solicitor. Unlike the vague conversation I'd encountered with Ian, he'd better have some damn good answers for me.

Whilst lost in my stupor of ridiculous thoughts about Ian, how he knew Mel and Jean, levitating objects, and a kind builder chap with his good Samaritan-cum-guardian angel act of stepping into that situation earlier, I spotted a figure whizz past the window.

Whilst on tiptoes, I stretched forward over the sink in order to gain a better view along the landing. I laid my hand on the glass just at the point when Viv poked his head back, offering a tight smile and a cursory nod before carrying on towards Deli's flat.

"Huh," I muttered. "You've got a bloody nerve." I grabbed the milk from the fridge, one of the few items I'd purchased from the convenience store on my way back to the flat. Not a particularly pleasant shopping excursion and was further mired when served by Fat-Oaf. The git actually tutted when having to haul his jogging-bottom-clad arse from his stool, place his lit cigarette in the already overflowing ashtray, and glance away from his mucky mag – which depicted a glossy picture of some girl squashing her breasts together – to rather uninterestingly scan my items and hand my receipt through the security hatch.

When I'd pointed out that smoking in shops was against the law, also mentioning that I thought reading those sorts of magazines when serving customers was unnecessary and quite vulgar, he stated, *"The law don't apply around here,"* also suggesting I could, and I quote, *"Whip my tits out, instead, if I liked."*

I didn't like. And in no uncertain terms, told the git as much. Whilst he offered a shrug in reply to my rebuff of his suggestion, a hoodie-wearing youth queuing behind me voiced his disappointment regarding my decision. What he actually stated was – *"Ah, go on. Reckon you've got a couple of nice pert-puppies hidden up that t-shirt."*

As shopping experiences go, my first two forays into Fat-Oaf's emporium hadn't panned out particularly well. Although I knew the Broxworth owned a reputation for being rough, I'd been oblivious to the extent to which this odious place seemed to be teaming full of muggers, perverts, thieves, drug dealers and vagabonds. However, on a positive note, I made it from Fat-Oaf's shop to my flat without further incident, which I considered a minor miracle in itself.

As I steeped my tea by repeatedly squashing the tea bag with the back of the spoon, I could hear a muffled conversation on the landing. I presumed Deli was disinclined to invite her brother into her flat. Akin to devout practising Catholics, when hastily shovelling their Jesuits clerics into a priest hole to conceal them from pursuivants during the Elizabethan era, I imagined Gabe would be in the process of stashing their ill-gotten-gained gear in various hidey-holes. Although, unlike those discovered priests, torture and death weren't on the cards for Deli and Gabe. However, if Viv unearthed their hidey-holes, that would leave the cheating officer with an impossible decision – a kind of *Sophie's Choice* – give up his career or arrest his family.

Tea in hand, I cracked open the kitchen window and hoisted the waist of my jeans over the edge of the sink. I employed the tactic of leaning my ear towards the window and squinting my eyes shut, as if that act would help me focus on the spoken words as I attempted to listen to their conversation.

Despite my best attempts and holding that position, I couldn't decipher any meaningful words, probably because of the shouting and hollering between a couple positioned outside a flat on the landing of the opposing tower block, which effectively drowned out Viv's and Deli's conversation.

As I clutched the hot tea to my chest, the heat emanating from the mug almost burnt my skin through my t-shirt. Despite my less-than-comfortable pose, I leaned closer to the window. For sure, I was determined to catch the conversation, thus hoping to glean evidence that Viv had spun me a pack of lies. Not that it mattered, but I just fancied getting the upper hand on the cheating git.

However, my efforts were in vain. The vulgar exchange that echoed and reverberated off the grey monolithic concrete five-storey tower blocks, which reared up in a circle formation akin to three standing stones placed there in the 1960s, continued to drown out my neighbour's conversation.

I heard the window hinges squeak.

"Hi, Ginny."

I cracked open one eye, spotting Viv quizzically raising his eyebrows.

"Are you in pain?"

"No," I barked, hopping back in surprise, resulting in the slopping of hot tea down my t-shirt. I glared at Viv, who'd pulled the window open enough to poke his head through.

"Oh, shit," I blurted, before glancing down at my stained t-shirt and feeling the hot liquid burn my cleavage.

"Sorry, didn't mean to make you jump."

"Yes, well, you did." I bit back and glared at him.

"Yeah, sorry. I thought I'd just say hi."

"Hi," I replied, offering a deadpan face. I hadn't consumed four glasses of wine, only two at lunchtime, so with my less inebriated state and knowledge of his philandering ways, I didn't feel the need to offer unnecessary pleasantries.

Viv nodded. "Sorry about last night."

"What about it?"

Viv shrugged, offering no reply as he dropped his eyes.

"I thought you should be in sunny Barbados by now. Or was that story about your mother all twaddle?"

Viv slowly raised his eyes. "Mum passed last night. I took a call from her partner in the early hours."

My mouth gaped.

"I cancelled my flight because I need to get Deli sorted with a passport so we can get over for the funeral."

"Oh," I muttered. My mind raced. Were these more lies? Could this bloke be the sort that trots out any old crap to seek attention? I presumed his girlfriend would also be making the trip if his mother had died. Perhaps no mother was living there in the first place. "Well, sorry to hear that, but I won't be looking after your thieving nephew whilst you're gone. Just to be clear."

Viv nodded. "No, I didn't think you would be. Anyway, I need to pick up my cousin. She's staying with me for a few days to check out some local universities. Take care, Ginny," he nodded, then hesitated. "Oh, and don't leave your flat at night. The estate is bad enough during the day. Even us lot try to avoid this shithole at night." Viv extracted his head from the gap and pushed the window closed.

Two and two equal four, not five. That young girl, arm in arm with Viv as they sauntered down Timber Hill at lunchtime, was presumably his cousin. They were arm in arm for comfort, Viv losing his mother and the young girl losing her aunt. And not, as I'd presumed, Viv and his young girlfriend linking arms like a couple of lovers.

Although I'd enjoyed his company last night, and he was absolutely a man I would have liked to get to know better, that was clearly not on the cards for reasons he stated or my husband's vulgar accusations about our private bedroom activities.

That all said, that didn't excuse my utter rudeness and suggestion about his lying. Also, I thought Viv could be a friend. Now I was living here, albeit hopefully only temporarily, I needed a friend who knew the lie of the land, so to speak. Also, that threat Alistair had levied at me in that pub could mean a friendly police officer on my side might be an asset if Alistair's dodgy dealings all came to light and the inevitable excrement smacked the air conditioning.

I flung open the window and bellowed down the landing, "Viv … Nelson." I waited for a second. "Viv," I hollered at the top of my voice. However, no reply seemed forthcoming. Assuming he'd already made it to the stairwell, I gave up and pulled the window shut. As I prepared to slide off the countertop, I noticed when hoisting my torso up against the worktop that I'd inadvertently nudged the mug of tea. The resulting upturned mug soaked the crotch of my jeans, which I could now feel seeping through to my knickers.

"Oh, brilliant!" I hopped down and assessed the carnage, which gave the appearance that I'd just wet myself before feverously and rather pointlessly scrubbing my hand down my crotch.

"You could get arrested for that."

My head shot up to spot Viv's hands cupping his face against the window. With my hand poised over the crotch of my jeans and my untied hair flailing in front of my eyes, I offered an embarrassed, exaggerated grin.

"You called," he shouted through the glass.

I nodded, stepped forward and flung the window open as Viv shimmied his head back and then through the gap.

"You could get arrested for that," he repeated and grinned.

"Yeah, hilarious. I spilt tea down my front."

"Again?"

"Yeah."

"What, d'you bath in the stuff? Does it have skin-soothing qualities?"

"No," I offered a thin smile in response to his babbling small talk. "I just wanted to apologise for what I said a moment ago. That was awful of me, insensitive, totally crass, and plain rude."

"It was. I ain't going to argue wiv you. But hey, apology accepted."

"I just assumed …" pausing, I hesitated with my hand positioned on my crotch and my mouth gaping.

"What?"

"Err, well …" pausing again, I chewed my lip, weighing up whether it was worth mentioning that I'd spotted him earlier and had come to the wrong conclusion. I deduced there was nothing to be gained by divulging my inaccurate assumptions. "Nothing."

"Okay. Anyway, I'd better get going," he shrugged, then nodded before scooting away, leaving me facing the window in wet clothes, covered in tea, and metaphorically soaked in regrets.

25

Pillow Talk

"There we go, darling. Earl Grey with lemon." Deana set the tray on the patio table before peering at Terry, who slouched in one of the rattan chairs while chain-smoking. "Now, remember, don't venture to the bottom of the garden. Otherwise, we'll have that nosey harridan, Dreary Drake, calling the police, claiming burglars are lurking in the bushes."

Terry glanced up, closing his left eye to avoid the smoke that drifted from the cigarette clamped securely between his lips.

"And by all means, you can remove your clothing, give me something to feast my eyes upon, but stay up this end near the patio and flower beds; otherwise, that pious old dragon will once again report lewd activities taking place at the Burton residence. Now, we wouldn't want that, would we?"

Terry tutted and dismissively shook his head.

"Oh, Terence, I'm just trying to lighten the mood. You've been nothing but a dolorous grunge since that incident in the pub. Now, come on, are you going to enlighten me as to what all this pent-up anger is regarding? You know, suppressing and keeping a tight lid on your emotions might be very British, but it's not healthy. I regularly poured my heart out to my therapist. Very empathetic they were … stimulating, you might say."

"You saw a shrink?" Terry quizzed, before taking another long drag on his cigarette.

"Therapist, darling. Everyone, who's anyone, has a therapist. It's about your social standing in life. You can't mix in certain circles without being in therapy. I mean, that's all us girls chatted about during our luncheon dates. Well, men as well, of course," she chortled. "Once a week, every Thursday morning, I enjoyed a session."

"Therapy," he scoffed. "So, you lie back on a couch and spout off your innermost thoughts to some old git, presumably wearing a white coat and peering at you over his half-moon glasses whilst analysing you? Ridiculous."

"No, not at all. Robin, my therapist, doesn't wear glasses, has only just turned forty, and there certainly isn't any leather couch involved. Pillow talk, mainly."

Terry shot her a look. "Pillow talk? I take it you're not referring to a film with Rock Hudson and Doris Day?"

"No, darling. Robin listened whilst pleasuring my senses."

"You paid for sex?"

"No, darling. I paid for therapy. The sex was part of the process of relaxing me so that I could talk freely and openly."

Terry raised an eyebrow.

"Rock Hudson, now that's a man who could make a girl quiver. My mother had a thing about that man."

"I presume he's dead now. Well, Doris Day, too, I suspect. I don't see them having to roam the earth completing missions." Terry muttered, before shifting in his seat to face Deana. "Also, I imagine that Rock Hudson would have experienced a slightly easier time with ghostly Doris than I have with you."

"Charming, I'm sure." Deana turned her nose up. "And, just to put you straight, Doris Day is very much alive. Unfortunately, poor Rock Hudson died many years ago, presumably sometime after you. I can't remember exactly when, but I recall it was due to an AIDS-related illness."

"AIDS?"

"Yes, darling."

"I thought ... I thought only—"

"Gay men?"

Terry nodded and went to speak, but Deana interrupted him.

"No, darling. That's not the case. Close your mouth; you're giving off an appearance which resembles a stuffed carp mounted on a plaque hanging from the wall of some smelly old fisherman's hut. An appearance that is not particularly flattering, I might add. Now, as I was saying, Rock Hudson was gay, but that's immaterial. The man demonstrated high levels of bravery and a valorous character when he came out. His death made bigots like you realise that AIDS is a disease, not an immoral affliction."

"Really?" Terry smirked. "Are you sure? Hudson, bent?"

"Oh, Terence. Christ, I keep forgetting you've been dragged out of some bygone heathen era with Pecksniffian, sanctimonious, outdated attitudes. You'll be calling him a poofter next."

"Pecksniffian?"

"Dickens, darling. Know your classics. Did you go to school, or were you consigned to the workhouses, begging for cups of gruel? Seth Pecksniff is a character from *Martin Chuzzlewit*, a cheat, and charlatan, who believed he held high moral values. In the story, he also happens to have two daughters, just like you, you bigot."

Terry offered his preferred po-faced frown, not knowing how to respond. "So, apart from humping your brains out, what did this Robin chap deduce from your rambling pillow talk?"

"I got the distinct impression you thought it all poppycock."

"Yes, well, good description. But just for entertainment purposes, what pearls of wisdom did he come up with during your weekly sessions?"

"He, darling, came up with nothing."

"There, told you. Poppycock," he chuckled.

"Robin is a she. A gorgeous virile, sensual lover who could assist me in reaching levels of sexual arousal that very few men have achieved."

Terry sat up, fumbling for another cigarette from the packet that lay on the table. "Really?" he grinned and repeatedly twitched his eyebrow. "Lezzy acts between you and her?" he smirked.

"My God. What are you, fourteen? That silly, smutty smirk affords you the look of a pubescent adolescent who's just discovered his father's stash of dirty mags."

Terry sniggered. "So, this Robin bird was a todger dodger type? What was she, all butch and macho?"

Deana slowly shook her head, offering him a contemptuous lip curl. "Robin is what is known as a lipstick lesbian. A stunning woman whose beauty is reminiscent of mine. That, according to her, makes me a dopplebanger, as in I like to bed people who appear similar to me."

"Wow."

"Darling, you're salivating. It's not a good look. Also, as I said, I find your childish, immature attitudes somewhat tiresome. I had no idea you were so ..."

"What?"

"Puerile!"

"Oh."

"Lilliputian, illiberal, narrow-minded, parochial, and ... and heterosexist!"

"You finished?"

"Probably. So, darling, are you suggesting, to satisfy your typical male smutty mind, if I can locate another willing woman ghost, you're up for a threesome? Can I then, finally, get my hands on the contents of your boxer shorts?"

"You know any other female ghosts?"

"Hmmm. No, pity." Deana screwed her face up as she plucked up her cup before popping in a slice of lemon. "Now, make yourself useful and light me a cigarette, darling."

Terry smirked as he made a grab for the packet of cigarettes before lighting one and handing it to Deana.

"Thank you."

"It's a man fantasy thing. Don't get all upset. It's ... it's just—"

"Puerile!"

"Yes, okay. Now, on the subject of female ghosts. Where d'you think that spectre-type woman snuck off to after you chased her?"

"I don't know. As I said, when I got out of the pub and scooted down the hill, she was nowhere to be seen. It was like the woman had just disappeared in a puff of smoke. Of course, then I spotted those two gits and thought I'd better nip back and warn you they were on their way in."

"She has to be a ghost, though."

"Well, the old witch must be. No one can see me apart from the dead and some small children." Deana sipped her tea before smacking her lips together. "Ah, that hits the spot." She gently placed her cup on the saucer before waving her cigarette at Terry. "What she said, vainglory ... you don't think I'm like that, do you, darling?"

"You ... conceited, arrogant, self-centred, egotistic, Scarlet O'Hara-ish, never," he scoffed, then smirked.

"Touché, darling. Touché."

"So, who do we think she is? And what about that warning? What was it? Don't go looking for Jean's killer."

Deana bristled before taking a long drag on her cigarette. "Makes me all aquiver thinking about it. I wonder if she's the killer." Deana shifted forward in her seat. "Darling, you think that old woman died under the knife? Jean was a surgeon. Perhaps she sneezed or got distracted when wielding her scalpel, killing the woman on the operating table. Could it be that she's meting out vengeance for Jean's cock up?"

"What about the other surgeon? She couldn't die twice, so then have two doctors to enact her revenge upon."

"Oh ... I see your point. Perhaps they were working together, like a tag team, taking it in turns to make incisions."

"What about Tetris?"

"Tetralogy, I think you mean. Tetris is that game you like to play on the iPad."

"Yes, alright. But you said something about four ... four will die. Unless the woman was undergoing multiple organ transplants, I can't imagine she had four surgeons digging their scalpels around in her body."

"No, probably not. Anyway, unless the police are incompetent, surely they would have already investigated that route. Relatives of the dead, not ghosts, of course."

"That probably means the woman who called herself the winged messenger is not the killer."

"Hermes ... the winged messenger of the Greek Gods. Hermes wore winged sandals and flew between the earth and the underworld."

"That's it then. She's from upstairs. The Powers-That-Be sent her to tell us to focus on Ginny and not to worry about Jean's killer."

"Oh, you think so? But, darling, how would she know you and me?"

"Maybe she didn't, as in met us before, but just read a briefing document about us."

"Oh, well, bloody charming, that is. So that bloody lot has a file that states I'm vainglory."

Terry smirked.

"Shut it, Walton," Deana warned with a wave of her cigarette.

"Can't you have a word?"

"A word?"

"The Powers-That-Be … y'know, grab a word in their shell-like. Find out if she works for them, or do we need to worry about a ghostly murderer lurking about whilst systematically knocking off doctors?"

"Oh, darling, it doesn't quite work like that."

"How does it work, then?"

"It's complicated."

Terry groaned.

"Come on, darling. Let's not get tetchy. Let's forget that gnarled old bag and get back on track. What's with this issue with Jean? Now, come on, tell me. I presume you knew her?"

Terry nodded, taking a few quick puffs on his cigarette before squishing the butt in the ashtray.

"Darling?"

"Jean Allsopp was my fiancée."

26

Bend It Like Beckham

Now feeling somewhat frustrated with myself, specifically that crass accusation levied at Viv, I barbarously yanked my t-shirt over my head, fighting with the material that stretched and caught on my elbow, refusing to comply. After a battle akin to watching a three-year-old attempt to undress, I hauled the garment free, thus causing my hair to cascade chaotically over my face.

"Sake," I growled, lobbing the offending item to the kitchen lino without inspecting the extent of the tea stain. Before hot-footing through to the bedroom, where I planned to rummage through my collection of suitcases in an attempt to locate some clean attire, I swung my foot at my crumpled t-shirt, resulting in said garment flying towards the window. I doubted even my teenage crush, David Beckham, could have done better.

At least my tea-spilling episode would force me into a spot of organised unpacking, rather than the somewhat skittish rummage I'd performed last night when searching for clean undies and a bed-shirt.

As I scraped my hair away from my face, I hollered in fright before swishing my left arm across my exposed bra-covered breasts.

Viv, who'd once again cupped his hands against the window, dropped his jaw, holding that position before glancing away. "Oh, shit. Sorry," he shouted.

Whilst dropping to a crouched position, with my arm still clutching my chest, I scurried away down the corridor to the bedroom. After a quick poke about in the one open suitcase, I snatched up and threw on a rumpled t-shirt and washed-out, although comfy, pair of black leggings before nipping back to the kitchen.

I hovered at the doorway and tentatively peered into the kitchen. Although fully expecting Viv would have sensibly skedaddled away due to the embarrassment, rather than bowl straight in, I thought it would be prudent to check he wasn't still standing there with his face pressed to the glass. As I peered around the door, I spotted him still in situ, leaning the back of his head against the window whilst facing the equally odious tower block opposite to the one I now called home.

Whether he just decided to perform an about-turn at that precise moment or benefited from extrasensory perception and thus detected my silent creep back into the kitchen, he again cupped his face against the window. He offered a one-handed finger wave as he spotted my furtive glances as I skulked near the door. Although not wearing attire I would generally like to be seen in, usually just worn for lounging in when having a slob day, I huffed, accepting I couldn't ignore him and padded over to fling open the window.

"Hi, Ginny."

"Hi again." I could feel my cheeks burning.

"Sorry about … you know," Viv gestured to my t-shirt with a wagging index finger. "I wasn't peeping."

"You could get arrested for that."

"Yeah … yeah, you could. Sorry, I didn't know you were going to perform a striptease at the window before flinging your clothes around the room like some lap dancer."

"Excuse me! I wasn't bloody stripping!"

"Oh, well, I'm no expert, but it looked like you were from where I'm standing."

"Frequently visit lap dancing clubs, do you?"

"Yeah, occasionally, when on official business. Some of them are used for money laundering."

"Yes, well, I was just removing my stained t-shirt, that's all."

"Oh, right," he replied with a cheeky grin.

"Was there something else? I thought you were in a hurry to collect your cousin. Or perhaps you spend your free time peeking into women's bedrooms."

"This is your kitchen, I fink." Viv moved his head from side to side to peer around my torso, presumably to recheck the accuracy of his statement. "You were getting changed in your kitchen, not your bedroom."

"Yeah, alright. Whatever," I snapped back, whilst subconsciously folding my arms across my chest. Whether that was a defensive act, or the need to cover my body, I don't know. However, I certainly wasn't the sort to flash. Also, now feeling self-conscious regarding my bedraggled appearance.

Not that I'm prudish, but I'd never felt particularly comfortable with nudity. Also, Alistair hadn't helped and would often tease me, no scrub that, ridicule me about what he described as my mimsy attitude. When on our regular two-week summer holiday, usually in one of the many Greek islands, he'd comment about my insistence regarding the need to keep my bikini top firmly in place.

"All the other birds have got their tits out. You should show off those pert fun-bags because there's nothing worse than gawping at your milky tits and strappy tan lines," he'd often quote before pointing out many other women splayed out on their towels, showing off their wares. My soon-to-be-ex-husband had such a way with words.

It had taken our break-up for me to realise what had clearly stared me in the face throughout our relationship. Alistair had never loved Ginny Goode, the young woman he wooed or Ginny Strachan, the mature woman he dumped. He just wanted a trophy wife. The shallow man needed a 'bird' to show off to his mates to prove that he, Alistair Strachan, could pull what he perceived was a good-looking girl.

Throughout my teens and twenties, friends and boyfriends regularly complimented me on my looks – Karen's FAF addition to my dating app profile being another example. Also, somewhat embarrassingly, my mother entered my name for some hideous teen beauty pageant when at the difficult age of fifteen. However, I'd never seen myself as a fit-bird trophy-wife type. In fact, the whole idea of those labels wanted to make me gag. I was just Ginny Goode, a girl from a small town, hoping to find love and have a family – none of which I've managed to achieve.

Perhaps those alarm bells should have sounded way before I discovered him on top of that panting starfish. Alistair's disturbing growing obsession with internet porn and the offer to pay for a breast enlargement operation perhaps were clear signs that my husband was only interested in the size of my *fun bags,* as he put it. *"They are your best asset. It'll be good to keep them that way as you get older,"* he'd stated.

Alistair was his father's son, alright. I'd been stupid enough not to see what my mother clearly could. Anyway, I was already top-heavy. So, the thought of lugging around two silicon barrage balloons protruding from my chest, making me appear like some desperate ageing glamour model, along with the inevitable accompanying back pain caused by hauling around G-cup breasts just to satisfy my tossy husband was not going to happen.

Perhaps, when I rebuffed his offer, that's why he looked elsewhere. I momentarily wondered how long before Vegan-Thigh-Gap got whisked off to the breast augmentation clinic for an enhancement, which, going by my knowledge of Alistair's fetishes, she sorely needed.

Viv hovered in position by the window, appearing awkward after accusing me of performing a lap dance for all and sundry to see. I imagined those highly polished Chelsea boots would be shuffling back and forth on the piss-stained concrete landing. He checked his phone before glancing up to answer. "Letisha, my cousin, just texted me to say she's got a lift. So, I don't need to pick her up," he waved his phone in my face as if to prove the point.

"Oh. So, you thought you'd nip back and peek through my window, did you?"

"No ... I came back to check you were okay. Alright? I thought you looked a bit naffed off, that's all."

"Right," I huffed. "Look, you want a cup of tea?" I offered, feeling guilty regarding my accusation that the story about his mother's illness was a lie, along with barking at him when suggesting he was a peeping tom.

Viv appeared to be about to say something but stopped himself, leaving his mouth gaping.

"Oh, sorry, you can't because of the case, right? Or, now you've seen me in my slob clothes, you're thinking it's time to run," I barked again in a less conciliatory tone than when offering refreshments.

"Jesus, woman, are you always this aggressive?"

"Sorry," I snapped back, whilst hauling handfuls of hair from my face as I leaned forward.

Viv backed up a pace, holding his hands in surrender. "Frig sake, Ginny. I was just asking if you're okay, that's all."

"I'm bloody fantastic. Never better. Life is just so frigging peachy, y'know."

"Great. I'll piss off then. Deli knows how to get hold of me if you need anyfink," he threw over his shoulder as he turned to leave.

"Like what? Perhaps a stripper's pole for my kitchen. I could offer live shows from my kitchen window. What d'you reckon? Like me, that lot in *The Full Monty* were unemployed, so perhaps I should just get my kit off like the girl who lived here before me!" I bellowed, my voice rising inflexion, sounding somewhat hoarse as I strained my head out of the window.

Viv halted a few feet away and swivelled on his heels. "No ... I was finking if you're worried or in trouble. As I said, Deli has my number. I wouldn't trouble her today, though. Not with losing her mum."

"Shit," I muttered. "Viv ... Viv, I'm sorry."

Viv nodded and offered a thin smile.

"Look, I'm making another brew to replace the one I threw over myself. You sure you don't want one?"

"Go on then, why not?" he nonchalantly replied with a shrug of his shoulders.

Although I didn't believe, not for one moment, that his concerns regarding becoming involved with someone connected to an ongoing investigation were the true reasons he'd made a rather swift exit last night, but I really didn't want to fall out with the guy. Anyway, despite his rule-book attitude, it seemed that was the usual trope in films, where every police detective character ended up in a relationship with either the suspect or the victim. However, this wasn't Hollywood, nor was I a suspect in the investigation – well, I assumed I wasn't. And if I were, well, yes, that really would be the cherry on top of a rather shitty cake that my life appeared to have morphed into.

Viv padded back to the window and leaned his elbows on the sill as if waiting for me to squirt out a Mr Whippy 99 and pass it through with a Flake poked in the side.

"You won't get into any trouble with your boss, Foxy?" I threw over my shoulder, as I slid off the counter and flicked the kettle on before grabbing a couple of mugs.

"Nah, that won't happen. Foxy don't give a shit about procedures. For him, it's about results, regardless of the methods used or who he gets involved wiv. Rumour has it he's usually in a relationship wiv another officer, suspects, or both. He's already on his third wife, and she used to be one of his DCs."

"Oh. He and my ex should get on well," I chuckled, whilst making a grab for the tea bags.

"You'd fink she'd know what he's like, wouldn't you?" he mumbled, nudging his head through the open window again.

"Perhaps she chooses to ignore it. Maybe she has her head in the sand, like me with Alistair. Milk? Sugar?"

"Just milk, please."

"Sweet enough already, are we?" I blushed. "Sorry."

"Somefink like that. Hey, as I said, I'm sorry about last night. I just got a bit jittery. Heather drums it into me about following procedure, and I fink I take her warnings to the nth degree."

"Heather, that retired DCI? You know, your saviour?"

"That's her," he nodded.

"Well, I have to say, it sounds like to me that the woman's got her head screwed on."

"She's as straight as a die, that's for sure. Oi, you going to hoik that tea bag out?" He gestured to where I aimlessly pummelled the bag at the bottom of the cup. "I like a reasonably strong cup, but I ain't a hairy-arsed builder."

"Oh, sorry. Force of habit, I'm afraid. I like tea strong enough to stand your spoon up in. Anyway, I understand. Taking me on a date could leave you compromised if I was discovered to have murdered my mother-in-law." I placed his cup on the windowsill, offering a whimsical smirk.

"I take it you didn't?"

"No, Officer. Not guilty. However, if you discover my husband's body parts cut up into bite-sized pieces and scattered liberally in the Thames, I'm your girl."

"I'll bear that in mind. Has somefink else happened?"

"Nothing like yours, I imagine, but I've had a super-shit day."

"Oh ... you wanna talk about it?"

"Maybe ... look, this is a bit odd ... you know, chatting through the window. You want to come in?"

Viv, mug in hand, hesitated.

"Oh ... forget it. The 'rule book'," I offered the bunny-ears gesture.

"Go on then, why not?"

"You want to check with Heather first?"

Viv frowned.

"I mean, d'you think you should check with your retired DCI before stepping into a woman's flat with the intention of drinking tea, bearing in mind said pole-dancing woman could be a suspect?"

"Oh ... I fink I'll risk it."

"Very brave of you."

"Anyway, by the sounds of it, you already know about the conversation my DCI had wiv Mel and Helen Strachan today, so I guess there's no harm."

I presume my surprised expression indicated I had no idea what he was jabbering on about, which I didn't.

"Shit ... I've blabbed without checking what you know. Heather would dish out one of her famous bollockings for that."

"I've never met the woman, but from what I gather, I guess she would." I nudged my head, indicating the front door. "Come on, Officer, you'd better come in and enlighten me."

27

Bang Bang – My Baby Shot Me Down

Once reunited with his mug of tea, Viv surveyed my kitchen, a collection of cheap fitted, '80s-styled honey-pine units. Similar to the white goods and basic furniture, I suspected all were purloined from skips, or at best, eBay. That said, although dilapidated, the flat was spotlessly clean. Either the landlord had installed a crack team of cleaners, or the outgoing porn star took pride in her housekeeping. After meeting my landlord last week and going by his apparent lack of interest in personal hygiene, I suspected the latter.

"You'll have to excuse the look," I winced, as I plucked my mug from the countertop. "Look, I've not had a chance to unpack my things, so this is all I could find to throw on." I rubbed my hands down my t-shirt in a pointless attempt to iron out the creases.

"I fink you'd look hot in anyfink."

"Christ, you sound like that barista boy in town. Although, if I'd bowled in there looking like this, I very much doubt he'd have offered to take me out to lunch at Maccy' D's or wherever."

"Ah, him. The git who I need to arrest for wielding an offensive ponytail."

"That's him. Anyway, now you don't need to, do you?"

"Sorry?" Viv lowered his mug from his lips.

"Well, that was when you thought ... y'know ... we might go on a date, sort of."

Viv performed that opening and closing mouth routine as if about to say something, but changed his mind.

"Hey. It's okay." I waved my hand as if to scrub away what I'd said, clearly clocking that I'd caused Viv to feel awkward. "So, come on then, apart from surveying this shithole, what was that meeting about with your DCI and Mel?"

"Okay, but listen. Ginny, I have to be careful about what I say." He raised his mug. "Nice cuppa, by the way."

"Viv!"

"Okay. So, apart from following procedure, I try to keep on the straight and narrow so as not to compromise my position. The last fing I can afford to do is throw away what I've earned because of a loose tongue."

"I get that. But come on. Now you'll have to spit it out. I promise I won't mouth off to anyone." I hooked my hair behind both ears to ensure I could hear what he was about to say, mindful that I'd already broken a promise when confronting Ali with the information Viv divulged the previous night.

Viv shrugged after taking a couple of sips of tea. "Jean Strachan *was* murdered. We know that for certain because we're already investigating another murder wiv basically the same MO."

"Oh, God. Who?"

"A doctor who worked with Jean Strachan up at Fairfield General. We discovered him earlier this year."

"You're joking! Two doctors died this year, and both in suspicious circumstances?"

Viv, mug poised at his lips, nodded.

"Christ, you've got a serial killer on the loose, hunting out doctors?"

"No. If it were a serial killer, there would need to be three or more murders. You remember the note Jean was holding?" Viv waited for my nod. "Well, so was the other victim when we discovered him wiv a broken neck at the bottom of the stairs."

"Christ," I muttered. "Revenge meted out by some patient's family? Jean and that other doctor screwed up an operation, perhaps?"

"The only connection *is* the hospital. We're not looking at anyone in the family, but there is definitely foul play."

"I presume Alistair knows?"

"I'd imagine so."

"Gotta say, I'm a bit shocked. I know Helen's been banging on about it, but I just thought that was her way of dealing with what happened."

"The DCI told them about the other murder to encourage Helen to stop her social media campaign in case it derailed the investigation or, if we catch the perpetrator, any impending court case."

"Wow. Well, apart from being a tosser, Ali was right all along. Like his sister, he wouldn't accept the suggestion about suicide."

"On the subject of your husband, I take it he's the cause of your crap day?" he questioned, skilfully diverting the direction of our conversation. "Not wishing to stick my nose in," he added, before slurping his tea.

I dismissively waved my hand as if swatting a hovering wasp. "Oh, nothing compared to yours. Look, I'm so sorry to hear about your mother."

"Fanks, although it's been on the cards for some time. As I said, her health has been an issue for some years. So, come on, that prat you're married to has presumably caused more irritation."

"Yeah, you could say. Another argument with that idiot, along with meeting a strange man and imagining flying beer glasses."

Viv raised his eyebrows.

"Not glasses that have been thrown like in a pub brawl. But actual glasses flying on their own, as if commanded to do so by some witch's spell."

"Oh," Viv slowly nodded. His po-faced frown and furtive side glances towards the front door suggested he was seriously considering it was time to leave.

"Yeah, I know. That sounds ridiculous." I offered a nervous giggle, realising how my suggestion of witchcraft at play might sound to this seemingly well-adjusted man.

"De dark arts at play, ma boy. Tis Satan who darken ya soul, as my mother would say," he chuckled. "Or used to say," he added in a sombre tone.

"Yes, I'm sure. Anyway, I'll come back to that. So, after ripping Alistair's head off for what he said about ... oh, shit," I winced. "Sorry, I know that what you told me was confidential."

An awkward silence hovered between us, which I felt compelled to fill. "I'd offer you a biscuit, but I haven't got any. Sorry, are you mad at me?"

"For breaking a promise not to blab to your husband or not having any biscuits on offer?"

"Err ... well, both, I guess. Probably more concerned about the blabbing issue." I offered my best repentance-styled wince, hoping that would be enough of an act of contrition.

Viv held his palm aloft. I wasn't sure if that was acceptance of the lack of Hobnobs or Digestives on offer or for me not to worry about confronting my husband about his taped statement where he'd suggested that our lovemaking was akin to banging some corpse in the morgue who was as dry as a bucket of sand.

"Kill Bill ... kill Alistair," I muttered to myself, thinking about his sodding comment about our lovemaking. Like *The Bride*, I wished vengeance upon the man who betrayed me, and perhaps I should have bitten his tongue off as I lay there corpse-like. However, unlike Uma Thurman, I didn't own a *Hattori Hanzo sword.* That said, even if I say so myself, I reckon I'd look pretty frigging hot in a yellow jumpsuit.

Due to the fact that Viv hadn't commented regarding my mutterings about committing murder, hadn't walked out for fear of being in the presence of some deranged scorned woman, and appeared to be content to continue sipping his tea, I decided he'd accepted my apology and bashed on with my story.

"Yes, well, what Alistair said to you incensed me. Sorry, but I just couldn't let it go." I placed my mug down to avoid slopping my tea, presumably a subconscious act that my brain decided upon, knowing my next statement would require hand signals to emphasise the point. "Then, can you believe, after I found out my tossy husband has also been screwing our receptionist, I somehow ended up going for a drink with some random bloke who seemed to know me. Well, know about me. Sort of. Well, no, he did, I think. But he was a nutter ... definitely a nutter. Well, I think he was. And then, as I said, a self-levitating glass threw beer in my father-in-law's face, if you see what I mean."

Viv frowned. "Not really. Are we back to de dark arts, or that black magic my DCI keeps asking me to employ? 'Come on Kananga, use that voodoo magic all you coloured lot have'," he imitated Foxy, who I presumed, going by the accent portrayed, possessed a gruff cockney accent.

"Christ, I still can't believe he said that and can get away with it."

"Yeah, that's not the worst of it. I made the mistake of pointing out that Dr Kananga doesn't possess voodoo powers. It's Solitaire who was the psychic medium, and Baron Samedi was a voodoo spirit."

"You know your Bond films."

"Yeah, classics, all of them."

"What did he say when you imparted your greater knowledge?"

"I fink he said that all us lot have links to witchcraft."

"Viv, you must report the man."

"I have, once ... the senior ranks all pulled together, so he got away wiv it. Most of the top brass are all members of some secret club."

"You should take it higher. That can't be allowed to continue."

"That's what Heather said."

"She's right!"

"Probably. Oh, and I remember the dick also said he wouldn't mind banging Jane Seymour as well."

"Yes, well, I suspect most men have said or thought that."

"You look a bit like her, you know."

"Viv ... don't go down that route. We know where we stand, don't we?"

"Yeah," he nodded, presumably accepting that throwaway compliments were not where our relationship was at.

Despite my concerns about my ability to make sensible choices, our failed romantic relationship was purely down to him and his holier-than-thou love of the rule book. So, complimenting me, or flirting, after making that decision outside my flat, were now pointless and unnecessary.

"So, let's assume Solitaire or Baron Samedi aren't involved, but you reckon you saw a glass fly?"

"Yeah, I guess that sounds a bit nuts, doesn't it?"

"Just a smidge."

"Well, it was ... nuts, I mean. But you should have seen it."

"I can imagine."

"Can you?"

"No. Sorry, I have no idea what you're talking about."

"Christ, sorry, I'm babbling. Are you annoyed I confronted Ali?"

Viv continued to sip his tea, presumably taking a moment to decide whether the sensible course of action was to get the hell out of my kitchen and as far from me, the witch-believing mad woman, as possible. Whilst his deadpan expression gave nothing away, I felt the need to keep babbling.

"You don't need to worry. Ali wouldn't say anything to your lot. I've discovered he's been dabbling in a bit of insider trading. I imagine he will want to avoid the police like the plague," I nervously chuckled, before my face dropped when remembering I was chatting with an officer of the law.

"Insider trading?"

"Oh. Shit. Yeah, I think so," I grimaced, regretting opening my big mouth. "He threatened me, saying that if it ever came to light, he could ensure that the trail led back to me, not him. He reckons he's covered his tracks, so I would end up going to prison." I chewed my lip, awaiting his reaction.

Viv placed his cup down before pushing his jean-clad bum away from the worktop and stepping towards me. I involuntarily stepped back, wide-eyed, fearing he was about to cuff me and haul me off to the police station.

"Hey, it's alright," he whispered, gently stroking my arm. "You've made me aware of a potential crime. Of course, I should probably act on that information. However, that's for Fraud to deal wiv. Also, as I know what my sister gets up to, I can hardly hold the moral high ground, can I?"

"No ... I guess not," I whispered, losing eye contact, instead choosing to focus on the pattern formed by the collection of cigarette burns in the faded-blue lino whilst trying to decide if it resembled Ursa Major. Not that I'd ever been interested in star gazing as such, but Alistair had set up a telescope in the living room of our penthouse flat. He would try to educate me about the constellations, or constipation, as I like to call it. He'd said star gazing is proven to ease the mind and rejuvenate our spirits. For sure, it had rejuvenated his desire for someone other than me. Unlike Sir Patrick Moore, and following my recent discoveries, I wondered if Alistair had used that equipment to spy on positions closer to earth. Perhaps the bedrooms of the flats opposite. *Sick pervert.*

"Ginny?" With his hand on my elbow, Viv tried to break my trance.

I glanced up, snorting in a lungful of air in an attempt to control my breathing.

"Sounds like he's chucking veiled threats at you, if you ask me."

I shook my head, causing my hair to uncouple from the back of my ears. "No, I don't think so. Somehow, I think my brother has found out and is trying to blackmail him."

"Your brother?"

I bowed my head and picked at my nails. "That's what Ali said. I've tried to ring Jules, my brother, but he's not picking up."

"Oh."

"Have I talked myself into an interview room?"

"No. Come on, drink your tea. There's no evidence of any crime. I'd suggest you get hold of that brother of yours and tell him to back off 'cos blackmail is a crime."

"I will," I groaned out. "What will happen? I don't think I can take much more," I squeaked out, my bottom lip starting to tremble.

"Hey, there's probably nothing to it. Your ex would be an idiot to dabble in something like that. Your brother has probably got the wrong end of the stick and thought he'd get back at your husband for what's happened between you two."

I offered a thin smile. However, from what Ali had said at lunchtime, he had dabbled. If it all came to light, I could sink further into that puddle of stinking excrement, which I was already wallowing around in at about chest height.

Letting go of my arm, Viv grabbed his tea. "So, come on then. Strange men and flying glasses. What's all that about?"

Although a meal in a country pub and our brief conversations thus far couldn't be enough to elevate Viv to close friend status, I found myself blurting out the day's events. Also, for some unknown reason, I felt it necessary to impart upon him the background information about Terry Walton. Details that I'd only previously divulged to Karen earlier in the week. However, I felt comfortable in his company. By employing his well-practised listening skills, he stayed attentive, not even raising a sceptical eyebrow when I finally got to the detail when describing self-levitating beer glasses.

"So, you have no idea who this bloke is?"

"Nope. Well, he reckoned he was that Deana woman's nephew."

"Have you looked him up?"

"Sorry?"

"Social media."

"Oh … I didn't think."

"Come on. You check out that name, and I'll make a call."

I plucked up my phone whilst Viv stepped into the hallway to make his call. Of the twenty or so Ian Beachams with a Facebook account, none sported a picture of the man I'd met at lunchtime. In fact, most appeared to resemble many profiles of those serial killer lookalikes that matchmaking website continued to fire at me with annoying regularity. I made a mental note to delete the app.

Due to my nosey nature, presuming Viv was making a call to a colleague, I stepped towards the open doorway, leaned through and hooked my hair around my ear as I tried to listen in. However, I couldn't grasp the conversation despite hearing him mention the name Ian Beacham.

Turning my attention back to my phone, I scrolled the Ian Beacham profiles on offer. Only one lived within a hundred miles of Fairfield, and he appeared to be a man well into retirement age. One account sported a profile picture of the Manchester United Club badge and, along with their privacy settings, that squashed any way of knowing that particular Ian's location or identity. I was led to believe that most Manchester United fans had never visited or been within the same area where that northern city nestled between the longitude and latitude lines. So, discounting the half a million or so Mancunians, that just left the other ninety-odd-thousand square miles he could reside in.

As I clicked off my phone, not bothering to investigate any other social media platforms, Viv stepped back into the kitchen, sporting a bemused look whilst still clamping his phone to his ear.

"Can you check that and get back to me? And remember, don't mention I've asked." Viv ended the call and bowed his head. With knitted brows, he studied the phone's blank screen, which he held in his palm.

"Viv?" I quizzed, presuming he'd asked a colleague to tap into the police database.

He glanced up. "Did you find anyfink?"

"No ... no Facebook profile, anyway. Well, not that I can see."

"I'm not surprised. However, listen to this. Deana Burton, previously Beacham, is on file, as is a certain Ian Beacham."

28

Rock the Boat

"Terence! Why on earth haven't you mentioned this before? All this time, we're running around trying to sort your Ginny out, and now you drop the bombshell that you were engaged to her damn mother-in-law. Christ!" Deana exclaimed, flinging her arms in the air.

Terry heartily dragged on his cigarette, allowing the smoke to funnel out of his nose before responding. "You finished your little rant?"

"No! I most certainly have not. Don't interrupt me, Terence. So, exactly how many women did you propose marriage to when you were alive? Don't tell me that was a ploy you used to lull them into a false sense of security so you could get your wicked way with them before you binned them off for your next conquest?"

"No, there were only two. Jean, then Sharon, who I married, of course. I'll ignore your little quip about multiple conquests."

"Alright. But why all the cloak-and-dagger theatrics? Why not mention before that you were engaged to Jean?" Deana lowered her voice and shifted forward in her seat.

"We're a team, darling. You and I shouldn't be harbouring secrets. If we're going to achieve a satisfactory result for our mission, we must pool our resources and share information."

"I didn't know Jean Strachan was Jean Allsopp. The penny dropped when Mel Strachan waltzed into that pub today. That name Strachan had been eating away at me, but I just couldn't place it. Then that parasitical, sanctimonious git stuck his ugly mug through the door and it all became clear."

"Hmmm." Deana topped up both cups, dropping a slice of lemon in each, whilst keeping her eyes on Terry, who seemed lost in his thoughts. "Darling, I think you'd better enlighten me."

Terry stubbed out his cigarette and snatched up the packet to light another before continuing his tale. "Jean and I stepped out together in the early seventies. I'd just got a job at Freshcom's and she was completing her medical training. We were young and thought we loved each other. Anyway—"

"So, you got down on bended knee? Oh, how romantic."

"I did." He pointed the cigarette lighter at her before lobbing it on the table, crossing his legs and taking a long drag on his cigarette. "No sooner did I have that ring on her finger, the cracks appeared in our relationship—"

"You found some floozy to fumble with in the electrical services cupboard behind the checkouts, perhaps?"

"No... please stop interrupting me."

"Can't help it, darling. You should know that by now. Come on, get on with it. If you don't spit it out soon, I'm liable to develop deep vein thrombosis if I sit here much longer."

Terry tutted. "As I was saying, we were young. She had her busy life as an intern up at Fairfield General, and Freshcom's shipped me all over the damn place, store to store. You know how food retail works."

"I do. So, you split up. Apart from sounding like some tear-jerking love story where Redford and Streisand can only reminisce about the way we were, what am I missing? What's the drama?"

"I'm coming to it."

"Well, hurry up. You're starting to sound like Dave Allen when he would famously trot out one of his long-winded stories. The only difference; Dave Allen was funny."

"Yes, he was. I take it he no longer performs?"

"Terence! Get on with it. And no, the poor man is like you and me. Dead!"

"Right, okay. After we split, I lost touch with Jean, only meeting up with her again at a party in '75."

"And which young floozy was hanging off your arm at that point? Was the perfect little Sharon on the scene, or were you still rogering your way through the female population of the south of England?"

"It was only a few years ago, so not that difficult to remember—"

"For you, darling," she interrupted. "As far as the rest of us are concerned, 1975 was half a lifetime ago."

"Yes, well. Anyway, the party was a shitty housewarming shindig that some bloke I knew from school and his girlfriend were throwing. I wasn't with anyone at the time, so I only showed my face to be polite before planning to nip off to the pub."

"Well, blow me down. Put the bloody flags out!"

"Sorry?"

"You ... not with someone."

"Oh ... yeah," he smirked. "Well, I met a girl there that night. So, the flags wouldn't be flying for long. Anyway, listen," Terry sipped his tea, then leaned over the table towards her, jabbing the cigarette's lit end in her direction. "Until that night, I hadn't seen Jean since we split up sometime in '74. The party was in full swing, and me and this girl I hooked up with, Suzy, if I remember her name correctly, were enjoying each other's company up in one of the bedrooms—"

"I can imagine. I don't need a blow-by-blow account of that part."

"Yes, quite. So, I nipped to the toilet, along from the bedroom where Suzy was getting comfortable—"

"Ripping her clothes off and waiting for you to return and pleasure her, I assume?"

"Something like that. So, I was just about to enter the bathroom when I heard this scream coming from one of the other bedrooms. Now, there I was bare-chested with the flies of my denims at half-mast, facing a dilemma ... do I nip to the loo and then back to enjoy the delights of Suzy, or investigate that scream—"

"I bet you went to the loo and back to Suzy, you horny little devil," she sniggered.

"No ... whilst contemplating what to do, the girl screamed again. Now, the record player was banging out a bit of *The Hues Corporation – Rock the Boat*, which I clearly remember because I thought perhaps I shouldn't—"

"Rock the boat. Don't stick your nose in and disturb them?"

"Precisely—"

"Oh, I loved that song. Soul music was my thing. *Band of Gold* by Freda Payne has to be my ultimate favourite. Did you like that tune, darling?" she quizzed, before closing her eyes and humming the ostinato of the chorus line. Now appearing to be in a trance, she waved her hands about, either conducting an imaginary orchestra or impersonating some hippy-type trip after partaking in some mind-altering drug.

"Quite apt for you. Seven marriages, most of which didn't last longer than a wine gum."

"Sorry, darling," she quizzed, halting her humming mid tune.

"Band of gold."

"Oh, yes, very droll."

"I can't believe anyone could amass seven marriages. It's just plain weird."

"I'm not weird, darling. I'm what you might call a limited edition."

"Limited edition," scoffed Terry.

"Hmmm. Yes, well, Dickie and I would have grown old together if it wasn't for Portly-Pete ramming his whopping great pantechnicon into the back of our car."

"Yes, whatever. You had your revenge when you murdered him."

"I did, didn't I? That was such fun," she chortled. "Now, come on, we digress. What happened next?"

"So, as I said, I heard another scream. Although it was none of my business, and that girl was waiting for me—"

"Suzy, the one whipping her knickers off, panting in anticipation of your return."

"Yes, the very same. As I was saying, although Suzy and I were about to get it on, I felt I couldn't ignore the situation. I was just about to knock on the bedroom door when I heard a crash and another shriek. So, sensing something untoward was afoot, I burst into the room. There I discovered Jean Allsopp pinned to the bed, her suede miniskirt up around her armpits, and her blouse ripped open with some bastard squirming on top of her with his denims positioned significantly lower than half-mast."

"He was raping her?"

"He was. He being Mel Strachan."

"Oh, Terry, no!" Deana shot her hands to her mouth before uttering the muffled question. "What did you do?"

"What any bloke should in those circumstances ... I punched that bastard's lights out."

"But ... hang on ...they got married. Why would Jean marry a man who raped her?"

"Well, good question. But I have a theory. After ramming my fist through Mel's nose, the ensuing commotion alerted a few others who were canoodling on the stairs. A couple of lads helped me throw Mel out of the house. Jean, who was obviously in a bit of a state, said she and Mel had been going steady for a while but wasn't sure if she was ready for ..." Terry paused and nodded to his lap.

"Play a game of hide the sausage."

"Correct. But Mel forced himself."

"That still doesn't explain why she would end up marrying the man who forced himself upon her against her will."

"That's what I've been stewing on. Alistair Strachan is thirty-nine. Born August 1976. That party was November 1975."

"You think Jean married him because that night Alistair was conceived?"

"Spot on."

"Oh, that's awful. I would have sent the git packing, not married the bastard."

"I guess Jean felt she didn't want to bring her child up on her own. Maybe Strachan convinced her it wouldn't happen again. Who knows what happens behind closed doors?"

"I can see why you've been pondering all afternoon. Right, darling, light me a cigarette whilst I recap our situation."

"Another one of your synopses?"

"Yes. So, Ginny is in a spot of bother. That tossy husband of hers has conned the poor girl out of her home and livelihood. As I explained on the way home, the git has dabbled in a bit of illegal insider trading, which he claims he can pin on your girl if it all goes belly up. Also, we have Jules, Ginny's brother, who is indulging in a spot of blackmail against Alistair. Then, we have a serial killer prowling around with a penchant for murdering those in the medical profession and some old, gnarled witch warning us off whilst accusing me of being vainglorious. To add to the plot, we know Mel, the pervert Strachan, raped his future wife back in '75, and he's now wondering how you, Terry Walton, have reappeared thirty-odd years later. To top it all off, Ginny, poor girl, is probably wondering how those spooky events in the pub took place—"

"Your Wicked-Witch-of-the-West antics, you apparently employed?"

"Yes … and also the poor woman is trying to work out who Ian Beacham is and how he's connected to you, her dead father, Terry Walton."

"A mess, as usual,"

"Hmmm. Quite." Deana accepted the lit cigarette that Terry offered. "Thank you, darling."

"Okay. Do we have addresses for this lot?"

"Yes, I have Alistair's and Mel's. Unfortunately, the address for Ginny is the same as Alistair's, so I don't have hers."

"Somewhere on that bloody Broxworth Estate."

"Oh, yes, you said. Good God, not that place again, for heaven's sake."

"I'm afraid so. Ginny mentioned something about renting a flat up there."

"Christ. I can't go back there again. You know, dead and invisible aside, I really can't be seen in that hideous dump three times in as many months."

"Agreed. So, the plan …"

"Yes, darling." Deana shifted forward and rubbed his knee. "I'm all ears, sweety. What clever idea has that beautiful head of yours conjured up?"

"We have to focus our efforts on solving Ginny's little crisis. That was the brief from the Powers-That-Be, so we need to stick to it. The murders are a side issue we can't get involved in—"

"Agreed."

"Blackmail and poltergeist-type acts are our game. Now, that Jules may be a problem because, if he persists, he could land Ginny in trouble. So, we need a new angle."

"What you thinking?"

"Tomorrow, we need to have a rummage through Alistair's and Mel's homes and see what we can turn up."

"Good idea."

"Obviously, I can't be seen breaking and entering. So, I think you'll have to go it alone whilst I keep watch."

"Marvellous, darling. Nothing I like better than rummaging around in men's drawers," she smirked, running her finger towards his crotch. "Apart from a collection of Y-fronts, what will I be searching for?"

"I'm not sure. However, from what I've seen so far, Ginny is a clever, switched-on sort of woman. Alistair, although clearly capable of using an abacus, is a bit of a dick. I know Mel, and I know what a twisted git he is. Alistair could not have orchestrated all this against Ginny on his own. Mel Strachan is involved, and you need to discover something we can use against the bastard."

"Yes, sir!" Deana saluted. "This angel is ready for action."

"It's Charlie, Angel. Time to go to work," chuckled Terry.

"Oh, that was such a good series. I think I could have played the part afforded to Cheryl Ladd when Farrah Fawcett left. With my stunning looks and physique gracing the TV screens, that series could have run forever. They missed a trick there, you know?"

"I'm sure they did. However, Deana, I very much doubt Hollywood could have coped with you. Anyway, tomorrow, you'll be employing your invisible woman skills, not flaunting your physique, as you put it."

"Hmmm, pity that. I'm sure that grunge, Mel Strachan, has never enjoyed a woman like me rummaging around in his Y-fronts, whether he's wearing them or not."

29

The Whole Nine Yards

Just at the point when Viv announced that Deana and Ian were known to the police, Karen called my mobile. I glanced at it, deciding whether to answer or ignore it and call her back after Viv had left. However, knowing she'd fear the worst if I didn't answer, I accepted the call before tipping my head to allow my hair to flop away from my face and slapped the phone to my ear whilst raising a finger at Viv to indicate I wouldn't be a moment.

"Karen, can you call me back in a few minutes?"

"Course honey. You're okay, though?"

"Yes, I'm fine."

"Alright, I'll call you back in a mo … when the girls have finished their tea."

I ended the call and lobbed the phone down. "Sorry about that. It's my friend Karen. She worries about me."

"Should I go?" Viv gestured to the hallway.

"No. I'll speak to her later. You were going to say about Deana and Ian Beacham being on the police database?"

Viv hesitated.

"Shit … you can't say, can you?"

"Oh, bollocks. I've said too much already. Look, don't go blabbing this time." Viv reinforced his demands with a well-practised police officer-style wag of his finger.

"Yes, Officer," I smirked.

Viv snorted a laugh. "Seriously, though … I have to be careful."

"I know. Look, please don't tell me if it will compromise you or make you feel uncomfortable."

Viv pursed his lips before nodding, presumably to himself. "Okay, both Deana and Ian are on the police database. We arrested Deana a few years back for indecent exposure—"

"You're joking!" I blurted, before my jaw sagged.

"Yeah," he chuckled. "Dogging in a layby up near that pub we went to last night."

"Christ—all—mighty! My mother said the woman was a trollop, but that takes the bloody biscuit."

"No charges were brought to bear, but obviously, we have her on record. The odd fing, though, she died a few months back. RTA … road traffic accident. But somehow, her fingerprints are all over a crime scene of a burglary at some private investigator's office a few weeks ago."

"Oh, odd. Presumably, the trollop visited there before she died."

"The obvious explanation. Trouble is, there were letters and envelopes with her dabs on which post-dated her death. The mate I just spoke to said there were also a couple of girly mags published after her death with the woman's fingerprints plastered on nearly every page."

"Girly mags?"

"Yeah, you know. Top shelf men's stuff."

"I'm aware of what you're referring to, but I'm a bit surprised that a woman, presumably in her fifties, would be thumbing through that sort of publication."

"Well, you're right. Dats de work of de Devil, as Mum would say."

"Hmmm, I'm sure. The git who runs the convenience store in the main square spends all day looking at that stuff."

"Craig Willock?"

"I don't know his name."

"Big geezer, needs a wash."

"That's him."

"Yeah, the bloke's a pervert. Well known to us."

"Oh, nice. Anyway, talking of which, I'm a bit shocked Deana would be into that sort of stuff. My mother would never have looked at anything like that, and she would only be a few years older."

"Remember, Deana may have been in her fifties, but we arrested the woman only a few years ago for performing lewd acts in a public place."

"Blimey. But how come that crime scene was smothered in her fingerprints when she's already dead?"

"Don't know. Apparently, it's got the Robbery Squad a tad confused."

"I bet. What about Ian Beacham?"

"So, we arrested him in 1983 for assault."

"Oh, who did he beat up?"

"His wife, Deana."

"Charming."

"Not really. Ian Beacham, who's now in his early sixties, was married to Deana at the time. According to my colleague, the report states that Ian assaulted her when he found out she had bunked up with some bloke in a hotel bedroom at a works conference."

"My father," I muttered.

"Do what?"

"The man in that hotel room with Deana was my father, Terry Walton. The man who Mel Strachan believes took me for a drink at lunchtime today."

"Well, it couldn't be him, could it?"

"No. But why did Mel think it was? Why did the Ian Beacham I met today recognise Mel from back in the 1970s? How come he knew Jean and her maiden name? And, more to the point, how come he looks the spitting image of Terry Walton who's been dead for over thirty years?"

Viv shrugged. "I've no idea. But it gets more complicated. Ian Beacham, the bloke who's very much alive, who we arrested in 1983, is an only child with no children. Deana Beacham, dead, had one sibling, a brother, also dead, who also had no children. The man you met today may well be called Ian Beacham, but he cannot be the nephew of Deana Beacham, who had a fling with your biological father back in the 1980s."

"I don't get it."

"Me neither."

"He knew so much about me. How could he know about Terry Walton? How come he looks just like the man in that old photo who *was* Terry Walton?"

"Ginny, I don't know. I fink you need to be careful, though. He didn't say anyfink about meeting up again?"

"No … as I said, he handed me that solicitor's letter that suggests my bastard husband is hell-bent on ruining me, had a spat with Mel, then took off."

"Okay. The mate I just spoke to will do some digging for me. Hopefully, we can get some answers."

"We?"

"We need to know who he is, don't we?"

"Yes … but is that we, the police, investigating a murder? Y'know, this bloke could be involved. Or is that us, as in you and me?"

"What's the difference?" shrugged Viv, clearly struggling to understand my point.

"Viv … I don't want to sound callous, but discovering who killed Jean Strachan and that other doctor is no longer my concern. I'm sorry Jean's dead, but her bloody son is trying to unfairly ruin my life. So, I guess I'm just saying that whoever is out there knocking off doctors is a police matter. The bloke I met today, whoever he is, appears to be involved with Mel, so by association is involved with Alistair. I want nothing more to do with them."

Viv held his palms wide. "I get that, but—"

"Hang on, let me finish. As I said, that man I met today is now on your radar … yours and that racist boss of yours.

He might have trotted out some crap about wanting to help me, giving me a letter which he reckons an acquaintance of his acquired, whatever that means, but I know I have to set my life back on track. Only I can do that. Firstly, I get my bloody solicitor to pull his finger out and do what I'm paying the useless git to do. And secondly, find a job and get out of this dump. Chasing ghosts of my father and some wanton woman won't help me."

Viv glanced down at his phone, which he repeatedly spun around in his hand whilst rhythmically nodding his head, appearing to consider what I'd said. I waited, the constant noise of the estate filling the void. I glanced out of the window to spot the couple on the landing of the tower block opposite, who appeared to have restarted their slanging match, or perhaps they'd not stopped and I just hadn't noticed.

"Ginny?"

I turned away from gawping at the couple just as the man stormed off, rudely gesturing with his middle finger. The tone of his voice suggested he was launching a barrage of obscenities at the woman, who appeared to have won the argument.

"Perhaps I just want to help you. Maybe what's happened today has made me re-fink …" Viv shrugged as he paused. "Re-evaluate my life."

"Re-evaluate."

Viv raised his head, stopping the hand rotation of his phone. "Mum passing. It's made me fink about my life."

"Oh."

"I could let the rule book control my life or start living it."

"What does that mean?"

"Well, y'know ... what I said about you and me."

"Right ... so are you asking me out ... again?"

"Ginny—" Viv's pause allowed the sound of my phone vibrating across the worktop to interrupt his flow.

I glanced at my phone as it juddered, causing the flimsy worktop to hum like a reverberating drum skin. "It's Karen again. I said to call back in a few minutes. Sorry, but I'd better take it." As I grabbed my phone, I noticed Viv step away towards the door leading to the hallway.

"Hi, Karen. Hang on." I clutched the phone to my chest and grabbed his hand, hauling him back. "Stay ... please."

"Okay," he mouthed.

With my fingers, I made a T shape and nodded to the kettle before flicking my hair over my shoulder and slapping my phone to my ear.

"Hi, Karen."

"Hun, you okay? What's going on?"

"I'm fine. Nothing's going on."

"You've not been raped or murdered, then?"

"Not yet."

"Don't joke! Christ, Ginny, it's no laughing matter."

"I know, I know. But honestly, I'm fine. Anyway, I have a police officer standing in my kitchen right now. So, I couldn't be safer," I chuckled, raising an eyebrow at Viv, who glanced around where he stood at the sink filling the kettle.

"Oh, shit! What's happened? I'm coming to get you. You're going to have to leave there and come back to ours. I'll call Danny now, and we—"

"Karen … Karen. Nothing's happened. Viv is just a friend—"

"Viv? Who's Viv?"

"He's the police officer."

"He? Viv's a he?"

"Yes."

"Oh, odd name for a bloke. So, is he married? Is he hot?"

"Oh, Karen. Come on, it's—"

"If he's hot and available, ask him out."

"He is … very. But it's complicated."

"No, it's not. Christ, if you've got him in the kitchen, it's only a few yards to drag him through to the bedroom! Get on with it, girl."

"Karen!"

"Alright, I'm just saying."

"I know what you're saying. But not all women are sex-crazed nymphomaniacs like you!" I chuckled, before glancing at Viv, who now sported a quizzical expression as he searched my Old-Mother-Hubbard-styled cupboards for the tea bags.

"I can't help it," she sniggered.

I turned away from Viv to lean on the worktop.

"Karen," I whispered. "I can't talk now. Can I call you later or in the morning?"

"Yes, alright. But you are okay? You're not in any trouble?"

I turned back to face Viv. "No, honestly, I'm fine."

"Can I talk to him?"

"Who?"

"Viv, of course."

"No!"

"Why not?"

"Because you'll say something stupid, that's why."

"Viv!" Karen bellowed, causing me to yank the phone from my ear, fearing her hollering would cause a ruptured eardrum. "Viv, Ginny fancies you!"

"Karen!" I screamed, before placing the phone back to my ear. "Karen, behave!"

"Did he hear me?"

I glanced at Viv, who now leaned against the counter sporting an embarrassed smirk whilst waiting for the kettle to boil. "Oh, yes, he heard you, alright."

"Ring me later. I want a blow-by-blow account, if you get what I mean," she sniggered before ending the call.

I slapped my phone on the counter and took a few seconds before glancing at Viv.

"She's very loud."

"You heard it all?"

"Uh-huh. Only a few yards to the bedroom, apparently," he chuckled.

"Christ. Sorry. She's a wonderful person. Larger than life, I think they say."

"No shit."

"Right. So that's my second embarrassing episode today. Please, let's put that one behind us like the lap dancing incident from earlier."

Viv offered an exaggerated nod.

I padded over to the sink and playfully poked him in the stomach. "So, you were saying about having an epiphany?"

"Was I?" he quizzed, whilst turning to grab the kettle.

I offered a grunt, similar to the noise received when offering up the wrong answer on a game show. "No ... forget the tea. What were you saying?"

"Well ... perhaps you could give me another go? See if I can't make a better job of a second date than I did on my first attempt."

"What about me being involved with a live investigation?"

Viv shrugged. "Too bad, I guess. I take it you didn't murder your mother-in-law?"

"Correct, Officer. Not guilty. However, please bear in mind that I still might dismember my husband at some point. Feed the fishes, as they say."

"Yeah, I fink I'm aware that you want to merk the bastard."

"Merk?"

"Gang talk … murder. Anyfink else I should know that might force me to arrest you?"

"Insider trading."

"You're not guilty of that, are you?"

"No … no, I most definitely am not," I swished my hair from side to side to enforce the denial.

"So, there's nothing else I might need to arrest you for?"

"No. Is this relevant, Officer?"

"Only if you agree to a second date. Otherwise, no, my questions have no relevance whatsoever."

"Yes … yes, to a second date."

"And you fink I'm hot?"

"Sorry," I blurted, leaning my head back.

"You said to your friend. A minute ago. She said, is he hot, and you said, yes, very."

"Did I?"

Viv nodded whilst forcing his tongue into his cheek.

"So?" I nonchalantly shrugged, trying to give off an aura in direct contrast to my burning cheeks.

"Shall I make that tea?"

I grabbed his hand. "No. You want to walk those few yards with me?"

30

Run Baby Run

Whether the sunlight streaming into the bedroom, as that golden orb fired its bolt of spring morning sunlight between the two tower blocks opposite, or sensing someone hovering by my bed were the reasons for waking, who could tell. That said, as I gingerly cracked open one eyelid, the vision in front of me was not the usual sight that greeted me upon awakening. Instead, Viv's nude torso, specifically the area between thighs and stomach, filled my field of vision.

"Tea, for you," he whispered, placing a cup on the threadbare polypropylene carpet beside the bed. His bending action caused his face to come into view and his exposed lower torso to disappear.

"Got nothing against your pretty face … but I preferred the view you offered a few moments ago," I mumbled, then giggled, maintaining my comatose position whilst only employing my eyelid and jaw muscles for movement.

"Glad you like what you see," he whispered, before nudging my body with his bottom in an attempt to gain space that allowed him to perch his bum on the edge of the bed.

"You been flashing at the kitchen window? Surely a police officer shouldn't perform lewd acts in public?" my mumblings muffled by the quilt I buried my head into.

"After your striptease in the kitchen yesterday afternoon, I thought I'd follow your lead."

I spun around, flinging the quilt down, just managing to keep my naked chest covered whilst huffing away some wayward strands of hair before assessing the smirk he appeared to have plastered across his face.

"Morning."

"Oh, God," I muttered, feeling the wave of embarrassment rise up my body akin to a tsunami of hot lava. With my flailing right hand, I grabbed his pillow and flung it over my face, thus hopefully avoiding Viv from spotting my embarrassment before the inevitable flow of adrenaline forced a humiliating blush.

"Are you trying to smother yourself?"

"No ... although that might not be a bad idea," my muffled words drowned out by the soundproofing qualities of the thin, off-cast pillow gifted to me by Karen.

I felt his weight shift before I noticed a set of fingers curl around the top edge of the pillow and gently tug. His smirking face appeared.

"That would be a shame because I've only just met you. Also, if you die now, I can't arrest you when you dismember your husband."

"You'll have to dredge the Thames to find the evidence."

"A body, or body parts, are not required to secure a conviction."

"Oh ... pity."

"Are you going to come out from hiding?" Viv gently tugged the pillow away from my grip.

I flung the pillow away before frantically thrashing at my hair to cover my face. "Am I blushing?"

Viv gently lifted a few strands away with his index finger and peered into the gap he'd created. "Yep. Either that or you've developed a nasty case of scarlet fever."

"Oh, great."

Viv leaned down and grabbed my tea before shifting further up the bed. "Here, before it gets cold."

I shimmied up the bed, trying to hold on to the quilt with one hand, my other attempting to assist both heels in their attempt to push my body into a sitting position. As I reached the required pose, I dragged my hair over my shoulder while keeping hold of the quilt high on my chest before accepting the mug. "Thanks," I whispered.

Viv gently nudged the cup away from my lips before kissing me. "You're welcome."

While gripping the quilt's hem and holding it as if my life depended on it, I offered a winsome smile before gulping the weak, tepid liquid. Viv Richards might have provided the best sexual experience I'd enjoyed in many a long year, but if the piss-weak crap in this cup was anything to go by, his tea-making skills were nothing but piss-poor.

Viv pointed to the quilt that I white-knuckled clutched to cover my chest. "I've seen it all already. No need to hide."

"I'm shy."

Viv snorted a laugh. "Not last night, you weren't."

That tidal wave of blood flowed again, an unstoppable river of embarrassment that morphed my appearance into that of a baboon's arse. I winced, my shoulders sinking. "Was I …" I giggled, not knowing what to say.

"A ravenous sex goddess who ravaged my body for hours on end. Does that cover it?"

"Christ … was I that bad? I know I got a bit excited, but—"

Viv whisked his finger to my lips, shaking his head. He gently prised the cup from my grip and placed it back on the carpet. "I've recovered. As a reward for making tea, perhaps I could experience a re-run?" he stood, exposing his naked form before lifting the quilt and raising an alluring eyebrow at my body.

"Oh, ha. Christ … yes, I can see you have definitely recovered," I sniggered, as I shimmied across to allow him to slide in beside me. "Although I'm up for a re-run, I can't reward you for your tea-making skills. Specifically, lack of."

"Oh," Viv quizzed, as he yanked me close.

"Piss-poor performance, I'd say … you're going to have to improve."

~

"Thanks, mate, I owe you one …" Viv paused as the caller presumably took up the conversation on the other end of the line. Dressed in only a towel wrapped around his midriff where he stood leaning against the kitchen worktop after we'd showered, he raised his eyebrows at me and rolled his eyes, indicating the caller was prattling on.

I, dressed similarly, wrapped in a towel, secured in my cleavage, finger combed my hair as I listened into the ten-minute call he'd taken after we'd hurriedly bundled out of the bathroom and scooted into the kitchen searching for his ringing mobile.

"Yeah … yeah, cheers, mate. Look, I've gotta go. I'll catch you next week. Oh, remember, this is between us." Viv clicked off his phone and laid it face down on the counter.

"*8 Mile … Lose Yourself.* Is your ringtone symbolic?" I asked, flicking my hair around to my left side before continuing with my finger-combing routine. Although I'd always had super-long hair, something Karen said I should be thankful for, washing, combing and drying took that long it could almost be classed as a hobby.

"You know your Eminem."

"My brother Jules was always playing it. So, that film, about a boy from a rough neighbourhood trying to make it. That storyline resonates with you?"

"I'm black, not white."

"Nooo … really?" I exclaimed, bulging my eyes in mock horror. "I'd have never known."

"You know what I mean," he chuckled. "Jimmy Smith Jr., Eminem's character in the film, was from a white neighbourhood … it's different."

"You've still got the ringtone on your phone."

"The film's nang."

"Nang? I take it that's Nelson the Yardie speaking and not from Viv, the police sergeant's vocabulary?"

"Yeah ... I meant the film is good. It's this bleedin' estate. I slip back to my old ways when I come up here."

"You're not going to mug me, are you?"

"No ... but I wouldn't mind plundering that towel off you."

"Would you, now?" I coyly replied, before beaming at him when recounting in my mind our earlier frolicking. "You are a horny little thing, aren't you?"

"I most definitely would. Anyway, you suggesting I'm rough?" Viv smirked as he padded over to me, releasing my combing hand before flicking my locks over my shoulder and pulling me close with his arms wrapped around my back.

"My bit of rough?" I quizzed, raising a seductive eyebrow.

Viv pouted whilst rocking his head from side to side.

"You were in a gang ... a Yardie."

"Yardie is strictly Jamaican. I'm from Barbadian heritage."

"Sorry ... I'm doing a Foxy."

"No ... you're not totally wrong. I'm just being pedantic. Anyway, although I got into a few scrapes, I wasn't exactly Nicky Cruz."

"Run Baby Run."

"Oh, have you read it?"

I nodded. "My dad, Paul, had the book. I read it years ago."

"Mum, bless her, suggested I read it when I got caught up wiv a drug-running gang on the estate. I fink, the fact that he became a reformed character and an evangelist, she hoped it might have some effect on me."

"Did it?"

"No … never read it. I fink I used the book to prop up the monitor to my Xbox."

"Who brought you up … you know, when she returned home?"

"No one," he shrugged. "DCI French had just got hold of me at that point. I left the streets, looked after Deli, and got on wiv it."

"Oh."

"Look, I guess that makes my mum sound a bit shit … leaving her kids behind. She had a troubled life, in and out of hospital, sectioned twice. Basically, Mum wasn't equipped to look after us. She did her best, which is more than I can say for my father."

I nodded and laid my head on his chest, not knowing what to say or how to respond. Viv had endured an upbringing that led him into a life akin to those reprobates depicted in *The Cross and the Switchblade*. However, his unlikely saviour came in the form of the apparently ferocious DCI Heather French and not a small-town priest. It brought home to me, despite my current predicament, that I'd been fortunate to have enjoyed a stable and mostly happy upbringing – well, apart from the Saturday morning pony rides.

A couple of loud bangs on the kitchen window hauled me from my thoughts. As I swivelled around to face the window, keeping my head rested on Viv's chest, I spotted a schoolboy copying Viv's pose from yesterday as he peered through the window with his hands cupping his face.

"Gabe," muttered Viv.

"Christ, I've got no clothes on," I whispered, attempting to swivel Viv around to hide my modesty. Although wrapped in a towel, parading half-naked in front of my kitchen window was not normal behaviour for me. Now, I'd performed the same act twice in as many days. Courteney, the porn star, might have liked to show off her wares to all and sundry who passed by on the landing, but I felt the urgent need to invest in a roller blind.

"Oi, bitch. You sucking that filth's black cock," shouted Gabe, before poking his tongue into his cheek and feigning oral sex.

"Piss off, Gabe."

I watched in horror as Gabriel leaned against the railings on the other side of the landing and proceeded to pump his hips back and forth, shouting, "Bang that soft white pussy, Nelson," before taking off down the landing.

"Sorry, Ginny."

"How old is he?"

"Ten ... not got the best role models, I'm afraid. It's not unkind to say that Deli ain't too particular who she invites into her bedroom."

I cuddled him tight, almost feeling I needed him close to protect me from a world I didn't understand or had limited exposure to. Although, the irony of that thought, being with Viv would only cement my closeness to a completely alien culture.

"That phone call," I whispered, keen to discover what his colleague had said and to change the subject away from schoolboy smut.

"That was the mate who I spoke to yesterday. He's had a good dig around for me. What's for certain, the bloke who you met yesterday ain't called Ian Beacham."

I leaned back and looked up at him. "Who was he, then?"

"Look, I guess this might be a bit arse about face, now that we've ..." Viv nodded to the bedroom. "You know."

"Enjoyed multiple orgasms, as my mother would say."

"Jesus ... did she really?"

"Long story ... but yes, she did."

"Okay. Well, as I was saying ... we're kinda going out together, yeah?"

I shrugged, then nodded. "That's what you want?"

Viv nodded. "Yep ... you said timing was off the other day. Is your divorce all too raw?"

I poked his chest with my nail. "No, you lobbed a police procedural guide-shaped spanner in the works."

"Foxy reckons I've got it stuck up my arse."

"Foxy is starting to grow on me," I smirked. "I'm joking!" I added when clocking the horror etched on his face.

"Right, so, you ... you and me, we're a fing, then?"

"Yes ... we are a thing. Now, what's you and me becoming a thing got to do with a bloke that I met who isn't called Ian Beacham?"

"Okay. So, now you're officially my girlfriend; I'm going to pluck that police procedural book from my arse—"

"A lovely arse, it is too," I interrupted.

"Fanks ... yours ain't bad either. But, as I—"

"Christ, you're a bit shit on the compliment front. Although it's better than Gabe's 'soft white pussy' comment, I suppose."

"Yeah, sorry about that. Your arse *is* lovely."

I raised my eyebrows.

"The best arse ever."

"Better."

"As I was saying. The rule book can go to hell. This week, apart from securing a passport for Deli and making sure my cousin behaves herself, we'll investigate who this bloke is and why he wanted to meet wiv you."

"Is this official ... official police business?"

"Nope ... off-piste."

"Is that allowed?"

"Not really," he shrugged.

"What if this bloke is in some way connected to Jean's murder?"

"Then we'll find out. If he is, and we can gather enough evidence, then I wouldn't mind nicking him and ramming that up the arse of my useless DCI."

"Okay, where do we start? How are we going to find him?"

"Ginny ... I'm a detective. It's my job."

"Oh, good point," I sniggered. "So, Sergeant Richards, what's the plan?"

"We need to start with your father-in-law. Although you said yesterday that Mel thought that bloke was your long-since-dead biological father, he appears to be the only person who knows who he is."

"Yes, but that man can't be Terry Walton, can he?"

"No ... but I think Mel Strachan needs to answer some questions. And I hold a warrant card, which tends to make people talk."

31

The Bard of Ayrshire

"I see that git, Strachan, has done alright for himself, then." Terry nodded to the stone-built Georgian house nestled behind a double-gated driveway which swept around a well-maintained lawn shrouded by mature trees.

"Well, yes, I suppose he has. Just shows you, doesn't it? Crime pays."

"He's a nonce, not a thief."

"That's as may be, but there are the proceeds of that little insider trading caper."

"Yes, but I imagine that's a drop in the ocean compared to what that damn great place is worth."

Deana peered back at Terry as they hovered close to a dilapidated fence panel, the thick hedge branches protruding through the rotting slats positioned at the corner of the road opposite Mel Strachan's home. "There's a car on the drive, so it appears the despicable git's at home."

"I used to know a couple who lived just around the corner from here. Pleasant area, this. Lovely house … I remember it had one of those Victorian-type conservatories on the back." Terry vacantly mumbled.

"Friends of yours and your precious little Sharon's, were they? How very interesting. Not," snorted Deana.

Terry glanced down at Deana, who peered up at him while holding her semi-crouched position. "Oh … no, not really. Sharon didn't know them. Vicar and his wife, lovely couple. Why are you crouching and hiding in the bush? You're invisible."

"Oh, yes … I keep forgetting. Anyway, despite your boring reminiscing regarding old acquaintances best forgot, I'd have thought that a vicar and his wife were unlikely friends for you to keep."

"I think you mean should old acquaintance *be* forgot, not *best* forget."

"Sorry?"

"*Auld Lang Syne*, Robert Burns, I believe," Terry grinned. Nothing he liked better than pulling Deana up when she made an error. Over the few weeks they'd spent together, it had become a kind of sport that Terry enjoyed – putting the ever so annoying Bossy-Boots-Deana, with her better-than-anyone-else attitude, firmly in her place.

Deana straightened up and thumped her hands on her hips before peering up at him. "Terence. I wasn't referring to a poem by the Scottish Bard. I was merely pointing out this is not the time or place for you to trot out some tedious episode of reminiscing about the good old days and some stuffy démodé clergy and his presumably pious old nag of a wife. And, to wipe, cleanly and rather swiftly, that smug look off your face, there is a certain amount of conjecture as to which lines of that poem can be attributed to Mr Burns. Many are believed to have been written by many other talented Scottish poets long before. So, Mr Burns, who certainly penned some of those lines, cobbled them together in a verse that is known as Auld Lang Syne. Capishe?" Deana rocked her head from side to side and bulged her eyes at him.

"Oh," Terry offered his now perfected po-faced nod.

"Anyway, if we must discuss your old friends whilst preparing to indulge in a spot of breaking and entering, I might point out that I'm a little surprised you and a vicar had much in common."

"I only met him on a couple of occasions. His wife, Clara, used to run charity collections at the front of my shop. Y'know, tin-shaking sort of thing. Although I can't remember what charity she and her posse of do-gooders were collecting for."

Deana, refocusing on Mel's house, gingerly lowered a branch of the overgrown Leylandii hedge that offered some cover, thus negating any chance Mel would spot Terry if he felt so inclined to peer out of one of his front windows. "Not that I'm remotely interested, but if she was just some tin-shaking bleeding-heart type, how did you know where they lived?"

Terry cleared his throat but didn't reply, only offering up a wicked grin when Deana turned to glance back at him.

"Oh, Terry … you didn't?"

"Sunday mornings," his grin widening before elaborating further. "Her husband would be delivering his sermon, and Sharon would be nipping over to visit her parents."

"And you were providing a Sunday servicing to the vicar's wife?"

"Rampant little thing she was."

"Terence, you were a wicked man," Deana slowly shook her head and tutted. "I'm presuming Clara wasn't some old frump wearing a floral dress and complaining about bunions whilst serving tea at the village fête."

"Err, I only saw her in her negligee … definitely no bunions."

"I presume she didn't rattle a tin outside your supermarket dressed in a see-through, skimpy negligee, though?"

"No," Terry shook his head. "Tight jeans and boots … always been a sucker for boots."

"That's where I've been going wrong. I thought prancing around naked would draw your eye. But, no. It appears that all I needed to do is hook out my old gum boots from the understairs cupboard, and hey presto, your boxer shorts would finally drop."

"I was thinking more on the lines of high-heeled—"

"Yes, yes, alright, I get it," she hissed. "Anyway, I imagine the Powers-That-Be will take a rather dim view of your little tryst with the vicar's wife when we have to finally present ourselves after our missions."

"You can talk. Based on your track record, I think you'll have a slightly trickier time of it."

"Hmmm, you may have a point. I suppose I may have dabbled with some men of the cloth on a few occasions."

"Christ. Don't you know if you did or didn't?"

"Darling, it's difficult to tell when you're in the melee of a packed hot tub. Sometimes, during our little pool parties, it became so tightly packed that it wasn't always apparent who was doing who, if you see what I mean?"

"Not really. But I assume you didn't invite a prudence of vicars to join your debauchery of hedonists at your little gang bangs?"

"Oh, we had all sorts, darling. To follow your collective nouns themes, I'm quite certain we enjoyed the company of a doctrine of doctors, a wiggery of barristers, a smear of gynaecologists, a worship of writers, not to mention a reflection of narcissists. Certainly not a rage of maidens, though," she sniggered. "So, as I say, there's a high possibility that some devilish cleric was having his wicked way with me in the bubbles whilst I focused on pleasuring one of our other guests."

"Wow … think I missed out."

"You most certainly did, my darling. Nothing I would have liked better than to have you in a jacuzzi wearing gum boots or not. Now, let's focus. As much as what a lovely thought that is, rather than discussing your plethora of Sunday morning conquests in suburbia, let's get back to the plan."

Terry nodded. "Okay. It appears Mel is home, which is good."

"Is it?" she hissed.

"Yes, that way, we don't have to break in."

"Oh."

"Of course, I can't come in with you. I suggest you use the same trick you employed when gaining access to Joseph Meyer's house when on our saving-Kim mission."

"Ring the bell, then sneak in when he opens the door?"

"Spot on."

"And what are you going to be doing?"

"I'll just hang around."

"Well, I suggest you don't get any ideas about looking up Clara because, by now, I fully expect she *will* be dressed in a floral dress, complaining about her bunions."

"Hmmm … I guess she would be about your age now, or even a bit older."

"Yes … and most women my age, not that I'm old, of course, don't look as ravishing as me. I, dear boy, am an enigma. A hot, nubile, beauteous woman who just happens to look rather bootylicious in a pair of Wellington boots, I might add."

"I'll take your word for it."

"You do so. If you're a good boy, I'll give you a showing later. Now, try not to draw attention to yourself whilst I go and rummage around." Deana straightened up, tapped Terry's bottom and strode across the road, only to halt her advance when a car pulled up and parked in front of her. "Oh, bloody charming! The git nearly ran me over," she announced, peering back at Terry, who was in the process of nestling himself into the bushes.

"The driver can't see you, remember," Terry hissed out from behind several branches.

"Hmmm. Well, he was still driving too fast."

"Deana, look."

Deana followed the line of Terry's pointing finger, specifically the couple who'd now hopped out of the car and hovered near the entrance to Mel's front garden. "Oh, darling," Deana purred. "He's delicious. What a fine specimen of a man. He reminds me of my personal trainer, Conrad."

"The woman!" hissed Terry.

"Ah … I see. It's your little Ginny. Now, the plot thickens." Deana nipped back to where Terry crouched, embedded amongst the undergrowth. "Looks like your girl has a rather dishy friend. What d'you suppose we do now?"

"Follow them. Suppose they're going in to see Mel. In that case, you can listen in on their conversation," Terry hissed, from somewhere behind a sizeable flowering forsythia which he'd managed to shoehorn himself between that and the Leylandii.

Using both hands, Deana parted the bright yellow flowers and peered in. "Oh, there you are. You look just like *Little Weed* all tucked up in that bush."

"Sorry?"

"Terence, darling. Has it ever occurred to you why women have to utter twice as many words as men?"

"Sorry?"

"My point exactly. The reason is that us girls have to repeat everything because you men don't listen."

"Oh."

"Oh, indeed."

"Sorry, but you're going to have to explain to me what the blue-blazes you're on about."

"Babap ickle weed. That's what Bill and Ben the *Flower Pot Men* said to *Little Weed* at the end of each show. Don't you remember?"

"Jesus, Deana. And you accuse me of blabbering on about irrelevant twaddle."

"Oh, well, you were the one a couple of weeks ago reminiscing about *Watch With Mother*."

"Yes, that as may be. However, apart from having some branch stuck up my rectum—"

"You should be so lucky," she chortled.

"I'm trying to remain incognito, woman," Terry growled. "And you spreading the branches of this bush apart, like an inquisitive David Bellamy, is going to expose me!"

"Oh … well, at least you're not naked."

"Deana …"

"Yes, darling?"

"Go and follow them."

"Right you are, darling."

Deana released the branches, allowing them to ping back into place, thus concealing Terry from view before hot-footing after Ginny and the dishy-looking man as they strode along the wide gravel path towards Mel's front door. As she caught up with the couple, Deana trotted around them, performing a corkscrew formation as she inspected them from each angle.

"Lovers ... I can tell. You lucky girl. I wouldn't mind betting you don't have to slip on a pair of Wellies to get your man to perform."

32

Spectre

"Viv ... Viv," I tugged his arm, effectively halting our purposeful advance towards my father-in-law's front door. Although not relishing the thought of spending a nanosecond in Mel's company following that odd incident in the pub yesterday lunchtime, I knew Viv was right. I needed to know the true identity of that bloke claiming to be Ian Beacham, Deana Beacham's nephew, which he clearly wasn't. So, starting our investigations here was as good as anywhere, based on the fact we had very little information to work with.

However, my trepidation about facing Mel was not the reason I encouraged Viv to check his stride. Whether or not Ian had spiked my drinks yesterday lunchtime, today I'd only consumed tea – one cup of Viv's piss-poor offering and two of my own, hairs-on-your-chest, builder-type cups – so that could only mean the hallucinations I now appeared to be suffering from were not due to some mind-altering drug.

"Ginny, you alright?" Viv halted, quizzically glancing at me before following my gaze down to the gravel drive.

"Can you hear that?"

"What?"

"Stand still a minute. The gravels crunching all around us." I swivelled around, following the crepitating sound. "There! Look, those stones moved."

"Ooh. She's a sharp one. Best I stand still for a wee moment, methinks." Deana glanced down at the thick mat of pea-shingle, specifically where her Michael Kors baby-pink ankle boots depressed the small stones, whilst praying Ginny or her man didn't spot the indented gravel which under her invisible designer footwear would presumably have formed two size-four, boot-shaped dents.

Viv stepped back towards me. "Stand still," I hissed, holding my position as I pivoted my waist to glance behind, performing a manoeuvre akin to as if I'd inadvertently stepped into a minefield and one false move could result in catastrophe.

"Good job I wore these today. Pea-shingle can play havoc with an opulent pair of four-inch-heeled Jimmy Choo's. Wouldn't you agree? Apart from the obvious problem of ruining a perfectly good pair of designer shoes, there's always the chance of tottering over and suffering a compound fracture," she chortled. "What d'you think, my dear girl?"

Whilst still focusing on maintaining her stance with her feet anchored steadfastly in position, Deana wagged a finger at Ginny as the woman continued to swivel her hips around, swishing that long ponytail back and forth. "Oh, Christ. Careful woman, I don't want your damn great mane in my face! Y'know, unlike your half-sister, plain-little Kimmy, who, of course, you've never met, I wouldn't mind betting you own an extensive collection of fetching high-heeled shoes and boots. Eh, am I right, or am I right? Anyway, you're not going to answer me, so come on, get on with it, girl. I can't stand here all day. I can feel my toes twitching."

"Ginny?"

Bemused, I glanced up at Viv.

"Come on. You're spooked, that's all."

"She most definitely is! Spook, that's me. Deana Burton, the sexiest spook around."

I accepted Viv's outstretched hand, entwining my fingers in his as we approached Mel's front door. Viv gave the bell a couple of elongated dings before adding a hefty rap of his knuckles to the door's obscured glass inlays. A typical police officer's calling card, I imagine. Although, without the 'police open up' comment, which I would assume would be his typical statement when visiting a suspect's home. That said, apart from a spot of insider trading illegally brokered by my soon-to-be ex-husband, which Viv and I were keen to ignore, I guessed Mel wasn't a suspect.

Half a minute passed before Viv repeated the routine. "Is that his motor?" He nodded to the ancient-looking Jaguar parked, or more abandoned, on the driveway.

"Hmmm," I nodded.

"Is he the sort to go for a walk?" Viv quizzed, as he attempted to peer through the obscured glass.

"Not really. Mel's not exactly a health freak. I guess he might walk to the pub, but they're not open yet."

"Christ, is this going to take all damn day, Deana tutted, leaning against the porch's wooden upright.

Viv squatted down on his haunches and lifted the letterbox to peer into the hall. "Hello. Mr Strachan, it's the police. Can you open up, please?"

"Police! Oh, that is interesting. So, Ginny, you've bagged yourself a cute little policeman, have we?"

"Viv, you're off duty," I hissed, worrying that his epiphany regarding previously being overly concerned with procedures had now morphed him from strutting around with the rule book shoved up his rectum into an intractable loose cannon.

"It's alright. I'm still a copper whether I'm on duty or not."

"But Mel will tell your boss you've been here. He's just the sort to cite police harassment."

"I'm with you, my girl. I'm not too fond of the Strachan clan. And as for your mother, well, she's got a nerve. I'll have you know that spat at Terry's funeral was quite uncalled for. If I ever cross paths with the woman again, I shan't be so deferential next time, I can tell you. You know, I was pregnant with your half-brother at the time," Deana accusingly wagged her finger. *"So, you could say your mother caught me at a vulnerable moment. She'll be treated to the wrath of my viperous tongue next time; I can assure you, my girl. Hmmm."* Pleased to have offered her thoughts regarding Ginny's mother, Deana raised her nose and folded her arms.

"Foxy's on thin ice if he wants to take me to task. I've got enough on that dick to have him dismissed." Viv rocked back and forth on his heels before bellowing through the letterbox. "Mr Strachan."

"Oh, waste of time!" On tippy-toes, Deana carefully nipped across the gravel drive before leaning over the small flower bed and grabbing the windowsill of one of the bay windows to peek inside.

"No doubt," I nervously laughed. "But, Viv, by all accounts, when you reported him last time, that didn't work. You said senior officers closed ranks."

"They did," he muttered before straightening up and pressing the bell again.

"So, if you have to report him again, why d'you think it will be different this time?"

"Foxy's close to retirement. If Mel complains, all Foxy will do is bawl me out. He knows what I've got on him, and the last fing he wants is to risk an internal enquiry this close to picking up his pension."

"Oh. I don't know how you work with the git."

"Oh, there he is. Sitting in that armchair. The old pervert must be deaf or drunk."

"I've applied for a transfer on God knows how many occasions. Unfortunately, top brass want me to stay put and keep DCI Reeves on the straight and narrow."

"They said that?"

"Yeah, pretty much. The Super suggested we make a good team. Foxy wiv his effective methods, none of which can be found laid down in any procedural manual, and me with a keen eye for process."

"Well, be prepared. My father-in-law will deffo complain, especially as I'm here."

"That may be. But we need to talk to him. Anyway, there's no answer, so I won't be harassing anyone today, it seems."

"Why isn't he answering? That dishy police officer bellowed loud enough to alert the whole neighbourhood. Come on, man, wake up, you idiot, or I'm going to have to break in," muttered Deana.

"What now, then?" I huffed. "Do we wait?"

"You got his mobile number?"

"Yeah, course."

"Give it here. I'll give him a ring when we get in the car. Hopefully, he'll pick up and tell us when he intends to be back."

"Err ... hello! Mr dishy policeman. Mel is sitting in his armchair!"

Whilst Viv peered into Mel's Jag and tried the door handle, I hooked out my mobile from my jeans back pocket and searched Mel's number. In recent years it wasn't a number that I would generally call, so I hoped he hadn't changed it.

"Oh, well, it's down to me then, is it? Men, you're all bloody useless." Deana raised her arm and slapped the window with her open palm, trying to awaken the old sleepyhead. "Come on, wakey-wakey. It will be a damn sight easier if you just come and open the front door. Otherwise, I'll need Terence to break in, and that will be difficult with a dishy police officer sitting in his car a few feet away. Come on, wake up, you git," she hollered, slapping the glass again.

Almost simultaneously, both Viv and I swivelled around when alerted by what sounded like someone slapping their hand on the window. We shot each other a look before glancing back at the house, our eyes shooting from one window to the next, trying to spot who'd just banged on the glass.

"Viv?"

"I can't see anyone."

"Over here, PC Plod!"

Together, we nipped up to the bay window and peered in, cupping our faces against the glass.

"See anything?" I asked.

"Not that window. This one! Christ, this is bloody hard work."

"No," muttered Viv, as he stepped back and glanced up at the first-floor windows.

"Oh, for Christ, sake, man. What's the matter with you? Over here, not up there! You might be dishy, but you're a bit dippy, too!"

"Someone definitely banged on the glass, though."

"Yeah," Viv replied, hand against his forehead to cover his eyes from the sun's glare as he scanned the upstairs windows.

I nipped over to the other bay window and carefully placed my foot between the wilting spring bulbs before peering in. Since Jean died, I'd only visited this house on the odd occasion and had never ventured into what I presumed to be Mel's study. Mel and Jean had been what you might call modernists in their tastes. The décor of his study appeared similar to the sitting room and was in direct contrast to the house's Georgian façade. I scanned around the room, from the cubism nude art and the iguana-tank-styled minimalist gas fire, to the enormous glass and steel coffee table.

"Good! At least you've worked it out. He might be rather ravishing, but he's dippy for a policeman, don't you think? I guess what he lacks up top, your man compensates with his performances under the sheets. A bit like Conrad, I suppose? Not exactly the conversationalist, but I was only employing his services for fitness training skills and that ravishing body of his. Anyway, dear, can you see him now? Look, there," Deana wagged a finger. *"Slumped in the leather armchair, snoring his head off."*

"Viv."

"Uh-huh?"

"Viv … he's in there. I can just make out him slumped in the chair."

"Hallelujah!"

Viv trotted over, stepped into the flowerbed and pressed his nose against the pane.

"Oh, well, don't mind me, will you? I'll move out of the way, shall I? Deana belligerently spat, as she hopped backwards to avoid being clattered by Viv's advance.

"See?"

"Yeah. Who tapped on the bleedin' window, then? Strachan lives alone, don't he?" Viv rapped his knuckles on the glass. "Mr Strachan?" he bellowed.

"D'you think he's alright?"

"Mel … Mel Strachan, can you hear me? It's Sergeant Richards from Fairfield Police."

"You think he's had a turn or something? Not that I'll shed any tears, but he might have suffered a stroke or a heart attack."

"Dunno. Unless we can find an unlocked door, I'll have to break in. Somefink ain't right here."

"You don't think he's asleep?"

"Nah, don't reckon so. The bloke must be comatose not to have heard my hollering and banging."

"Don't you have to call it in or something like that?"

"Yeah, I may have to. But first, I need to get in there and check he's alright." Grabbing my hand, Viv helped me negotiate out of the drooping daffodils and neatly trimmed bushes that made up the well-kept borders below the window before we hot-footed around to the side gate.

Deana carefully extracted herself from the flower bed and stood back on the gravel, wondering if she should follow or locate Terry and update him on developments. She presumed if Mel didn't answer, Sergeant Richards would break in to check the man was alright. If she were nimble, she would gain entry to the house without having to ask Terry to nip over from his hiding place and force a door or break a window.

Whilst pondering her decision, when Terry's daughter and her policeman boyfriend disappeared out of sight, Deana became distracted when detecting movement in the room on the other side of the front door. As she glanced around to the other bay window, Deana spotted that woman with the sunken eyes who could have performed as an extra in Thriller – The Spectre – who she'd chased yesterday lunchtime.

The zombie-looking woman flung open the front window and leaned out. "Hello, Deana. Like the proverbial bad penny, you turn up everywhere you're not wanted, I see."

"You," blurted Deana.

"Yes, me, dear."

"Who are you? And how come you can see me?"

"That's irrelevant. However, I'm rather delighted to inform you that the bastard is dead."

"Mel?"

"He's the only bastard I know. Yes, Mel."

Part 3

33

1987

Pulp Fiction

Lizzy and Paul hadn't uttered a word during those few minutes that elapsed since Mel had stepped away from their table, leaving that indecent proposal hanging in the air. Whilst Paul continued to fiddle with the table confetti, Lizzy became distracted by the band, who now bashed out a version of Bill Haley's *Rock Around the Clock*. She watched as couples, mostly worse for wear as a result of many hours of drinking, attempted the Jive, Jitterbug, and some more energetic types, dangerously undertaking what appeared to be an inebriated, chaotic version of the Bunny Hop.

"Lizzy?" whispered Paul, glancing up to look at her with teary eyes whilst taking a break from pinging sparkly 'Happy New Year' confetti across the tablecloth.

"What?" she barked, without looking at him.

"What the hell are we going to do?"

Lizzy, prising her eyes from the dancers, turned to face her husband. The vision of his sad, almost pathetic expression instantly dissolved the memories of happier times when Paul would expertly whisk her around the dance floor as they tripped the light fantastic together.

"What do you suggest?" she somewhat aggressively spat.

"I don't know," he whispered, dropping his gaze to the tablecloth.

"Well, as I see it, you can work for that bastard. Of course, we'll have to sell the house, and because of your idiotic obsession with gambling, that will leave us having to rent some shithole. I really can't see any bank thinking we're a safe risk and being prepared to offer us a mortgage, can you?"

Paul shook his head whilst keeping his focus on the tablecloth.

"The other option ... I agree to Mel's—"

"No!" he blurted, whisking his head up.

"What damn choice do we have? Your wife and daughter will end up homeless unless we do something," Lizzy paused before clarifying the situation. "I have to do something."

"You're not suggesting you sleep with him?" he hissed.

Lizzy huffed. "No ... the thought makes me feel physically sick."

"You and me both."

"I can't see why on earth it would bother you! It's years since you've come to my bed."

Paul tutted and glanced away from her. "You know why ... anyway, Ginny isn't my daughter."

"What the hell has that got to do with anything? Are you saying because she's not the fruit of your loins, you don't care what happens to her?"

"No ... you know that's not what I mean."

"What then?"

"You said about you and my daughter being homeless. I'm just saying Ginny's not my daughter."

"Don't, Paul. Just don't."

"Well, she ain't, is she?"

Lizzy leaned across the table, lowering her voice. "No ... she's not. However, I am your wife, albeit in name only."

"You could divorce me."

"I could. And probably should."

"Why don't you then?"

Lizzy took hold of his hand, waiting for her husband to look at her. "Because I don't want to. I love my husband, despite the fact he's an idiot."

Paul sniffed and wiped the back of his hand across his nose. "Sorry, Lizzy. I'll take the job and get a second job at the weekends so we can save up. Perhaps, in a few years, we can get back to where we are now."

"Broke?"

"No ... before now. When we had money."

Lizzy snorted a reply whilst letting go of his hand.

"What about Ginny's father?"

"What about him?"

"You could leave me for him … take Ginny with you. You'll be better off without me, that's for sure."

"Paul … I've told you 'til I'm sick to the back teeth with it. Ginny's natural father is a closed subject. If this is some pathetic attempt to find out who he is, I suggest you forget it and focus all your energy on what we are going to do."

"Christ … fucking mess," he muttered, whilst rummaging in his jacket pocket before extracting a handkerchief to wipe his wet nose properly.

The band completed their rendition of *Rock Around the Clock* and, after a rapturous round of applause, the saxophonist announced they were about to perform their last number before the disco saw in the New Year. Then, with the aid of his saxophone, he pointed to all corners of the ballroom, encouraging everyone to get up on their feet before the quintet launched into bashing out their version of *The Twist*.

With only a few notes played, the vast majority of partygoers who weren't previously dancing were up on their feet. Lizzy spotted that even Brian, the stuffed-shirted club captain, was attempting to wiggle his hips. If her mood wasn't so morose, she might have giggled at the sight of his dreadful attempt to strut his stuff. Everyone except three were dancing – Lizzy and Paul Goode sat at their table, and Mel Strachan, who sipped his whisky as he leaned against the bar ogling Lizzy.

As Lizzy's eyes drifted from the dancers to the bar, specifically Mel, he clocked her glance and raised his glass at her. Then, breaking eye contact, she peered at the ruddy face of her husband, who continued to sniff and snivel like a child who'd lost his teddy bear.

Life had dealt a cruel hand. Terry Walton was the man she'd always wanted. Although they'd only enjoyed those few hours together, she'd known the moment Terry lifted her nighty over her head as they fumbled on the couch in that quaint little holiday cottage back in '77 that no one would ever make her feel that way again.

However, prior to that holiday, Paul had gotten on bended knee, and she'd accepted that offer of marriage. Lizzy knew that breaking the engagement and facing the impending fallout of that decision, which would have inevitably ensued with her parents, wasn't something she was prepared to face. So, she'd stupidly decided to try and put Terry out of her mind. Anyway, at the time, Terry already had a girlfriend, who, like Paul, had soundly slept in their beds the night Terry pleasured her.

Lizzy could still recall the utter devastation when she learned that Terry and his girlfriend had split and realised he was a free agent, but she wasn't. However, that paled into insignificance when a few years later he then married Sharon Bradshaw. Even then, she'd harboured thoughts that perhaps they would still be together in the future.

Not until 10th July 1985, when that NHS letter dropped on the doormat advising Paul that he was incapable of procreating children, could she be sure that Ginny was Terry's. In her heart, if she'd known for certain before he died, she would have told Terry, hoping that the pull of a daughter would be enough for him to leave his wife for her.

The day of Terry Walton's funeral would have to be the worst day of her life. Now, contemplating that his daughter's life was about to be ruined by Paul's stupidity, she made a decision – well, someone had to. And, going by the state of her husband, he appeared incapable in more ways than one.

"Paul, I suggest you get yourself up to bed."

"You want to go up already? We haven't seen in the New Year, yet."

"Not me, you. I suggest you go to bed."

"What are you going to do?"

Lizzy slowly raised herself from her chair before leaning across the table to hiss her reply in his ear. "Deal with that git ... sort out our situation."

Paul swivelled his head and looked up at her. Apart from the thunderous look she offered back, Paul thought that the way she held herself in that tight-fitting gown, it was obvious why men would want her – his wife was stunning. The self-loathing which tormented his every waking moment had only served to destroy their relationship. Notwithstanding his utter stupidity when gambling their life away, Lizzy was prepared to stay with him – see it through – 'til death do us part. However, despite her commitment, the knowledge that she'd been with another after they'd become engaged ate away at him like a cancer, leaving all but a shell of a man who no longer possessed the fight to survive.

"What are you going to say to him?"

"You don't need to know. Just go to bed."

"Don't blow my chances of a job ... that's all we have left."

"My daughter isn't going to suffer because of you. Now, go to bed. I'll see you in the morning." Lizzy turned, leaving Paul sporting a sagging mouth as she headed for the bar.

Paul gripped the back of the chair as he slowly stood and watched his wife approach Mel. "You wouldn't," he muttered. Unwittingly, he held his breath whilst he witnessed his wife and Mel exchange words. Paul tentatively took a pace forward, intent on joining the conversation, but halted when Mel glanced at him and raised his glass before downing the content, grabbing his wife's arm and heading for the ballroom's exit – the exit that led to the bedroom suites.

Paul slumped back down in his chair and hung his head. As his chin trembled, the tears rolled.

34

2016

Doctor Zhivago

"Hello Lizzy."

Deana swivelled around, open-mouthed, to spot Terry purposefully striding into the driveway.

"Oh, Terry, my sweetheart, you're here too. And I see you can now recognise me. Would you be a love and do me a favour? I'm going to need some help to clamber out of here. You see, I'm not as agile as I used to be, and scampering through windows can be tricky at my age."

"What … but how, what?" blustered a baffled Deana, as she shot quizzical looks between Terry and the woman, who now attempted to shimmy through the open window.

Lizzy Goode perched her bottom on the windowsill before rather ungainly swinging her legs out and, with open arms, waited for Terry to assist her. "Thank you, Terry. I so wanted to hug you yesterday, but simply couldn't. As I'm sure you realise, just like that vainglory bitch you've been paired up with, I'm invisible to mere mortals." Whilst waiting for Terry to negotiate the thick shingle driveway,

Lizzy dropped her arms and scowled at Deana. "Yes, that's you I'm referring to."

"How dare you! Terence, don't you dare help her. She can drop out of that window and break her scrawny neck."

Lizzy dismissed Deana's bark with a shrug and a flick of her head as she turned back to offer a benevolent smile to Terry whilst wiggling her legs and thrusting out her arms like an expectant child waiting to be plucked up and cuddled. "So, as I was saying, it was difficult to show you my true feelings when in that packed pub. Especially with *her* in the way." As Terry approached, she glanced across at Deana. "Although we've only met the twice ... well, three times now, I can see you're still the stuck-up bitch you always were. By all accounts, thirty-odd years and a bout of death hasn't improved your character."

"Terence!"

"Hang on," he mumbled, whilst attempting to lift Lizzy by way of placing his right arm under her bent knees, just below the hemline of her skirt, before encircling her back and shoulders with his left.

Lizzy swished her arms around his neck and buried her head in his chest as he took her weight and hauled her out through the open window. "Oh, Terry, I've missed you so," she whispered. "I so wished we could have met again long before now."

Deana screwed up her nose. "Oh, Terry, I've missed you so. I wished we could have met again long before now," Deana mocked, imitating Lizzy's demure tone whilst clutching her hands to her chest and shaking her head from side to side. "Pathetic!" she barked. "Who the hell d'you think you are, bloody Julie Christie, gazing up into Omar Sharif's eyes?"

"There, you go. I'll settle you down here. Can you stand? Are you alright?" Terry enquired, as he gently set Lizzy on her feet. "Mind you don't come a cropper. That loose shingle is so thick it's like walking up Brighton Beach," he chuckled. "I wouldn't want you to slip over."

"Oh, Lizzy, be careful, don't slip over. Let me hold you in my arms so you don't fall," Deana scoffed in that mocking tone.

Terry shot a disparaging glare at Deana. "I was just being a gent and helping Lizzy to stand. There is no need to become so childish, woman."

"Childish! How dare you? And how come it's all 'Lizzy' today? Yesterday, you had no idea who the old hag was."

"It just came to me when I spotted her open that window." He turned to Lizzy. "I hope you're not too offended when I say you're a little older than I remember."

"No, of course not, sweetheart. It's a good thirty-five years ago, isn't it?"

"I could never forget those beautiful green eyes of yours, Lizzy. Captivating eyes. Still as beautiful today as they ever were."

"Oh, pass the bucket!" barked Deana.

"Thank you, sweetheart. You still look as handsome as the last day I saw you," Lizzy purred, gazing up at him. "Can you remember that day?"

Terry nodded, offering a mischievous grin. "How could I forget?" he raised his eyebrows and smirked. "My wedding day, I believe."

Lizzy offered Terry a wide smile before replying. "It was, you're right. Little did we both know back then that Ginny, one of your bridesmaids, was your daughter."

"So I've discovered," he chuckled.

"Would it have been different if you knew? Could we have been together?"

Terry shrugged. "I don't know. I loved Sharon too ... and you were married to Paul."

"Unfortunately, I was. Still, that stolen moment we had together at the reception will stay in my heart forever."

"Yeah, that was a close one. We nearly got caught, didn't we? It's a good job my best man warned us Sharon was looking for me. I take it Paul never found out?"

"No," she giggled. "What about Sharon?"

"No ... although, unfortunately, I'm afraid there were a few affairs which she unearthed. But she never knew about you and me."

"You naughty boy," she smirked, playfully slapping his chest.

"Terence! My God. Surely, you're not suggesting you and her," Deana, with hands on hips, nodded at Lizzy. "You and this trollop dilly dallied at your wedding reception."

Terry shot her a nervous grin. "It kind of just happened in the cloakroom."

"A bunk up in the bogs!"

"No … amongst the guest coats behind reception."

"The best orgasm I've ever had … no one ever made me feel like you could, sweetheart."

"Well, you're still just as beautiful."

"Oh, my God, Terence. The woman looks like a bloody corpse. If it's beauty you're looking for, I'm right here!"

Lizzy laid her hand on his chest. "I endured a tough few months before I died. What with losing a few stone and my hair not at its best, I accept I don't offer up an appearance that is quite as alluring to when in the flush of my youth."

"Walking bloody dead, more like," muttered Deana.

"Your hair is lovely." Terry gently stroked her cheek before swishing her long, greying hair over her shoulder. "I can certainly see where our Ginny gets her looks from."

"She's a beauty, isn't she?" Lizzy cooed.

"Err … hello! Terence, have you lost all sense of proportion? I might add that this bloody woman is a damn sight older than me. And … and, she is not exactly in the greatest of shape!"

Terry arched his back and glanced at Deana, who aggressively glared back with her hands still thrust upon her hips. "Deana, please remember Lizzy has suffered. There is no need to be rude."

"Yes, well, that as may be. However, whilst you're doing your Dr Zhivago impression, and this trollop acts out her damsel in distress performance, it might have escaped your attention that she's just snuck out from the house where that pervert Strachan lay dead!" boomed Deana, waving her hand in the direction to where she'd earlier spotted Mel slumped in his chair.

"Good riddance," mumbled Lizzy, still holding on to Terry's arm.

"Also, Terence, darling. Me and good-old Lara Antipova here are invisible to all except you and some snotty offspring of some undesirables, who probably should all have been sterilised at birth. However, spawn of the swinish multitude aside, you," Deana paused while belligerently thrusting a digit at Terry. "Yes, you … you are very much visible. So, just like in that epic film, which probably lasts a good hour longer than the happy periods of the vast majority of my marriages, you have a long-lost daughter who just happens to be around the corner with her dishy policeman trying to gain entry. I think it might be a bit tricky if she comes bowling back around to find you here with her dead mother in your arms, cooing over you like some lovesick teenager."

"You finished?"

"Yes!"

"Well, as you pointed out, Lizzy, like you, is invisible. So, Ginny won't be able to see her mother."

"That as well maybe. But she'll see you," Deana enforced her point by jabbing her accusing finger at him once more. "And, after yesterday's debacle, that could be a bit on the tricky side, don't you think?"

"Yes, okay. But what's this about Mel being dead?"

"That thing," Deana grimaced, pinching up her nose whilst wagging a finger at Lizzy as if indicating to a stinking dog turd. "Old cooing-dead-eyes, here. She said the git's dead."

"Who is *she*? The cat's mother? Vainglory, rude and obnoxious," retorted Lizzy.

Terry shot looks between the two women, who, baring teeth, both appeared ready to pounce and tear each other limb from limb like a couple of deranged vampires. "Hang on, hang on. Lizzy, what's happened to Mel?"

Lizzy snorted a grunt at Deana before turning to glance up at Terry. "He is my sweetheart ... Mel is dead. I found him there this morning. The despicable git is at last dead. Put the flags out and celebrate, I say."

Deana stepped a pace towards her. "Presumably, you murdered him, you twisted evil piece of dead strumpet."

"Deana," hissed Terry.

"No. I most certainly did not," Lizzy barked, before releasing her hold of Terry's arm and stepping towards Deana. "Take that back. How dare you accuse me? I'll accept that seeing the bastard dead is more than pleasurable, but I'm no murderer, thank you very much."

"Well ... as you said, the bastard's dead. You can deny it all you like, but sneaking out of the window suggests to me to be the act of the guilty." Deana aggressively folded her arms and jutted her chin in the air.

Lizzy jabbed a finger at her. "Oh, don't you get all clever with me, you filthy hussy. I spotted Ginny and that policeman, so thought I should make a swift exit. I didn't kill Mel!"

"You're invisible. You didn't need to scamper out of that window, you old strumpet."

"I keep forgetting I'm invisible, you bitch. And I'm not a piece of strumpet. You are!"

"Ladies ... ladies, please."

Lowering her chin, Deana offered a curled-lipped sneer as she leaned in towards Lizzy, only halting when her nose ended up inches from her face. "Hussy," she hissed. "Terry would never have stayed with you. It was me he wanted ... me! You're deluded if you think he would want some gutter trash like you—"

"You! Debauched Deana ... in your dreams, you slut. Terry and I loved each other—"

"Love! Don't give me love. You were just a one-night fling ... a bit of fluff he banged on the sofa to pass the time!"

"Wha—"

"Alright, a two-night fling, what with your illicit tryst amongst the fur coats," Deana interrupted. "That about sums you up. All fur coat and nae knickers!"

"Terry loved me. We had a child! A beautiful daughter—"

"So did we! Damian, a true love child."

"What? No, you can't have ..."

Deana leaned back and grinned whilst smugly nodding her head. "I bet that's pissed on your strawberries, hasn't it?" she chuckled. "I was carrying when you shouted like a fishwife at me after Terry's funeral. Carrying *his* child," Deana reinforced her point by way of waving a digit at Terry, who shot his head back to avoid receiving a poke in the eye. "Terry and I have a beautiful son, who's a damn sight more switched on than that dizzy blonde you pushed out of that trollop fanny of yours—"

"Ladies, for Christ—"

"Good God, woman, you've got a nerve. I heard you've taken more love trains than the Channel Tunnel!"

"Stop!" hissed Terry. "For God sake, ladies, stop."

"Terence, surely you're not going to allow this bloody woman to speak to me like that." Deana doe-eyed him as he rammed his head into the gap between them.

"Terry, sweetheart, she was horrible to me," whined Lizzy.

"Christ sake. Both of you put a ruddy sock in it," Terry demanded, swishing his head from side to side. "Now look, this isn't getting us anywhere, is it? I loved both of you, alright."

"Huh," both ladies huffed in reply.

"Can we at least be civil?" Terry quizzed, glancing back and forth at the icy glares. "Deana?" he asked, raising an eyebrow.

"Oh, very well, if I must. Lizzy, I'm sorry to hear you were unwell before you died. My brother died the same way, and I know how distressing that must have been," Deana mumbled.

"Thank you," whispered Terry, before turning to Lizzy. "Would you like to say something to Deana?"

Lizzy bristled. "Sorry you got crushed by a big lorry."

Deana nodded. "You don't look as awful as I said, I suppose."

"Thank you. You should know I'm not here to take Terry from you, Deana. I'm no threat to you."

"Huh … okay," Deana nonchalantly replied.

"That's better, ladies. All friends again?"

Deana tiptoed up and whispered in his ear.

"What did she say?" blurted Lizzy, grabbing Terry's arm.

Terry jolted back as Deana settled her heels back on the gravel, sporting a wicked smirk. "You've got to be joking!" he exclaimed.

"I'm just saying, darling. Not ideal, I grant you that. But you did say if we found another female ghost—"

"Deana!"

"Alright, alright. Don't go off on one. As I said, it was only a suggestion."

"What did you say?" Lizzy jabbed her finger at Deana, who continued to offer that lascivious smirk at Terry.

"Trust me. You don't want to know."

Lizzy leered at Deana. "Trollop," she muttered.

"Scrubber," Deana hissed back.

"Oh, I give up," Terry announced as he threw his arms in the air before marching towards the bay window where he'd earlier spotted Deana peeking through.

Deana and Lizzy exchanged glances before hot-footing after Terry. With Terry positioned between them, all three slowly raised their heads above the windowsill and peered inside, just at the point Ginny glanced through the window.

"Shit!" blurted Terry.

35

The Untouchables

As we hovered in the side passage, appearing like a couple up to no good, I furtively glanced around, harbouring a growing concern that any active members of the neighbourhood watch scheme might be twitching their curtains.

Whilst I pondered that thought, along with why Mel hadn't answered the door, Viv clambered up the wooden gate, gripping the top with one hand whilst releasing the bolt with the other. Fortunately, Mel had left the back door unlocked, thus negating the need for Viv to force entry.

"Viv." I grabbed his arm as he gently pushed open the door. "Should we just go? If he's dead, we're not going to be able to probe him about Ian Beacham, or whatever his real name is."

"He might have collapsed. Maybe the bloke's had a stroke and needs medical attention."

"Oh ... okay," I shrugged.

"Hey, you stay here, and I'll go see what's going on."

I shook my head. "No, I'll come with you." Although not particularly keen to see Mel Strachan, dead or alive, I didn't fancy hanging around on the patio.

Viv nodded before stealthily opening the door. "Mr Strachan. Mr Strachan, are you there? It's the police. Sergeant Richards from the police."

We hovered – Viv, a foot inside the door, me on the threshold, waiting for a reply.

All that came back from Viv's announcement was a deathly silence. Viv took the lead as we nipped through to Mel's study, where an open-eyed, although sightless, Mel Strachan appeared to gormlessly grin back at us.

"Oh, my God," I whispered, my hand involuntarily shooting to my chest as I hovered in the doorway.

"Hey, you okay?" Viv questioned, placing a comforting hand on my elbow.

"Yeah," I nodded. "Is he …?"

"Yeah, looks that way. As he's your father-in-law, I'm guessing your DNA and prints will be all over this place. But I fink it's best you don't go near the body and try not to touch anyfink." Viv waited for my nod before padding over to Mel. I held my breath as he gently teased away his open-necked shirt collar, where he placed two fingers on his neck.

I glanced around the room before movement at the window distracted me. With knitted brows, I focused on the middle pane, where I'm convinced I'd spotted movement as if someone had ducked below the windowsill.

"Ginny?" quizzed Viv, presumably spotting my worried expression.

"Nothing." I shook my head, removing the silly thought. We'd only just come from the front of the property and, with all the crazy happenings over the past few days, I guess my mind was on high alert, now imagining the ridiculous and spotting bogey men who weren't there.

Viv shook his head at me, pulling his fingers away from his neck.

"Is he?"

Viv nodded.

"Viv, look." I pointed to a scrap of paper which lay tucked under the front of the chair directly below Mel's slack right hand.

Whilst squatting on his haunches and with the aid of his car key, Viv carefully scraped the page, which appeared to have been torn from a reporter's notebook, from its half-concealed position. "Need gloves," he muttered whilst attempting to flip open the folded sheet.

"Is it …"

Viv hesitated before glancing up at me. "Same … handwritten in block capitals. The quote from that author bloke."

"Dumas? How did I escape? With difficulty. How did I plan this moment? With pleasure."

"Yeah. It's got those three words on the back, just like the other notes."

"Tetralogy not trilogy. Meaning four, not three."

Viv glanced up at me as I hovered just inside the study. "Yeah, same. I don't fink I need to worry about gloves. The other two crime scenes were as clean as a whistle. I reckon this will be the same."

"Oh, God. But … I thought …"

"What?"

"Does this mean he was murdered?"

Viv nodded at me before straightening up and peering into Mel's dead eyes.

"What you looking for?" I whispered, glancing around to the hallway, now concerned when we entered through the back door we may have disturbed the killer whilst in the throes of murdering his victim. Through the half-light emanating from the hallway, the coats and boots, on and below the coat stand, morphed in to a menacing appearance. My overactive imagination, now half expecting the perpetrator to leap from their hiding place.

"I spotted it a moment ago. Petechial haemorrhages of the conjunctiva."

"What's that," I stammered, still with half an eye on the coat stand whilst keeping a watchful eye on the dark vista of the stairs.

Viv continued to scrutinise Mel's eyes. "Haemorrhaged blood vessels in the eyes. I reckon Mel died of asphyxia. I've seen this before when we discovered a body up at one of the flats on the Broxworth. Rival drug gang suffocated some lowlife shit with a plastic bag over his head."

Not wishing to suffer the same fate and fearing the murderer would zip down the stairs waving a Tesco carrier bag, I nipped into the study and positioned myself behind Viv. "What if they're still here?" I hissed, the palpable fear in my voice plain to hear.

Viv swivelled his head around. "Ginny, he's as cold as my ex's heart. I reckon he's been dead for hours."

I raised my hand to my forehead and sighed in relief. "Oh, good! Thank God for that," I chuckled. "I was about to shit myself that some bastard was about to leap out at us."

Viv raised an eyebrow.

"Oh … ha, sorry. I didn't mean, well, you know. I know I said I really didn't care if Mel was dead or not. But—"

"Ginny, it's alright," he interrupted. "Whoever's responsible didn't kill him then head upstairs to take a nap. Let's get you back to the car. I'll nip back, give the house a quick once-over, and call it in." Viv followed my gaze to the window. "What?" he quizzed.

"There, can you see it? There on the window."

We both stepped forward and witnessed two misting patches appear on the glass. It reminded me of when enduring long car journeys to Cornwall for our annual holiday. Jules would huff and mist his side window before drawing pictures to relieve the boredom, interspersed with moans of 'are we nearly there yet'. I, an adolescent teenager suffering from a cocktail of hormonal emotions, would sulk and listen to *Ace of Base* on my Walkman, dreading the two weeks of utter hell at a caravan park, knowing full well my parents would expect me to entertain my little brother. Jenny Berggren might have been singing about *all that she wants is another baby* … whereas all I wanted was to be anywhere but in that car.

My mind whirred – Jules. Why wasn't he answering my calls? Not that we'd ever been close, what with the huge age gap between us. However, for whatever reason, we'd drifted further apart after Mum passed away. As I gormlessly gaped at the growing circles of mist forming on the windowpanes, I considered the thought that I'd better pay Jules a visit and see what was up with him. After what that weirdo Beacham and my bastard husband had mentioned, I knew something wasn't right.

Viv stepped up to the window and peered out, then down to the gravel. "Odd," he muttered.

"Come on. This place is giving me the damn creeps. I didn't exactly enjoy Mel's company when he was alive and, to be honest with you, I'm not enjoying it much when he's dead either." I nodded to Mel, who continued to stare at the cubism nude art as if his dead eyes were appraising the artists brush strokes. For me, a lamebrain when it came to the arts, those paintings were grotesque images depicting angular-shaped nude women in degrading positions. Porn, dressed up to be a piece of fine art and no better than the glossy mags Fat-Oaf leered at when perched on his stool in his grubby emporium.

Viv nodded as he turned to face me. "This blows bleedin' great holes in our investigation. The focus of our inquiries has been around the two doctors' connection to Fairfield General Hospital. Now Mel Strachan has suffered the same fate, it suggests the avenue of inquiries we've been pursuing are completely off track."

"I don't see how they can be connected. Well, apart from the note, of course. But how can the deaths of Alistair's parents be linked to the murder of that other doctor?"

Viv shrugged. "At the moment, I've got no idea. The DCI is going to go off on one, that much I do know."

"Also, we're no closer to finding out who Ian Beacham is. I suppose your leave will be cancelled now that you have a third body?"

Viv, who now appeared to be vacantly staring at the wall opposite, specifically the floor-to-ceiling bookshelves, didn't answer.

"Viv," I quizzed, glancing from his pained expression to where he appeared mesmerised by a neatly stacked collection of *Encyclopaedia Britannica*. Based on the fact that these publications didn't appear to be first editions and were largely outdated and superseded by such platforms as Wikipedia, I failed to see the attraction. "Viv, what's the matter?"

"Somefink friggin' stinks."

"Is it him? Has he started to rot already?" I whimsically suggested, waving my hand at Mel's dead body. Although a rather insensitive joke, as far as I was concerned, since the day he stroked my breasts, Mel Strachan had always stunk.

Viv padded over to the bookcase, leaned forward and inspected the collection of framed photographs positioned on a shelf below the stack of books. "I had no idea they knew each other," he mumbled.

"Who?" I shimmied over to see what he was peering at.

"Mel Strachan and this git." Viv pointed to the photo of two men shaking hands. Both appeared dressed in some odd regalia, which I presumed was something to do with their club, or secret men's society, to which Mel had belonged to for years. I recall he tried to convince Alistair to join. My husband had declined, saying he didn't have the time. With all his extra-curricular activities with a certain well-proportioned personal trainer, I could now see Alistair's point.

"Who is that with Mel?"

Viv, still holding that bent-over pose, glanced at me. "That is DCI Kevin Reeves."

"Foxy?"

"The very same. I find it odd the DCI hasn't mentioned they know each other." Viv pointed to another photo tucked at the back. "Look, there they are together again."

"So," I shrugged. "What does it matter?"

Viv straightened up. "It matters because we've been investigating the death of Strachan's ex-wife, and my tossy DCI thought never to mention it. Also, the case against your father-in-law, five or six years ago, fell apart at the trial, if you remember. Evidence against Mel went missing ... police error was cited."

"You don't think—"

"No, I don't fink. I bleedin' well know," Viv interrupted. "CCTV footage disappeared from the evidence store. That taped footage was the principal evidence against Mel. Otherwise, it was simply her word against his. I remember the bloody shit hitting the fan and the internal police review. Only one officer entered that evidence lock up the day that VHS tape disappeared."

"DCI Kevin Reeves?"

"Yup. Being a DCI, he wasn't under suspicion. I recall he said he was reviewing evidence of another case." Viv pointed to the pictures. "My DCI is not only a misogynistic, racist tosser, but he's bent as well. I've always known it, but could never prove the fact."

"You think Foxy removed and destroyed the tape?"

"Well, these photos suggest Mel and him were pretty tight. Every time we've spoken with Mel about Jean's death, not once did either man give away that they knew each other."

"Because of what happened six years ago, and both men needing to keep their relationship a secret."

"Yep."

"What you gonna do?"

"Dunno. The DCI has so far avoided any internal reviews because senior management are all in the same bleedin' club."

"Old boys' network."

"Yeah. Untouchables. That's all dying out now. But there's one senior officer who I know is clean." Viv turned and faced me.

"And?"

"The Chief Super, Adele Megson. Although she's come up through the ranks, she ain't part of that old boys' network. And more to the point, retired DCI French knows her well. Chief Superintendent Megson was a DS working under Heather years ago."

"You going to blow the whistle on Foxy?"

Viv shrugged before turning back to scrutinise the pictures. "The bastard's had it coming for years," he muttered whilst wagging an accusing finger at a third picture of the two men positioned standing in line with five others posing on a golf course.

"What you going to do?"

"Firstly, I'm going to have to call this in. I need the Scene of Crimes team down here and a forensic team to inspect the body."

"Then what?"

Viv turned to face me. "I don't know. Trouble is, as soon as I call this in, the DCI will be down here, and that's somefink I need to avoid," he huffed. "We have a body, so I'll have to get the ball rolling. I'll secure the back door, then we'll nip out to the car and I'll make some calls."

Whilst Viv nipped back to the kitchen, I plucked up the frame Viv had just pointed to. Although the other five men were not known to me, I studied the faces of Mel and Kevin Reeves. Going by the fact that Mel sported a full head of hair, a feature he'd lost some years back, I surmised this picture was taken a good ten years ago.

Whilst narrowing my eyes, I could sense bile rising in my throat as I jabbed my finger at the image of a grinning Kevin Reeves. "I know you," I whispered.

36

It's A Wonderful Life

"Shit," blurted Terry, before ducking down below the windowsill, closely followed by both ladies positioned on either side of him. "Did she see us?" he hissed, shooting his head back and forth between Lizzy and Deana, who just shrugged as they crouched in the flower bed.

"Who's the bloke with Ginny?" Terry hissed.

"A police officer called Viv," whispered Deana.

"Odd name."

"He stayed at Ginny's flat last night. I think they're an item," added Lizzy.

"She never mentioned him yesterday," Terry shot out the side of his mouth at Lizzy.

"I think they've just met. Anything has got to be better than that idiot son of Mel's."

"We agree on something, then," hissed Deana. "From what I've seen of Alistair, he's a right snivelling little weasel. I can't for the life of me see how any mother would let their daughter marry such a runt."

"Well, easy for you to say," Lizzy hissed, poking her head forward. "Paul and I tried our best to dissuade her. However, the girl is headstrong and was adamant about marrying him."

"I suggest you didn't try hard enough. Terry's other daughter is stepping out with a millionaire. She's done rather well for herself. Unlike your girl," scoffed Deana.

"Kim? Kim Mayer? I heard she was just a cleaner," Lizzy shot back, leaving Terry playing head tennis between the two ladies.

"Not anymore. The girl's bagged herself a rather dashing Italian chap. Terry and I assisted with that matchmaking a couple of weeks ago."

Terry glanced at Deana and raised an eyebrow.

"Well, darling. We did. If we hadn't gotten involved, little Kimmy and that Vinny chap might not have got it on."

"Why are you both whispering and hiding?"

Deana and Lizzy exchanged glances and shrugged before standing from their crouched position.

"Darling, you know I keep forgetting that I'm invisible. It's not as easy as you might think."

"Oh, you're right ... so do I. Even though I've been roaming around for months, I seem to forget I'm see-through, which is rather peculiar and difficult to get used to," chortled Lizzy, as she peeked through the study window. "You know, I had a right go at some bloke yesterday. There I was, walking into that pub after following Ginny and Terry, when some bloody bloke rudely shut the door in my face. When I barked at him about his lack of manners, I remembered he couldn't see me."

"Oh, me too!" guffawed Deana. "It happens all the time. Yesterday, when I chased after you, just after you accused me of being a vainglory bitch, I might add," Deana wagged an accusing finger at Lizzy. "Hmmm, anyway, I had an unfortunate incident with a group of tossers who blocked my path and wouldn't step aside when I politely said excuse me."

"So rude of them."

"You're not wrong, Lizzy. Although, I had the last laugh when I tipped his pint down his shirt. That showed the git! Manners cost nothing, do they?"

"Well said. I have to say I quite enjoy getting up to a little mischief. Only the other day, when minding my own business waiting at the bus stop, some scummy lowlife blew cigarette smoke in my face."

"Revolting."

"Absolutely! As you say, I had the last laugh."

"Oh, pray tell, what did you do to the git?"

"Well, you'll like this one. The repugnant oaf is still probably in some considerable pain …" Lizzy hesitated, adding to the drama when detecting Deana appeared to be hanging on her every word. "So, I snatched the cigarette out of his gob and thrust the lit end to his lips!"

"You didn't! Really?"

"I did. You should have seen the git jump," Lizzy chortled.

"I can imagine. What fun! Now, you'll like this little story. Last week, when Terry and I—"

"Ladies!" Terry hissed, interrupting Deana's flow. "Not that I'm upset that you seem to be getting along rather better than before, and although your tales of ghostly acts are mildly amusing, do you think we could get back to the task in hand?" barked Terry. "It's not that comfortable down here, and I've had my fill of hiding in bushes for one day."

Lizzy and Deana peered down at Terry crouched amongst the daffodils.

"Good point, darling," Deana nodded. "We'll save my little amusing anecdote for another day."

"What's happening in there?" Terry quizzed, as the two ladies cupped their faces to the window.

"That policeman is crouched down by Mel. He appears to be reading the note."

"Note?" blurted Terry.

Lizzy glanced down at Terry and then across to Deana. "A quote from Alexander Dumas, I'm led to believe."

"How did I escape? With difficulty. How did I plan this moment? With pleasure."

"Well done, sweetheart." Lizzy offered a thin smile at Terry before turning around to plant her nose against the window.

Deana and Terry exchanged glances. Terry shrugged before Deana copied Lizzy and peered back into the room.

"What's happening now?" hissed Terry.

"Our Ginny is staring straight at me. Oh, I wish I could talk to her. I do miss her so."

"Uh-oh ... oh, hell," mumbled Deana.

"Christ, what now?" blurted Terry.

"Darling, you'd better flatten yourself against the wall because that rather dishy police officer is walking towards the window. You don't have time to make a dash for it, so try to pin yourself in as tightly as possible."

Lizzy leaned back as Viv peered out of the window. "I'll agree with you, Deana. He's definitely a lot more handsome than Alistair. I hope he treats Ginny well. She deserves someone to make her happy. Something that stupid husband of hers could never achieve."

Due to Viv's face almost pressed against the glass and thus now blocking her view, Deana shifted her head sideways. "Your girl looks a little shocked. Has she seen a dead body before?"

"Yes ... mine. Oh, and Paul's, of course. Ginny stayed with me until the end, holding my hand."

"Oh, that's very sweet of her," Deana replied, rolling her eyes.

"You'll be with your darling Terry again ... that's the last thing I remember Ginny saying to me."

Deana glanced down at Terry, sticking two fingers in her mouth whilst feigning to gag.

"Of course, that wasn't to be the case. Neither did I find Paul, the little scallywag."

"Did you reawaken as soon as you died?" Deana enquired, as both ladies cupped their hands around their faces and peered back into the study.

At the moment that Viv shifted away from the window and padded back into the room, Lizzy turned to face Deana.

"Yes ... yes, I did. Seeing Ginny in floods of tears was so distressing."

"Is he still there?" whispered Terry.

Both ladies peered down at Terry, who, with his face hugging the brickwork, sported a pained expression.

"Darling, you're doing your Steptoe impression again," she giggled. "No, he stepped away. You can refrain from sandpapering your face on the brickwork now." Deana peered into the room again. "Sorry, Lizzy, you were saying?"

"Oh, yes. So, no sooner had I taken my last breath, and there I was, awake again. No pain, feeling as fresh as a daisy. For a brief moment, I thought I'd miraculously been cured. Of course, when I spotted Ginny in floods of tears and the fact that she seemed unable to hear me, I realised something was amiss. That's when I heard this guiding voice suggesting that Paul had gone rogue."

Terry glanced up as Deana shot him a bug-eyed look. "Rogue," they stated in unison.

"Yes, they informed me that my dead husband was operating off-piste, to coin a phrase. So, I've been afforded the dubious mission of pulling Paul back ... stopping his little caper, you might say. Although, so far, I'm doing a rather shoddy job of it," she wheezily chuckled.

"Lizzy," hissed Terry. "Are you suggesting Paul is wandering around here as well?"

"Oh, yes. Somewhere. And clearly, my dead husband was here recently."

"Bloody hell! Lizzy, you're suggesting that Paul killed Mel, Jean Strachan, and some other poor fellow?"

"Another doctor, like Jean," added Deana.

"Yes, of course. Paul is on a mission of vengeance, and good on him, I say. The Powers-That-Be might want me to put a stop to his little caper, but bugger that. I'm dragging my heels on this one."

"Lizzy!" hissed Terry from his crouched position. "What do you mean by gone rogue and vengeance?"

"Paul has gone AWOL, for want of a better word. I'm sure Deana is fully aware that once you pass to the other side, you're not allowed to step back into the land of the living unless on an authorised mission."

Deana nonchalantly shrugged and nodded, confirming she was up to speed with the rules by which the dead were expected to comply with.

"Now, I'm led to believe that my husband, who died six years back, a few months ago, managed to escape and step back into the land of the living. If you see what I mean?"

"Paul is roaming around unauthorised?"

"Spot on, Deana."

"That explains the first part of that little riddle … How did I escape? With difficulty."

"Correct, Terry. Rather fitting, don't you think? Although Edmond Dantès was referring to prison, Paul was referencing the afterlife."

"What the hell have those three done to Paul? The three he murdered, assuming he murdered Mel as well."

"Did, Terry, did. Whilst you lay in that grave for over a quarter of a century, these despicable gits wronged my husband. It appears my dead husband is on a mission to mete out revenge on the Strachan family, who have to pay the price for their wrongdoing to us Goodes."

Deana, her mind whirring, raised a finger. "Hang on; there are four who will die."

"Correct. Paul has been quite clear on his little notes. Four will die."

"Who's the fourth?" quizzed Terry.

Lizzy smirked and shook her head. "No, that's on a need-to-know basis. Besides knowing the circumstances surrounding my husband's death, fortunately, the Powers-That-Be are clueless. However, I'm pretty sure of the identity of the next victim Paul has firmly in his crosshairs."

"Lizzy, you can't allow Paul to roam around knocking people off," hissed Terry, shooting a look at Deana for support.

"Oh, I can, and I will. I plan to fail my mission so my husband can take vengeance."

"Where is he?" Deana cut in.

"I wouldn't tell you if I knew, and I don't. Unfortunately, despite my valiant efforts, I haven't been able to track the man down. Of course, Paul is also invisible to mere mortals, but my husband seems to be able to avoid me, too. He's a sneaky little one, you know. I struggled to keep track of him when we were alive. So, now we're both dead, it's nigh on impossible," she again concluded her statement with a wheezy chortle.

"Hang on. Lizzy, you said those three wronged him. So that must mean you know what they did to Paul."

"I do. Well, I didn't, but I do now."

Deana knitted her brows as she peered at Lizzy, leaning against the windowsill. "What does that mean?"

"Mel Strachan is obvious—"

"Why?" Deana aggressively stabbed back.

"Let's just say that we have history with that man. As for Jean Strachan and Dr Rawlinson, I didn't know why Paul wanted them dead until the Powers-That-Be enlightened me to the exact circumstances of Paul's death. Then it all became clear."

"Dr Rawlinson is the name of this other chap who Paul has murdered?" quizzed Terry from his crouched position.

"And?" chimed in Deana with open palms. "What exactly did they do to Paul that has incensed him enough to nip back to perform a spot of murdering?"

"Oh, no. I'm not telling you that. Paul has good reason. Damn good reason."

"And you say you reckon you know the identity of his next victim?" chipped in Terry, wincing due to feeling pins and needles setting into his legs.

"Oh ... I've said too much." Lizzy stepped out of the flower bed before brushing away some foliage from her skirt. "Now, as I warned you both, do not chase after Paul. Instead, focus on your mission ... as in helping our girl get back on her feet. Paul has good reason for the retribution he's meted out so far, and I am going to make damn sure nobody, you or the Powers-That-Be, step in his way. When my husband has completed his quest, I'm sure he will find me. Then, and only then, we can trot off together into the bowels of hell."

"But—"

"No." Lizzy whisked up her hand to effectively halt Terry's protestations. "Paul was a weak man, and I would have preferred to spend my life with you. Of course, I would. However, I married Paul and, in later life, we found companionship. I let the man down during our marriage, and even with the knowledge that Ginny and Jules couldn't biologically be his, he stayed with me. I think the very least I can do is make sure I screw up my mission and help the poor man achieve his goals."

"Ginny's brother, this Jules bloke, isn't Paul's?"

"No, Terry. Paul was infertile."

"Who's his father then?"

"The man lying dead in that chair."

"You and Mel?"

"Unfortunately, yes. Paul knew it was Mel. Despite what that bloody man put us through, he doted on Jules as if he was his own son. For that very reason, I'm more than happy to ensure my husband gets his revenge. I am his guardian angel, a Clarence Odbody type if you like. Paul *will* have his vengeance."

"Darling?" Deana shakily whispered.

"Goodbye, Terry," Lizzy threw over her shoulder as she negotiated the deep gravel path before stopping at the entrance to the driveway and turning around. "I did love you. However, I suspect we will never meet again. Well, not in this life. Maybe we can enjoy a catch-up in hell if we all end up there. Toodle pip."

"Terence, get after her! We can't let her escape."

"I'm stuck. I can't move because Ginny and that policeman will see me."

"Bugger!" Deana swivelled around and peered through the window again.

"Are they still there?"

"They are, darling."

"Well, you'll have to go and chase after her, then."

Deana peered down at him. "Me? Oh, no, darling, I can't go chasing down ghosts, and certainly not in my Michael Kors boots."

"Oh, great!" he hissed. "So, I'm stuck in a flower bed whilst our only lead to putting a halt to Paul's rampage of murder has just scooted off up the road."

"Sorry, darling, but these boots were built for their looks, not comfort. They weren't designed for walking in, and certainly not running, despite what Nancy Sinatra might think. Anyway, I believe your Lizzy has a point."

"Sorry?"

"We need to focus on our mission. We can't very well get involved in hers, can we now?"

"Yes, but we can't stand back and let Paul continue his killing spree."

"Why not? They all probably deserve to die. Mel, the pervert, definitely was due for some comeuppance. As for his wife and that other doctor, I don't know. However, I guess there's a good reason, as Lizzy suggested."

"Deana, that's not the point. Our missions are linked. She said that Paul was on a campaign of vengeance against the Strachan family who've wronged the Goodes."

"So?"

"So, the obvious person with the name Strachan who has wronged a Goode is Ginny's husband."

"Oh ... yes, I see your point." Deana shifted her stance to lean her elbow on the windowsill as she continued to peer down at Terry in his hunched position. "Oh bugger, I've got mud on my boots. How annoying," she tutted, before offering her boot up to Terry. "Be a love and brush that off for me."

"Deana, this is serious!"

"So is mud on my boots! You think Paul is planning to kill Alistair next?"

"Makes sense, doesn't it?"

"Yes, I suppose it does. Boots, darling." Deana wiggled her foot in Terry's face.

Huffing, Terry complied, slapping away the mud. "You agree then, Alistair is the next target?"

"Yes, I suppose so," Deana wagged a finger at her boot. "You missed some, darling. Come on, do the job properly. What does that mean for our mission?"

Terry, boot in hand, shot a look up at her. "Deana, wake up! Going by that episode in that office yesterday and the solicitor's letter you nabbed, I suggest the split with Ginny and Alistair is somewhat acrimonious, to say the least. By now, he will have changed his will. So, if Paul kills Alistair, that will potentially leave Ginny screwed."

"The business and their flat will end up going to someone else?"

"Precisely. We can mete out blackmail and ghostly acts until the cows come home. However, if Alistair is dead, that will mean we fail our mission."

"Oh, bugger."

"Yes, oh bugger. The Powers-That-Be have already got the hump with us. So, we screw this up and God knows what punishment we'll have to face."

"You're right, darling. What's the plan?"

Terry straightened up whilst rubbing the small of his back. "Nothing for it, but I'm going to have to tell Ginny the truth."

37

White Star Line

When Viv disappeared from view, I whipped out my phone and carefully captured shots of every framed picture which depicted DCI Kevin Reeves – a face I recognised from some years back. And, under the circumstances of the one time I met this man, a face I would never forget. However, until today, I never knew his name.

Although I'd perfected that skill of calculating that two plus two equals five, this time I wasn't wrong. Pieces of the puzzle were missing or perhaps were slotted in the wrong way around, causing the picture to become muddled. However, that man's connection to Mel Strachan was too much of a coincidence to be unrelated to what spun around my mind. What I would tell Viv, at this point, I couldn't decide. Also, I guess what my befuddled brain was trying to compute was probably totally unrelated to Mel's death.

Not wishing to spend any more time in the company of Mel, although his character had significantly improved since dying, I scooted out of the sitting room to find Viv, who'd presumably nipped outside to secure the side gate and was now striding back across the patio towards the open back door.

Whilst waiting for Viv, I glanced around the kitchen, musing about the last time I'd visited this house. At that point, I believed Jean had committed suicide. Although Alistair struggled to hold that view, I'd assumed Jean had decided to end it all because of her husband's behaviour. Despite Mel's acquittal, as the years passed, I guessed the stigma caused by her ex-husband's trial was all too much for her. Although, at the time, some of their close-knit friends had supported Mel, many drifted away, presumably not wishing to be associated with a man accused of such a heinous act.

As for Jean, well, I guessed I'd always got on reasonably well with her, despite my parents' utter loathing of Mel, even before my lecherous father-in-law's arrest. However, during the trial, although as a family of Strachans we all rallied around to support Mel, something about how Jean acted suggested that she wasn't convinced of Mel's innocence. Like me, I believed Jean probably suspected that Mel Strachan was guilty, and I wondered if she knew of previously unreported incidents in the past.

Also, going by that vile violation with me in this very kitchen years before Ali and I were married, that confirmed Mel thought it acceptable to touch women when it took his fancy. The breast fondle he claimed to be accidental was nothing less than the grope of a pervert when manhandling a young woman. I imagined it wasn't the first time he'd committed such an act – scum like Mel Strachan think they can take what they want when they want.

Of course, despite my beliefs regarding Mel and suspecting that Jean had taken her own life because of being unable to live with the guilt of not reporting her husband's probable misdemeanours in the past, I appeared to have got it wrong. The information Viv divulged yesterday, confirmed that Jean hadn't taken her own life. As for a reason for her murder, along with that other doctor, who knew? However, whoever the murderer was, they'd done the world a great service by ridding it of Mel Strachan.

The day after Alistair's sister discovered their mother's body in her flat, which she'd moved into when she and Mel split, was the day that I, with Ali, came around to spend some time with Mel. Despite my utter loathing for the man and the fact that I'd always been convinced he was guilty of raping that girl in his office, I recall feeling how pathetically sad the situation was. Little did I know then, how pathetic my situation would pan out to be in just a few short months. My life was akin to the Titanic, going down fast at the bow, lacking lifesaving equipment, with probably low odds of survival.

However, something suggested that the man, now slipping the bolt across at the top of the back door, could be the catalyst to help me turn my life around. For sure, we had one thing in common – we both had an issue with DCI Kevin Reeves.

"You ready?"

I nodded.

"We'll leave by the front door. I'll call it in, then you'll have to wait in the car while I wait for the circus to start."

"Circus?" I quizzed, presuming that a pratfall of clowns and a troupe of jugglers weren't about to pitch a big top on the front lawn.

"When SOCO turn up, along wiv my tossy DCI. It will be like a bleedin' circus."

"DCI Reeves will be the one with oversized shoes, sporting a big red nose, I take it?"

"You've already met him then," Viv chuckled, gesturing we should head out to the hallway.

I smirked back, not wishing to verbalise my one previous meeting with the man. That day, there had been nothing clownish about him. As I recalled that incident, I now had the vision of that evil shapeshifting titular antagonist in that Stephen King horror movie *It* firmly lodged in my mind.

I complied with Viv's gesture and stepped into the hall. "Will it be like the TV shows? You know, everyone donning those white hazmat suits with some Quincy-type bloke predicting the time of death?"

"Quincy?"

"Oh, it was one of those detective shows my mother used to watch on daytime TV. Quincy was a medical examiner, pulling all the clues together. Some old show from the '70s. Mum used to watch any old crap after Dad died."

"Yeah, well, daytime TV's never really been my fing."

"You ain't missed much. It's a bit like *Silent Witness*, with Emilia Fox replaced by some ageing actor playing a pathologist who miraculously solves the case, always gets the girl, who is probably half his age, leaving the police looking like numbskulls."

"Oh, okay. Yeah, somefink like that, but the pathologist won't be solving anyfink. That's our job. Hopefully, in this case, the police sergeant will get the girl," he smirked.

I side-eyed him and raised my eyebrows.

"Oh, not a girl half my age … that would be, well, weird."

"Not to mention illegal."

"Only just."

"Hmmm, anyway, I take it you were referring to the old bird standing before you?"

"Yeah."

"Oi, careful, young boy. This old bird might change her mind," I threw over my shoulder as I hovered by the open door to the study, unintentionally grabbing one last look at Mel Strachan's lifeless body whilst heading for the front door.

Viv nudged my arm. "Come on," he whispered, encouraging me to move.

Although I was there when my mother passed and had visited Dad's body in the chapel of rest, Mel's was the first dead body I'd seen in these circumstances. I could almost feel him haunting me as he remained slumped in position. Despite my abhorrence of the man, I shuddered at the terror he must have suffered if Viv's assessment of how he died was to be found accurate.

"Will …" I cleared my throat, which now seemed as dry as a bucket of sand, to coin a phrase my git of a husband seemed fond of. "Will your leave be cancelled?"

"I don't know, maybe. I'm probably gonna have to get Uniform to run you back to your flat if I'm stuck here."

Viv stepped past me and thumbed back the Yale lock to the front door before glancing back at me as I became mesmerised by Mel's dead eyes. "Ginny?" he questioned, breaking my trance.

"Sorry," I mumbled, padding to the now open door where Viv hovered half in, half out of the hallway.

"You know, I fink the spotlight will turn on your family. Well, Alistair and Helen. Those two have lost their parents, and presumably at the hands of the same killer."

"Will that involve me and Helen's husband, too?"

Viv nodded. "It will be more around background checking, diving into your affairs to see if we can identify why someone wants your husband's parents dead."

As I stepped onto the quarry-tiled porch, I swivelled around and looked up at Viv. Whilst he pulled the door closed, leaving the latch up, that conversation with Alistair yesterday lunchtime filled my mind. I slowly blinked, allowing my mouth to gape.

Viv nodded as he clocked my vacant stare, presumably realising what was going through my mind. "If your husband has been involved in dodgy dealings, it will come to light."

"Oh, no. The bastard said he'd planted a trail of evidence that points to me," I mumbled. "Viv, Ali might be a complete knob—"

"Might?"

I offered half an eye roll. "No, you're right. He *is* a complete knob. But he's also damn clever. Whatever financial scam he's been running with his bloody dead father, he will have made damn sure he's covered his tracks. If you lot start digging around his business affairs, I could end up taking the fall for something I haven't done," I exclaimed, as the realisation of how dire my predicament might become.

"Hey. Hang on. You're getting ahead of yourself." Viv re-pocketed his phone, which he'd just pulled from his jeans pocket, before taking my hands in his and giving them a shake as if to calm me. "He might fink he's covered his tracks, but I guarantee the Fraud boys will pull that apart. The one fing he's forgetting about—"

"What?" I interrupted.

"Fraud investigations follow the money. Who's benefited from financial gain is where they'll be poking about."

"What d'you mean?"

"Fraud ... that usually results in someone gaining financially, yes?"

I nodded.

"Well, you haven't, have you?"

"Err ... no. In case you're not fully aware, I'm as good as bankrupt. You're dating a financially ruined old bird."

"As long as I'm dating her, I'm not worried she's broke."

"Really?" I whined. Although kind of super happy he wasn't bothered about dating a woman in financial ruin and potentially only a few short steps away from seeing the inside of a prison cell, I found it baffling that Viv could be attracted to me. I imagined he would spend most of his time fending off women, all of whom were probably nearly half my age.

"Yes! Really. Jesus, you're hard work. Why can't you accept that I kinda like you?"

"Kinda?"

"Or-right … you're peng."

"Oh, I know that one. That means you think I'm well fit, doesn't it?"

Viv nodded and smirked. "Come on, stop shitting yourself about that dick of a husband of yours and whatever stupid scams he's cooking up."

I chewed my lip, gripping his hands to prevent him from letting go. "Yes, but—"

"No," he uttered, followed by that wrong-answer-game-show honk.

"Hang on. I was just saying that Ali suggested his dad, that git lying dead in there, gained financially from his illegal dealings. If he's laid a trail pointing to evidence indicating that I've committed fraud with my father-in-law as the beneficiary, that would stick, wouldn't it?"

"Ginny, calm down. You said that Alistair has taken everyfink—"

"Yes! The bastard is now trying to take the proceeds from our penthouse flat! All I've got left is a whole heap of debt, a short tenancy agreement for that squalid shithole in that ghetto you came from, and the prospect of my new boyfriend left with no choice but to arrest me!"

"There you go, then," he smirked.

"There you go then, what?" I aggressively batted back.

"You have no financial gain. If a charge is to be levied at you, the fact you're as good as bankrupt ain't going to make that charge stick."

"Oh. You think?"

"Yeah, course. Hey, no one's going to arrest you. You're getting ahead of yourself."

"Christ, Viv. This is getting worse. Not for one moment did I think Mel Strachan dying would cause me issues. But now the bastard's dead, he can't be investigated."

"He can, and he will be. We will investigate everything connected to the potential murders of your in-laws and Dr Rawlinson. That's what the Chief Super will push us to get to the bottom of, not your husband's dabbling in a bit of insider trading. Now, if that comes to light during our investigations, we'll deal wiv it then."

I narrowed my eyes at him, my mind whirring like a washing machine on a spin cycle.

"Ginny?"

"Dr Rawlinson? That other victim was a Dr Rawlinson?"

"Yeah ... the first murder with a note left by the body. Back in early February."

"And he is the same Dr Rawlinson who works up at the private health care place on the Haverhill Road?"

"Well, he did until someone shoved him down the stairs. What's going on in that head of yours?"

"It's just another odd coincidence. My father, Paul, that is, went in for a heart operation after a series of heart attacks. Routine stuff, we were told. Anyway, there were complications and, basically, Dad died under the knife."

"And David Rawlinson was the surgeon who operated?"

I nodded. "I mean, it has nothing to do with this, I know. It's just a coincidence, I guess. Ali's mum, Jean, also performed private work up there. She's the one who investigated Dad's death, concluding that it was unfortunate. She said although a routine operation, there was always a risk. Dr Rawlinson wasn't to blame, and my dad was just unlucky."

"Jean Strachan, who was also murdered," Viv muttered, appearing lost in his thoughts.

"Yeah ... what does that mean?"

"Probably nothing. We know from our investigations that both surgeons had a better-than-average track record with operations. Being that they neither appeared incompetent in their work, relatives of dead patients have never been a line of inquiry we've pursued."

"I didn't murder them!"

"Ginny, I'm not suggesting you did," he chuckled. "Christ, you're impossible."

"Oh ... sorry, as I said yesterday, I'm a bit of a nutter." I offered a wincing grimace, wondering why I seemed hell-bent on informing Viv of all my poor qualities. Perhaps I could write him a list, let him peruse it at his leisure and decide if he really was prepared to take on a no hoper, with dwindling prospects, not to mention a recently new odd affliction of believing in witch's spells.

'Unless you want to lose this man, I'd keep that list to yourself, girl.'

I offered a nod to my mind talk. For once, I pondered that my brain made a good point.

"As I said, it was probably just a coincidence. Apart from a professional relationship to link Jean Strachan and David Rawlinson, we have nothing else that ties those two together. But now we have Mel Strachan, our investigations will take a significantly different route. I'd imagine the connection of David Rawlinson operating on your father is just a coincidence and has piss all to do with Mel's last few minutes on this earth when staring into the inside of a plastic carrier bag."

I shivered at the thought.

"Right, come on, I need to call this in. At this rate, Queeny or Nikki Alexander will only have a skeleton to cut open."

"It's Quincy," I giggled. "As I said, the character always got the girl. If he was called Queeny, he would probably prefer the men."

"Yeah, whatever." Viv let go of my hands as he prepared to step onto the gravel drive.

"Oh."

"What?" he quizzed.

"You believe Mel was guilty of raping that girl, yes?"

"I don't know. I wasn't involved in the case. All I can remember is the team investigating it said he was bang to rights."

"So …" I raised my finger, Columbo style. "What if he was murdered by one of his rape victims? Maybe someone related to that girl … a boyfriend, perhaps."

"What about Jean Strachan and Dr Rawlinson? Were they also involved in rape?"

"Oh … see your point. Not very good at this detective work, am I?"

"A little rough around the edges, to coin a phrase Heather likes to trot out," he chuckled.

"Yeah, maybe. But I'll bet you anything you like; Mel Strachan has raped before."

Viv and I spun around when a figure appeared from the bushes that flanked the porch.

"He did. I witnessed that bastard rape Jean Allsopp at a party in 1975."

38

The Eyes of Laura Mars

"Oh, my God, it's him!" I broadcasted to the whole neighbourhood whilst offering an animated finger wag at the bloke who'd seemingly appeared from nowhere. "It's Ian Beacham, or whoever he damn well is."

With one hand grappling on my forearm, Viv encouraged me to step behind him when fronting up the weirdo who, since yesterday, appeared to have become my stalker – oh, lucky me.

"Who are you? And what are you doing here?" Viv demanded, his tone and demeanour morphing from the caring, quiet man to something more akin to Yellow-Eye's temperament as he aggressively jutted his chin forward. I guess Viv's history had equipped him well to deal with confrontation. Presumably, these days, trained to take the legal route rather than what he learned when growing up on that odious estate.

"Oh dear, darling. The dishy policeman doesn't appear overly pleased to see you. Also, the expression on your girl's face suggests she's nae too chuffed about it, either." Deana gripped Terry's arm with both hands and peered up at him.

"Terence, my darling, I know we're fresh out of ideas, and I'm fully aware that it's your job to devise the plans, but I really don't think this is one of your better ones."

"Get off," my stalker muttered whilst rather oddly wriggling his arm, akin to watching someone as they battled with an errant pullover that just wouldn't offer up the sleeve when dressing. "I'll come to that. But first, you need to be aware that Mel Strachan has raped before. I had to drag the bastard off Jean at a party in 1975."

Whilst wrapping both arms around Viv's biceps, I peered over his shoulder at my stalker and, presumably like Viv, somewhat stunned by his ridiculous statement and peculiar wriggling movements.

"Don't dick me around, you twat. You need to start talking. Who the frig are you?"

"Viv," I hissed, concerned that his tone appeared far from the official lilt required by an officer of the law. For sure, my newly acquired boyfriend could no longer be accused of having that rule book stuck up his rectum. I momentarily wondered what his mentor would make of this regression.

"Charming. I was just showing a scintilla of affection and trying to advise, that's all. No need to get tetchy."

Ian side-eyed to his left before focusing his attention on me as I tiptoed up and rested my chin on Viv's shoulder. "Ginny, I'm sorry that I lied to you yesterday. But, the simple truth of the matter," he paused, glancing left. "I am the man in that photo with Paul and your mother."

"What photo?" barked Viv.

"My God, he really is frigging deluded," I muttered, after shifting my head to peer around Viv's shoulder.

"Viv, this weirdo reckons he's the same bloke in an old photo I have of Mum and Dad taken in 1977." I could detect Viv's muscles tense, suspecting he was about to take this odd man to task, either by pinning him to the ground and reading him his rights or just a straight-out punch. So, not wishing Viv to land in trouble on my account, I squeezed his arm, thus encouraging him not to act. Although this bloke clearly suffered from delusions, he probably needed counselling rather than a bloody nose.

"Oh, Christ! What now? I suppose you want me to perform some of my party tricks to prove we're dead, do you? What shall I do today, eh? Shall I fling some of this shingle around? Shake some bushes whilst you make ghostly moaning noises?" Deana exasperatedly flung her arms in the air as she stepped away from Terry's side before turning around and jabbing a finger at him. "No, wait, I've got it! I'll magically make a penny rise up from the ground and hover in the air whilst you can harmonise along whistling a rendition of The Righteous Brothers' Unchained Melody!" she barked before lowering her digit and aggressively thumping her hands on her hips.

My stalker defensively held his palms up to his chest. I guess sensing that Viv didn't appear overly friendly. "Look, I know this will be all rather difficult to believe. Christ, it's hard enough for me, let alone you," he chuckled. "See, the simple fact is … I am Terry Walton … your real father."

"Oh, terrific!" Deana exclaimed, as she stepped towards Terry before again jabbing a finger in his face. "Terence, I'm fully aware that we're in a tight spot here with our mission rather rapidly going south, but Christ almighty, you're making a fool of yourself."

I allowed my forehead to thump on Viv's shoulder and groaned at the idiot's statement. "Terry Walton is dead," I muttered. Although I didn't feel particularly threatened by the poor, delusional idiot, I maintained my grip on Viv's arm. "You should know Viv is a police officer. So, before you trot out any more bull, I suggest you start telling the truth."

"I suggest you avoid the truth at all costs!"

The strange man claiming to be my reincarnated father appeared to perform that odd sideways glance that he'd enacted with some regularity during our meeting yesterday lunchtime.

"Ginny, I can prove it to you—"

"What the hell are you doing here?" When striding into the drive, the sound of the dulcet tones of my soon-to-be-ex-husband halted the man claiming to be my dead father from uttering anything else that was liable to land him with a set of regulation police handcuffs slapped around his wrist. Not that I thought, for one moment, that Viv carried them around on his day off, but I detected he was close to arresting him.

"Oh, shit," I muttered.

Viv pointed at Ian, Terry, or whoever he was. "Don't you dare move, or I'll arrest you on suspicion of murder," he hissed before swivelling around to me. "Stay there. Let me deal wiv this."

"See, I told you. This is a right sodding mess. I really don't know what you expect me to do when this dishy policeman arrests you. Due to an unfortunate incident some years ago, I'm fully aware that the cells up at Fairfield

Police Station aren't exactly Alcatraz, but a spot of jail breaking might be beyond my many talents."

"What's going on?" bellowed Alistair, as he trotted forward.

"Mr Strachan. I'm DS Richards. We spoke some months back if you remember?" Viv called out as he stepped towards Alistair, meeting him halfway across the drive.

"Christ, now we've got this git here as well. I suppose, at least we know where he is and can protect him from Paul. Pity, though, as I wouldn't mind watching your old friend murder this snivelling little weasel."

Whilst Viv presumably prepared to explain to Alistair that his father had died, I turned to the idiot who'd complied with Viv's instruction to stay put. "I have no idea what your game is, but what was all that about Mel and Jean in '75?"

Although not at the level of what I'd witnessed in that pub, I considered something strange was occurring. The man claiming to be my dead father had blurted a similar accusation at Mel when they fronted each other up like a couple of rutting stags yesterday lunchtime. Clearly, the two men were not fond of each other and, based on the fact that Mel lay dead only a few feet from where we now stood, I became a smidge concerned that this bloke could be the supermarket-carrier-bag killer.

"Ginny, we don't have much time. But listen, I was at that party in '75, and I did step in and help Jean when Mel took advantage of her."

"Terence! It was rape. Rape is not taking advantage; it's a damn sight more serious than that." Deana barked, as she approached the two men in deep conversation.

"At a party that you attended about eight or nine years before you were born, you say," I scoffed, keeping half an eye on Viv in case I needed him, just on the off chance this nutter had secured that carrier bag in his back pocket and planned to whip it out at any moment. Although I couldn't hear the verbal exchange between Viv and Ali, I detected my husband's agitation.

"Yeah. Okay, I know this is a tad difficult to believe, but I am Terry, and I was at that party when Mel raped Jean—"

"Oh, get real, you idiot," I interrupted. "You're as much Terry Walton as I'm Lady Gaga."

"Who?" He offered a bemused shake of his head before continuing. "No, honestly, you have to listen to me." He reached out his arm; I leaned back to maintain the distance between us – well, *every little helps,* as they say. "I'm not gaga. Honestly, I'm telling the truth."

I narrowed my eyes at him. Surely, he knew who Lady Gaga was? Everyone on the bloody planet had heard of her, even my mother, who believed popular music died when ABBA split. "Are you for real? You're suggesting that Jean would marry a man who raped her?"

"I suspect it was the night Alistair was conceived. I wouldn't mind betting Alistair came on the scene soon after they were married."

"This dishy officer is first-class, darling. If I had to be informed about a relative's death, I think I would have liked him to deliver the news. What a wonderful bedside manner the man has," Deana announced as she performed her circling routine around the two men. "He might very well arrest you, but he really is a lush," she purred.

I narrowed my eyes at him. I knew Alistair was born five months after his parents married. However, the guessing of a madman didn't make him my reincarnated dead father.

"I presume you are aware that you were conceived on the night of the Jubilee?"

"Excuse me?" I exclaimed, thinking what an odd remark to make. Although my mother and I had discussed that very night, namely that excruciatingly embarrassing conversation when my dying sixty-four-year-old mother had felt it necessary to describe the man who gave her multiple orgasms, the thought of picking up that conversation with this weirdo didn't bear thinking about. Out of the corner of my eye, I noticed Viv almost having to hold Ali back as my husband attempted to barge past him.

"Your mother, Lizzy and me. We had an affair whilst in a holiday cottage in Hunstanton. We ... well, you know. Let's just say we both nipped into the kitchen for a glass of water at the same time in the middle of the night," he chuckled, whilst seemingly suggestively raising his eyebrows.

Despite the rather odd expression, which I couldn't decide if he was flirting or was just part of his repertoire of odd tics, the fact he knew the exact circumstances of that night which my mother had chosen to describe in entirely unnecessary detail, rendered me speechless.

Whilst Viv and Alistair's conversation appeared to become heated, the man claiming to be my father notched up the lunacy to another level when conversing with someone called Deana. A woman, I could only assume, was an imaginary figure and part of his schizophrenic tendencies, or this Deana was invisible and stood somewhere near Viv and

Alistair. I recalled when he mentioned her name in that coffee shop and his ridiculous claim to be Deana Beacham's nephew. As he held that conversation, I found myself playing head tennis from him to a point about ten feet further up the driveway.

"Deana ... Deana," he hissed.

Deana shot her head around from where she'd been focusing on the two men's conversation. "Terence! Shush. What on earth are you doing? You can't call out my name in public!"

My jaw slowly sunk downwards as I witnessed the actions of a man whose mind suggested it was in a state of psychosis.

"Deana," he hissed again, this time with his hand on the side of his face covering his mouth, shooting me a look out of the corner of his eye.

"Terence, why are you calling my name?"

"Can you remember what Lizzy said earlier about when she died?"

"What specifically?"

"Something Ginny said to her on her deathbed."

"Oh ... err. Hang on."

"Hurry! By the look on my daughter's face, she probably thinks I've lost my marbles."

"Oh, we're way past that, darling."

"Deana!"

"Oh, yes. She said something like ... you can be with your darling Terry again. I'm paraphrasing, of course, darling."

Whilst the nutter continued his conversation with thin air, I edged towards Viv, who'd spread his arms wide presumably in an attempt to block Alistair's path.

"Ginny. When your mother died, you were with her."

"So," I blurted, stepping further away as he advanced.

"The last thing you said to her was that she would be with her darling Terry again."

Stunned by his statement, I halted my backward staggering. Whether or not this man was the carrier-bag killer, and realising I could be about to place myself in danger, I stepped towards him. "How ... how could you know that?" I stammered.

"Because your mother told Deana and me only a few minutes ago."

"Sorry?" I bulged my eyes at him whilst my mind skittishly trawled my memory banks, trying to determine if I'd ever told anyone what I'd said to my mother during those last few moments together.

"Ginny, I am who I said I am. Your mother was here, and Deana and I know Paul is running around killing people."

"Viv ... Viv," I shrieked, stepping back.

"Ginny! Your father is going to kill Alistair next."

"Well, nothing like putting it out there, darling, is there? I'm quite sure if you holler a smidge louder, I expect the damn Powers-That-Be could hear you as well!"

Despite my shrieking, the heated exchange between Viv and Alistair meant my plea for help fell on deaf ears. However, the deluded nutters hollering, claiming that Paul had risen from the grave and planned to murder my husband, was enough for Viv and Ali to swivel around.

Presumably like me, Ali and Viv gawped at the odd man as he offered that nervous, almost serial-killer-type grin. Apart from a temperate spring breeze ruffling the leaves of the trees circling the half-moon front lawn and that crepitating sound of crunching gravel, silence pressed down upon proceedings until Viv pointed at the grinning man. "What did you say?"

Before my stalker answered, he appeared to follow the sound of the visibly shifting gravel, causing Viv, Ali and me to glance down to witness depressions form half a yard apart and halt about a foot from where the nutter stood.

"Darling, please tell me you know what you're doing. Because I think blurting out that a ghost is roaming about murdering folk is probably one of your less well-thought-out ideas."

"I'm doing my best," he hissed.

Whilst Ali and I continued to gawp, our heads rhythmically swivelling from the gravel indents and my new stalker, Viv pushed for answers.

"Oi, I asked you what you said."

"I said that I know who the fourth victim will be." He nodded at Alistair. "Paul Goode is exacting revenge on the Strachan family. Unless we can stop him, you, Alistair, will be his fourth victim."

"Who's Paul Goode," growled Viv.

"My dead father," I mumbled.

"Sorry?" Viv shot across to me. "Sorry, is this twat suggesting your dead father …" Viv's voice trailed away, presumably preventing himself from uttering the ridiculous.

"Yeah, Paul, my father," I mumbled. Akin to a cricket umpire indicating the batsman's innings had concluded following an incident of LBW, I slowly elevated my arm and pointed my index finger at the man who knew information that could only mean he *was* my reincarnated biological father, as ridiculous as that thought was. However, what I whispered to my mother as she took her last breath was something only the two of us could know. "This … this man knows stuff, which means he must be … must be Terry."

Clocking my vacant stare, Viv stepped towards me, presumably now concerned about my mental state. "I know your father was Paul Goode, but he's dead. Who's this other Paul Goode?"

Keeping my finger aloft, I ignored Viv's question and focused on Terry. "You can communicate with the dead?"

"Frig sake, Ginny, what are you talking about?"

My stalker, who I rather surreally considered must be Terry, nodded. "I can, indeed. Just a moment ago, your mother informed me that Paul was responsible for all three deaths where that note has been left." Before continuing, he performed that odd glance to his right, akin to a person suffering from a lazy eye. "I can see what others can't if you like."

Viv, presumably sensing the situation was becoming a farce, turned his attention to the man claiming to be Terry. "Oi, this ain't time for bleedin' jokes, mate. Claiming you can speak or see through the eyes of a ghost is going to get you arrested."

Now that Viv had stepped away from barring Alistair's passage to the house, my husband, who presumably was still processing the information that his father had died in similar circumstances to his mother, bolted past me and up into the porch.

"Shit!" blurted Viv, giving chase, just at the point I heard a car door slam and a figure appear from around the gatepost.

"What the hell are you doing here?" I mumbled, somewhat shocked by his presence.

39

Dead Man's Chest

Unsurprisingly and somewhat thankfully, Mel Strachan remained slouched in his leather armchair, just as he had been when we exited the house only a few minutes ago. However, based on my concerns regarding the state of my mental health, I'm not sure if I'd have been overly surprised if Mel hadn't suddenly sprung back to life.

Well, yes, I know that's a slightly deranged thought. However, let's face it, yesterday I witnessed levitating beer glasses and chairs that appeared to have taken on a life of their own. And now this bloke, a doppelgänger for my biological father, claiming to be that very person who'd miraculously come back from the dead, spouting that he's just held a conversation with my deceased mother and that my father, Paul, was roaming around murdering whoever took his fancy.

So, with this list of ridiculous events, who could blame me for half expecting my father-in-law's heart to transcendentally spring back to life akin to Captain Barbossa's dramatic return after Johnny Depp – incidentally, another one of my heart throbs, that I'd swooned over ever since Freddie Krueger murdered him, who definitely rivalled David Beckham – had shot the man dead in one of the final scenes of *The Curse of the Black Pearl*, only to reappear in one of the many lesser sequels, the titles of which now escape me.

Sensing Viv's concern regarding contaminating the crime scene as he attempted to drag Alistair away from Mel's body, with my arms slapped to either side of the doorframe, I barricaded the entrance to the study, thus preventing Terry, if that's who he really was, and my little brother, Jules, who'd just turned up, from entering.

With my back to Viv, who'd successfully managed to grapple with Alistair and hold him away from Mel's body before switching to a more comforting stance when my husband started to sob, I turned my attentions to Jules, who'd followed Terry and me into the house when chasing after Viv and my husband.

Deana flicked Mel's right earlobe as she pinched up her nose whilst inspecting the man's vacant, staring eyes. "As the proverbial doornail, darling. He's definitely dead. Lord knows what went through his mind when the invisible Paul finished him off. I wonder how he did it?" Deana glanced up at Terry, who peered over his daughter's outstretched arms that effectively blocked entry.

"Jules, what the frigging hell are you doing here?" I hissed, before puffing away some errant strands of hair that had uncoupled from my scrunchie during all the excitement.

"Jesus, Ginny ... is he?" Jules paused and gestured with a nod towards Mel. "Is he actually dead?"

"As the proverbial doornail!" Deana boomed. "Christ, doesn't anyone listen to me these days?" She glanced up again. "Oh, no, I suppose not."

"Yeah, he is. But what are you doing here?"

Whilst continuing to gawp at the scene behind me, Jules offered a slight nod towards Terry, who stood by his side. As my brother raised his eyebrows, he exaggeratedly mouthed, "Who's he?"

"Oh, don't ask," I shook my head whilst maintaining my grip on the door frame to bar entry. "Apparently, this idiot believes he's my real father." I glanced at Terry, who maintained his open-mouthed expression. "Isn't that so?" I quizzed, raising an eyebrow.

"What the fu—" Jules started to say before Viv interjected.

"I need you all to leave the house. This is a crime scene," instructed Viv, guiding a distraught Alistair to take a seat on the Chesterfield sofa, which matched the armchair his father's body occupied.

"Jesus … I can't believe that letter actually told the truth," muttered Jules.

Viv, presumably satisfied that my husband's catatonic state meant he would no longer contaminate the crime scene any further, turned on Jules. "What letter," he demanded.

"Who's he?" my little brother quizzed.

"I'm DS Richards. Who the hell are you, and what letter?"

"This is my little brother Jules."

"This," Jules waved a folded note. The ragged top suggested it had been torn from a reporter's notebook.

Viv snatched the note and read aloud —

Dear Julian,

I beg your forgiveness.

Following my note last month, I must inform you that I have ended Mel Strachan's life. The man simply had to die. In 1987 my business fell into some difficulties, and thus your mother and I faced bankruptcy. The only option open to us was to accept a cash injection from Mel Strachan. Unfortunately, a condition of that deal required your mother to accept an indecent proposal from Mel.

I'm so sorry to inform you, but you are the product of that indecent proposal. It pains me to tell you that Mel Strachan is your biological father. Please do not judge your mother – she only accepted that proposal to save our failing business. Also, please understand, although Mel was your biological father, I had to gain vengeance for what he put your mother through.

As odd as this may be, as in receiving notes from your dead father, I see that you have acted upon my letter from last month regarding Alistair's illegal affairs. So, although you will rightly question who has written this note, you know now that what I told you is the truth. I urge you to see this through to a conclusion and assist your sister, thus ensuring she receives what she's entitled to from that conniving husband of hers. As before, please keep this information from Ginny because I don't believe she would be open to accepting that her father has returned from the dead.

Unfortunately, my excursion from the afterlife must come to an end. I've gone AWOL from death, to coin a phrase. Although your mother has kindly dragged her heels in finding me, I'm aware that my disappearance has now alerted less savoury characters, so I must make haste and finish what I started. Later today, I will eliminate my fourth target. Then, my quest for vengeance will be complete. The four who ruined my life will all have paid the ultimate price.

Although I knew you weren't my son, I always treated you as such and loved you with all my heart.

Live and be happy, beloved children of my heart, and never forget that, until the day comes when God will deign to reveal the future to man, all human wisdom is contained in these words – Wait and hope!

My final quote from Dumas.

Your father

Paul Goode

I recall reading an article in some magazine, probably whilst slowly dying in the waiting room of the doctor's surgery, that silence doesn't actually exist. Some neuroscientist, whose name escapes me, claimed that a state of silence cannot be achieved because the ear will still detect the sound of vibrating air molecules. According to the author, anywhere there is energy, sound is produced. As Viv concluded the recital of the note, although no one uttered a word, there was plenty of energy in the room.

"Where did you get this from?" Viv asked, breaking the non-silence.

"Someone stuck it through my door this morning."

"And this Paul Goode is your father?" Viv mumbled, not a question, as such, more the musing of a man trying to compute the ridiculous.

"Was," I muttered, letting my arms flop and swivelling around to face Viv. "It's some crank, playing games."

"We have a dead body here. This is no game."

"No, I know," I paused. "But Viv, my dad is dead!"

"I thought I'd come round and speak to Mel, see if he would corroborate what that letter states about him being my real dad."

"You've received other letters like this?"

"Yeah. Two. The first one was ages ago. I assumed it was some sick joke by one of my mates. So, I just ignored it."

"What did it say?" I fired back at my brother before Viv had the chance.

"Something about that the doctor who operated on Dad was under the influence of alcohol, which resulted in Dad dying because he botched the operation."

"Dr Rawlinson," chimed in Viv.

"Yeah … and it also said that Jean Strachan knew he'd caused Dad's death and covered it up to protect her colleague."

"When exactly did you receive that note?"

"A day or two after Jean committed suicide."

"Jules, you credulous knob. Why the hell didn't you say anything about it?" I aggressively fired back at him.

Jules shrugged, the dynamics between us reverting to a big sister berating her little brother of years gone by.

That Bart and Lisa Simpson arguing scenario. Although, unlike the Simpson siblings, I was the eldest and not a nitwit like Jules-Bart-Goode. "Because I thought it was a shit joke from a mate. I didn't want to get anyone in trouble."

"What about the other note? You said you had two," chipped in Viv.

"That was a month or so ago, just after Ginny and Ali split. It claimed Alistair and Mel were involved in dodgy dealings." Jules jabbed a finger towards my husband, who held his head buried in his lap. "I've always thought he was a bit of a twat, so I thought I'd chance my arm and see if there was any truth to what that letter claimed. As soon as I mentioned that I was aware of what he was up to, I knew from his tone that what the letter claimed was the truth."

"So, you thought you'd blackmail him rather than tell me?"

"I was trying to help you!"

"Jesus, Jules, no wonder you're frigging stupid! It's in your bloody genes. If Mel is your father, you're as dippy as your bloody half-brother, my cheating git of a husband, the man you've been trying to blackmail."

My verbalisation that Jules and Alistair were blood-related and not through my marriage was enough to allow that non-silence to halt proceedings. Jules and I locked eyes whilst Viv, the detective, presumably tried to piece together the clues on how my dead father had risen from the grave to murder the doctor, who apparently failed him, along with Jean and Mel, for reasons stated.

"Darling. Whilst this lot continue with their slanging match, it might be prudent to mention that detailed in that

letter, which this rather dishy officer kindly read aloud, it stated that Paul will complete his mission today. Assuming this snivelling weasel is his next target, that suggests Paul may very well be close. Following on from your point, as in our mission is to assist Ginny, we need a plan to protect this gob shite of a man."

"Shit! Good point, Deana. Any ideas?" Terry announced, breaking that non-silence.

"No, darling. That's your department, remember? However, we don't have much time, do we? And as much as I'm already dead, I really don't fancy being murdered trying to save this git!"

40

Moulin Rouge

The information contained in that handwritten note cleared up two mysteries. Whether written by my father's ghost or some other nutter hell-bent in sending me completely doolally, claiming that my mother had willingly, albeit with saving my father's business in mind, hopped into bed with Mel Strachan, who knew? However, ghosts penning letters from the grave aside, now I knew why my parents hadn't been overly supportive when Alistair and I started dating. Also, the identity of Jules's father.

Despite my babbling statement regarding Jules's parentage, which appeared to have stunted our conversation, the three of us shot a look at Terry and then across to where Mel quietly perched – the precise point where my new stalker appeared to be focused upon and, once again, in conversation with this imaginary person called Deana.

"Who you talking to?" Viv quizzed, causing Jules and me to swivel our heads back to face Terry, awaiting his answer.

"It's clear to see this place has missed the woman's touch. Why are men so averse to housework, d'you think? Even my darling Dickie was allergic to domestic chores and

never could be spotted with a duster in his hand, despite getting excited when I donned my sexy French maid outfit."

"Deana!" hissed Terry.

"I'm just saying, darling. Look at the dust on that coffee table. It's thick enough to grow spuds in. If Paul hadn't killed him, I could imagine the pervert would have died of consumption going by the amount of dust his lungs must have hoovered up in this place."

"Deana, we haven't got time to discuss the whys or the wherefores of your husband's sexual preferences regarding your French maid outfit you wore or his lack of desire to wave around a feather duster. We need to focus on the fact that Paul may have already killed someone else!"

"Frigging hell, who d'you say this twat was? What was all that crap about claiming to be your father?" chipped in Jules, appearing as stunned as the rest of us were by Terry's outburst.

"Darling, time to spring into action. I'm going to perform some of my Wicked-Witch-of-the-West antics. Now, eyes down, and focus. Get them all to look at the coffee table."

Terry nodded towards Mel, ignoring Jules's outburst. "Okay, give me a second and I can show—"

"Did you say French maid outfit?" interrupted Viv.

I shot looks between Jules, Alistair, Terry, and then Viv. "My, God, really!" I exclaimed, causing all four to glance at me. "Come on, why do all men have that salacious grin when it comes to French maids?" I thumped my hands on my hips and raised my eyebrows.

The four men exchanged glances.

"It's the way they're made, my dear. All men are cavemen at heart. You should know because your husband is a prime example. Your father, Terry, can't help himself. As for your new fella, well, I don't know, but I can't deny I wouldn't mind slipping on something sexy for him."

Terry shot a look in the general direction of Mel, whilst huffing and exasperatingly raising his hands.

"Well, I would, what a lush. Now, eyes down to the coffee table."

Terry broke the silence. "Hang on, all of you. You need to understand that all is not as it seems. I am Terry Walton. Ginny, I am your father. Now, if you'll kindly look at the coffee table, you'll see that I'm not some nutter talking to myself."

"What the—" blurted Viv, but halted his statement when stunned into that non-silence again when witnessing the thick layer of dust on the glass coffee table move as if pushed by an invisible finger.

Alistair raised his tear-stained face as the four of us stepped closer to witness the odd phenomenon which formed five capital letters.

D-E-A-N-A.

"Far out, man."

Viv, Alistair and I passed no comment as we stared at the letters, then watched as a smiley face appeared to form next to the word.

"It's called an Emoji, darling. They are all the rage. Bit like the Smiley face LSD tabs that I'm sure you indulged in back in the day."

Whilst leaving my teary husband mesmerised by the magically appearing letters and my brother to continue his hippy-styled muttering regarding the odd phenomena, Viv and I searched each other's eyes for answers before turning to face Terry, who offered that well-perfected exaggerated grin. Fortunately, Mel didn't move or utter his opinion on proceedings – what a relief.

"Deana, the woman your mother didn't hold in high regard—"

"Rather unfairly, I might add."

Terry paused and nodded, then continued. "As I was saying, Deana is here in this room with us." He held up the palm of his hand to stop any interruptions.

However, I, and it appeared by his expression, Viv, were too flummoxed to offer up anything coherent other than a, "Huh."

"Deana and I are both dead. As you are aware, so are your parents, Lizzy and Paul. However, for some bloody obscure reason, I appear to be the only one visible, if you get my drift," he chuckled, but continued when clocking that neither of us seemed to be able to join in with the conversation. "Deana has made a good point, which I know you couldn't hear her say—"

"Is Mum here now?" I interrupted. The sound of my words flowing from my mouth surprised me, as if my vocal cords had detached from my brain and acted independently.

"No," Terry paused. "No, your mother was with Deana and me earlier, but she's gone now." Terry turned and addressed one of the cubism art paintings. Although I presumed, rather ridiculously, I might add, he was addressing the invisible Deana, who I assumed now stood in front of it. "Deana, they seem a little perplexed. How about nudging that odd-looking picture frame down a few inches?"

"Right you are, darling. This is so much more fun than pretending to be a spook. It's actually nice to be 'in the room' if you get my drift." Deana chuckled, whilst performing the old bunny ears with her fingers before reaching across and nudging the frame as Terry suggested. *"Pity they can't hear me,"* Deana muttered as she stepped back to appraise the picture by way of tipping her head sideways. *"My darling Dickie would have liked that print. Right up his street, that is."*

"Wow ... that's real cool."

"How did you do that?" Viv chipped in, leaving Jules to ponder the bizarre happenings whilst sporting a childlike expression of wonder.

"Deana moved the picture, not me."

"Oh, piss off! You're making these things happen."

Terry offered that joker-type grin again whilst slowly shaking his head. "No, I'm not. Okay, so I don't have a six-foot one-inch rabbit as an imaginary friend, which I once accused Deana of being when trying to fathom out how I'd risen from the dead, but she is here. Deana, another demonstration is required. Something a little more convincing, perhaps."

"Oh, they're a tough lot to crack. I'd have thought writing my name was good enough. Err ..." Deana spun around, searching for inspiration. *"Mind out, you snivelling little weasel,"* she boomed at Alistair as she shimmied around his knees.

"Deana, he can't hear you."

Viv and I shot each other a look as Terry appeared to be following the invisible Deana around the room, halting his gaze beside the sofa where my unusually taciturn husband perched whilst appearing to have sunk into a stupor of bewilderment and grief.

"Yes, pity that. Right, eyes down, photo frames."

"You need to look at the photo frames on the bookcase."

One by one, all the pictures which Viv and I had earlier studied hovered in the air before gently landing on the coffee table. Without taking my eyes from the phenomenon of levitating photo frames, my right hand flailed by my side as I searched for Viv's hand whilst, along with Jules, we all stepped backwards until the wall behind us halted our retreat.

"Fuck this! I'm going," exclaimed Jules, before making a bolt for the front door.

"Viv … what just happened?" I stammered, glancing up at him. He didn't reply, keeping his focus on the frames and sporting a similar expression to Mel, who, fortunately, still hadn't moved. I figured this was all too nuts. So, if Mel suddenly decided to chip in with his opinion, I'd be following my little brother's lead.

Terry clapped his hands and swivelled around to address us as we pushed our backs to the wall. "Okay, so I assume that's enough for you to understand that Deana is here with us. Now, the point she made earlier is what we need to discuss."

I heard Viv swallow. For me, my mouth was as dry as that bucket of sand.

"Paul states in that letter," Terry nodded to the stapled sheets still clasped in Viv's hand. "The fourth victim will die today. Now, Deana and I assume the fourth will be Alistair," he waved his hand at my husband, who shot his head up at hearing his name. "Obviously, Paul had an issue with that doctor for operating on him when drunk and with Jean for covering up the malpractice. Why he wanted Mel dead is blatantly obvious, and what Alistair has been getting up to suggests he must be the intended fourth victim."

"Oh dear, darling. Your girl and Mr Dishy appear a smidge overwhelmed. That vacant expression they're giving off suggests they are a couple of gormless half-wits. I'm not sure they're listening."

"Ginny, Viv, you agree?" Terry quizzed, holding out his palms.

"I think you've flummoxed them, my darling."

Although not sure why, I managed to nod.

"Good. So, although your husband is dabbling in a spot of illegal accounting and is trying his best to ruin you, we're going to have to protect him from Paul."

Whilst this Terry bloke droned on about his ridiculous theory about my dead father planning to kill my husband, I focussed on the picture frames now newly arranged on the coffee table. I could detect Terry continuing to talk, but the words became indecipherable white noise.

"Ali … Alistair," I heard my voice call out. My verbalisation of my husband's name was enough to halt the white noise. "When that money went missing from the golf club, you and your father engineered that scam and tried to frame my father, didn't you?"

Alistair held my glare, his watery eyes conveying that I spoke the truth.

"After Mel's trial, his business collapsed, and you both thought you could embezzle funds from the club and pin it on Paul."

Alistair offered a slight, somewhat pathetic nod.

"It all went wrong, didn't it? Mel's mate, Kevin Reeves, arrested Dad but couldn't get the charges to stick." I aggressively jabbed my index finger towards him. "So, I'm guessing you had to perform some creative accounting to get the money back."

"Sorry," he muttered.

"What a little shit. I don't know about you, darling, but I'd happily assist Paul with the deadly deed if there weren't the need to protect Ginny's inheritance."

"I agree!"

"You agree, what?"

"Sorry, I was answering Deana."

"What did she say?" I quizzed, waving my hand in the general direction of the bookcase. "Christ, what am I saying?" I muttered, confused as to whether I actually believed Deana Beacham was standing in the room with us.

Terry pointed to his left, just behind Mel. "She's standing over there now."

"Oh." Although a pointless act, I glanced to where Terry nodded to.

"Deana was saying that she wouldn't mind helping Paul despatch this git into the afterlife." Terry waved his hand at Alistair, who now snivelled and repeatedly wiped the end of his nose on his shirtsleeve. Whether that was continued grief for the loss of his father, the fact that according to the note delivered to Jules a ghost was hunting him down, intent on sending him on his way along with Mel, or for playing his part in my father's downfall, I couldn't tell. However, now learning what I should have realised years ago, I suspected his snivelling repetitive routine was a concern for his own skin. *Bastard.*

"Hang on. Sorry, what did you say about Kevin Reeves?" Viv chipped in, now surfacing from his comatose state.

"It came to me a little earlier when we looked at those photos of Mel and your DCI together."

"What did?"

"Look, my father's health suffered after an incident at his golf club. Basically, he was the treasurer up at the Calthorpe Golf Club. To cut a long story short, fifty grand went missing, and the police questioned Dad …"

Viv knitted his brows as I paused.

"There wasn't enough evidence, and then the fifty grand just magically reappeared. Basically, someone, namely my scheming, conniving git of a husband and his pervert father, fiddled the accounts thinking they could get away with it. They tried to pin it on Dad, then replaced the money when the police couldn't get the charge to stick."

"When was this?"

"A year before he died. The whole affair caused him so much stress he had a heart attack."

"Then had a routine operation, which led—"

"Yep," I nodded. "What they did to Paul ended up with him on the slab being operated on by a pissed surgeon … it killed him."

"You think Reeves was colluding with them?"

"Ali?" I barked.

My husband nodded.

"Viv, that day, I met with Mum and Dad at the club. Not that I often met them there for lunch, but Mum and Dad suggested we meet up. I think Jules must have been at university because he didn't come. Anyway, that's when it happened. A club member, who also just happened to be a police officer, arrested Dad whilst we enjoyed lunch—"

"And you say that was DCI Kevin Reeves?"

"Definitely. I never knew his name. But he's the same man in those pictures with Mel Strachan, who you said is your DCI."

"Shit!"

I nodded whilst chewing my lip.

"When was this? When did your father die?"

"Dad died in 2010. They investigated him in 2009."

"And presumably, your father played golf at the same club as my DCI and Mel?"

"Yeah."

I waited as Viv appeared to take a moment to run this information through his mind.

I turned to face Alistair. "So, you admit that you, your father, and DCI Reeves attempted to fit Dad up so Mel could get his hands on the cash when his business failed."

Alistair chose not to answer.

Viv seemed to have concluded his musing and pushed his back away from the wall. "Right, this is a crime scene. I need you all out of here. I can't have you, whoever the hell you are, and Alistair in the room."

"What about Deana?" I asked.

"There isn't any Deana. I have no bleedin' idea what the frig's going on, but the only ghost in the room is this git," Viv jabbed a finger at Mel.

"Okay … I get it about being a crime scene. However, whether you believe Deana is here with us, you can't deny that the notes left at each murder scene suggest four deaths," chipped in Terry.

"So?"

"So, I suggest, Alistair Strachan has to be the next target. I think you're right; you should get him into safety. Call your lot, and secure this place."

"I'll be wanting to see some ID from you as well. I can't rule out that you're not responsible for this murder."

"Sorry, but I'm dead. I don't have ID."

"Fuck sake, this is ridiculous. Come on, all of you, out."

Terry held his hand aloft. "I have a suggestion."

Viv raised his eyebrows at Terry as he gestured to Alistair to stand. "Alistair Strachan, based on the fact of what you have already admitted, I'm arresting you for false accounting—"

"Can I just interject?" Terry leaned towards Viv. "Before you arrest him, I may have a better idea. Take a breath and hear me out."

"Oh, darling, I love it when you become all domineering. Makes me go all gooey and weak at the knees."

41

Sex, Lies, and Videotape

DCI Kevin Reeves slotted his black BMW Seven Series into his usual parking space in the little-used area tucked at the back of the hotel car park situated three miles south of Fairfield. From here, only the flock of the newly sheared sheep grazing on the rolling Hertfordshire farmland could spot his car. Plus, this area of the car park was devoid of any CCTV cameras.

Once a week, and every week for the last five months, Kevin parked in the same spot at 2 pm. On most occasions, a black Range Rover would already be parked in the next bay, and today was no different.

Superintendent Miles Bronckhorst, although Kevin's senior manager, had been a close friend for over twenty years. They were members of the same club, and Kevin and his wife regularly enjoyed dinner parties at the Bronckhorst's home, a six-bedroom mansion set in the leafy suburbs just north of Fairfield.

Like Kevin, Miles had divorced twice, not an uncommon situation for police officers who were married to their jobs. A couple of years ago, Miles married his third wife, a woman of significantly younger years, with many alluring qualities. Now in his mid-fifties, like Kevin, Miles, a competent officer, was close to retirement. However, unlike Kevin, Miles was none too skilled in the bedroom department. Well, that was according to Sarah Bronckhorst, the owner of the black Range Rover.

Kevin pinged open the glove compartment, lobbed his iPhone on the top of the service manual, and plucked out his burner phone. Kevin was a careful man. He'd switched his iPhone off before leaving Fairfield and wouldn't turn it back on until he returned to the Station later that afternoon – two hours after a tumble in the sheets with the Superintendent's wife.

Whilst holding his thumb on the green button, he waited for the cheap mobile to spring into life. After two short beeps, confirming the phone was ready, he tapped out the usual text message – *'I'm here'* – and then waited. Eight seconds later, the usual reply landed – *'Clear'* – Sarah had confirmed she was in the room waiting, and there appeared to be no one in the lobby who would recognise either of them.

Of course, there was always the chance that he might bump into an acquaintance when traversing the short skitter across the car park to the hotel entrance and the thirty feet from the revolving doors to the bank of lifts. However, the philandering DCI always had a credible back-up story planned out in his head to cover such eventuality, which so far hadn't occurred.

Whilst sporting a smug smirk, Kevin slotted the burner phone in his jacket pocket. Although his wife was nothing to be sneezed at and could rival the Superintendent's wife in the gorgeous woman stakes, Debbie Reeves had become a tiresome nag. Sarah provided two hours of erotic lovemaking without the moaning and constant snipes about his long working hours, which his wife claimed had started to sour their marriage.

~

Paul Goode, whilst leaning up against one of the three industrial-sized, roll-top commercial bins positioned at the rear of the hotel, patiently waited and soaked up the warm spring sunshine.

Of course, there was no need to hide from view. Although no CCTV cameras covered this area, he couldn't be spotted because he was dead and invisible. Well, invisible to all in the land of the living, that is.

Earlier that morning, he'd narrowly avoided a particularly close call when leaving Mel Strachan's home after suffocating the git with a plastic bag. As Paul had sauntered across the drive after a spot of murder, he'd spotted his wife alighting a bus a few hundred yards away, causing him to take swift evasive action to avoid detection. After diving behind a tree to take cover, he'd watched as Lizzy prised open a front window that he'd earlier jemmied to gain access. Although he suspected Lizzy wouldn't try to stop his little campaign of vengeance, he couldn't risk any interference with his carefully laid plans.

Paul lit another cigarette and rechecked his watch – 1:55. The black Range Rover arrived five minutes ago, dead on time. The thirty-something woman, dressed in gym gear and a baseball hat with her ponytail poking out the back, had hopped out and sashayed her way across to the hotel entrance as she did every week like clockwork. Paul had completed his reconnaissance and knew that the woman and Kevin Reeves kept to a strict routine.

He chuckled as he read the sign clamped to the lamppost, which stated that users of the hotel car park did so at their own risk and that management would not accept responsibility for damage, accidents, or loss. As he took a drag on his cigarette, Paul wondered if that also included loss of life.

In a little over five minutes from now, Paul would have completed his mission. Not an authorised mission like his wife had been afforded, but *his* mission to set the record straight.

Of course, there were others he could have *taken,* along with his four targets. Unfortunately, however, and rather disappointingly, Terry Walton, the man who'd enjoyed his wife's company whilst holidaying in Hunstanton all those years ago, was already dead. And then there was Alistair Strachan, that little shit, who'd married Ginny. He deserved to die, not only for how he treated his daughter but also for assisting Mel when trying to frame him for embezzling funds from the golf club.

Notwithstanding his desire to inflict misery and pain upon all of the Strachan family, Paul was mindful that murdering Alistair could result in Ginny losing the inheritance to which she was fully entitled. So, despite Strachan's boy having the opportunity to live, at least his son Jules seemed to have got the ball rolling to expose Alistair. Paul, although he'd doted on Jules, suspected that his son would be the easier – more gullible if you like – of his two children to convince that he'd come back from the dead. Anyway, with any luck, Ginny's husband would mourn the loss of his parents from the inside of a prison cell.

Kevin Reeves would undoubtedly be his most challenging kill. As for David Rawlinson, that murder could only be described as a piece of cake. The man was so inebriated, all that was required was a simple well-timed shove to send the drunk cartwheeling down to the foot of the stairs. As for Jean, well, now that was disappointing. Although married to Mel, he'd always harboured a bit of a soft spot for the woman. However, she'd made her bed when covering up Rawlinson's malpractice. Paul chuckled as he recalled the horror etched on her face whilst a seemingly invisible force held her head under the bath water as he watched the life drift from her eyes.

Mel was trickier. Although in his sixties and not particularly healthy, Paul knew the man would put up a fight, even though his attacker was invisible. Suffocation can take up to seven minutes, apparently. However, Paul banked on the fact that Mel, being a heavy smoker, along with his age, would reduce that significantly. He'd been right – just under four minutes for Mel to stop struggling.

Now it was Kevin Reeves's turn. Okay, so the man had only taken part in Mel's scheme to frame him, but that was enough. Although in his fifties, Kevin appeared healthy, regularly used the gym, and could keep up with his younger wife while also entertaining the fit young lady in the baseball cap. Paul knew murdering Kevin Reeves would not be as easy, even though he benefited from the element of surprise.

Right on cue, the black BMW Seven Series swung into its usual parking space. Paul dropped his cigarette and strode towards the car while hooking out Mel's club tie, which he'd previously purloined and secured in his jacket pocket. He leaned down and peered through the driver's door window, watching Kevin as he waited for the mobile in his hand to load. Then, as his quarry turned to gaze apathetically out of the car window, he stared directly at him.

Paul offered a little finger wave before stretching the tie that he held wrapped around both fists.

"Hi, Kevin. No shagging today, mate. In a couple of minutes, your bladder will open, and your eyes will bulge as I strangle the life out of you," he chuckled.

~

Just at the point when Kevin hit the engine stop button, the offside back door opened and then closed, seemingly of its own volition.

"What the ..." he blurted whilst shifting in his seat to peer behind him through the gap between the front seats.

"Af'noon, Kevin."

Bemused and now wondering if he'd imagined the door opening and closing, Kevin knitted his brows as he focused on the empty back seat. He sniffed, grimacing at the odour that now appeared to emanate from somewhere behind him. "Jesus, what's that smell?" he muttered.

"Yeah, sorry about that, old chap. I've not had the chance to shower for a couple of days, and it's been what you might call a busy morning. You should have seen your old mate Mel struggle," he chuckled.

Kevin edged his torso an inch or two further through the gap and sniffed again.

"Would you Adam and Eve it, but even ghosts have to wash. As I was saying, not had the chance to use any deodorant for a few days, so I probably do whiff a bit."

"Cigarettes," Kevin muttered, as he repeatedly sniffed.

Although, back in his younger days, Kevin had been a forty-a-day man, mostly Embassy, interspersed with a brief foray with Gauloises when trying to impress some French bird, he hadn't smoked for nearly twenty years. Now, a reformed smoker, he regarded the smell of cigarettes as repulsive.

"Oh, well, yes, that would be me, my old mucker. I've just put one out."

"Huh," Kevin shook his head and shifted back in his seat, snatched up his keys and made a grab for the door handle.

"Woah, not so fast, my friend." Paul whipped Mel's tie over the headrest, down to Kevin's throat, and then pulled with all his might by way of gaining purchase with his knees digging into the back of his quarry's seat.

Kevin's head shot backwards, thumping into the headrest. Instinctively, he grappled with both hands at the garotte that strangled his throat. Unable to squeeze his finger tips between whatever was tight around his neck and his skin, he shifted in his seat in an attempt to wriggle free. Unfortunately, although able to raise his bottom from the leather chair, the unseeable force which held his neck pinned to the headrest negated any chance to squirm free.

"Sit still, you bastard," grunted Paul through gritted teeth, as he yanked back on the two ends of the tie.

As Kevin attempted to breathe, panic set in when realising the cord around his neck had constricted his airways. Whilst continuing to writhe on his seat, his flailing arms floundered when the blood flow to and from his brain slowed. When noticing, in the rear-view mirror, the taught ends of a Calthorpe Golf club tie seemingly hovering in thin air, painful pressure built in his ears as he detected the warmth of his own urine seeping onto his thigh.

Paul held on for dear life as Kevin's body became limp. Although the bastard had slipped into an unconscious state, he knew he would have to starve the brain of oxygen for several minutes, presumably many more than it had taken Mel Strachan to give up the fight.

After holding his position, allowing three or four minutes to pass, Paul released the pressure to enable him to reach around and secure the tie around Kevin's neck. Paul nudged through the gap between the front seats and pulled the knot tight as Kevin's head flopped sideways. That momentary release of pressure allowed Kevin's bloodshot eyes to flicker open.

"Oh, no you don't, matey-boy." Paul afforded another tug on the knot to ensure he could fully achieve strangulation, thus sending Kevin off to the afterlife. Probably, to the bowels of hell, a place he knew he himself would soon be taking up residence in.

Paul slumped onto the back seat, now exhausted from his labours. Then, after pulling out his cigarettes and enjoying a post-murder smoke, he set about securing his pre-prepared note into the grip of Kevin's slack right hand that now limply lay on the centre consul.

'How did I escape? With difficulty. How did I plan this moment? With pleasure.'

Cigarette in hand, Paul opened the car door. Before hauling himself out of the car and back into the spring sunshine, he tapped Kevin on the shoulder. "See you soon, old chap. I'd better go and find my Lizzy. Oh, perhaps we could have a coffee and catch up in hell. Reminisce about old times, perhaps," he chuckled.

42

8 Mile

When interrupted by Terry, Viv hovered by the pathetic figure of my husband, who remained slouched on the sofa. Alistair appeared resigned to his fate, offering no verbal rebuff to Viv when my police officer boyfriend attempted to arrest him.

"Look, you could arrest him for fraudulent activity, but why not take this opportunity to help your girlfriend?"

"Oh, you clever boy," purred Deana.

Viv reeled around, facing Terry up. "I don't know who you are, but I'll arrest you for obstructing a police officer if you don't step out of the way."

Terry took a pace back. "Viv, all I'm saying is your primary focus is the murder of Mel Strachan, not his son's dodgy financial dealings."

"So? And anyway, Alistair has just confessed."

Appearing like a small boy awaiting his punishment, Alistair peered up at Viv and Terry, his head shooting back and forth as he followed their verbal exchange.

"I agree, he has. However, I think it's unlikely that Alistair Strachan murdered his father. So, rather than wasting your limited resources on nicking this git for his accounting fraud some years ago, focus on preventing the fourth murder. This bloke is in danger because Paul Goode plans to kill him."

"Jesus wept! You're not suggesting I listen to your bull about their father returning from the dead, are you?"

"I am. Because that is what's happening here."

Viv dismissively shook his head. "I'll be arresting you for perverting the course of justice, as well as nicking him." Viv jabbed a finger at Alistair, who continued to follow the conversation.

"Please, just hang on and listen to me. I reckon Alistair would be up for a deal." Terry glanced down at Alistair, who nodded vigorously.

"A deal? What kind of deal?" quizzed Viv.

Terry glanced at me. "Ginny, Alistair has financially ruined you, yes?"

I nodded.

"How much is your flat worth?"

"Oh, seven, eight-hundred thousand. There, or thereabouts," I shrugged, wondering where the hell this bloke was going with this while still trying to decide who he was and whether he had an invisible friend who could make picture frames magically fly.

"Oh, right. Wow, must be some flat," Terry muttered, seemingly bemused at my estimated valuation.

"Inflation, darling. You need to remember everything's gone up whilst you've been dead."

"Clearly," he chuckled.

Viv and I exchanged a glance. What was going through his head, I couldn't fathom. Whether I believed Terry was holding a conversation with the ghost of a woman who got herself arrested for indecent exposure, I didn't know either. That said, some batshit weirdo things were definitely afoot.

"So, Alistair, I'm guessing that you would be open to signing over your flat to Ginny in exchange for your fraudulent activity getting lost under a heap of paperwork, never to see the light of day again."

"Hang on, mate. You're suggesting I ignore his confession?"

"Yep ... Ginny gets to move off the Broxworth, Alistair avoids prison and can go back to running his business. My mission will be complete, as in my daughter here will no longer be destitute. Then Deana and I can turn our exclusive skills to hunting down Paul Goode. Hopefully, we can stop him from killing Alistair."

"Oh, darling, let's not bother. I think we should leave well alone. If Paul wants to kill him, let him, I say."

Viv shot a look at me, then back to Terry. "You're bleedin' deluded."

"Viv, think about it. This gives Ginny a chance to escape the shit she's in."

Although I could detect from Alistair's expression he was open to Terry's suggestion, I knew Viv wouldn't entertain such an idea. So, notwithstanding the golden opportunity to escape my dire situation, Viv had procedures and processes to follow – that rule book previously stuck up his rectum.

"Alistair Strachan, I'm arresting you—"

"Viv, please, think about this."

When Terry interrupted Viv, as he once again attempted to arrest my husband, Eminem rapping *'back to reality'* from *'Lose yourself'* interrupted proceedings. Viv whipped out his mobile from his jean pocket and studied the caller ID with knitted brows.

"Viv?" I quizzed.

"Work," he mumbled, before stepping to the doorway, leaving Terry, Alistair and me to exchange glances. Mel remained silent. As for Deana, well, what she was up to was anyone's guess.

Now Eminem had been cut short, we all listened to one half of the conversation between Viv and someone called Sir.

"I was just going to call it in, sir," Viv paused before informing whoever that he was at Mel Strachan's home and the circumstances of his death.

As the exchange continued, Viv mentioned the word girlfriend, presumably referring to me, and explained why he was at Mel's home. At no point did he mention Alistair, Terry, or an invisible ghost called Deana were apparently also present. Well, if she wasn't, this Terry bloke could perform some pretty neat tricks. Viv's omittance regarding their presence sent my mind whirring. Now I wondered why Viv appeared to have not only extracted the police procedure manual from his rectum and lobbed it out of the window, but also seemingly had metaphorically torn it into pieces and burnt it.

"My God! When?" Viv shot a look at me whilst 'Sir' presumably took up the conversation.

I raised my eyebrows at him as he again glanced my way and threw in a few 'Uh-huhs' and a couple of 'Hmmms' into the flow of the conversation. A couple of minutes later, following a fair amount of head scratching from Viv, 'Sir' presumably relented, allowing space for Viv to speak more coherent words.

"No, sir," he paused. "Yes, sir, that's no problem. The funeral won't be for a couple of weeks. I'll hand over to SOCO when they arrive and then meet you there."

"From what I can gather, this dishy boy has just been promoted. He's officially an Acting Detective Inspector. And, would you believe there's been another murder." Deana, whilst carefully trying not to nudge into Viv, strained up on tiptoe as she attempted to earwig the conversation.

"Another murder," muttered Terry.

"Whatever eau de toilette he wears, it's ravishing." With her nose to his t-shirt, Deana snorted at the aroma and closed her eyes. *"What a lush,"* she purred.

I swivelled my head from where I'd been gawping at Viv to shoot a look at Terry. "Excuse me?"

Terry pointed at Viv. "Deana said she's heard there's been another murder."

"Oh, is she over there now?" I quizzed, before slowly closing my eyes and shaking my head in despair regarding my utterance of such a stupid comment.

"Dad's ... been murdered," snivelled Alistair, as he started to hyperventilate before burying his head in his hands again and proceeding to sob.

Terry and I glanced at my wailing husband before looking at each other and offering a disinterested shrug.

"Yes, sir. And fank you, sir." Viv killed the call and glanced back into the room whilst twiddling his mobile around in the palm of his hand.

"Who's been murdered?"

Viv narrowed his eyes.

"Deana was listening to your conversation." Terry wagged his finger to the left of Viv's position.

Viv side-eyed the area indicated by Terry's outstretched arm before tutting to himself. "You ain't going to believe this. That was Superintendent Bronckhorst. Twenty minutes ago, an anonymous woman called the police to report that someone had strangled a man in his car which is parked up at a hotel just south of Fairfield—"

"Not with a note," I blurted.

Viv nodded.

"The same note as all the others?"

"Yep."

"That's four ... if the note is the same as all the others, Paul has completed his Tetris."

"Tetralogy, darling. Not Tetris," sniggered Deana.

"The back of the notes denotes four murders," I vacantly muttered.

"The victim was alive an hour ago, so that puts you both in the clear." Viv waved his finger between Terry and Alistair.

"How d'you know?" I chipped in.

"Because he made a call to Fairfield Station less than an hour ago."

"The victim?" I wide-eyed quizzed. "What, a distress call whilst being murdered?"

Viv shook his head at me, then glanced at Terry. I could tell his mind was whirring.

"Viv ... Viv, who's died?"

"You're not going to believe this. The victim is DCI Kevin Reeves."

"Oh, well, that's it, darling. Paul never intended to kill Alistair. Thank goodness for that," she chortled. "What a relief. I really didn't fancy hunting him down, I can tell you."

I pointed to the picture frame on the coffee table, specifically the one of Mel and Kevin standing on the golf course. "Mel, Kevin, Jean and that doctor ... their only connection is my dead father, Paul Goode." I glanced around at Viv, who slowly shook his head at me. "Oh, Paul, what have you done?" I whispered.

"Ginny, you can't be suggesting ..." Viv's voice trailed away, leaving us both, once again, pondering the absurd.

"Darling, I can hear sirens. I'm alright, but I think you need to make yourself scarce. I'm going to cause a distraction in the kitchen. Now, when they all scoot through to see what's going on, you make a run for it."

Terry broke the silence between Viv and me as we continued to contemplate my preposterous statement regarding my father's ghost. "Viv, by the sounds of it, the cavalry are on their way. You have an opportunity to save Ginny." Terry nudged Alistair with his shoe. "You agree to give the flat to Ginny in return for the police not delving into your affairs?"

Alistair nodded before glancing up at Viv.

The wail of sirens suggested a fleet of police cars was minutes away.

"Ginny?" quizzed Viv.

"What would Heather tell you to do?" I replied. Notwithstanding my desire to grab this opportunity, which Terry appeared keen to broker, I needed Viv to do the right thing.

If Alistair signed the flat over to me, I could sell it and, with the proceeds, set myself up for the future. However, whatever my future would pan out to be, whether financially secure or bankrupt and living on the Broxworth Estate, I just yearned to find happiness. Within the short time I'd started to get to know this man, who stood pondering my question, I'd come to realise he could be the catalyst to finally putting my crappy, loveless past behind me.

"Heather would tell me to do the right thing. Right over easy, as she always says."

I nodded and offered a tight smile. Although that condemned me to a life on the Broxworth Estate, a part of me felt relieved that my new boyfriend hadn't wholly decimated the rule book.

"Alistair," Viv barked at him.

My husband sighed, presumably knowing what was coming, before glancing up at Viv.

"You sign over the flat to Ginny today. Failure to do that and I will arrest you."

"Wha—"

Viv grabbed my hand. "Right over easy doesn't always mean follow procedures … that's another one of Heather's doctrines."

"Oh."

As the wailing sirens filled the void in our conversation, a cacophony of breaking crockery harmonised with the Doppler effect of the frequency changes to those police sirens.

Leaving Terry and Alistair with Mel, Viv and I barrelled our way through to the kitchen, where we witnessed flying crockery and glassware as if the house was rolling around on the high seas. Before our eyes, the contents of open cupboards levitated before shattering on the floor, as if some poltergeist had royally got the hump and felt the need to make a point. The resulting carnage afforded the tiled floor the appearance of the aftermath of a Greek wedding, where the smashing of plates was considered a way to ward off evil spirits. Mesmerised by the vision in front of us, we hovered at the doorway, watching each cupboard systematically empty to the floor.

"Cheap rubbish, anyway. I presume some of that crap, like this dinner service, was probably some of Jean and Mel's wedding presents. It looks like it's come out of the Ark." Deana held up a teapot, waving it at Viv and Ginny *"Look at this bloody awful thing. You'd think they would*

have updated this old crap years ago, wouldn't you?" she announced before sending it flying to join the rest of the tea service, which now covered the vast majority of the kitchen floor. "Always wanted to do something like this. Such fun, you know," Deana chortled, as she swept her hand across another stack of bowls and side dishes, sending them flying.

43

Good Night Charlie

Trent Lescott woke with a start when the front door to his flat, situated on the third level of Dublin House, took a fist hammering. "Fuck off," he boomed, confident this wasn't a drugs raid because the filth were always stupid enough to announce their arrival with a 'police, open up' shout, or they just battered the door down without knocking, neither of which had occurred.

His front door took another pummelling. "Fuck sake," he muttered. Although probably already mid-morning, Trent was naffed off about being woken so early. After enjoying a heavy night of drinking, snorting a few lines of Charlie, and the attentions of the two naked girls, whose names escaped him, who lay in a comatose state on either side of him, the last thing he needed was some wanker hammering their fist on his front door.

"Oi, move your arse," he barked at the girl on his left before flinging her limp arm from his chest and clambering over her. She muttered something incoherent in response as he hoisted up a pair of boxer shorts and padded to the front door.

"Or-right, Or-right. Fuck sake, stop banging on the door, you wanker," he hollered, before grabbing the latch and pinging open the door.

Trent peered around the doorframe before stepping onto the landing. Whilst offering a wide yawn, he glanced up and down, bemused as to why there appeared to be no one there. "Fucking kids," he mumbled, before flinging the door shut and padding into the kitchen, where he snatched up his cigarettes.

As he flicked the kettle on, after giving it a shake, he swivelled around to spot one of last night's conquests leaning against the door frame. Her hair hung limply as the girl turned her face up towards him, rolling saliva around on her tongue.

"You got any blow?" she mumbled.

Trent dragged on his cigarette as he appraised what stood before him. For sure, she'd looked a sight better last night when her makeup wasn't streaked across her face. "Get your gear and fuck off. And take that other slag wiv ya."

"Ah, come on, babe. You must have some blow," she whined, before stepping into the kitchen and tentatively placing her hand on one of the small plastic packets of white powder that lay heaped on the worktop.

"Get your fucking mitts off that."

"Oh, go on, man. Just a line," she whined.

Trent snatched her wrist and squeezed. "I said, leave it."

"Yeah, but you got loads of gear."

"Yeah, and it ain't yours," he aggressively barked.

"Or-right, fuck sake. Get off me, that fuckin' 'urts."

Trent blew smoke in her face as he shoved her hand away. "Now, go on, fuck off."

"What about those rings ... can I 'ave 'em?"

Trent glanced at the heap of assorted crap that lay abandoned where he'd slung the content of his pockets beside his stash. A haul that he would need to move on later today because his supplier would be expecting payment. Although being a violent thug, and the fact that most of the scum on the estate sensibly avoided Trent, his supplier wasn't the sort to be messed with. Trent moved drugs for one of the Gowers, and everyone knew you didn't mess with that family.

The Gowers, the leading light in the drugs distribution scene in Fairfield, weren't of a mind to offer second chances to those who were stupid enough to cross them. Trent was fully aware that failure to pay up when required would more than likely result in receiving a 9mm slug lodged in his skull.

The naked girl folded her arms across her breasts and apathetically glanced up at Trent, the act of lifting her head appearing to be a task in itself. Trent assessed the heap of crap where two rings lay nestled with a broken gold chain, a cigarette lighter, pocket fluff, and some scrunched-up receipts.

Trent plucked up the rings and rolled them around in the palm of his hand. Initially he'd forgotten where they came from, but then remembered that Virginia woman in the stairwell from a couple of days ago. He snorted a chuckle as he assessed the girl's vacant, dilated pupil appearance. Although that Virginia woman was at least twice the age of the girl who stood swaying in front of him, he considered she would probably be a better shag than this druggy bitch.

"Can I 'ave 'em, then?"

Trent threw the rings on the counter. "Yeah, they're just pieces of crap, anyway."

The girl made a grab for the rings as they spun on the work surface where Trent had lobbed them.

Trent smacked his hand on top of hers. "Get your gear and that other slag out of my bed before you take these." After releasing her hand, he scraped the rings along the counter and out of her reach. With the hand holding his cigarette, he gripped her neck before forcing her backwards out of the kitchen, thus propelling the naked girl back along the corridor towards the bedroom.

"Or-right," she gargled whilst struggling to maintain an upright stance before Trent unceremoniously shoved her onto the stained mattress.

"What's going on?" the other girl mumbled, as their two naked bodies collided.

"You need to piss off." Trent dropped the cigarette butt in a glass of undeterminable liquid positioned on the chest of drawers whilst the two girls staggered about, scrabbling around, trying to locate their clothing. "Fuck sake, what a state," he muttered, shaking his head as he wondered how pissed he must have been to shag these two.

~

Lizzy hopped backwards out of the way of the man with disturbing yellow eyes, as he thrust his hand around the girl's throat and forced her along the corridor towards the bedroom.

"My God, how some people live," she tutted. *"Scum, total scum."* Lizzy nipped into the kitchen and plucked up her rings before poking her head around the door and shouting to the man wearing a pair of boxers as he leaned against a set of dilapidated chest of drawers. *"I'll have you know, those rings cost my Paul a week's wages back in the day. You might regard them as crap, but they're not yours, you low-life piece of shit."*

Lizzy pocketed her and Paul's wedding rings and nipped into the hallway before glancing back into the kitchen. She chewed her lip whilst weighing up whether she had enough time. Of course, Lizzy only planned to retrieve the rings this reprobate had stolen from Ginny. However, now the situation presented an opportunity for vengeance. Well, her Paul seemed to be able to get away with it, so why shouldn't she have some fun? It wasn't like she was going to murder him, just cause enough problems that might lead to someone else doing the deed. Lizzy padded to the bedroom and peered in, spotting two near-naked women stumbling about trying to dress.

"My God. There's two of them. Looks like the sort of debauched behaviour that slapper Deana would indulge in."

Satisfied that both girls appeared incapable of putting their arms through the bra straps, and Yellow-Eye seemed quite content to stand and watch them, she nipped back to the kitchen. After grabbing all the packets of white powder, she turned the tap on and emptied each packet's content into the sink. "I presume this is going to put you in a spot of bother, you revolting man," she announced, before chuckling to herself as she revelled in the sight of flushing *away what she presumed was thousands of pounds worth of cocaine.*

After emptying the last packet, Lizzy left the tap running, zipped along the grubby hall to the front door and carefully twizzled the Yale lock. "I'll be off now. You've caused my girl so much distress. So, you revolting piece of trash, I do hope you have a thoroughly rotten day. I'm quite confident, after you see what I've done to your little stash, that will be the case."

44

New Year's Day 2024

A Finger of Fudge

"Daddy, where's your mum and dad?" enquired Noah, as he glanced up at his father whilst his innocent six-year-old brain tried to fathom where his grandparents were. Unlike him, all of his friends at school had grandparents. Like all his mates, he knew you should have two grannies and two granddads. That said, Noah knew that some of them had many more, which was all too confusing, especially as he had none.

Noah knew his mother's parents were in the grave, which she knelt by whilst laying a posy of fresh flowers. However, it suddenly occurred to him he didn't know where Daddy's parents were.

Noah's father ruffled his hair before squatting to be at eye level with him. "Your grandmother is with Jesus. There's a grave for her in Barbados."

"Where's Barb ... Barbidos?" he asked, frowning whilst trying to fathom how she could be in two places simultaneously.

After flicking a few twigs away that lay near the headstone of the double grave of Paul and Elizabeth Goode, I glanced around at my son. "It's called Barbados, sweety. Daddy's mum lived there, but she's with Jesus now ... with my mum and dad."

Viv raised an eyebrow at me as he rubbed our son's mitten-clad, tiny hands in his. Although a bright sunny January day, a stiff northerly breeze that weaved through the graveyard reduced the temperature to somewhere around freezing point. Anyway, a few hours to blow away the cobwebs of the old year was just what we needed after seeing in the new year well into the wee hours.

Whether my parents were with Jesus was a matter of conjecture. Of course, you could debate if Jesus existed, and if he did, would my father, Paul Goode, be with him or locked in some hideous dungeon in the bowels of hell – who knew?

Seven years had passed since that day at Mel's house when Viv and I stood and gawped as some invisible force ransacked the kitchen and its contents like a demented evil spirit intent on causing a path of destruction. Unfortunately, Terry, or whoever he was, had disappeared when Viv's colleagues arrived, and we never crossed paths again despite Viv and his team's best efforts to track him down.

To this day the four murders, culminating with the death of DCI Kevin Reeves, remain as unsolved cases. What actually took place in that house? Well, that was still anyone's guess. The lines of enquiry took on many strands, one of which involved investigating how a dead woman's fingerprints could be lifted from the coffee table and six photo frames, not to mention the vast majority of the fragments of crockery and glass that pretty much carpeted the tiles on the kitchen floor.

Viv and I had long since accepted the ghost of Deana had been there, as ridiculous as that sounds. The only other explanation for how her fingerprints could be on all of Alistair's parents' dinner service was that at some point in the past she'd touched every item in their kitchen, which was as probable as the imbecilic idea that her ghost had been there in the room with us.

Alistair complied with the deal, signed over the freehold to our penthouse flat, and vacated the premises later that week. I didn't move back in, choosing to move in with Viv and place my flat, which held too many bad memories, on the market.

Despite my plans to move to London, which I'd mooted with Karen that day I first spotted Terry in that coffee shop, I stayed in my hometown and married a police officer, who now held the rank of Detective Chief Inspector. I happily endured the calls to his mobile at all hours of the night when my husband was investigating a big case. Something his previous girlfriend wasn't prepared to put up with.

I, Ginny Goode, an average girl from a small town, had finally achieved what I'd always wanted – a family and the simple desire to be happy. Now, of course, you could accuse me of harbouring low ambition – fair point.

However, as Noah's honorary grandmother, the wise old woman, Heather French, would say – happiness equals success, not the size of your bank balance. As I'd previously proved that I struggled to accurately add two and two and achieve four, I thought it prudent to believe the retired DCI's calculations. Anyway, a DCI's pay wasn't too shabby, and with the proceeds of the sale of mine and Alistair's flat, we'd carved out a comfortable and, as far as we were concerned, idyllic life.

Whilst grabbing the top of the gravestone, I straightened up and brushed away the dirt from my knees before gently stroking my right hand across the top of the headstone. The sound of my ring as I tapped my hand echoed off the granite.

My usual thoughts when visiting my parents' grave – and today was no different – were regarding Terry Walton. Specifically, about that day at Mel's and what that bloke Terry had said about my mother being there earlier that day. I guess I would forever wonder if my mother's ghost had been within touching distance as we'd come to believe that Deana's had been. I shook my head, dismissing my silly thoughts as I turned to Viv and Noah.

"Come on, let's go."

Viv nodded before hoisting Noah into his arms as we stepped away from my parents' final resting place – presuming they still weren't roaming around as ghosts – and negotiated the gravel path that circumnavigated the church. As we purposefully strode back to the car, keen to put a lick on to duck out of the chilly wind, I fiddled with my ring which I wore on my right ring finger that earlier had echoed off the granite headstone.

A few years back, I'd asked a local jeweller to fashion me a ring from the gold of my parents' rings. Although their marriage had experienced difficulties, and if the events of seven years ago were to be believed far more problematic than I'd thought, I'd wanted something to remember them by. Of course, I used to wear them together on a chain around my neck. Well, I did until the day I met my husband, the day

I moved on to the Broxworth, the very day Yellow-Eye and his band of merry men mugged me and stole them when he'd barbarously torn the chain from my neck.

How they came back into my possession, you may ask. Well, that's as ridiculous a situation as that conversation with Terry and the invisible Deana. Two days after that ludicrous event, the day Viv, with the help of Karen and Danny, hauled my suitcases back down that piss-stinking stairwell, an envelope appeared on the worktop. I nearly missed it, just spotting it as I completed a final sweep of the flat before closing the door for the last time.

The plain white envelope, propped up against the kettle, simply had 'Ginny' penned on the outside. The handwriting was distinctly my mother's. Inside were both rings and a note, again in my mother's hand, with just three words.

'Please forgive Paul.'

The day after being reunited with my parents' rings, Viv and his team were presented with another murder to investigate as if they didn't have enough. However, this time there was no note with a quote from Dumas, and the cause of death was a single gunshot wound to the head – an execution carried out by an enforcer for one of the drug gangs. However, unlike the investigation into the four 'Dumas' murders, Viv's team apprehended the perp and arrested him within a few days. So, who was the victim? I hear you ask. Yes, well, he was a low-life drug dealer called Trent Lescott, or as I knew him, with my less than affectionate moniker, Yellow-Eye.

Whilst lost in my thoughts, I hadn't noticed Viv halt until Noah called out.

"Mummy, wait."

I swivelled around, glancing at where Viv appeared to be fixated on something on the far side of the graveyard. "Viv?"

With Noah in his arms, he turned and nudged his head in the direction he'd been gazing. "There's someone up at your father's grave."

I stepped back, grabbing hold of Viv's free arm. "Terry Walton's?"

"Yeah, look, looks like a family."

Although we weren't regular visitors to my biological father's final resting place, it was clear that someone was. On the odd occasion, when we'd wandered over there after visiting my parents' grave, fresh flowers would be placed by the headstone, so clearly tended to by someone who must have loved him. Of course, I had no idea about his family and, although he was my biological father, I'd never bothered to investigate the family tree.

Although Viv and I had settled on the conclusion that Deana's ghost existed, simply because of the irrefutable evidence and the absence of any other explanation, we rarely discussed the matter, thus avoiding disappearing down that particular rabbit hole of nuttiness. As for Terry, the visible man in that house seven years ago, well, that was just too much to consider. So, we didn't visit his grave, just occasionally stepping past and hovering long enough to offer a polite nod before moving on.

Now, for the first time, we were here when some of that man's family were too. The itch was too much to ignore. I just had to scratch it.

I glanced up at Viv, who nodded before we weaved our way towards the family, who were undoubtedly visiting the final resting place of Terry Walton.

As we grew ever closer, I could make out a man, perhaps in his late thirties, and a woman holding onto a pushchair. Two little girls of similar age to Noah patiently waited as the man, who I presumed to be their father, fussed about removing a pitiable festive wreath.

Viv grabbed my arm, halting my advance as we came within a few yards of the group. Detecting that my husband was non-verbally suggesting that we should give them some space, I halted my advance and laid my cheek on his arm as I watched the two girls hop up and down while their father whispered something to them before pointing at Noah.

Children have an innocence that breaks down barriers, something we adults seem unwittingly to put in place. The two girls skipped over to Noah, who Viv had settled down on the ground.

"I'm Katlin. What's your name?" confidently enquired the slightly taller of the two. Both girls were nothing short of beautiful, and I suspected they could forge a modelling career in the future.

Viv nudged Noah. "Say hello," he encouraged him.

My son, a shy boy, smiled back before Katlin plucked out a small chocolate bar from her baby-pink coat pocket and offered it to him.

"You can have it ... it's the last one from my selection box."

Noah glanced up at me with that 'can I?' expression. I nodded and smiled back before mouthing, "Say thank you." I think Noah and Katlin had found love.

"Hiya," boomed the woman, who swivelled around, keeping a firm grip on the pushchair. "Your little 'un okay wiv chocolate?" she joyfully asked. The woman was a stunner, late twenties, with long blonde hair and a smile that could stop aeroplanes in mid-flight, let alone cause multiple pile-ups on the M25.

"Yes, that's very kind of Katlin. You have beautiful children." I offered.

"Fanks, your boy's a cutie too. I'm Courteney, and this 'ere is my other 'alf, Damian. Y'know, like the antichrist, Damien Thorn. Although you spell it wiv an a, not an e. Ain't that right, babe?" she gestured with her cerise-pink gloved hand to the man who turned away from Terry's grave and stepped towards us.

"I'm Ginny, and this is my husband, Viv." Viv offered a wave; ever the strong silent type was my husband. "And this shy little one is Noah." My son, munching on his chocolate, didn't seem to mind that Katlin held his other hand. My six-year-old had acquired himself an admirer by the look on the little girl's face.

"Hi there ... did you know Terry Walton?" Damian asked, brushing away some dirt from his fingers before reapplying his black gloves.

I glanced at Viv, who shrugged back, his eyes indicating that I should tell them who Terry Walton was to me. "Err ... yeah, sort off ... although I never met him," I paused, concerned if I told him who Terry was to me, I could blow a ship-sinking-sized hole in his family. "Well, I don't think I met him," I nervously chuckled. "You see, Terry Walton was …"

"Your father?" Damian questioned, finishing my sentence.

45

Dead Goode

"Yeah ... you're right. Terry was ... err ... my biological father," I stammered, confirming what Damian suggested whilst inwardly wincing. Of course, divulging this information might become problematic if Damian also happened to be one of Terry's offspring. Let's face it, suddenly discovering your father's infidelity might not be such welcome news. However, judging his age and how long ago Terry died, I surmised that Damian probably would struggle to remember him.

Despite Damian paving the way, so to speak, for my announcement, my statement hung in the air, hovering like an invisible cloud between the four adults. Whether I'd made an error of judgement by announcing that the man, who I assumed was six feet below that headstone, was my father or not, Damian's expression suggested that my statement was either unwelcome or I was going to have to elaborate further.

"Babe?" chimed in Courteney, shooting her husband a quizzical look, presumably trying to nudge him from the vacant stare he now offered. "After last night, there's no time like the present."

Whilst Damian presumably mulled over an appropriate response, that first encounter with my sister-in-law churned around my brain. That day, when Deli had hollered at me, calling me bitch, when I'd scooted along the landing outside my flat intent on buying copious amounts of wine from Fat-Oaf's emporium, I recall she mentioned her friend called Courts. That apparently stunning porn star who previously rented that shithole I'd moved into for less than a week made a mint from her dubious lifestyle before running off into the sunset with a posh boy called Damian.

Now, I'm not suggesting that this woman previously dabbled in a spot of internet porn, but Deli had mentioned that Courts was a bit of a stunner. Deli also reckoned Damian was a posh boy, but the one sentence this man had so far uttered didn't suggest he was posh – no, far from it. Although to be fair to my sister-in-law, now living in Barbados with a gentle giant who'd wooed and calmed the girl, I guess anyone who didn't live on the Broxworth could be labelled high-born in Deli's eyes. However, on the subject of that odious place, Damian's gorgeous wife's diction suggested that she had once called the Broxworth Estate her home.

Damian nodded to Courteney, a gesture that suggested he would divulge what she appeared to urge him to. "Okay, it's Ginny, yes?"

"Yes … Virginia, but I prefer to be called Ginny."

"Well," he chuckled. "Here's the thing, Terry Walton was also my father."

"Oh," I exclaimed, shooting a look at Viv, who offered that smug grin, presumably pleased that his constant pushing for me to delve into Terry's past had now afforded me a little brother.

"Babe, you've got anover sister," grinned Courteney.

Damian stepped forward and nervously offered his hand, which I accepted. "This is a bit odd," he smirked.

"I hope I haven't caused any issues with your family."

While holding my hand, Damian knitted his brows, seemingly confused by my statement.

"Y'know, if discovering that your father had other relations than with your mother, if you see what I mean," I offered a nervous whining giggle. Christ, this was awkward.

Damian, letting go of my hand, raised a quizzical eyebrow at Courteney.

"Granny's custard," she tutted. "Bleedin' hell, babe, you are fick at times. What Ginny's saying, will your mother be upset to find out that your father has played away."

"Oh," he chortled. "Christ, no. Look, Terry died before I was born. As for my mother, well, we enjoyed minimal contact over the years. Anyway, my dear mother was far more skilled in the playing away department, if you get my drift."

"Oh, that's a relief," I nervously giggled, pleased to hear that Damian and I both appeared to have experienced a similar upbringing, as in our parents' propensity to dabble in extracurricular activities. Well, okay, that was a little unfair on Paul. However, as for my mother, Lizzy … hmmm, multiple orgasms Terry, springs to mind, let alone anyone else she might have dabbled with on a holiday sofa or whatever she got up to with Mel Strachan.

Viv thumped his large hand on Damian's elbow. "Good to meet you. I'm Viv. I guess you're my brother-in-law."

Before I knew it, a whirlwind of blonde hair flew at me as Courteney offered a hug, something that would have been rude not to reciprocate. While the four of us exchanged, what was for me, awkward hugs and cheek kissing, I spotted Noah offer his half-chewed chocolate bar to Katlin. The little beauty's opened mouth, waiting to accept his saliva-gunked offering, suggested she was more than happy to swap bodily fluids. Whilst noisily chomping the chocolate, she emulated her mother by way of hugging my shy little boy before planting a chocolate-infused kiss on his cheek.

Noah, benefiting from that mixed-race perfect skin, blushed.

"I might be wrong here, so please excuse me if I have, you know, made an assumption that's not true, if you see what I mean," I babbled before Viv nudged my arm, effectively encouraging me to get to the point. "Did either of you live up at the Broxworth Estate at some point?"

"Yeah, right bleedin' shithole. That's where me and my babe, Damian Statham, met."

"I think you know my sister-in-law. Delfina Richards."

"Deli?" exclaimed Courteney. "Friggin' hell, Deli's your sister?"

"She is ... she's my little sister," chipped in Viv.

"Oh, shit, you're the bleedin' filth, ain't you?"

Viv chuckled and nodded. "DCI Richards, pleased to meet you," he smirked.

"Shit," she hissed.

"Hey, don't worry, I might be the filth, but I don't nick my own family if I can help it."

"Oh, I ain't no lawbreaker. It's just I had a few run-ins wiv your lot back in the day."

"Courteney, did you say that your name was Statham?"

"Yeah," she grabbed Damian's arm. "We've been married for nearly seven years. I wasn't gonna get married 'cos I hate fruit cake, but Damian was very persuasive. Weren't you, babe?" she kissed his cheek, copying her daughter, although without the chocolate-infused lips.

"Oh, wow, you're that author … Courteney Statham," I exclaimed.

"That's me," she grinned. "And your sister was my inspiration for my main protagonist, Deli Klein. Well, without the love of vodka, that is. How is she? I heard she went back to Barbados?"

"She did. Happily living with a kind-hearted man who peddles the old ganja on the beach to the tourists."

"Oh, that's a bit awkward, ain't it? Y'know, what wiv you being the filth?"

"Winston, that's his name, might sail close to the wind, but apart from Viv, he's the loveliest man I know. Deli has landed on her feet with that man." I glanced up at Viv, awaiting confirmation. Although Winston dabbled in the illegal drug trade, my assessment of the man was accurate, and Viv knew it.

"Well, I'm just well happy she's okay."

Damian nodded to the path, a hundred or so feet away, where a couple strolled along with a girl who appeared to be a similar age to Katlin. "Ginny, you're having one hell of a day," he chuckled. "See that couple?" he pointed to the three as they headed our way. "Well, that's Vinny and Kim. Now, Courteney and I have known Kim for many years. I also knew that Kim's father is Terry Walton, but for some reason, until last night, I never told her that we're related."

My mouth sagged, and I bulged my eyes as I gawped at the approaching couple.

"Ginny, you have a brother and a sister," he whispered before shouting across to them. "Kim! Kim, you ain't gonna believe this," he beckoned with both arms, encouraging them to hurry.

As the couple approached, the little girl ran off to chat with Noah, Katlin, and Courteney's middle child, whose name I didn't know. I wondered if Katlin would have competition for Noah's attention.

Kim and Vinny exchanged kisses with Courteney and Damian before Kim caught her breath and asked what all the excitement was. "Damian?" she quizzed, glancing at Viv and me.

"Kim, I know I blew your mind last night about Terry also being my father, but wait till you hear this!" Damian shot me an exaggerated grin, presumably encouraging me to spill the beans.

Whilst gripping my husband's hand, I tried to find the words. Stunned by the revelation of my ever-growing family, my mind refused to play ball, and my bucket-of-sand mouth failed to comply. However, Kim filled the void.

"You're my big sister, aren't you?"

I offered a tiny nod, unable to find the appropriate words, although a simple yes would have sufficed. We all started another round of that awkward hugging and cheek kissing as I willingly allowed my eyes to water.

Now, of course, those weren't tears of displeasure. No, tears of joy. I, Ginny Goode, that ordinary girl from a small town, had finally got everything I wanted – a family, which appeared to exponentially grow larger by the minute.

"So, who are the mothers, then?" Damian announced with a cheerful grin. "I think we can all agree our father, God rest his soul, liked the ladies. So, which three lucky ladies produced us?"

"Oh, yes," I chuckled, wiping away the tears from my cheeks with the heel of my hand. "So, Elizabeth Goode is mine."

"Sharon Walton," announced Kim.

I detected a darkening cloud across her and Vinny's faces when it came to Damian's turn.

"Deana ... was Statham, previously Beacham, and Burton, and God knows how many others," he chortled.

I shot Viv a look, then back at Kim and across to Vinny. "Damian, did you say Deana?" I blurted.

Vinny answered for him. "I'm afraid he did."

As my mind raced while trying to compute the impossible, my eyes focused on our four children, who now sat perched in a row on a grave. "Noah ... Noah, please don't sit there. That's someone's grave. That's not a nice thing to do," I boomed.

With her arm around my son, Katlin replied, as the four children turned around, pointing with her free hand behind her. "It's okay. This is Deana's grave and she said we can sit here while she tells us a story."

That non-silence I hadn't heard for many a year seemed to fill the soundscape, as if some celestial power watching over us had hit the pause button. Finally, after an indeterminate time, Vinny broke the silence.

"For the love of God, please, not her."

Deana peered over at Terry's offspring and their partners before clapping her hands together to gain the four children's attention. "Now, children, do you want Aunty Deana to tell you the story about the most handsome man in all the land?"

All four children enthusiastically nodded.

"Super," she chortled. "Because it's a dead good story. So, there was once a handsome man called Terry."

Katlin raised her hand.

"Yes, dear? And well done for raising your hand. Your mother and father taught you well."

"Deana, was Terry a prince?"

"Oh, yes ... yes, Terry was the most handsome prince there ever was."

∼

So, what's next ...?

Coming up later this year, and due to popular demand, I plan to publish a fourth book in the Jason Apsley Series.

After that, a sequel to Eye of Time. You can keep up to date with my progress and pre-order releases on my website or by following me on Amazon – or, hey, why not both.

Thank you for reading this book, and may I ask a small favour? If you enjoyed this book, could I invite you to leave a review on Amazon? Just a few lines will help other readers discover my books – I'll hugely appreciate it.

For more information and to sign-up for updates on new releases, please drop onto my website. You can also find my page on Facebook and follow me on Amazon.

www.adriancousins.co.uk

Facebook.com/adriancousinsauthor

~

Author's note ...

I do hope you weren't offended by some of the vocabulary used by Terry because that wasn't my intention. Unfortunately, Terry came from an era when language was very different from today. Also, due to Terry wallowing in that grave for thirty-odd years, he missed out on our evolving world as we head towards a more tolerant society. Perhaps we can forgive the man? Anyway, wherever our philandering hero ended up, I'm quietly confident that the diva, Deana, will sort the poor boy out, one way or another.

However, as for that total knob, DCI Reeves, again, I hope you weren't offended by the language he used or the quotes from Viv regarding the DCI's vocabulary – as stated this wasn't my intention. You may remember Kevin Reeves from *Force of Time* when, as a rather immature DC, working for the fabulous DI Heather French, or Frenchie, as many affectionately like to know her as. I guess it's fair to say that Kevin never matured despite Frenchie's best efforts. Also, although I'm not condoning his actions, I venture to suggest that Paul Goode did the world a favour when he eliminated *Foxy*, thus paving the way for Viv to continue Frenchie's great work in helping the Fairfield Police to modernise.

Thankfully, for the vast majority, education has led the world to a more tolerant and inclusive society – although I accept that we still have many miles of that journey to tread.

~

Other titles by Adrian Cousins: -

<u>The Jason Apsley Series</u>

Jason Apsley's Second Chance

Ahead of his Time

Force of Time

Beyond his Time (Novella due to be published late summer 2023)

Calling Time (Due to be published late autumn 2023)

<u>Standalone Novels</u>

Eye of Time.

<u>Deana – Demon or Diva Series</u>

It's Payback Time

Death Becomes Them

Dead Goode

∼

Acknowledgements ...

Thank you to the following: your feedback and support has been invaluable.

> Adele Walpole
>
> Brenda Bennett
>
> Tracy Fisher
>
> Patrick Walpole
>
> Andy Wise

And, of course, Sian Phillips, who makes everything come together, I'm so grateful.

Printed in Great Britain
by Amazon